A qualified parachutist, Harvey Black served with British Army Intelligence for over ten years. His experience ranges from covert surveillance in Northern Ireland to operating in Communist East Berlin during the Cold War where he feared for his life after being dragged from his car by KGB soldiers. Since then he has lived a more sedate life in the private sector as a director for an international company and now enjoys the pleasures of writing. Harvey is married with four children. For more from Harvey, visit his website at www.harveyblackauthor.org.

Also by Harvey Black:

DEVILS WITH WINGS SERIES
Devils with Wings
Silk Drop
Frozen Sun

THE COLD WAR SERIES
The Red Effect
The Black Effect
The Blue Effect

GW00383272

Praise for Harvey Black

"Harvey Black's geopolitical survey is beautifully intertwined with personal stories of his characters. He builds tension relentlessly... looking forward to the next book!" – Author Alison Morton

"...tension, suspense, action, intrigue and moments of tenderness too which are a nice touch. I recommend the book entirely." – Steven Bird

"Factual along with gripping, takes me back to the days of the BAOR and what we all trained for... look forward to the next instalments." – Jon Wallace

"This book needs another one to follow on and complete the story. A similar story to Tom Clancy and his *Red Storm Rising*." – A Jones

"This is the best read I have had in ages very techno and extremely fast moving. It could have happened." – TPK Alvis

"This is a thriller in the style of Robert Ludlum or Tom Clancy. Credible characters and fast pace... thoroughly enjoyed the roller coaster ride!" – Author David Ebsworth

"The build-up is gripping and enthralling." – Author Sue Fortin

"If you have enjoyed *Chieftans, Red Gambit, Red Storm Rising, Team Yankee* etc, then don't miss this. Well written, realistic, unputdownable." – R Hampshire

HARVEY BLACK

THE BLUE EFFECT

SilverWood

Published in 2014 by SilverWood Books

SilverWood Books
30 Queen Charlotte Street, Bristol, BS1 4HJ
www.silverwoodbooks.co.uk

ISBN 978-1-78132-221-5 (paperback)
ISBN 978-1-78132-223-9 (ebook)

British Library Cataloguing in Publication Data
A CIP catalogue record for this book is available from the British Library

Set in Bembo by SilverWood Books
Printed in the UK on responsibly sourced paper.

Dedicated to my four children
Elaine, Lee, Darren and Annabelle

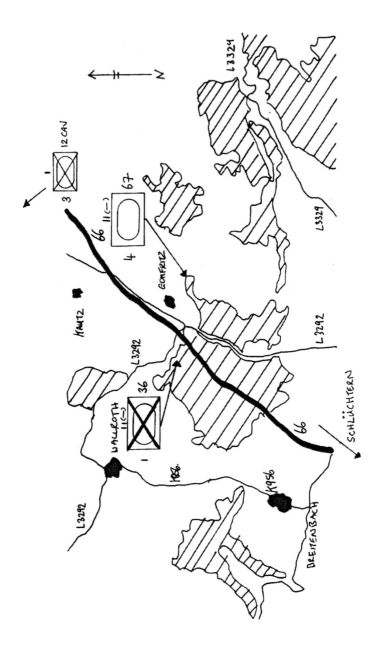

Gomfritz – 3rd Brigade/3rd US Armoured Division

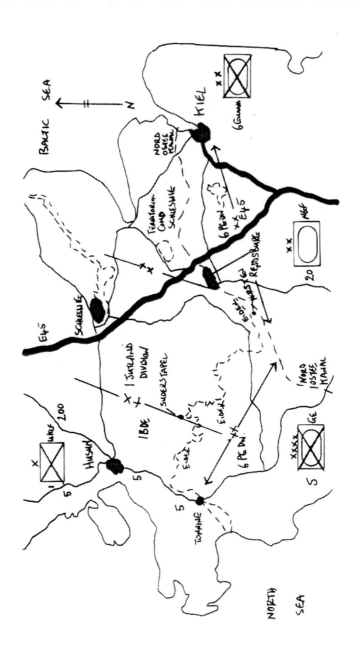

Schleswig Holstein – Landjut Forces

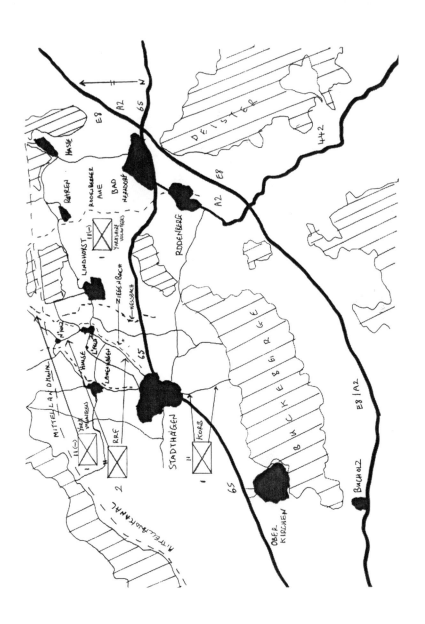

Stadthagen – 24th Brigade, 1 British Corps

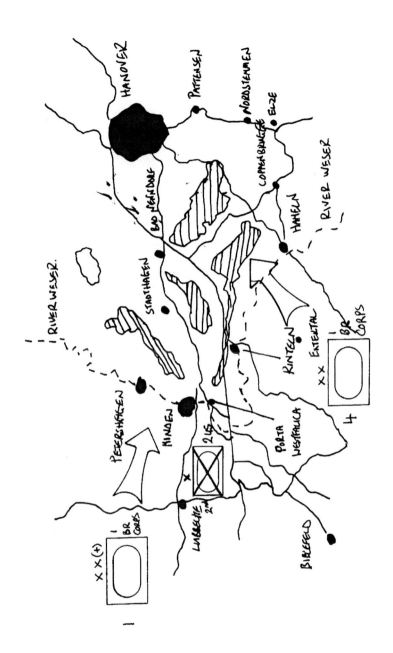

River Weser – 1 British Corps Counterattack

The 'Layer Cake' deployment of NORTHAG and CENTAG forces

Preface

I hope you have enjoyed the first two novels in my Cold War series. As you are about to read *The Blue Effect*, I just wanted to take this opportunity to thank you for your support to date.

It is never easy to write about an alternative history. People quite naturally have their own opinion of how events might pan out, and they may well be right. But, this is just my opinion of what may have happened. Also, reference material is not always available, or is contradictory. I have attempted to be as accurate as possible, but in order to focus on writing and not getting bogged down in endless research, I have occasionally used my prerogative, as an author, to determine the direction of the story.

I have set out with the intention of entertaining my readers with a fast flowing, exciting read and I believe I have achieved that. I have added extra maps to support *The Blue Effect*, but should you like to have access to further maps, then please drop me a line at harvey.black_author@yahoo.com and I will endeavour to include them on my site at harveyblackauthor.org.

Chapter 1

1900, 8 July 1984. Combat Team Alpha/2nd Battalion Royal Green
Jackets Battle Group, 4th Armoured Division.
Area of Coppenbrugge, West Germany.
The Black Effect +15 hours

Lieutenant Dean Russell ducked, tucking his head down deep inside
the foxhole as another explosion boomed nearby, causing the ground
to quake and showering him with clods of earth. He peered again over
the top, seeing a Chieftain tank explode, an anti-tank missile rupturing
the engine deck and sheering off the rear drive-sprocket. Another anti-
tank missile, fired by a second Hind-D, struck the opposite rear side,
propelling the armoured giant's back end sideways, until it eventually
came to a stop. The commander's hatch flew open, smoke pouring
from the turret and fighting compartment of the stricken tank,
and the commander clambered out, his lower uniform tattered and
smouldering. Sparks festooned the turret, and the tank commander
flopped forward, his body jerking as if on puppet strings as round after
round, fired by a deadly attack-helicopter, pierced his body.

The driver was next to attempt to escape the inferno boiling up
inside. Initially, he had been relatively safe due to his position furthest
away from the two deadly strikes, but it was a race against time
before the Chieftain brewed up. He lifted himself up with his arms,
threw his legs over onto the glacis and slid down, his headphones
ripped off his head, taking his beret with it, the cable still connected
inside. Dean watched as the driver dropped down from the tank and
started to run towards the British lines, the run turning into a sprint,
throwing his legs forward, pushing himself, arms pumping, fear and
panic driving him faster and faster. Three hundred metres was a long
way to run at that speed, and the soldier quickly tired.

Dean started to chant inside his head, the chant slowly becoming
audible: "Run…run…run."

The soldier started to stagger. Looking back over his shoulder, his eyes went wide with fear as flames shot up from what was once his home from home. A BMP-2 caught up with him, gunfire from the coaxial machine gun bracketing the fleeing driver with a swathe of fire. He flung his arms upwards, high into the air, bullets piercing his fragile body as the force of the blows hurled him forward, he was dead before he hit the ground. The BMP-2 heaved as a HESH round forced a scab of skin to break off inside the troop compartment, hot fragments puncturing the soft flesh of the Soviet infantrymen inside. A second strike, this time a sabot round, struck the now angled mechanised infantry combat vehicle with such force that it flipped it over onto its turret top. None of the crew would leave the now blazing vehicle.

One of the Hind-Ds was also ripped apart as a missile, fired from a Tracked Rapier brought to Coppenbrugge to support the fleeing NATO forces, scored a direct hit. The assault helicopter plummeted to the ground, crashing in front of a T-80, causing the tank to swerve sideways, a 14/20th King's Hussars' Chieftain taking advantage of the now exposed vulnerable side of the tank, and a sabot round punching a hole right through it.

The left side of Dean's face suddenly felt hot as a Chieftain tank from Alpha Troop, 14/20th King's Hussars, brewed up, hit simultaneously by two AT-5 Spandrel missiles fired from Soviet BMP-2s. He quickly put his hand up to his cheek, his neoprene NBC gloves partially protecting him from the fierce heat as the main battle tank was engulfed in flames. One of the crew could be heard screaming above the noise of the battle as he unsuccessfully attempted to escape the inferno inside.

Dean dropped to the floor of his hole again as the tank, the ammunition inside ignited by the heat, rocked again and again as a tumult of explosions took it through its final death throes. Between the cracks and thuds of exploding ordnance, firecracker-like sounds could be heard as the 7.62mm ammunition for the coaxial machine gun also succumbed.

Back up again, Dean held his SLR at the ready, two sharp cracks of gunfire in his right ear indicating that Colour Sergeant Rose was firing his SLR, hitting back. He too pulled his rifle into his shoulder and fired two shots at a Soviet airborne soldier advancing at less than 200 metres away. Both shots missed.

The Soviet soldier retained his life for a mere three seconds longer before a British Chieftain tank ran him down. This one was powering back in reverse, the commander choosing the superior protection of the front glacis and turret rather than exposing the rear of his tank to the enemy, just to gain greater speed. The tank crashed through a shallow berm that had once been protecting an infantry position. Its tracks tore up the ground, collapsing what had once been a rapidly dug foxhole, the dead soldier still within not caring. Once inside the British forward line that stretched from the high ground of Nesselberg in the north to Hohenstein in the south, with Coppenbrugge in the centre, the driver of Two-Two-Alpha, Bravo Troop, 14/20th King's Hussars, spun the Chieftain slightly on the spot, ensuring they were lined up with the enemy. The barrel jerked as a sabot round left it, its deadly charge striking a BMD, the penetrator rod perforating the vehicle's turret and knocking it out instantly.

Maverick anti-tank missiles struck two T-80s. A glowing orange mass, intermingled with white-hot gases and black fumes, engulfed the two machines, destroying them both, killing all inside. Then the pair of Harrier Jump Jets banked left, then right, to fly out of the danger area, swing round and come back in for a second attack.

"Zero-Bravo, Two-Two-Alpha. In position. Over."

"Roger that. One-One and Three-Three moving now," answered the Squadron Commander.

Alex peered through the vision blocks, turning the cupola, trying to make some sense of the chaos out there. Three-Three-Bravo and Three-Three-Charlie shot past. Charlie Troop would get into a position where they could cover Alpha and Bravo Troop for when it was their turn to pull back – if you could call the single tank, One-One-Alpha, a troop. One-One-Bravo had just been destroyed and One-One-Charlie moments earlier.

Alex observed a platoon of three BMP-2s. Their senior commanders, noticing a potential opening, had ordered them forward to break the British line, at whatever cost.

"BMP-2, 500 metres, left, sabot," Alex screamed.

Ellis, his arms aching, his head banging, went through the motions, robot-like: sabot, bag-charge, breech, small charge, gate. "Up!"

Patsy fired, stopping the BMP-2 dead. A second MICV flared up violently as a Milan missile blew the turret completely off the main body. Two more Maverick missiles hit home, but one failed to kill its target. Only one of the Harriers banked left this time to return to its base to refuel and rearm, the second aircraft in the flight having flown directly into a hail of fire from two ZSU 23-4s.

"*Two-Two-Alpha, Zero-Bravo. Mechanised infantry units withdrawing. Cover for figures five. No longer. Figures five. Understood?*"

"Roger that. Who do I have for company? Over."

"*One-One-Alpha and Two-Two-Charlie. Pass through Three-Three. Out.*"

Three tanks. That's all he had: three tanks to hold back an entire Soviet tank regiment and an airborne force bent on revenge. But, he knew they would have to commit to staying the full five minutes if the infantry were to get out of this maelstrom alive. The breech of the 120mm main gun slammed back again, Patsy identifying his own targets. Alex checked through the rear vision blocks. He could see the two tanks of Charlie Troop, about 200 metres further back, getting into position. He also spotted a dip in the ground.

"Two-Two-Charlie. We're moving back fifty. We hold for figures five. Over." He ordered the second tank in his troop.

"*Roger, we'll over-watch.*"

"Mackinson. Take us back fifty metres. There's a dip in the ground. It will give us some cover."

"Sir."

The engine groaned slightly before increasing power, and the driver reversed the vehicle, guided by his troop commander, until they dropped slightly, now with a shallow ridge across their front providing some additional cover.

"Two-Two-Charlie. We're in a good defilade position. Move now."

"*Roger.*"

"Get ready to bug out quickly, Mackinson. What can you see, Patsy?"

"Just fucking dust, sir. Bastards will sneak up on us." Responded Corporal Patterson.

"*Two-Two-Alpha, Zero-Bravo. You have company. Alpha Squadron to your left and Charlie Squadron to your right. Standby to move while they cover.*"

"Roger."

Thank god, thought Alex. The remnants of Alpha and Charlie Squadrons, with only fourteen tanks between them, had managed to extract themselves from the melee and pull back. A forward line was slowly forming. If they could get into some decent cover, they could hit back; perhaps hold the Soviets off until darkness covered the area and restricted their massed tank attacks.

"Two-Two-Alpha, Zero-Bravo. Pull back, pull back. Alpha and Charlie covering."

"Location? Over."

"November Charlie three, two, five, eight, one, four."

"Roger. Who's with me? Over."

"You plus Three-Three. Over."

"Roger that. Moving now."

"We'll meet you there. We will cover you until then. Then we can get the hell out of here. Zero-Bravo out."

"Two-Two-Charlie, Two-Two-Alpha."

"Go ahead. Over."

"Go to grid, November Charlie three, two, five, eight, one, four. I repeat, November Charlie three, two, five, eight, one, four. Pull back beyond Alpha and Charlie, then flat out and we'll see you there."

"What about you? Over."

"We'll cover for figures one. Then we'll be right behind you. Out."

Alex grabbed the map and did a quick calculation of the approximate area east of Bad Munder. He warned Mackinson to be prepared to move; then he turned the cupola, sussing out the activity to his front. The tank rocked as Patsy fired another sabot round, a BMP-2 suffering the same fate as the last. Alex's head shot back, his bone dome striking the rear of the cupola as he recoiled back from a now chipped and clouded vision block. Round after round pummelled the Chieftain as a Hind-D fired short bursts of 12.7mm rounds at its target.

Thump, thump, thump. Clang…clang. The turret and fighting compartment resonated as round after round battered the Chieftain's armour. The attack-helicopter had used up its stock of anti-tank missiles, but the pilot was determined to keep the pressure on, pushing the enemy back.

"Back! Back!" yelled Alex.

The tank jolted, the roar of the engine mingling with the heavy-calibre bullet strikes. A tremor racked the tank as Mackey depressed the accelerator and the battle tank surged rearwards, clawing its way back, the tracks gripping the earth and laying a metal carpet for the giant to escape over. Alex peered through one of the clear vision blocks, observing plumes of smoke and dust as their own artillery had finally managed to relocate and put down a short bombardment before they too were forced to move again, escaping any Soviet counter-battery fire. The fighting compartment juddered and the tracks ceased moving, the diesel engine coughing into silence.

"Fuck, fuck, fuck," hollered Mackinson as he desperately tried to restart the engine that had now left them stranded and vulnerable. The Hind had left but, once the British artillery barrage petered out, the enemy would push west even harder, leaving Two-Two-Alpha high and dry. The engine spluttered, hesitated, and then burst into life only to cut out again.

"For fuck's sake, Mackey, get it sorted. We're in the shit here," screamed Ellis, the Loader.

The engine caught again as the driver played with the starting motor and accelerator pedal. A sudden roar was followed by an unwelcome squeal from the L-60 diesel engine, and the Chieftain jolted backwards, steadily gaining momentum but achieving little more than ten kilometres an hour.

"Well done, Mackinson. Is that all we have?"

"Yes, sir. If I change gear again, I'm worried she'll give up the ghost."

Alex squinted through the rear vision blocks. "OK. Just keep it moving. Corporal Patterson, how are we for ammo?"

"OK with HESH, sir, but seven sabot."

"Two-Two-Alpha, Zero-Bravo. Pull back, pull back, now. Acknowledge. Over."

"Two-Two-Alpha. Received. Engine playing up. Over."

"Roger that. We'll direct you to a safe location. Just get out of there. We'll cover."

"Roger. Out." Alex keyed the internal comms. "Mackinson, will we be able to spin and go forward?"

"Tricky, sir, but I can try."

Alex did a quick scan of the area: no immediate threats were spotted. British gunners were putting down more artillery fire, making it difficult for the Soviets to go in pursuit of the two battered Battle Groups.

*"Two-Two-Alpha, Zero-Alpha. Start pulling back to the high ground
now; then head west to Behrensen. Acknowledge. Over,"* radioed the
Company Commander.

Dean had to shout into the mouthpiece, such was the noise erupting
all around him. "Two-Two-Alpha. Received and understood. Over."

*"Armoured units will cover your withdrawal. Make it quick, Dean.
Alpha will consolidate there. Out."*

Dean held up two digits to Colour Sergeant Rose who nodded
his understanding. He knew the order to pull back was due. They
couldn't hold out here for much longer. Casualties were stacking up,
and the losses of Chieftains had been steadily climbing.

Dean keyed his handset and notified all his units that they would
be withdrawing in two minutes. The mortar section was still going
strong. It had miraculously survived a counter-battery strike, having
moved location two minutes prior to the salvo of 122mm shells
landing on their old firing base. Dean ordered them to fire a salvo
of 82mm bombs for the full two minutes before they too would
race to their next location northwest of Coppenbrugge. He knew it
wouldn't be long before they were outflanked. The Soviet airborne,
tasked with pushing the British units back, had headed for the high
ground on both sides of Coppenbrugge so they could make headway
and come in behind the Royal Green Jackets (RGJ) and 14/20th
King's Hussars situated in the valley.

It was falling apart.

With the enemy across the River Leine to the north, 22nd
Armoured Brigade, positioned further south, had been hit on their
left flank. After the remnants of the 62nd Guards Tank Regiment
and the Independent Tank Regiment, had crossed the River
Leine south of Hanover, they had smashed into the flanks of the
Royal Green Jackets. Taking advantage, two of the Soviet airborne
battalions fighting around Gronau had pressed the three 14/20th
King's Hussars' combat teams west of the River Leine. One airborne
battalion had attacked from the south, moving deep into Gronau,
nearly cutting off Bravo Troop and the supporting units who were
still on the eastern bank. A second airborne battalion thrust south,

to help close the trap. The British units had raced across the first of the Gronau bridges, the engineers destroying it as the tracks of Lieutenant Alex Wesley-Jones's Chieftain, the last British unit to cross, had barely touched the opposite bank. A small engineer unit, supported by a mixed force consisting of drivers from the Royal Corps of Transport, signallers and a small detachment of Royal Military Police, held the second bridge as Alex and his small force raced to get off the small island that sat between the two bridges.

The final bridge was blown five minutes before the southernmost airborne battalion closed the trap. All British units were ordered to withdraw, at speed, towards Coppenbrugge. 14/20th King's Hussars were to defend the Coppenbrugge gap, along with Combat Team Alpha of the 2RGJ. The rest of the 2RGJ Battle Group, held back from the 4th Armoured Division, had been ordered to defend the high ground to the north and south.

Further south, the 2nd Royal Tank Regiment had been badly mauled by a massed attack from the air. Thirty sorties by ground-attack aircraft struck hard. Before the dust had even settled, elements of the 3rd Shock Helicopter Attack Regiment, twenty Hind-D helicopters, hit them before they could recover. They finally managed to extract themselves from the carnage with thirty-two Chieftains surviving to fight another day.

The dilemma for the commander of 22nd Armoured Brigade was whether to counter-attack and risk losing his remaining tanks in the mess that was once a frontline around Gronau or to pull them back to new defensive positions to plug the gaps that were forming as the 1st and 2nd Battalions, the Royal Green Jackets and the 14/20th King's Hussars battled for survival. He chose the latter, keeping his only relatively intact armoured regiment to reform further to the rear. 2RTR raced west, heading for a position west of Hameln.

For half an hour, all three Battle Groups, in particular the RGJ and 14/20th, had got to grips with the remaining 800 men of the Soviet air-assault battalions from the 34th Airborne Assault Brigade around Benstorf. Two battalions had been parachuted into the area east of Coppenbrugge to cut off any British withdrawal and secure a passage for the following armour between the two sections of high ground. Two-Two-Alpha and Two-Two-Charlie had crashed straight through the Soviet airborne brigade's D-30 artillery positions, Two-Two-Charlie nearly losing a track as it crushed the trails of one of the 122mm artillery guns.

22nd Armoured Brigade's extraction from the battle was chaotic. At one point, the entire 1st Division's area of responsibility from south of Hanover to the north of Alfeld was a mass of intermingled Soviet and British forces. At least one flight of Sepecat Jaguar ground-attack aircraft had returned to base with their full weapons' load, unable to distinguish the boundaries between friend and foe. The Soviet 7th and 12th Guards Tank Divisions, from the 3rd Shock Army, took full advantage of the chaos. Within an hour of their advance forces crossing the River Leine, using GSP, PTS and K-61s, the first PMP pontoon bridging section was being dropped. As more and more of their forces crossed to the western bank, expanding the bridgehead and threatening to trap the retreating Western forces between themselves and the airborne forces behind, they broke out from the bridgehead.

Having battled their way out of the clutches of the Soviet airborne battalions, and now joined by a few elements of the 1st Battalion, the Royal Green Jackets, also retreating, the 14/20th collided with the Soviet airborne battalion assaulting Coppenbrugge. The 14/20th ploughed through the Soviet airborne elite, rounds from BMDs ricocheting off the Chieftain's armour, an ASU-85 taking out a Chieftain from A-Squadron, a BRDM-Sagger damaging another from C-Squadron. Covered by the now consolidated elements of A-Company, 2RGJ, Alex and his regiment believed they were on the home run – at least, until the dreaded Hind tank hunters were unleashed, destroying two more Chieftains before they were all able to join the thin British line and turn to defend their corner.

1930, 8 July 1984. Recce troop and Combat Team Bravo/2nd Battalion Royal Green Jackets, 4th Armoured Division. Hohenstein, West Germany. The Black Effect +15.5 hours

The Scorpion tank rocked as the 76mm gun fired one of its two canister rounds that were stored on board the light reconnaissance tank. Nearly 800 pellets tore into the Soviet airborne forces attempting to outflank Combat Team Bravo, the Royal Green Jackets.

"Back, back," ordered Lieutenant Baty.

Thomas, the tank's driver, powered the Jaguar engine and the Scorpion, a Combat Vehicle Reconnaissance (Tracked), a CVR(T), moved back fifty metres.

"Stop, stop, stop. Infantry, 200 metres, MG," ordered Baty.

The turret vibrated as the coaxial 7.62mm machine gun sent

round after deadly round down range, ripping into trees and bodies alike. After one long burst, Lance Corporal Alan Reid then fired short five to ten-round bursts. Ammunition was low: perhaps only 250 rounds left. They had been conducting a fighting withdrawal for over four hours after escaping from the confines of Gronau. Gronau was now in the clutches of the Soviet airborne. A pincer movement by the airborne force had nearly trapped them, slowly squeezing them and the British Mechanised Infantry section, along with a scattered German Jaeger unit, into a smaller and tighter space.

Once the second bridge was blown, they were released by high command, along with their sister unit, from the defence of Gronau, to bug out and race west to safety. Baty pitied the German reservists who provided cover while they fled. The Jaeger unit were having to drag their wounded and dying, some suffering horrific injuries from bombs, bullets and the dreaded chemical blister agent, to safety, yet still fight a rearguard action. Baty had seen one soldier in his early forties, his face and hands a mass of septic-looking blisters. Some of those that had burst were either red-raw or congealed. Reluctantly, he had ordered his small troop to run, seeing the staring eyes of a Jaeger captain, watching them go as he bravely rallied his men to defend themselves, care for their wounded *kameraden*, and attempt to escape the slowly closing claws of the enemy.

Baty watched through a vision block as a gun-group flung themselves down behind one of the tall trees of the Hohenstein Forest. Within seconds, the butt of the general-purpose machine gun was up and into the infantryman's shoulder, the ammunition belt flying through his oppo's fingers as he ensured a smooth feed.

He turned to face the front again, looking for the enemy ahead as another burst of fire from Reid kept the enemy's heads down. The tang of cordite soured his tongue, and acrid fumes irritated his nostrils. The metal shot had devastated a Soviet section, killing two and wounding two as the deadly bullets tore into the airborne ranks.

"As soon as the infantry relocate, we move again. Fifty metres, got that, Thomas?"

"Sir," responded the driver, a slight tremor in his voice.

The Scorpion rocked as half a dozen 30mm rounds from an AGS-17 exploded on and around Baty's vehicle.

He heard the *thump...thump...thump* as Two-One-Alpha, Sergeant Gough, his second-in-command, the second surviving tank of his troop, fired three rounds in the direction of the enemy firing position.

"Two-One-Alpha, Two-One, moving back now."

"*Roger.*"

"Fifty metres, Thomas."

"Sir."

The Jaguar engine purred as power was initiated and Thomas took them back a further fifty metres.

"Watch for the infantry. They'll be pulling back now."

The turret turned slightly as Reid adjusted his sights so he was aiming directly at a point between two large trees, a route the Soviets would come through to follow the retreating British troops.

"*Two-One, Two-One-Alpha. Covering now.*"

"Roger," responded Baty.

The gun-group was up and running as Sergeant Gough's Scorpion fired short bursts of 7.62.

"There," yelled Reid as he fired a 76mm round into a Soviet half-section coming through the gap as he had suspected they would. The soldiers withdrew, dragging one of their wounded with them. The infantry unit, B-Company, Royal Green Jackets, used the opportunity to pull back even further. Space was running out though. Now on the Fahnenstein, the ground dropped away behind them. Half a kilometre further and the ground would drop from 300 metres down to 200 metres, and the enemy would then be above them. Not only that but they would be clear of the forest, in open ground, exposed. Their only option then would be to run northwest towards Bad Munder, or southwest towards Hameln. To their north was Coppenbrugge where Combat Teams Alpha, 2RGJ, and Bravo, 14/20th, were also being relentlessly pushed back. If they didn't coordinate their withdrawal, one unit giving ground too quickly, eventually an unlucky unit would find itself trapped, surrounded and destroyed.

"*Two-One, this is Two. Orders. Over.*"

"Two-One, over."

"*Five minutes, figures five. Then get the hell out of there. Head for Grid November, Charlie, three, three, zero, seven, three, four. Your other friendlies have the same orders. Understood? Over.*"

"Roger that, Two. Over."

"*Don't hang about. It's a bloody mess back here. Once you get into position, cover and report. Two, out.*"

"All Two-One call signs. Figures five and we're out of here. Acknowledge. Over."

Chapter 2

2000, 8 July 1984. 1st Battalion, 108th Guards Cossacks Air
Assault 'Kuban' Regiment, 7th Guards Airborne Division.
West of Pattensen, West Germany.
The Blue Effect -3 days

Two Phantom jets roared overhead. The shells from their six-barrelled guns gouged deep ruts in the ground as short bursts of 20mm rounds, at one hundred rounds per second, ploughed a furrow of destruction through the airborne company crouching behind their BMD MICVs. The fighters, an older aircraft in the NATO armoury nicknamed the 'Wood Burner', were from 19 Squadron RAF based at RAF Wildenrath near Geilenkirchen, West Germany. They were both Supersonic Interceptors, not close-support aircraft; such was the desperation being felt back at the headquarters of the British Army of the Rhine (BAOR) and the Northern Army Group (NORTHAG). Two surface-to-air missiles fired from shoulder-launched SA-14 Gremlins trailed the tail end aircraft, both failing to hit their target. An SA-9 Gaskin, positioned alongside its burning companion hit earlier by a West German Tornado sortie, fired its last missile from the quadruple mounted launcher, set on top of a BRDM2 chassis. At Mach 1.5, one and a half times the speed of sound, it streaked after the Phantom. The missile wavered, matching the Phantom's speed, hunting it down, toying with it. The pilot flipped his craft left and right in an attempt to shake it off; then the afterburners kicked in pushing the aircraft towards its top speed of Mach 1.9, the pilot pulling back on the stick to take it into a steep climb. The missile flicked right, exploding close to the tail, smoke and flame engulfing the back end of the now crippled aircraft, and two blurred shapes launched from the cockpit as the pilot and navigator escaped death.

Lieutenant Colonel Stanislav Yezhov, Commander of the 1st Battalion, 108th Air Assault Regiment, crouching behind his command BMD, pulled one of his company commanders in close as the Phantom exploded in mid-air almost above their position. "Baryshev, I want your company to push for Gehrden and secure the eastern outskirts of the town. We have to create a passage for 12th Guards. How many casualties?"

"Seven killed, eight wounded so far, Comrade Colonel. Three vehicles lost. Are they heading for route 65?" Major Nestor Baryshev, Commander of the 1st Company, shouted above the sound of explosions, as an artillery salvo landed not more than 200 metres away.

"Yes, I have already sent Gorshkov to secure Ronnenberg, so watch where you shoot. They'll be practically opposite your location."

"Any other support, sir?"

"I'm giving you two of the ASU-85s and two BRDM2 Sagger's from Regiment. I've sent the AGS-17 platoon; air-defence platoon and mortar battery with Gorshkov and the anti-tank platoon is with Volkov. Make good use of your RPGs. How many warheads do you have?"

"Should have at least six left. Have we any idea where the enemy are, sir?"

"None, Nestor. They're all over the place. Three-Company is fighting with a troop of tanks as we speak. The British are trying to break off contact with 12th Guards so they can establish a line further west. We have to clear a passage for the 12th. That's the priority, that's our job, nothing else matters. Once you and Gorshkov have secured your sectors, Volkov's company will leapfrog you and secure access to the road. Once he can extract, that is. Then they are on their own."

"Where are the rest of the regiment then, sir?"

"I've no idea where Two-Battalion is. They were sent towards the River Leine, to come at the British from behind. Three-Battalion were providing all-round protection, but are now consolidating. General Boykov will direct them towards the canal, and create as much mayhem as possible."

"Are we done then, sir?"

"Yes, Nestor, go. Good luck."

They both pulled themselves tighter against the side of the BMD as bullets ricocheted off the other side of the armoured vehicle. Fleeing British units were still fighting a running battle.

★

With the River Leine breached, the Soviet air-to-ground strikes increased in intensity, and armour and infantry flooded across. Elements of the battered 10th Guards Tank Division had created a bridgehead before releasing elements to strike south increasing the pressure on the British 22nd Armoured Brigade who were desperately attempting to hold back the deluge that was building up to their front. In the meantime, the three battalions of the 108th Air Assault Regiment continued to expand their own bridgehead, creating space and a passage through which 12th Guards Tank Division of 3 Shock Army could transit, quickly overpowering the NATO defence, getting behind them, and cutting them off from their higher command. Once complete, they would push west, at speed, giving the British 1st Armoured Division little time to reform their defence lines. The intermediate objective of the 12th was to link up with 247th Caucasian Cossacks Air Assault Regiment near the Mittellandkanal. The 247th was commanded by Colonel Vydina who had conducted a descent, a parachute assault, further west, securing the western end of the gap. Together, the 12th and the 247th would ensure a crossing of the River Weser before 1st British Corps could complete their defensive preparations.

2000, 8 July 1984. Combat Team Delta, Royal Hussars.
Ditterke, West Germany.
The Blue Effect -3 days

Corporal Mason helped drag Trooper Mann from the damaged Challenger tank. The crewman had a minor wound to his head from a ricochet, and a more serious wound: a smashed shoulder. The other two men were safe, ensconced with an infantry section. A mere 500 metres away, the BMD, responsible for the tank's demise after hitting it with a Sagger missile, was still smouldering, an airborne soldier broken and battered lay close to the rear hatch, the rest of the soldiers blackened and unrecognisable in the troop compartment to the rear. After a HESH round had demolished the airborne infantry vehicle, the crew, those who had been able to escape the inferno inside, had been immediately cut down by a pintle-mounted Gympy on top of a British 432. The infantry were from the 3rd Battalion, the Queen's Regiment, having got separated from their parent unit, and seeking support and protection from their much larger cousins. A second BMD was burning furiously a further 100 metres east. Clouds of thick, black, oily smoke funnelled upwards, an advert to anyone watching that there had been a clash between opposing forces.

The 1st Royal Tank Regiment, Royal Hussars, and 3rd Battalion, the Queen's Regiment, had been fighting a running battle with the Soviet army between Hanover in the north and Bennigsen in the south. Not only had they been trying to prevent a crossing of the River Leine, but also to hold off repeated attacks from behind them as two battalions of Soviet airborne forces that had landed in the vicinity of Pattensen continuously harassed the British defenders.

"Lay him down here." Lieutenant Barrett looked at Corporal Mason. "You've got less than a minute to get him patched up. Then we need to get out of here."

"I'll do my best, sir."

The wind shifted slightly and the acrid smoke from the burning BMD drifted across, causing Barrett to gag. A rasping cough was needed to clear his lungs. The wind shifted again, and he looked out across the ground in front, an array of arable fields, some needing attention from the farmers who owned them. They had been pulling back between Wettbergen and Ronnenberg, making it as far as Ditterke, when they had been bounced by an airborne platoon. Two BMDs had been destroyed, but not before crippling Delta-Four-Charlie. One BMD escaped, no doubt informing their masters of the location of the British units. The unit had been pulling into a farmyard east of a small village, seeking cover from Hind-D attack-helicopters they had seen in the distance, when they were hit.

They couldn't stay here for long. Lieutenant Barrett climbed up onto the glacis of his troop command tank, surveying the open fields to his front. To the northeast, the high ground of Benther Berg, and to the southeast, the much larger village of Gehrden. If he had a squadron of tanks here, he could see and hit any Soviet armour as soon as they were in range, such was the levelled ground.

Sergeant Glover came over from Delta-Four-Bravo. "We've patched up Mann as best we can, sir. He'll be OK for a while. His shoulder's a bloody mess though. The shrapnel that hit him almost took his arm off."

Barrett dropped down from the Challenger and beckoned Sergeant Glover over, spreading out a map in front of him.

"Still no contact with the Squadron or Regiment as yet, sir?"

"Once they've sorted themselves out, I'm sure they'll give us a rendezvous. But we need to get out of here, and soon."

"I'm with you on that, sir." Glover placed his personal machine gun, an SMG, on the glacis and pointed to the Mittellandkanal on the map. "We know they'll initiate a stop-line along here somewhere. But where? It's a bloody pig's ear at the moment."

"Definitely the canal. It's a natural barrier before the Weser, but it won't be the first one. They'll want to slow the advance down before the Soviets reach it."

"Should we head for Route 65 and run like hell until we meet up with the rest of our Squadron?"

"That would make sense, Sergeant, but the Soviets will be wanting to use that route to move their armour west as fast as possible. Get behind us for one thing, and keep One-Div moving back. They'll be provided with air support to facilitate that."

"Particularly those blasted Hinds. They're bloody everywhere. We don't seem to have anything to stop them."

"So, we need to get back to our own area of operations. We're currently in 1RTR's area. We keep away from the 65; go west to Grossgoltern, then south to Barsinghausen. It's a choke point, the town to the south and the high ground of Stemmer Berg to the north. We may find the rest of our unit regrouping."

The corner of one of the farm's outbuildings, the one Barrett's Challenger tank was sheltering next to, exploded into a hundred fragments as the Spandrel anti-tank missile detonated, having missed its target by less than a metre. Sergeant Glover yelped as a large chunk of masonry struck him in the back, a second smaller piece smashing into the side of his knee. He dropped to the ground, his injured leg giving way.

Boompf.

Delta-Four-Bravo, on seeing the BMP-2 that had fired, despatched the enemy MICV almost immediately after the gunner who was keeping watch spotted the dust trail kicked up by the rapidly retreating vehicle attempting to make its escape and seeking out new cover to target the British tanks again. It failed, the sabot round crippling it, but four Soviet infantry escaped.

"Mount up! Mount up!" screamed Barrett as he dropped to the floor, grabbing Sergeant Glover's webbing and pulling him onto his feet. "Can you walk?"

"Just about."

"We need to mount up quick and get the hell out of here."

"Move back," yelled Lieutenant Barrett to his driver, the man's head popping out above the driver's hatch.

28

The engine, which had been ticking over, picked up revs as Tyler reversed the Challenger until it was completely hidden from view. Barrett helped Sergeant Glover to his vehicle and, with the help of the gunner and loader, secreted him into the turret where the tank would support his crippled back and weak knee.

"Sergeant Glover, give us two minutes then follow. I'll inform you of our location on the move. Make it quick when you do move. We need to get away from this area."

"That was a BMP-2, sir," called Lance Corporal Frith.

"Fuck," responded Glover. "That means they have advance elements of the new Soviet division making progress."

"It does. Here." Barrett handed Sergeant Glover's SMG to the driver. "See you in two minutes." Then he called over to the infantry section to mount up and follow him in their 432, keeping to his left flank at all times.

With that, he ran towards his own tank and clambered on board. On the orders from his commander, the driver reversed around the end of the building, stopped, turned right, then rattled in between the farm and an outbuilding, picking up speed as they crossed an open field. Barrett frantically scanned for some cover so they could protect Delta-Four-Bravo when it was their turn to pull back. He glimpsed something, a small copse a thousand metres away just southwest of the village. That would do the trick.

"A copse. There's a minor road coming up. Take it, left. Three hundred metres south, then right on the next track. You should see the copse by then. Go for it."

"Got it," responded the driver.

Barrett spun the cupola round, watching the 120mm gun moving up and down above the engine deck as it maintained its level on whatever point Corporal Farre, his gunner, was tracking.

"See anything?"

"Sod all, sir."

"Keep your eyes peeled."

"No worries about that, sir."

Lieutenant Barrett pulled down the hatch as the sixty-ton giant made its way south, Tyler steering left as he came across the track. Within 700 metres, they reached the copse and the Challenger crashed through the foliage, brushing aside that which the driver couldn't avoid. Spinning it round on its tracks, he brought them back to the eastern edge of the copse. The 432 had gone straight through.

The infantrymen and the three surviving tank crew dismounted, setting up a position along the outer edge. The gun-group, with barely 600 rounds of belted ammunition, set up and watched for any sign of the enemy in pursuit. The 432 then spun round, the pintle-mounted machine gun adding to the section's firepower. The tankies lay alongside their comrades, their SMGs of no real use at long range, but up to fifty metres they would provide a significant boost to any close-quarter fighting.

The corporal issued arcs of fire to his section, now down to five men. He had lost his second-in-command and three men on the outskirts of Hanover: two as a consequence of the chemical strike, the other two from an attack by Spetsnaz forces. He spoke calmly to his soldiers, but inside he was still shaking. He and his men had been bombed, shelled, strafed, ambushed and poisoned. When ordered to pull back, fighting for every metre of ground as they did, he still looked at his small section with incredulity, astonished that they had escaped at all, let alone survived. The platoon, separated from its Company, had tried to push further west, but came across Soviet airborne troops and were deflected south. They were later ambushed and the section became separated from their platoon. It was then that they met up with the retreating units of the Royal Hussars Battle Group. That was a great relief for the young twenty-four year-old corporal.

"Delta-Four-Bravo, this is Delta-Four-Alpha. In position. Copse 1000 metres west your location. I'll talk you in. Over."

"Understood. Moving now. Out."

2000, 8 July 1984. 48th Guards Tank Regiment, 12th Guards Tank Division, 3rd Shock Army. West of Pattensen, West Germany. The Blue Effect -3 days

Colonel Kharzin pressed his regiment hard. The Bear had left him in no doubt of the consequences of failure. Artillery shells airburst above his head, and he dropped into the turret, the turret cover quickly pulled down to secure the tank. Moments later, his regiment felt the effects of the 155mm rounds as they discharged sub munitions above their heads, showering the racing T-80s with a rain of small, almost insignificant-looking, armoured-piercing projectiles. His regiment, spread out across the open fields, charged west to maintain the Operational Manoeuvre Group's momentum. Elements of his forward units were brought to a halt as four salvos, of nearly 3,000 sub munitions, fired by the Royal Artillery, struck. The sub munitions, small shaped-charge warheads, smashed into the top cover of the speeding tanks. The ERA blocks secured across the armour deflected many. Although limited in capability, penetrating only tens of millimetres of armour some got through causing devastation. One managed to penetrate a tank's ammunition carousel. The explosion was catastrophic. For some of the T-80s, the thinner armour on top of the turret succumbed, crewmen inside injured, but several drivers were able to keep their tanks on the move. One ground to a halt, the thin engine deck failing to resist the hot molten metal as it bit into the gas-turbine motor, rupturing the engine, engulfing the armoured vehicle in a steadily growing ball of flame. Black, oily smoke identified those tanks most badly hit.

Kharzin ordered his spearhead company to halt as the last salvo of Improved Conventional Munitions struck. A company of BMP-2s had been ordered forward to provide right-flanking protection from the British Mechanised Infantry Battalion that he knew to be out there somewhere to the north. In fact, the two antagonists had been in parallel, racing west: the British to escape and reform further back, the Soviets to link up with the airborne carpet that had been laid out in front of their axis of attack.

The smaller armoured vehicles fared worse, the company of ten mechanised infantry combat vehicles, MICVs, each carrying a Soviet motor-rifle section, losing half of their force. A concentrated salvo had straddled the small group on three separate occasions in less than a minute. Soldiers had huddled in their dark, cramped troop compartments, some feeling sick after being thrown from side to side inside the claustrophobic space as the BMP-2s raced across the undulating ground as if the devil himself was after them. In some respects, he was, in the form of their divisional commander, the Bear. Then they were met by a searing heat as jets of molten metal penetrated the thin armour, splaying out inside in a plume of destructive energy that ate into the flesh and bone of the cowering human beings who had nowhere to go but die a horrible, painful death as their vehicles continued on. The driver, in his own world of fear, carried on, deaf to the screams of his comrades dying less than a metre behind him.

A second vehicle erupted in a violent ball of flame. First, it was struck by a single charge which tore off a track rendering the BMP motionless; then by two more of the small but deadly charges, one

31

piercing the troop compartment killing four men as they scrambled to escape the stricken vehicle, the second penetrating the turret, setting off the anti-tank missiles and the large calibre ammunition from the 30mm gun.

The platoon commanders, those that had survived, were terrified by the cacophony of sound battering what they'd hoped was their safe haven. They had to use every ounce of persuasiveness to keep their soldiers from panicking. One infantryman opened the rear door as the BMP was on the move. The sound from without horrified his comrades even more as they heaved the door shut, one soldier striking his comrade with the butt of the gun he had retrieved from the clip at his side. The lieutenants and sergeants either used threats or attempted to cajole their men to keep order. One sergeant, cramped in the back of a troop compartment with his subordinates, even begged the soldiers to keep their alarm in check, promising them they would survive. They just needed to remain calm and trust in the protection of their armour. His cries fell on deaf ears as two charges struck the top armour, punching through, savagely tearing into the helpless men inside, mutilating their bodies. Prisoners, trapped inside their own steel coffin.

The BMP Company was brought to a halt; the commander dead, killed in the first salvo, the rest of the unit either crippled, dying or leaderless and floundering. Kharzin radioed his force, establishing the state of his leading unit, and ordering the following units to make best speed and catch up. He was immediately in contact with the 1st Battalion Commander having him order his second and third company to bypass the crippled lead company and continue to push ahead.

Kharzin's tank approached his lead company and received reports from the battered unit. He then waited for the second and third company to pass through. Out of the ten T-80s and ten BMP-2s he had pushed forward, three of the main battle tanks were ablaze, their engines afire, fuel and exploding ordnance feeding it, forcing back any rescuers attempting to recover the crews. One had a track split in two places: recoverable, but out of commission for at least half a day. The fifth had survived, mainly intact, but the turret was frozen in place, the repair time unknown. As for the rest of the company, plus his own T-80K, they were fully operational, but many had lost explosive reactive blocks from the surface of their armour, the blocks fulfilling their role in protecting the tanks.

For the infantry company, it was a similar story: three completely destroyed, a fourth with both tracks lost, and a fifth with minor damage to the turret but capable of continuing with the battle if called upon. Twenty-six infantrymen had been either killed or severely wounded. Some of those that had survived were in a serious state of shock and temporarily deaf. But they would be expected by their leaders to remain with the unit and fight when called upon. Ten tank crewmen had been killed. Kharzin had also lost a ZSU 23/4 and an SA-9. *The British have drawn real blood for the first time in regard to the 12th Guards Tank Division*, he thought.

"Four-Eight-Zero, this is Four-Eight-One. Passing your location. Orders. Over."

"Push for Ronnenberg. Link up with the airborne. I'm right behind you." He ordered 1st Battalion forward.

With that, he gave the order to move to his driver, who was still slightly shaken after experiencing his first taste of being under artillery fire. He pressed the pedal and the armoured giant surged forward. Not far away was a T-80K, followed by two MTLB command vehicles belonging to the 1st Battalion HQ, as the commander came forward with his third tank company. Soon, Kharzin would have a full battalion, minus the casualties, starting to make progress.

"Four-Eight-Zero, this is Zero-One-Two. What is your situation? Over?"

"Artillery strike. Temporary halt. First-battalion pressing forward," replied Kharzin.

"Keep up the pressure, Yury. There's to be no stopping," responded the Bear.

"Understood. The British artillery will strike again once they relocate."

"We will deal with them. Forward, Yury, you must move forward. Out."

"Four-Eight-Four, this is Four-Eight-Zero. Report. Over."

"We have sight of Four-Eight-One. Situation Report. Over," responded Captain Kalyagin, the commander of the regimental recce company, from his BMP command vehicle.

"Go ahead."

"Contact with airborne. Two elements have secured Ronnenberg and Wettbergen. You have free passage. Over."

"Understood. Make your way to Ditterke and report. You must secure the gap."

"Understood. Will contact you when we have a visual. Out."

Chapter 3

2030, 8 July 1984. 1st Battalion, 36th Mechanised Infantry
Regiment, 3rd Brigade, 3rd Armoured Division, US V Corps.
Stop-Line Dallas, northeast of Schluchtern, West Germany.
The Blue Effect -3 days

The Soviet planners of the invasion of West Germany had a number
of routes, options, available to them. Two consisted of a strike into
Western Europe from the area of the River Danube in the south,
or across the flat, open plains of Germany in the north. Crossing the
River Danube would allow the Warsaw Pact to attack through Austria
and into the soft underbelly of West Germany, in between Nuremberg
and Stuttgart, supporting any attack from Czechoslovakia. In the north,
the flat open plains straddling Minden, north and south, would allow
the fast movement of massed tank armies, although the growth of the
West German population and subsequent expansion of the towns and
villages would in effect provide small defendable fortresses. A third and
fourth option was to cut through the two corridors of the Fulda-Gap:
an area that stretched between East Germany and Frankfurt am Main
where two low-lying corridors linked Bad Hersfeld in the north and
Fulda in the south with the River Main. Situated close to the banks
of this major German river sits Frankfurt. Napoleon's armies used
these very routes after they were defeated at Leipzig. Over 100 years
later, during WW2, it was the route taken by the US XII Corps as
they advanced on the Germans in 1945. The northernmost corridor
passes south of Knullgebirge and continues around the northern
slopes of the Vogelsberg Mountains, a volcanic massif reaching a
height of 773 metres. The southern corridor stretches from the town
of Fulda to Frankfurt via the Flieden and Kinzig valleys, straddled by
the Vogelsberg Mountains to the north with the Rhon and Spessart
Mountains to the south.

Emerging from the western exit of these two routes, the Soviet army would encounter less undulating terrain, speeding up their advance after the slow, restricted corridors they would have initially navigated. From there, they could strike out for the River Rhine and attack deep into the heart of the US military, centred on Frankfurt am Main. The Rhein-Main Air Base, designated to receive a huge bulk of the US reinforcements, had to be defended at all costs.

Beyond Frankfurt, the US army garrison of Wiesbaden was a mere thirty kilometres away. The defence of this gap was in the hands of the US V Corps. With the 11th Cavalry Regiment, the 'Black Horse' Regiment, completing its role as a covering force after being pushed back by the advancing forces of the Soviet 8th Guards Army. General Stilwell, commander of US V Corps, had now committed the rest of his forces to the defence of this critical sector. His toughest unit was that of the 3rd US Armoured Division, and it was this unit that would take the brunt of the next phase of the Soviet attack.

The most famous soldier in the 3rd Armoured Division during the 1950s was Elvis Presley, assigned to Company A, 1st Battalion, 32nd Armoured Regiment, Combat Command C, at Ray Barracks in Friedberg. After his time in service, Elvis made the famous movie *G.I. Blues* in which he portrays a 3rd Armoured Division tank crewman with a singing career. Former Secretary of State, General Colin Powell, also served in the 3rd Armoured Division and went on to command V Corps in Germany. However, the Spearhead Division was about to face its toughest task yet.

The M113 Armoured Personnel Carrier, the first armoured vehicle of its kind to have an aluminium hull, slewed left, coming to a halt, depositing the HQ element of the platoon it carried. The soldiers dismounted as a second APC pulled up alongside them. The platoon leader beckoned for his men to deploy along the edge of the wood on the lower part of the slope, northwest of Schluchtern, they were assigned to defend. A third and fourth M113 manoeuvred further into the trees where their squads would also dig in overlooking the L3292, a minor road that ran west from the Autobahn that snaked southwest through the 3rd Brigade's position.

The platoon leader, Lieutenant Garcia, and his four squads had the task of protecting two units from the anti-tank platoon sent from the support company. They were expected within the next ten minutes.

Garcia made his way into the trees and met up with his platoon sergeant, Sergeant First Class Ricardo Park.

"LT, I've put first and second squad on the far left, weapons squad in the middle with third squad on the right."

"What are the foxholes like?"

"Good, sir, a decent size. The engineers have done a half decent job. The squads just need to sort out some top-cover."

"Let's go take a look then, Platoon Sergeant. We need to get the APCs moved pretty soon."

Before they could take a step towards the lower slope, the sound of the ITVs could be heard making their way through the trees. Although the forested area was very large, the trees themselves were fairly widely spaced, allowing smaller armoured vehicles to weave their way through slowly, providing someone guided them on foot. They turned around and headed back towards where the M113s were parked up and were met by an infantryman on foot guiding one of the M109 ITVs through the trees. Behind the lead ITV, they could see a second one following. The gunner who was the guide raised his hand and called a halt, and Garcia and Sergeant Park made their way over to the vehicle. The driver's helmeted head, goggles pushed up and back, could be seen peering out of the driver's hatch.

Behind him, the squad leader was sitting higher up. He called down, "Where do you want us, sir?"

"If you follow us in, we'll take you to your positions."

"Have they dug some berms for us?"

Lieutenant Garcia turned to Park and the platoon sergeant answered, "Yes. You have two facing the northeast and two to the southeast. I suggest you place one ITV each side. That'll give you two berms for each track."

"Your men, sir?"

"You'll have two squads on your left," answered Garcia. "Along with the weapons squad, that's where they'll probably try and flank us. There's a squad on your right, so watch where you go." The lieutenant laughed. "I don't want you running over my boys."

"I'll lead then, LT," suggested Park. "You can hitch a ride."

"You're on, Sergeant."

Garcia clambered up onto the M109 ITV, an Improved TOW Vehicle, crouching down next to the squad leader, Sergeant Dowling. To his left was the lowered 'hammerhead' turret, the TOW weapon launcher. He nearly fell off as the driver applied power to the tracks and the vehicle jerked forward.

"They coming tomorrow, Lieutenant?"

"They'll be here alright, so get yourselves organised quickly."

"Who's holding them off?"

"Twelve-Cav and two companies from 2nd Battalion. But they'll be here before the night's out. We'll probably see their recce first thing."

Sergeant Park turned round and jabbed his left arm in the direction of the southeast.

"Tell your second unit to follow my platoon sergeant, and I'll lead you to your location. I'll set up my platoon HQ close by."

"We'll need to ride in behind our positions, sir. Confirm our landmarks; then pull back out of sight."

"Yeah, fine." Garcia tapped the hammerhead. "These babies do a good job then?"

"You bet, sir. Eighty per cent probability of a hit."

"Keep your boys tight, Sergeant. Popov will looking to hit you during the twenty per cent."

"Gotcha, LT."

The vehicle spun on its tracks and headed northeast, the lieutenant guiding the driver.

"How far are we from your squads, sir?"

Garcia thought for a moment. "I've not looked at the positions yet, but we instructed your berms to be dug at least fifty metres from our positions."

"When these things fire, we'll draw their attention, that's for sure. Once the Red Army's tanks are less than 1,000 metres, we have orders to pull back."

"They'll be close enough for our Dragons then," answered Garcia. "Here we are."

The ITV stopped with a jolt, close to the edge of the forest, a berm carved out in front of them and the lieutenant slid down the front and off.

"I'll need to go further forward, sir. Check out the scenery."

"I'll leave you to it." Garcia patted the slab side of the ITV as it picked up speed, one of the crew now leading it through the trees.

The M109 ITV picked its way forward slowly and drove closer to the edge of the forest, only far enough so it was in a position for the squad leader to check out the lay of the land. The ground behind him was about 500 metres at its highest point, and his vehicle, along with the supporting infantry, was at roughly 200 to 300 metres. It gave him a great view of not only the valley where the Autobahn ran across the open fields towards his position, but he could also see across the open ground, apart from a few small buildings, to his left. The second ITV, 100 metres off to his right, would cover any blind spots. To his right was the berm dug out by the engineers from where he could support the mechanised infantry company dug in close by. And they, in turn, would reciprocate. His M109 ITV, replacing the older M113A1 TOW, would finally get an opportunity to show the enemy what it was capable of.

Dowling laughed to himself. The Russians were about to come up against the 3rd Armoured Division, so God help them. "Back up. I want to see the view from the berm."

2030, 8 July 1984. 4th Battalion, 67th Armoured Regiment, 3rd Brigade, 3rd Armoured Division, US V Corps. Stop-Line Dallas, southeast of Schluchtern, West Germany.
The Blue Effect -3 days

Two-Company, and its seventeen M1 Abram's, occupied the forward slope of a set of hills that looked out onto a valley, just south of the village of Gomfritz, facing the Autobahn coming from the northeast. A company from the 1st Mechanised Infantry Battalion had been given the northern side of the valley to defend, and a company of tanks from 4th Armoured Battalion the southern. The Major checked the positions of his armour, conferring with his platoon leaders, agreeing which platoons would pull out first and which would provide over-watch.

The road was now quiet. A long column of evacuees had passed by earlier in the day. Major Anderson dropped down beside his personal Abram's and rested his back against one of the bogie wheels where Lieutenant Hendricks, one of his platoon leaders, joined him. Anderson had a map on his knee and was examining the layout of the area the Spearhead Division had to defend.

"They're going to roll right into us tomorrow, sir."

"That they are, Ed, so keep your boys on the ball."

A rumble of explosions, no more than three kilometres away, shattered the relative silence.

"Son of a bitch. The Cav and the 2nd are getting some Soviet attention."

Major Anderson turned to his junior officer. "Yeah, but I hear the Russians are getting a bit of a stonking too."

"Those Cobras scare me, and they're on our side. Is Dallas ready, sir?"

Anderson slid the map across and briefed his subordinate on what he believed was the current status of Stop-Line Dallas.

As part of the preparation, for a potential invasion by the Warsaw Pact, which had been conducted over the last five years, the commander of US V Corps had instigated a number of stop-lines where his defence of the Fulda Gap and, in turn, the city of Frankfurt, would be conducted. Two of those had already been crossed. 11th Cavalry, using a rolling defence, provided the initial resistance to the Soviet invasion. Now, the responsibility had fallen to the 3rd Armoured Division to hold the final two stop-lines. The immediate one, Stop-Line Dallas, named after an American city, ran from Grafendorf northwest to Schluchtern, where the 3rd Brigade were centred, north to Freinsteinau, then west through Shotton, and north-east to Alsfeld. 1st Brigade had Alsfeld, and 2nd Brigade was on 3rd Brigade's left flank around Freinsteinau and Shotton, the towering Vogelsberg Mountains in the middle. If they were unsuccessful in holding, the Division would pull back to Stop-Line Phoenix, a line that ran from Lohr to Friedberg, passing through Geinhausen and Glauburg. Behind the 3rd Armoured Division sat the 8th Mechanised Infantry Division, deploying behind Phoenix ready to hold ground until more reinforcements arrived.

Beyond that line, the US military was still assessing what their next action would be. All that depended on speed: speed of the Soviet advance, speed at which reinforcements could be brought into the country, and the speed at which the US air force, and other NATO air forces for that matter, could hold their ground, gain air superiority, and hit back hard at the marauding Soviet armies.

US V Corps' primary role was the defence of the Fulda Gap and, ultimately, Frankfurt. On its right flank, US VII Corps was also battling with an advancing Soviet force, where 4th Armoured Division was digging in. Further right again, 2nd German Corps was holding. On their left flank, 3rd German Corps was fighting a bitter battle to hold ground. 1st Belgian Corps, having finally taken up their position to the German's left flank, took considerable pressure off the German Corps that had effectively been fighting a two Corps front. Although under the command of the Central Army Group (CENTAG), and following the orders of their American Army Group commander, the German Bundeswehr was impatient to hit back.

Having been forced to constantly retreat towards the west, watching their soldiers and civilians suffer from horrendous injuries and the devastating effects of chemical agents launched by the Soviet army, they were ready to release a brigade to support a counter-attack, catch the Soviets off guard, blunt their advance, and take the battle to the enemy. Their argument was that it would force the Soviets to halt and take stock, taking some pressure off the mauled Bundeswehr brigades, giving them time to consolidate and rearm. But, for now, their American commander was holding firm and reining them in.

"Looking good, sir."

"It does Ed. But for us, it all starts tomorrow. Let's mosey and check out the crews."

They both left the berm where one of the HQ's M1s was hull down, and moved off to check on the lieutenant's platoon of five tanks.

Of the three platoons in Two-Company, Lieutenant Kendrick's platoon held the centre, covering the gap between Gomfritz, off to their front left, and the wooded area to their front right, the high ground of Drasenberg behind them. The crews were edgy, knowing they were about to meet the enemy for the first time. They had seen the remnants of the Cavalry Regiment, bruised and battered, pulling back. Some of the men who were suffering from the effects of nerve agent poisoning had been pulled well back, way behind the front line, closer to the city of Frankfurt. Casualties had been high: losses of up to sixty per cent for some of the squadrons. And those that had survived were in no fit state to fight. Also the survivors of the chemical attacks were still suffering from the consequences of the absorption of the lethal toxins, the after-effects persistent. Those that had survived, through being appropriately protected and with a small amount of luck, were exhausted and traumatised. Their recent battle was over, but there was no way they would entirely be released from duty by their generals. They had an opportunity to eat and sleep, rearm and repair their vehicles, then rest some more. There was no doubt that if Frankfurt was threatened, they would be quickly designated as a reserve and brought back into the fight, used as fire brigade troops or a stopgap to cover any Soviet breakthroughs. Should the battle go well for the US forces, they could also be pulled in and used as part of any counter-attacking force.

The terrain to the platoon's front was good, but not perfect. The few buildings of Gomfritz to the northeast were in their line of sight, so Lieutenant Hendricks' platoon were unable to see the Autobahn as it passed the other side of the village. But Two-Platoon, further to the left, had a clear line of sight and would be able to target any enemy tanks fool enough to charge down the road, or either side of it. However, Hendricks' platoon did have a view out to their front that was well over four kilometres. They could see as far as the village of Ruckers where the forward elements of the Brigade, 12th Cavalry, had already pulled back too, disentangling themselves from the enemy. To the right, a small wood about a kilometre long restricted their view, but the Third-Platoon had that covered. The Third could also switch their fire east, towards the village of Elm. The high ground of the Ebertsberg, east of Elm, was covered by elements of the 2nd Armoured Battalion. The platoons were also equipped with the M1 Abram's, a tank the men had confidence in after changing the old M-60 for it. Whatever Soviet forces came at them, they would put up a good fight. This time, it wasn't a mere cavalry squadron, as powerful as it was, but a full armoured brigade of some 4,000 men.

Hendricks looked over his spot again. They had a good hull-down position, and all his crew knew the location of a further two should they need to pull back. To his right was a second position for his tank, a shallow ditch with a fallen tree perpendicular to it. Once they had fired a couple of rounds from his current berm, he would shift to this new location, covered by other tanks in the platoon as he did so. They, in turn, would conduct a similar manoeuvre while Tango-One-One and Tango-One-Two covered them. There was nothing out in front of them now but the enemy would be here soon. Two Medium Atomic Demolition Munitions, small nuclear devices of one kiloton each, had been detonated between Eichenzell and Neuhof on the valley floor along the Autobahn route. Other areas, north and south, had been treated in the same way, using nuclear landmines, powerful demolitions, to degrade the route the Soviet forces would have to take. Two more had been detonated west of Hutten and Gundhelm, obstructing the entrance to two further valleys. Before detonation, German civilian police and Jaeger troops had evacuated civilians in the local areas. Although many civilians had earlier become refugees, flooding west in front of the wave of Soviet forces behind them and fleeing the battle before they became engulfed in it, a few had decided to remain with their homes. When advised of what was about to happen close to their villages, to a man and a woman, they chose to leave.

41

Hendricks' men had felt the earth shake when the devices had exploded, tearing the earth apart, even vibrating the sixty-ton main battle tanks. They had received a warning when the detonations would be initiated, giving them time to ensure their eyes were protected. Even facing away from the location of the blast, night suddenly turned to day. The estimate of casualties had been as few as ten killed and thirty injured at each ground zero. In the immediate vicinity of the blast, the fireball would have expanded to a radius of nearly 100 metres, and a powerful blast out to four times that distance which would easily destroy heavy buildings, and most residential buildings would collapse. Anyone within three quarters of a kilometre from ground zero would be exposed to a high rem radiation dose and, without swift medication; it was likely that the mortality rate would be as high as ninety per cent. More importantly, torn up trees and disturbed earth, deeply rutted, would degrade the route that the Soviets would have to take.

Fallout would also be an issue for the advancing Soviet soldiers. The wind, blowing a steady five to ten kilometres per hour, would take the fallout away from the US troops and towards the enemy. From each ground zero, there would be a cloud moving slowly east, out to about twenty kilometres, where exposure would drop to around one rad per hour. In total, over fifty square kilometres would be affected.

Hendricks mounted his M1 and dropped down into the turret, checked in with his crew, and confirmed there had been no messages from HQ. He laid his map on the rim of the hatch and ran his finger along the stop-line they were defending. Moving his finger further east, he picked out the areas designated as artillery targets, committing them to memory as best he could. A FIST, Fire Support Team Vehicle would be close by, ready to call in fire when needed. M109s, nine kilometres to the rear were ready to support him, and the rest of the battalion, when called upon.

He then picked up his binoculars and scanned those sectors, making sure that, if it were up to him to make the call, he would get it right. The night was drawing in and he had been warned by his battalion commander that the Soviet unit, elements of 8th Guards Army Division, once 12th Cav had pulled right back, might probe their positions during the hours of darkness. Scouts in vehicles and on foot would shortly be sent out ready to interdict any such reconnaissance, replacing the helicopters of the 2nd Attack

Helicopter Battalion that would attempt to track the Soviet armours' progress right up until the last minute. He'd heard reports that the aviation regiment was getting a hard time. The ZSU-23/4s were proving to be an excellent weapon of choice for air defence, taking out three helicopters, two AH1Fs and one OH58C in the last few hours. All he could do now though was wait.

Chapter 4

2210, 8 July 1984. Ministerium fur Staatssicherheit, MfS state prison, Hohenschonhausen, East Berlin.
The Blue Effect -3 days

Bradley slowly woke up, his senses reeling, nearly causing him to black out again. With pulsing temples and a pounding headache, the black bag over his head and face was stifling. He was curled up on the floor, his knees up, arms cradling them, almost foetal-like. He wriggled his fingers, and then flexed his hands: they were free of restraint. He slowly stretched out his legs, yelping with pain where soldiers wearing heavy military boots had repeatedly kicked him. The sound uttered from his cracked lips was swallowed up instantly and, for a moment, he wasn't actually sure he'd made a sound. He shifted his body again, spitting a piece of the bag out of his mouth after sucking it in when taking a deep breath. He could feel something behind him and used its soft surface to gain traction and lever his body into a sitting position. This made him feel nauseous and he heaved, retching, his head pounding even harder, white flashes of light, like shooting stars racing away from his eyes. He stopped moving, resting his back against the padded wall.

Once his stomach had settled and he had swallowed back the bitter taste of bile, he reached up to remove the hood, wanting a view of his surroundings. With the coarse material removed, the dark was replaced by yet more darkness: a blackness that ordinary eyesight couldn't possibly penetrate; a blackness that was suffocating in itself. Bradley's fingers explored his body, assessing his injuries. They didn't have to move far before they discovered egg-shaped lumps on various parts of his anatomy, and a particularly large swelling on the side of his head.

He attempted to stand, slapping his hand against the thick, black, ribbed sides of the isolation cell. Beneath his hands were rubber-coated walls, thick soundproof insulation that completely encapsulated the cell, top to bottom, in a waterproof and soundproof shield. He eventually pushed himself upright, his legs trembling as his stomach suddenly heaved again, vile-tasting stomach acids burning his throat and tongue. He retched again. Only greenish brown bile left his mouth and stomach as he slumped back to the floor.

He suddenly had a raging thirst and called out, "I need some water...hello."

He could barely hear his own voice as he tried to shout louder, the sounds dampened and going nowhere.

"I need water," he almost whispered.

He ran the last twenty-four hours through his mind. At least, he thought it had been twenty-four hours, or thereabouts.

Once caught, he had been beaten and dragged to one of the trucks on the Autobahn and thrown in the back with two guards and one of their dogs. He was curled up at the front end, next to the cab, coming to terms with his condition and, more importantly, his circumstances. The flap at the rear was pulled down and secured, and what little light there was was now blocked out. The dog and his handler took great delight in tormenting Bradley further. The dog's sharp teeth gripped his boot, not quite piercing it, but the grip was so firm that it crushed his toes. Then the war-dog would yank at it, twisting its head and shoulders violently in order to drag Bradley closer and rend his foot from his leg.

It eventually stopped as the commotion was annoying the guards, who lit up a cigarette and discussed the war that was in progress. Bradley's German was fair and he got the gist that the war had well and truly kicked off, and NATO were not holding their ground. He wasn't sure what to believe. *Are the guards continuing to taunt me in a different manner?* He thought. But they sounded fairly nonchalant, now disinterested in their captive, looking forward to getting back to barracks and catching up with some sleep.

Bradley attempted to register distances, speed, sound, and taking note of when the vehicle turned; more as a distraction than through any expectation of an escape. Within only fifteen minutes, he started to lose track, and his concentration waned. After what he perceived to be an hour, he gave up completely. The journey progressed for what must have been two to three hours. He just lay there numbed. Unknown to Bradley, the route of their journey was deliberate, literally driving round in circles at times, the intention to disorientate their captive.

On arrival at his destination, he was hooded and dragged off the lorry, duck-walked until inside a building and thrown into a small brick or concrete-lined cell, remaining there with a guard for no more than five minutes. Picked up again, he was taken along a corridor before turning left where he was placed on a seat in what felt like, from the confined sounds reflected off the walls, a smallish room, the edge of something hard touching his knee. He couldn't hear anyone else there, but could sense he was not alone. He was sure someone was standing behind him, and perhaps another of his captors was sitting across from him on the other side of what could be a desk or table.

"Well, Mr Spy."

Bradley jumped at the sound of a man's voice coming from the other side of the object in between them. The accent was clearly German, but his English sounded near perfect.

"I shall start by explaining to you how life is going to be for you, going forward. But, first, I need you to fully understand the position in which you now find yourself."

The voice picked up an object, followed by the sound of a liquid being sipped and swallowed.

"Either you, or your comrade, have killed a member of the *National Volksarmee:* a soldier of the German Democratic Republic who was just doing his duty for his country. A family man, I might add; a good man, protecting his country from intruders such as yourself. He is now dead and leaves a wife and two young children to fend for themselves. No, that is not strictly true: their country will take care of them. So, Mr Spy, you will eventually be charged with murder."

Bradley could pick out the sound of shuffling papers through the throbbing in his temples. The splitting headache returned and it felt like his skull wanted to burst open.

"You are, at the moment," continued the voice, "in the custody of the MfS, the *Ministerium fur Staatssicherheit.* You have been caught spying on the German Democratic Republic at a time of war. Because, Mr Spy, we are at war with your country, so you come under my control now. But, I have a dilemma."

Bradley heard the rasp of material and caught a whiff of stale cigarette smoke. "And," he said quietly, leaning forward, "I hope you can help me out with this. You are in uniform, I can see that. But, I don't believe you are a soldier. I think you are one of those spies that hide away in the bowels of the British Government buildings in the occupied portion of our city of Berlin. When ordered, you leave your nests to spread your filth across decent nations like ourselves. So, you see, in my mind you are here, disguised as a soldier, in order to pass back information on our forces and operations to your masters back in the West."

A door opened behind him and Bradley felt something brush against him; then heard a cup being placed on a hard surface. He could sense a warm vapour, then the smell of hot chocolate assailed his nostrils through the hood. The voice took a sip and made a sound of satisfaction.

"Also, you have killed one of our soldiers. His *Kameraden* waiting outside are very keen to get hold of you. They want to extract revenge. It was only through my intervention that you are actually alive and sitting here in my office."

The voice took another sip of hot chocolate, and Bradley could hear the sound of smacking lips. He resisted the temptation to point out that they had killed his comrade: Jacko was dead, killed by one of those very men that were standing outside wanting to get to him. He kept quiet.

"So," the voice carried on, "soon, very soon, I will be asking you some questions. But not just yet. I am in no hurry. I want you to reflect on your situation and come forward willingly with any information that you think may be of use to us."

Another slurp of hot chocolate.

"Is there anything you would like to inform me of now?"

Bradley went to speak, but nothing came out. He tried again. "24388749, Bradley Reynolds, Sergeant, Royal Corps of Transport," he finally managed to get out.

"Ah, the classic. Wonderful. We are going to get along just fine, you and I, Herr Bradley."

Another drink of his chocolate.

"I recognise your cap badge. But I have one slight problem with that statement." The voice sounded distorted, like he was bent over. *Crash.* An object was slammed down on the on the hard surface in front, and Bradley not only felt the residue of brackish water splash over him but also smelt it.

"We have some very bright people in our organisation. You have some very bright people in yours. Some of them have willingly passed information on to us. For money, I might add. From the information that we have gathered on the British forces, I know this to be a Clansman PRC, and it is no ordinary radio. A PRC-319, I have been informed. A fifty-watt microprocessor-based radio transceiver. And this," he said, "would allow you to type a message and send the data at high speed to your masters. It is of a type used by spies and Special

Forces. Now, what would a driver want with one of these?"

Bradley knew exactly what it was, the radio, along with the small alphanumeric keyboard; he had pushed into the ditch just before he was captured. "I cannot answer that question."

The blow from behind came out of the blue, and the shock of it was almost as devastating as the blow itself. Bradley's ears rang, and the painful swellings on the side of his head felt as if someone had thrust a white-hot poker into them.

"You see, Herr Bradley. You lie to me. Next time we speak, I hope you will be more cooperative. Take him out."

Bradley's mind raced. He wasn't sure what to expect. During his training he had been taken through 'Resistance to Interrogation'. It wasn't pleasant. But he had no real idea of what was in store for him now. It was not as if there was a political stalemate to rely on. His boss knowing he was missing. A protest made to the Soviets, their WW2 Allies, to secure his release. A few slapped wrists, and he would be back home in a matter of hours. But that wasn't going to happen: they were at war.

He was manhandled along what appeared to be a well-lit corridor, a light occasionally passing underneath the folds of his hood. His escort said nothing, and he heard no sound other than the slap of his bare feet and the boots of his captors. The guards stopped suddenly, and he was pushed into a narrow room. The door was slammed in his hooded face. Calling the room narrow would be an understatement. The concrete floor was cold on his feet, and his shoulders touched an equally cold wall either side. In fact, he was trapped. He couldn't move in any direction, couldn't sit or lie down. It wasn't long before the cold started to creep up his body, and he flexed his feet and toes as best he could. He was tired, desperate to close his eyes and fall asleep, but his body was already starting to scream in pain, his well-muscled body suffering at being pinned in this one position. He felt sick, but forced it back down. His mind raced, fear gripping him. Yes, they had driven around for two or three hours. But he now knew that they had travelled only a few miles. He was in the 'Submarine', the subterranean cell block run by the DDR's Ministry of State Security, the *Ministerium fur Staatssicherheit*, the MfS, the infamous Stasi. He was at Hohenschonhausen, the MfS prison where they held political prisoners and those caught attempting to escape from the DDR. He had driven past it many times in the past, reminding the Stasi that the West was watching. Now, he found himself on the inside.

48

His legs felt like jelly and, had he been able to, he would have collapsed, but he couldn't. Fear welled up inside him, gripping his stomach like a vice; the pounding in his head multiplied ten-fold, and tears welled up in his eyes. His thoughts before he passed out were that he was going to die in this place.

After drifting in and out of consciousness for an unknown number of hours, his body was racked with pain on a level he had never experienced before. He was eventually released. He asked his escort where they were taking him to, could he have some food, some water. But they remained silent. His cramped legs protested painfully, his upper thighs burning from the urine he'd had to release while confined, as he was dragged to the cell he was in now, given a reprieve, if that was what you could call it.

His head snapped round as the grey steel door was pulled open, the sudden blinding light from the corridor stabbing his eyes. Pulled to his feet by two of his captors, the hood reapplied, he was taken out of his padded isolation cell and transported painfully elsewhere to the upper part of the prison block, the new four-storey section built in the late 50s. He knew, from reports received by ex-prisoners who had eventually been released and subsequently escaped across the Berlin Wall that the prison had a traffic-light system. This ensured that prisoners never got to meet, ensuring their isolation at all times.

He was thrust into a small room, pushed down on a lightly padded steel chair, and his hood was yanked off. The door was closed behind him as he placed his hands over his eyes to protect them from the bright light. Once accustomed to the glare, he took stock of the room. He was sitting at a small square table, not much wider than the seat of his chair. This was butted up against a steel-legged desk, topped in a light brown with a set of matching drawers attached each side. Sitting behind the desk, on a much more comfortably upholstered chair with wooden arms, sat an MfS officer, his grey uniform with its distinctive piping. A major.

The major said nothing, but continued to make notes in a small notebook. To the right of the MfS officer, there was a tall, green cabinet and behind him a dark cream, cast-iron radiator. A flimsy set of pale green curtains prevented Bradley seeing what was outside. On the desk was a phone and, alongside, a reel-to-reel tape recorder. Did the voice now have a face?

The major finally looked up from his scribbling. "Herr Bradley,

I won't ask after your health as I'm sure you are not at your best. There was a very good reason why I allowed you to spend some time getting acquainted with our special room." He opened one of the left-hand desk drawers and extracted a packet of cigarettes and a Zippo lighter. Taking a plain cigarette from the packet, he lit it and took a slow, satisfying drag. He picked a loose shred of tobacco from his lips as he held up the Zippo lighter. "I love this lighter. It has a picture of a red London bus on it – so quaint. I bought it the last time I visited your country when I had other duties to perform. So, I know a little about you British." He took another draw, the tip of the cigarette glowing a bright red, before tapping the ash off onto a saucer on the desk. His chair creaked as he leant back, savouring the smoke as he exhaled.

"I want you to fully understand there are no political games to play here. Your government are not coming to your rescue." He laughed lightly. "In fact, they have no idea where you are, or if indeed you are still alive. They will have no doubt logged your lack of radio transmissions by now." He made eye contact with Bradley, who shifted on his seat trying to get as comfortable as possible, pain lancing through his cramped muscles. "So, Herr Bradley, let's not mess about. Just tell me what I want to know, and I can have you medically treated and get some hot food inside you. Eh?"

Bradley remained silent, his stomach cramping at the thought of food. He was in constant pain, the hunger and thirst only making matters worse. There was a terrible smell emanating from him, he was sure. His jumper had been removed, but he still wore his No. 2 shirt. It was soiled and slightly damp, as were his green trousers.

Bradley lifted his head up as he heard a clink. The major was stirring his coffee after adding three teaspoons of sugar.

"I don't know how you English can drink tea. It has no bite to it. Would you like a cup of coffee, Herr Bradley? Of course not. You have been trained to keep a stiff upper lip." He laughed to himself.

"All I want to know is how many other spies there are in the vicinity of Berlin? And beyond, of course. How many teams do you have out there? Well?"

Bradley remained silent. He knew that he and Jacko were the only Intelligence acquisition team out on the circuit, but there were at least two operatives from the security section. They had a very different task to perform within the confines of the city of East Berlin itself. Bradley had taken two across, individually, over two days, hidden under a blanket in the back of the Range Rover. It hadn't been the first time he'd done that. He and his section worked closely with their sister unit, photographing buildings of potential significance, completing Close Target Reconnaissance on their behalf; hunting for installations that the Soviets and East Germans tried to keep hidden.

Bradley thought back to the day they had discovered a secret hospital in the middle of the forest of Wernsdorf, surrounded by high walls, topped with barbed wire, and with watchtowers at each corner. The response from the occupants had been aggressive. Within minutes, two Ural-375 trucks had appeared, loaded with MfS troops. Before they could surround the Range Rover, Jacko manoeuvred the vehicle between the trees, pursued by soldiers on foot, one of the Ural-375s crashing through the trees behind them. Just as Jacko and Bradley thought they had made it, a UAZ-469, a Soviet jeep, cut across their front. Jacko twisted the steering wheel, driving the vehicle through a gap in the trees, pressed hard on the accelerator and, with a spray of debris from the rear wheels, extracted them from the trap, but it left them with two of the tyres punctured. The two right-hand side wheels bumbled over the ground as the air escaped. But they kept moving until they could hold up somewhere and review their position. Accessing an abandoned forestry compound, they pulled up behind a small hut and waited. Once they believed themselves to be safe, they assessed the damage: two tyres were shredded, and both of the wheels badly damaged. Another team would have to come out and bring replacements.

"What about a drink?" the major asked as he slid a small glass of water across the desk until it rested in front of Bradley.

Bradley looked at the glass, and then into the eyes of his interrogator, because that's what he was, then back to the glass. He had been taught to take food and water at every opportunity. His lips and throat were dry, his tongue swollen. He reached out with shaking hands, one badly bruised and swollen after being stepped on by a studded boot. Gripping the glass as best he could, he lifted it to his lips, the glass rattling against his teeth. He closed his eyes and savoured the tepid water, an elixir. His spirits rose slightly and he replaced the empty glass on the table.

"See, there is no need for all this unpleasantness. So, tell me about your friends."

"24388749, Bradley Reynolds, Sergeant, Royal Corps of Transport."

Chapter 5

0100, 9 July 1984. Corps Patrol Unit (CPU). Southeast of Pattensen, West Germany.
The Blue Effect -2 days

The Corps Patrol Unit was currently positioned in a deep ditch close to a water feature northwest of Heisede, about a kilometre from the east bank of the River Leine. Wilf had chosen their location due to the patchy water catchment areas surrounding the water feature, an unfriendly area for vehicles, and particularly armoured ones. As a consequence of Wilf's choice of location, they were damp, and Badger's gripes about it being gopping were fairly frequent, unsurprisingly.

The CPU, on receiving new orders from headquarters back at 1 BR Corps, had moved from Lehrte to their current location on the banks of the River Leine, which they now planned to cross. After the aborted reconnaissance of the 12th Guards Tank Division headquarters, their planned return to their Mexe-hide was suspended and they were ordered west. They had moved as far as possible in the early hours of the 8th but, with a heavy Soviet presence and troops crossing the River Leine to reinforce the rapidly growing bridgehead, they had finally been forced to go to ground. That gave the soldiers an opportunity to rest up before moving out again during dusk of the same day. Before the light of day finally died, as they headed towards Sarstedt, they witnessed more of the carnage of the fierce battles that had been fought by the British and West German forces to hold up the pressing Soviet advance. Once they had extracted themselves from the forward headquarters of 12th Guards Tank Division, the team's next mission was to report on Soviet units crossing the River Leine, looking particularly for reinforcements following on in support of GSFG's main thrust south of Hanover and Gronau. Following that, a particularly important mission had been assigned to them. It had been a long tab, travelling in the dark for cover but constantly on the alert for enemy forces that were either consolidating in the area or passing through. On occasion, what they took to be campfires of Soviet military units often turned out to be still burning tanks and armoured personnel carriers. Some hulks had been doused and would no doubt be recovered by the Soviet engineers at some point. Up until now, the four SAS soldiers had only seen enemy equipment and soldiers, other than RAF or other NATO countries' ground-attack aircraft harassing the Soviet forces' rapid advance. One shock they did encounter though was coming across a burnt-out Challenger tank, with its crew still on board, which brought home to them that they were well and truly behind enemy lines and were becoming more and more isolated from their own forces as every day passed by. The team had considered rummaging through the bodies in order to get hold of their dog tags. But the bodies were so badly burnt, the crew's clothing practically none existent that, even the hardened soldiers that they were, they couldn't bring themselves to rummage around the human debris to search for the articles in question. Apart from that, they still had a mission to perform. The Challenger was far from being the only hulk on the battlefield. They came across two more of these latest model British tanks, but the open ground was also strewn with T-80s, BMPs, SA9s, ZSUs and the odd Jeep or box-bodied vehicle. The Soviets had plainly paid a heavy price to take the ground that was now theirs.

As darkness had closed in, all Wilf's team could see of the still smoking hulks was the occasional flicker of flame or glowing metal. It wouldn't be long before the Soviet engineers started to recover their own damaged vehicles with a view to repairing those they could and quickly putting them back into the battle.

It had taken the CPU nearly six hours to get to their current location, prepare their kit, and move closer to the riverbank. Their route had been through a golf club, then some wetlands, an area scattered with close-lying mini lakes of water. They made their way down to the riverbank, keeping their movements as quiet as possible. This was difficult when their kit was wet, and they couldn't help but squelch as they picked their way through the sodden earth. Wilf had chosen this way deliberately. He looked about him, smelling the damp earth and grass around them. Thick clumps of coarse vegetation provided them with good cover. But soon they would have to leave it and make their way across the river and west. While they were heading deeper and deeper into what was now enemy territory, there was a comfort in the fact that they were moving closer to their homeland. All four crouched next to the water, watching and listening. Tag, their strongest swimmer, would go across first and check out the far bank. Wilf had chosen a level stretch of water, with a light-coloured sandbank downstream on the opposite side.

Wilf tapped Tag on the shoulder, and the SAS trooper took his first steps into the water. He, like the rest of them, was stripped down to his underwear and boots. Out in front was his rucksack, all the contents in a waterproof sack inside, helping it maintain neutral buoyancy. An additional bag had been filled with air, tied off, and was adding to the buoyancy of the heavy Bergen. His combat uniform was bagged and tied to the top, along with his personal weapon. He took small steps ensuring his boots had a good footing before the depth of the water forced him to swim, keeping his body as flat as possible, pushing his pack out in front of him. He allowed the slow current to take him, not fighting it, but swimming at a forty-five degree angle, aiming for the sandbank on the other side.

Once across, he heaved his bag out, released his SLR, and moved up the bank. He was cold, very cold, but needed to be sure they hadn't been discovered. He gave it ten minutes, returned to his pack, put on his dry clothing, and signalled the rest of the patrol with a red-filtered torch. The three men started their crossing. It was 0235, so they still had the cover of darkness to get as far west as possible. CPU headquarters were adamant that speed was of the essence. Once all were across and fully dressed, the patrol crowded around peering at the 1:50,000 map that Wilf had lain on the damp ground.

"Well, boys, it's a bit warmer now," he whispered.

"A bloody hot drink would be a godsend," muttered Badger.

His friends just grinned. All was well if Badger was moaning.

"We need to push as far as we can while it's still dark. We have to get as close to the Deister as possible. That tab will give our bodies a chance to warm up," advised Wilf.

"We could just go in a straight line," suggested Tag.

"Risky," warned Hacker. "The place will be crawling with soldiers."

"Yes, but they'll want to be under the cover of a canopy, near buildings or snug in a barn," countered Wilf.

"Let's just do it," advocated Badger. "Get under some decent cover. We're pretty exposed out here."

The other three couldn't disagree with that so, with Wilf in the lead and Bergen's on their backs, the four men headed across the cultivated fields that stretched from south-east of Pattensen to the southern tip of the Deister. Weapons were always at the ready: Badger in the rear with his C7 carbine; Hacker next with his M-16 A2; Tag with his SLR; and Wilf's M-16 swinging left and right as he scanned the route ahead. They stuck to hedge lines as often as possible, stopping every thirty minutes to look and listen. Apart from the popping of guns to the north and the occasional rumble of aircraft at high level, they heard and saw very little.

It was only as they got closer to the village of Hupede that enemy activity increased, so Wilf led them southwest in between the villages of Hupede and Oeire to a small copse where they could hide up during daylight hours. There they could rest, catch up on some sleep, and, more importantly, recce their surroundings as they were sure that the missile unit they were seeking wouldn't be more than a few kilometres away.

Chapter 6

A Tomcat taxied through the steam given off by the steam-catapult from the previously launched aircraft. The plane handler looked on as a third and fourth Grumman F-14D Tomcat lined up on the carrier's deck. The plane handler, distinguishable by his blue coat and blue helmet, lined the first one up with the catapult shuttle that lay ready on the four and a half acre deck. Two one-hundred-metre long tubes, an open slit between them, ran along at deck level, a shuttle protruding just above the deck. The nose wheel of the 27,000-kilogram aircraft nudged up against the shuttle, and the pilot lowered the tow bar until it connected with the slot in the shuttle. The holdback was attached to the rear of the nose gear strut. Jet blast deflector-number one was raised as the F-14 powered up its engines. It wasn't possible to mistake an F-14 fighter, the 'King' of the US CVN flight decks: it was both powerful and noisy. Neither was it modest in size with its large wings spread ready for take-off. It dominated the flight deck as much as it did the airways. A green shirt checked the aircraft was correctly hooked up. Once the engines powered up ready for take-off, without the holdback, the brakes would not be able to hold the aircraft on their own. A second green shirt held up a chalkboard, showing the aircraft's take-off weight for the benefit of the pilot and catapult officer. The pilot, and the catapult officer who is located in the catapult control pod, give each other a hand signal confirming they both agreed the weight being displayed was correct. Final checks completed, Lieutenant Higgs selected full power for the two General-Electric turbofan engines, and both he and his radar intercept officer braced themselves for the force of the launch. The catapult shooter depressed the button in the control pod, the holdback was jerked away from its grip on the Tomcat, and the aircraft was thrown down the aircraft carrier deck at forty-five metres per second, the fighter dipping slightly as it left the deck. Reaching its flying speed of 150 knots, the fighter was finally launched. These two Tomcats would relieve the two already providing a Combat Air Patrol protecting the 'The Boat', as they fondly referred to the aircraft carrier.

Their primary mission, air superiority, had a key role to play in defending the carrier and its accompanying ships. One of the key threats was from the deadly AS-4 Kitchen and AS-6 Kingfish Soviet long-range, radar-guided missiles that packed a punch. The AS-6, in particular, carried a 1,000-kilogram warhead. Carried by the Soviet long-range bombers, TU-16 Badger, TU-95 Bear and the TU-22M Backfire, they were a major threat to the aircraft carrier and its escorting ships. The Tomcat's Phoenix air-to-air missiles, with a range of 185 kilometres, had been specifically designed to counter that threat.

Lining up behind the fighters that had just launched, a selection of aircraft were preparing to support the US Army battling against overwhelming forces that were arrayed up against them. An EC-2 airborne early warning aircraft was already on watch, but a second one would join it soon, moving closer to the proposed target area west of the Fulda Gap. A strike force was being assembled: two EA-6Bs, electronic warfare aircraft, an attack squadron of twelve A-7Es, a fighter squadron of twelve F/A-18s, and three KA-ED tankers for inflight refuelling. A convoy brought safely to the European Continent, the USS Carl Vinson was now tasked with assisting the US air force in supporting the US ground forces.

Six storeys above, on the 'Island', in the Primary Flight Control, Pri-Fly, two senior officers watched the activity down below on the flight deck. Surrounding them, windows angled away from the bulkhead providing an excellent view of the flight deck, comms and consul displays, the centre of operations for controlling the air activity in the vicinity of the ship was a hive of activity.

"Any more from Providence, sir?" asked the air boss, Commander Chilvers.

"No, just the emergency signal," responded Captain Kiely, the skipper of the 100,000-ton aircraft carrier USS Carl Vinson (CVN-70).

"What's your plan, sir?"

The Captain turned to Commander Chilvers, the commander of the carrier's air wing, Air-Wing 15. Chilvers' himself had been a pilot for a number of years, but now commanded over ninety aircraft from the 'Island' as opposed to in the air.

"I've despatched a destroyer, that's all I can do for now. I can't release anyone else. We have the convoy to protect as well as our next mission once we're released from this babysitting duty."

"Not sure how many would have made it without us sir. They've pulled out all the stops to get submarines in the vicinity to interrupt our progress."

"At a price, Kyle. We've killed two of them."

"And a possible."

"Yes, but that one worries me. Let's hope to God it's on the bottom somewhere."

"And we don't know what kills Providence has under her belt."

"Losing that fuel tanker was bad news."

"We'll need to be on the alert for some more. If Providence has intercepted more of our Soviet comrades, we could have visitors very soon."

F/A-18 Hornets blasted their way down the flight deck, joining the squadron that was forming up. They would provide a Combat Air Patrol for the ground-strike force that was also in the process of forming up. Two Tomcats would also be sent up to protect the ever-growing array of aircraft circling above. It wasn't only submarines that the Soviets were sending to prevent the US convoy from reaching its destination, bringing badly needed supplies, equipment and men to the European continent to help stem the Warsaw Pact tide. Long-range Soviet bombers would also be out hunting.

"What have we got up at the moment – for subs, that is?"

"The usual, sir, but I've sent two Vikings fifty miles astern. Have a sneak around for any sign of subs trying to creep up on us."

"Good. We've been promised some air cover from the mainland. The Brits have promised us two or three of their Nimrod anti-submarine aircraft."

"Good, that will take some pressure off the Vikings."

"Tomorrow, we go through a full debrief of your air group. Once they've completed their mission, that is. The convoy will be ready to go any day soon, so the escort needs to be ready for the return journey."

"My boys will be ready, sir, don't you worry about that."

"I know, Kyle. Right, I'll leave you to watch over your fledglings. By the way, how are the two new boys doing?"

"Fine, sir. Both have good scores on the greenie board so far."

"Great. Leave you to it."

The captain left the CAG to control his air ops and headed for the bridge, high up on the 'Island' between the flag bridge below and the Primary Flight Control level above it. He passed through an entryway hatch, turning right, stepping over a 'knee-knocker', a tall step over one of the many structural members that gave the Vinson its structural integrity. Then he made his way down the narrow corridor, crew coming from the opposite direction stepping aside to allow their captain to pass by freely. The captain clattered down a set of long metal steps taking him to level-09 where he was able to enter his domain, the bridge.

On the port side, the left of the bridge was his elevated leather seat, currently occupied by his Executive Officer, Commander Chuck Summers. The XO went to rise and give up the seat but was waved back down by his commander.

"All quiet, Chuck?"

"For the moment, sir. I'll feel better when we get some air cover from the land bases."

"Me too. Our jet jockeys need to be able to slow the tempo if the Aircraft Maintenance Division are to get on top of the backlog of repairs that are building up."

"Will they have breathing space after the mission?"

"Twenty-four hours, tops. Once we are out of range of the land bases, we'll need twenty-four-hour top cover again." He cast his eye over the computer screens that flanked the captain's chair. All looked to be in order. Over to the starboard side, stood the wheel, chart table, and the conning stations. Lookouts stood peering through their binoculars, backing up the electronic aids that provided the captain with an electronic picture of the surrounding area. "I want to go through the convoy return plans again later today."

"You worried, sir?"

The captain took off his dark blue baseball cap, bought by his wife for his forty-fifth birthday, and brushed his fingers through his brown but slowly greying hair. Placing his cap back on, he responded, "Our air wing is primarily for defence, Chuck, not attack. Certainly not attacking land-based targets."

"Our boys on the ground are putting up a pretty good fight by all accounts, but are getting hit damn hard. A bit of help from us won't go amiss."

"I know that, Chuck, dammit. Sorry. You saw the last report. The Soviets are right up against the Fulda Gap. If we can't support our troops on the ground then the enemy could be at the gates of Frankfurt in less than three days. But air-to-ground strikes are not our forte."

"Kyle's boys will do the job, sir."

A young lieutenant interrupted their conversation. "The escort group has a possible sighting, sir."

"Bearing?"

"One-Nine-Two, fifteen miles, sir."

"Right, Chuck, you still have the con. I'm going down to the CDC."

Chapter 7

0600, 9 July 1984. 4th Battalion, 67th Armoured Regiment,
3rd Brigade, 3rd Armoured Division, US V Corps.
Stop-Line Dallas, northeast of Schluchtern, West Germany.
The Blue Effect -2 days

Lieutenant Hendricks could feel the perspiration running down his back. The inside of the tank suddenly felt stifling, and there was a huge desire to tear off his MOPP suit. They were at MOPP Level 2 – suits and boots on, gloves and Pro-Mask carried. Although taking his gloves on and off was such a pain in the ass, he'd decided to keep them on. The nuclear and chemical protective suit just added another layer, its bulk preventing the heat that was building up inside from escaping. He wasn't scared, but there was a heavy feeling of apprehension tugging at his mind. His hands inside his rubber gloves were clammy with sweat. However, he relaxed slightly once he realised he had been clenching and unclenching his hands, forming tight fists as his mind raced.

He started as he heard shells flying overhead, their target the US troops, a company dug in 500 metres further back. Peering through the scope, he watched another Cobra swoop in, drop down below treetop level; then, having been given information by one of the OH-58 spotter helicopters, it popped back up and launched a missile. He watched helicopters progress before it flew to the rear again.

"Tango-One-One, Tango Zero. Enemy four kilometres out. The flyboys tell us that the poor ground is causing them to bunch. Give them hell. Out."

"Company HQ say they're getting close, boys. Four thousand metres. Keep focussed, everyone. Malone, you OK up front?" Queried Lieutenant Hendricks.

"Sure, LT. Just let me know when to move, and I'll have this baby relocated like a shot."

"Good. Tate?"

"Yessir. Popov's not getting past us today," responded Tate, his gunner.

"We're the best. We're the Spearhead Division. Right, LT?" added Orfila, his loader.

"You're right about that. Just keep those rounds coming."

"Tango-One-One, Tango-Zero. Incoming friendlies. Out."

"Standby boys. We have aircraft about to hit the enemy."

"A-10s, LT?" asked Tate.

"Not this time. I've been told the navy is coming to the rescue."

"I'll shout when I see the first destroyer." Tate laughed.

Moments later, any chatter was disturbed by the roar of jet bombers roaring overhead as the A7-Es flew in, two at a time, dropping their ordnance on top of the targets they had been designated. Above, F/A-18 Hornets battled it out with the Soviet air force. They were unable to do too much, only carrying two air-to-air missiles, the long range reducing the weapons load they could carry so they could loiter while the bombers did their job. Once finished, the surviving bombers returned to 'the boat' where they could prepare for their next mission: protecting the convoy as it returned stateside.

It's getting close, Hendricks thought as he secured the hatch and squinted through the vision blocks. He didn't need his binoculars to see the two Cobras hovering up ahead, waiting to ambush the Soviet T-64s. *That will give them something to think about.* He hoped that he and his platoon would give a good account of themselves. He had confidence in his M1 but was fully aware that their 105mm main gun was disadvantaged by the Soviet tank's 125mm-calibre smoothbore gun. The tank's armour was solid and he felt safe within its confines. *We will sure give the invaders a bloody nose.*

Way out to the front, probably in excess of 3,500 metres, he watched as a cloud slowly rose up across the horizon. The Lance battalion, subordinated to the heavy artillery brigade, was also showing its teeth in the ongoing battle. The Lance missiles, with their M251 warheads carrying hundreds of sub munitions, sprayed the advancing Soviet forces with a deadly storm. They might not defeat the enemy, but they could sway the forthcoming battle shifting the advantage to the defending US forces. The crew were now quiet as the tank commander settled himself in the fighting compartment. There had been some inane chatter, guessing at the location where the T-64s would appear first, reiterating the tactics they would apply once the fight started. Even families had been a part of the four-way discussion between the crew, and at one point politics came into the frame, at which time they had all laughed, realising they had been babbling about anything and everything for the last thirty minutes. It had helped to ease their nerves, but now they were silent, deep within their own thoughts, preparing themselves in their own way for what was about to transpire. Only the throbbing of the tank's engine could be heard.

Hendricks opened the hatch again and pushed himself up for one last look. Somewhere out there, not too far away, a giant, possibly unstoppable, steamroller was heading in their direction.

The nearest Cobra flared, and a trail of jet exhaust left one of the rails as a TOW anti-tank missile headed towards its target.

"Tango One-One. The flyboys have contact. Recce, three 64s and two BMP. Over."

"Understood, Tango-Zero. Over."

"You are clear to engage, you are clear to engage. Hit the big boys first. Leave BMPs to the TOWs. Over."

"Roger that, sir. Out."

Hendricks switched his comms to internal and pulled the hatch down again, sealing him and his crew in their armoured shell.

"They're on their way, boys. Keep your eyes peeled."

The gunner, sitting at the feet of the tank commander, watched as another missile left the Cobra. Less than a minute later, the attack-helicopter banked and headed back behind the line of American armour, ready to pick off the enemy tanks as they battled with the Abram's below.

The first T-64 rolled into view, and the Abrams' laser rangefinder detected the enemy tank, the on-board computer determining the correct elevation and angle of the gun.

"Standby," called the commander.

The gunner, with narrowed eyes, peered into his scope.

"Gunner, sabot, tank, designate," ordered the Hendricks.

"Up," informed the loader after shoving a sabot round into the breech.

"Fire and adjust."

"Away."

The barrel shot back as the round left, the hardened penetrator hitting the Soviet tank in just over a second. It hit, but the tank kept moving.

"Gunner, same target, sabot, designate."

"Up."

"Fire and adjust."

"Away."

This time, they were more successful as the enemy tank was struck by the penetrator, turning the steel of the tank to molten metal, igniting the interior, and causing a catastrophic explosion that wrenched the tank apart.

The commander was already calling out a new target, but soon they would need to move.

A second T-64 was hit, along with two BMPs. The Soviet recce platoon had just been wiped out. It was time to move.

"Gunner, take over. Driver, back, back, back."

Malone, the driver, reclining in a space that wasn't much bigger than his frame, accelerated and, under the guidance of his commander, shifted position ready for the inevitable much larger wave of tanks.

Chapter 8

0700, 9 July 1984. 13th/18th Royal Hussars, Reconnaissance
Regiment. Area of Husum, West Germany.

The Blue Effect -2 days

The two Scimitars, followed by two Scorpions, tore down Route 5,
putting aside the risk they were taking in travelling along a road in
broad daylight. They had just crossed the water feature of Arlau that cut
across from the coast, west to east, for about ten kilometres. The troop
was roughly five kilometres from the village of Hattstedt. Their first
checkpoint, the town of Husum, a further ten kilometres away. Five
minutes behind them, a second troop raced south. Two-Troop, Second
Squadron, of the 13th/18th Royal Hussars, part of the British 1st Infantry
Brigade, had disembarked from ships docking at Esbjerg in Denmark
the previous night. The Brigade, part of the United Kingdom Land
Forces and under the command of NORTHAG Landjut, had been sent
in to support the Territorial Command Schleswig-Holstein. 6th Panzer
Grenadier Division, supported by an array of German Jaeger units, was
hard-pressed and there was a real danger of the front line collapsing,
threatening the Landjut and eventually Denmark. The Soviet and East
German forces had broken the Kiel Canal defence line to the west
and were racing to the River Eider. If the East German army crossed
that barrier, there was a danger that the Landjut forces would end up
in constant retreat, never able to establish a proper defence, eventually
being pushed up into Denmark threatening NATO's northern flank.
NATO forces in place along the Kiel Canal had not been expected to
hold the line for long, depending on West German reservists to support
6th Panzer Grenadier Division. But the canal had now been breached.

A new stop-line was being rapidly set up from the west of
Rendsburg, following the section of the canal still being held west
where it met the River Eider, then north-west to Tonning where
Schleswig-Holstein butted up against the North Sea.

1st Infantry Brigade, led by the reconnaissance regiment, had been given the responsibility of defending the ground between Tonning and Suderstapel. It was a task the Brigade could achieve with its four battalions and tank squadron so long as they had the time to prepare. But, as usual, it was a race against time. The 5th German Army, consisting of the 8th Motor-Schutz Division and 9th Panzer Division, along with the Northern Group of Soviet Forces (NGSF) consisting of the 6th Motor Rifle Division and the 20th Tank Division, were advancing rapidly. NGSF had been reunited with their helicopter attack regiment with its remaining twenty-seven MI-24 Hind and fourteen MI-8 Hip helicopters that had previously been tasked with other duties. The Warsaw Pact forces in this sector were ready for the next big push. Should they cross the stretch of the Kiel Canal between the east of Rendsburg and the east coast, the enemy was confident that the NATO defence would crumble, and their entire northern flank would quickly fold.

6th Panzer Grenadier Division, part of the German Bundeswehr, although only a division was a significant part of the Northern Army Group's defence strategy, and had an essential mission: the defence of Schleswig-Holstein. In peacetime, the three brigades, the 16th and 17th Panzer Grenadier Brigades and the 18th Panzer Brigade, came under the command of NORTHAG. But, in the event of an invasion by the Soviets and the Warsaw Pact, the units would revert to the control of the Landjut. This force, known as the Baltic Approaches (BALTAP), headquartered in Karup, Denmark, was created to defend Denmark, Hamburg and Schleswig-Holstein. The current commander, Lieutenant-General Pedersen, a Danish officer, was a worried man. The reinforcements coming into theatre were desperately needed if the General was to prevent the Soviet and East German forces from crossing the Kiel Canal, north of Kiel, along with the River Eider. Although reinforcements were now pouring into the country, it would be touch and go if his depleted force could hold long enough for these additional troops to reach their assigned positions.

The 1st Infantry Brigade had landed at two ports in the north and were pushing hard to get into position and add to the defending troops desperately battling to prevent the enemy from crossing. Once across those two water barriers, the Warsaw Pact would be difficult to contain.

Two-Troop, plus three further troops, consisting of a mix of Scimitars and Scorpions, had a long journey ahead of them. Once through Husum, west of the peninsular, they would split up. Two-

Troop had been tasked with assisting the defenders of the bridge at Tonning, preventing any crossing of the River Eider at that point. They were also to conduct a reconnaissance of the area and report back to brigade command.

Three-Troop had been given Friedrichstadt and Four-Troop the north of Suderstapel. One-Troop would cross the river, head for Heide, and establish where the forward elements of the East German army had reached. Equally as important, they were to report back on the condition of the German forces defending the line and the estimated period of time they would be able to hold on. Between Tonning and Suderstapel would be the extent of 1st Brigade's area of responsibility. From Suderstapel to the north of Kiel, the Allied Command Europe (ACE) Mobile Force, the second reinforcement for the region, along with Jutland Division, would be expected to defend. Behind the British reconnaissance regiment, the 1st Battalion, Devonshire and Dorset Regiment, were powering along the same road as fast as their Saxon armoured personnel carriers would allow. A battalion of the Queen's Regiment, the 2nd Battalion, the Light Infantry, and a tank squadron would travel at a much more leisurely pace, ready to switch direction or deploy quickly should the enemy suddenly cross the river and attempt to push north as rapidly as possible, striving to encircle the defenders and destroy the Landjut forces in one quick strike. The 1st Battalion, the Wessex Regiment, a Territorial Army unit with its recruitment grounds the south-west of England, was mounted in Bedford 4-ton trucks, and would deploy around Husum and as far as Oster-Ohrstedt, acting as the Brigade's reserve, either to be called forward to support or to bear the brunt of a Soviet breakthrough should the bulk of the Brigade find themselves on the run.

The Brigadier was far from happy with the way events were unfolding. It was one thing to split his reconnaissance regiment across a fifteen-kilometre front; it was another to split the four companies of the Devonshire and Dorset's. He was leaving a fifth of his force behind in Husum.

0715, 9 July 1984. Jutland Division, Allied Land Forces, Schleswig-Holstein and Jutland, Flensburg, West Germany. The Blue Effect -2 days

Eyes peered from behind curtains. German civilians stared through their windows as tank after tank thundered through the town of

Flensburg. Leopard 1s, interspersed with M113s, some of the APCs armed with TOW anti-tank missiles, and M109 self-propelled howitzers, travelled at best speed. They moved with urgency, now finally committed to the battle for northern Germany and Denmark. Having left Denmark in the early hours of the morning, they were finally in Germany, on their way to reinforce elements of the Jutland Division already in position. The 3rd Jutland Brigade would act as rear security, ready to block an enemy breakthrough or reinforce parts of the line that were under threat of collapsing. The 1st and 2nd Jutland Brigades were already south of Schleswig, moving into position. They would deploy west of Rendsburg, plugging the gaps that were threatening the security of that part of the front line. They would be responsible for the stretch of the Kiel Canal and River Eider as far as Oldenbuttel, then northwest, covering the River Eider as far as Suderstapel, linking with the British 1st Brigade.

Danish Military Police, supported by their Bundeswehr counterparts, waved the convoy through, watching nervously for any signs of the Warsaw Pact air force. They had got off lightly so far, but knew the quiet couldn't last. The Soviets were not going to allow NATO to reinforce this sector so easily. Elements of the ACE mobile force were also starting to make an appearance. One British battalion, along with a strong force from the British Royal Marine Commando, were in the process of landing further north, along with a battalion from Luxembourg. The arrival of the US 6th Marine Expeditionary Brigade, with its six battalions, one of them a tank battalion, was expected within the next twenty-four hours. 9th (US) Infantry Division was at least one week away, if not more. The clock was ticking, and a storm was brewing.

0730, 9 July 1984. 60th Field Replacement Regiment, Territorial Command, Schleswig Holstein. Area of Rendsburg, West Germany. The Blue Effect -2 days

Colonel Faust looked over the shoulder of the battalion commander responsible for the defence of this sector of the city, and followed Leutnant-Colonel Keortig's eye line. The water in front of them, an extension of the Audorfer Sea and the Kiel Canal, looked black and uninviting.

"They're going to try again before the day's out," suggested Keortig, commander of the 602nd Field Replacement Battalion (Reserve), 60th Field Replacement Regiment.

They could hear the sound of distant explosions coming from the direction of Kiel, some thirty kilometres to the east. A major battle was in progress. Just as the Soviet 6th Guards Motor Rifle Division had thought it had succeeded in forcing the German reserves defending the city of Kiel to withdraw, the 612th Infantry Battalion (Reserve), from the 61st Home Defence Brigade, were sent in to bolster the flagging troops. Using their seven Leopard-1s to support the infantry, the German forces counter-attacked, throwing the enemy back, forcing the Soviet infantry into a retreat, street by street, threatening the flank of the motor rifle regiment to the west of the city. The Soviets had got as far as placing a platoon on the opposite bank, crossing under the cover of darkness in BMK bridging boats, but the follow-up forces were stopped midstream, and the stranded infantrymen surrendered when they recognised they were surrounded, separated from their mother unit, and rapidly running out of ammunition. The Soviet troops across the other side of the river were themselves nearly cut off from the main force as security platoons from the *Verteidigungskreiskommando* (VKK), West German territorial troops from the local sub-regional command, that had been in hiding in the city waiting for such an opportunity, were reinforced and attacked the Soviet regiment's flank and rear. Their intention, however, was not to hold the ground taken but to keep the Soviet army on edge, and prevent them from establishing a safe area along the southern bank from where they could launch a full-scale assault river crossing.

"They have no option," responded Faust. "They'd hoped to take Kiel and cross somewhere along that stretch of the canal."

"We can't hold it forever, sir."

"I agree. Soon, they'll hold the entire length of the southern bank. Then it won't take them long to find a weak point, and force a crossing somewhere. If they attempt to cross in our sector, I've put a company from the 603rd on standby to either act as a blocking force or support you in a counter-attack."

"Have the British committed any support for our sector yet?"

"Not for us personally, but elements of the ACE mobile force have started to land, and a battalion has been allocated as a tactical reserve in this sector."

"They have to be at least twenty-four hours away. And a strategic reserve, sir?"

The senior officer didn't answer, which said it all.

The 2nd Battalion, *Jydske Dragonregiment*, or Jutland Dragoon Regiment, manoeuvred their tanks into position, ready to react to any attempted assault river crossing by the enemy. Although only Leopard 1s, the twenty main battle tanks could still disrupt any Soviet intentions to expand a bridgehead once they were able to secure a foothold on the northern bank of the Kiel Canal. The small force was split into two units. Half the force was secreted in a large forested area directly south of Horsten; the other half was closer to the canal west of the L126. The tunnel that passed under the canal had been blocked at both ends and booby-trapped, so it would not be passable by enemy soldiers.

Further forward, infantry companies, transported by their M113s, camouflaged themselves and their vehicles, waiting to pounce when called upon. Close support was provided by four M113s with TOW anti-tank missiles and four Land Rovers also mounted with the TOW anti-tank weapon. Dug in, providing they survived Soviet artillery and air-to-ground strikes, they were the perfect weapon to hit any Soviet armour across the other side of the man-made canal. Although the canal was actually wider than the River Eider, because of its solid, man-made banks, it would actually be easier to cross than the riverbanks that had been carved by nature.

The 2nd Jutland Brigade was responsible for the stretch of the canal from the west of Rendsburg where it ran parallel to the River Eider, a mere two to three-kilometre gap at the widest point, to where the river linked up with the canal again near Oldenbuttel. From there, the 1st Jutland Brigade would take over, linking up with the 1st British Brigade at Suderstapel.

The Leopard 1 clawed its way across a farmer's field until it reached the hedge line at the far side. Two hundred metres to the left, a second Leopard manoeuvred into position at the edge of a road, overlooking the open ground to their front. Other main battle tanks of the unit twisted on their tracks until they too were in a position where they

70

could see forward; yet the bulk of their tanks were hidden by foliage at the side or to the front.

The company commander checked in with his men, getting confirmation that they were ready. This would be the third ambush instigated in the last three hours. He was down to seven tanks after amalgamating two weaker platoons. They had to keep hitting the advancing units if they were to give the rest of their division, and the rest of the army, a chance to dig in along the next stop-line. The British were on their way as, further east, was the ACE mobile force.

"They're coming," the young company commander informed the remnants of his tank company. "As soon as we've fired, we'll pull straight back through you. Acknowledge."

"*Seven-One-Alpha, understood.*"

"*Seven-One-Bravo, understood.*"

He peered through his scope, watching for the East German T-72s he had been warned were on their way. He shook his head to try and clear his thoughts, focus on the task ahead, sleep clawing at his eyes. They had been battling since the first day of the battle. Leapfrogging the defending reserve units, they doing the same when it was their turn. But always backwards. They had made some counter-attacks to push the Volksarmee forces onto the back foot, but in the end they'd had to retreat. Hamburg had fallen, their defence of the Kiel Canal in this sector had been broken, and apart from a brief respite during the night whilst the Warsaw Pact forces consolidated their position, they had been fighting for four days solid. This was the start of their fifth. Morale was OK but, after losing Hamburg and Lubeck to the enemy, the company commander had to work hard to keep his men focussed. His company, part of 171st Grenadier Battalion, 17th Panzer Grenadier Brigade, 6th Panzer Grenadier Division, started out with thirteen Leopard 1s. Now the major was down to seven.

"Contact, 1500 metres. T-72."

Before the tank commander could give any more orders, his gunner yelled, "It's been hit!"

The T-72 slid at an uncontrollable angle as its track unravelled, leaving the Soviet-made, National Volskarmee commanded tank, stranded.

"Fire!" There were no fancy orders, just the commander wanting the enemy main battle tank finished off before its *Kameraden* joined in the fight. The turret was torn sideways as the armoured piercing round smashed into it. A second T-72 oscillated, its armour smouldering before being immersed in flames. A vehicle shot out from a group of trees where it had been hidden. After firing into the side of the T-72, the low silhouetted *Kanonenjagdpanzer*, a tank destroyer, reversed at speed, desperate to put some distance between it and the advancing East German unit. Three more T-72 tanks appeared in front of the Bundeswehr defenders. Although weighing in at over forty tons, the T-72 profile was incredibly low, uncomfortable for the crew, but this low silhouette made it difficult to see and hard to hit. Smoke puffed out of the barrels of two of the enemy tanks as the Major's gunner thrust a fresh round into the breech.

The *Kanonenjagdpanzer* crashed through the foliage of a low hanging tree as it slipped out of sight and into relative safety. They would move back a few hundred metres and wait to spring a trap all over again.

The Leopard rocked when the gun fired; the 105mm round seemed to arc towards its target.

"A hit! Back, back now!"

The Major was relieved they were up against the T-72M and not the T-64. The East German army had been sold an inferior model of T-72 as opposed to the ones in the Soviet Army. The T-72M had inferior armour and a downgraded weapons system. The Volksarmee were paying the price as a consequence.

The engine strained as the driver applied power, and the tracks gained traction, pulling the tank further into the trees. A 125mm round from one of the enemy tanks stripped branches from the trees as it ploughed into the foliage alongside the rapidly accelerating tank. Three more T-72s had appeared and Seven-One-Foxtrot was no more. The Major winced when he received the call. His company strength was rapidly diminishing, and for the first time in the war, he had doubts about his and his men's survivability.

0735, 9 July 1984. 2nd Zealand Battle Group. Southeast of
Ringsted, Denmark.
The Blue Effect -2 days

The Centurion tank trundled forward. It may have been over twenty years old, but it was the core mobile weapon of the 2nd Zealand Battle Group (Reserve). It had settled on the edge of a small copse, and the crew were out within seconds, dragging the camouflage netting over the top, tying one edge to the trees they were alongside. A second tank, one of eight tanks belonging to 2nd Squadron, 5th Battalion of the Guards Hussars Regiment, weaved through the trees, stopping just before the edge of the treeline. The small group of tanks, held back in reserve until now, were finally being redeployed further forward, there being an expectation of a Soviet force landing somewhere along the East Zealand coast in the next few days.

Although old, the Centurion had proved its worth. During the Yom Kippur War in 1973, in 'The Valley of Tears', an Israeli Defence Force Brigade with less than 100 Centurion tanks defeated an assault by 500 Syrian T-55s and T-62s. With their 84mm guns, 2nd Squadron would also be depending on its legendary status. Two battalions of Infantry, the 2nd and the 4th, were digging in further forward but ready to move within two hours' notice should they need to relocate and isolate any attempt by the Soviets to force a bridgehead on Danish soil.

The 1st Zealand Battle Group (Reserve), with its tank squadron, two Infantry battalions and artillery battalion, had responsibility for the coast from Koge to Naestved, in the south. The 3rd Zealand Battle Group (Reserve) held the west coast from Naestved to the thin peninsular of Kalundborg, and the 4th Zealand Battle Group (Reserve) was on the southern island based around Nykobing. The three Battle Groups had deployed at the outbreak of the war, the 2nd Battle Group being held in reserve. The 1st Zealand and 2nd Zealand Brigades, much larger formations than the Battle Groups, manned by regular soldiers, were being held more centrally. The 1st Zealand Brigade was being kept close to Copenhagen, the capital of Denmark. Once the landing point, or points, had been identified, these two heavy brigades, with their eighty Centurion tanks between them, along with their mobile infantry battalions, would attempt to stop the Soviet invasion in its tracks.

2nd Squadron wasn't destined to finish its preparations to hide because, at that moment, they received an urgent call. A large Soviet airborne force was in the process of landing east of Ringsted, the location of the headquarters of the Allied Land Forces of Zealand. Camouflage netting was quickly dragged off the tanks again and literally thrown on the rear decks. The Centurion's Rolls Royce Meteor engine was turned over, and the lead tank pulled out from the trees and spun round until it faced the northwest. An M113 pulled up alongside it, and Lieutenant Colonel Jensen jumped out from the

73

back of the APC and ran to the front of the Centurion yelling up to Captain Petersen, the commander of the squadron of eight tanks.

"You're to get to Ringsted as fast as possible," ordered the commander of the 4th Battalion, *Gardehusarregimentet*, the infantry element of the Battle Group. "It seems a significant force has landed, and the local troops are not holding."

"Do we know the size of the force, sir?"

"Not entirely, but they estimate at least a battalion."

"How the hell did we miss them coming in?"

"It's not surprising. Command has been leeching aircraft from Zealand to help support the Landjut forces."

"So the Soviets are coming through the back door."

"You need to move," ordered the Colonel. "Time isn't an asset that we have much of."

"Let me know when the Infantry moves out, sir. We'll be pretty vulnerable out there on our own."

"I've not received any sightings of armour yet, Captain."

"It's not the armour I'm worried about," responded the captain.

"We'll get there as soon as we can."

"Right, we're moving out now, sir."

"Good luck."

The Colonel stepped back as the Centurion reared up at the front, the driver pressing hard on the accelerator pedal as soon as he received the order to pull out. Petersen estimated they had about twenty-five kilometres to travel. With a top speed of roughly thirty-kilometres per hour, and bearing in mind the undulating ground, they could be on the eastern outskirts of Ringsted in less than two hours.

They bypassed Tureby then headed northwest along the Slimmingevej, maintaining a steady speed. After a drive of roughly twelve kilometres, Captain Petersen planned on taking a left turn, using the Kogevej that ran parallel to the Vestmotorvejen, a major motorway, to take his small force direct to the town of Ringsted. The last report had the Soviet airborne soldiers on the eastern outskirts of the town. The squadron passed cultivated fields either side of the road and made their way through the occasional small village. Thirty minutes later found the squadron of eight tanks 2,000 metres from the turning. A large forest of pine trees loomed up on the left. Once they left that behind, Petersen knew they should be less than 1500 metres from the turning.

The tall, straight pines dominated his view, as he looked left at the proud line of trees 300 metres away. Suddenly, a huge explosion sent a pressure wave of heat that whipped past his back and head. He twisted his body around so he was facing to the rear as a streak of light emanated from a ditch in front of him and to his right, as an anti-tank grenade headed for its target. The target of the rocket-propelled grenade quickly became apparent as the Centurion, fifty metres behind his, seemed to surge upwards as the hollow-charge warhead slammed into the side of the main battle tank, slicing through it with ease, killing the crew inside instantly. Beyond that, he could see a second Centurion in flames, a firework display shooting skyward as the ammunition cooked.

"Put your foot down!" he screamed at his driver. "Gun left," he ordered his gunner as he gripped the handles of the .50-calibre machine gun. He swung round as the turret started to turn, the tank rapidly increasing speed until it reached its maximum of thirty kilometres per hour. The machine gun vibrated in his hands as he aimed at the likely location of the ditch where he had seen the rocket grenade launch, the rounds curving towards it, now over 1,000 metres away. He watched the spurts of dust from the strikes of the heavy calibre bullets as he played them across the likely enemy location.

"One-eighty, one-eighty," the captain called down to his driver as he saw a third Centurion brew up as it attempted to escape the carnage that was ensuing. He needed to provide support while he still had some tanks left. The fifty-ton Centurion slowed then spun on its tracks.

"Fifteen hundred metres, one o'clock, ditch right of road, HE," he ordered his gunner as he fired another burst towards the enemy location.

Something exploded in the road on the southern flank of his squadron as one of his tanks drove over an anti-tank mine laid by the Soviet airborne soldiers as soon as the convoy had passed them.

"Up," informed the Loader.

"Fire."

The tank snatched as a round left the barrel. Moments later, the High Explosive shell exploded in close proximity to the ditch he had fired on earlier. He had the satisfaction of seeing a number of soldiers running from the vicinity, two of them with a wounded comrade draped between them. Peterson suddenly realised the danger as they approached the forest, they had passed earlier, now on their right.

"Left stick, left, left." He swung the machine gun round to face

75

the potential danger just as a smoking flame streaked alongside the turret, missing him and his tank by mere centimetres. He fired into the trees as the tank bounced across the rough earth, the engine growling as the driver changed down to negotiate the undulating ground. He sprayed the trees but doubted he had hit anything as he rocked back and forth in the turret.

He shouted into his mike, "All call signs report. Right stick." The tank slewed to the right as the driver steered the heavy tank round.

"Forward." They were now heading south, parallel with the road, but they had at least passed the forest.

"Juliet-Zero, Juliet-Five. Lost track, immobile but functional."

"Juliet-Zero, Juliet-Six. Road, south of forest, 2,000 metres, in position to cover. Over."

"Juliet-Zero, Juliet-Seven. 200 metres east of Juliet-Six. Over."

"Roger, all call signs, this is Juliet-Zero. Hold position, hold position. Cover Juliet-Five. Coming to you. Out."

The turret turned slightly, the gunner keeping track of the likely enemy positions. Peterson looked across at his three burning tanks, and the crippled one stranded still close to the enemy.

Suddenly he was thrown violently against the side of the turret, the force so great it nearly broke his right arm. He grasped it in agony as he heard the screams below, the tank turning left, out of control, the glacis dipping down into a ditch, the tracks bogged down in the mud at the bottom.

Captain Peterson scrambled out onto the turret, captivated by the three burning tanks he could see, a column of thick, black, oily smoke poured skyward, yellow and orange flames still flickering around the armoured vehicles. Turning around, he watched, mesmerised as a main battle tank was being hungrily devoured by flame and exploding ordnance from within, jolting the armoured vehicle. He had just lost over half of his squadron. Only the infantry could help them now.

0915, 9 July 1984. Motor-Schutz Regiment, 8th Motor-Schutz Division, 5th German Army. Area of Albersdorf, West Germany. The Blue Effect -2 days.

Oberst Keller walked alongside Colonel Gachev, commander of the Soviet tank regiment in the local area. T-64s lined the streets. The tank crews had made a poor attempt at camouflaging their main battle tanks. Like everyone else, they were weary. Also, there was an air of over confidence. Before Oberst Keller, from the 8th Motor-Schutz Division, 5th German Army, could make his next move, he needed to ensure that his troops were locked in with the Northern Group of Soviet Forces, particularly the 6th Guards Motor Rifle Division, if they were to advance at the same time and put pressure on the enemy. Whenever Keller spoke aloud, referring to the West German Bundeswehr as the enemy, it left a sour taste in his mouth. On their way to the Soviet regimental headquarters, they passed a hospital. It was clearly overcrowded; overflowing with wounded soldiers, most of them East German, but some of them West German, as well as Soviet motor rifle and tank troops. A number of UAZ 452s, small glass-sided utility vehicles, with a Red Cross sign indicating they were ambulances, along with Gaz-66 vehicles similarly marked, were offloading even more wounded. Space inside the hospital was obviously at a premium as, once triaged, those deemed not severely wounded were left outside on stretchers. But what horrified Oberst Keller more was the queue of German civilians lined up along the pavement, clearly seeking treatment for various injuries as a consequence of being caught up in the fighting. He did a quick mental count: there must be at least 100, he surmised. At least seven had horrific facial and arm injuries, reminiscent of exposure to a blister gas. Evidently, many of the blisters had burst, and now looked red and raw, weeping, the pain they were causing etched in the people's faces. Others were obviously traumatised, their wounds caused by exploding bombs or a stray large calibre bullet or splinters from a shattered tank shell.

Oberst Keller stopped. "Do they have some civilian doctors or medical staff that can treat these people?" he said, looking at the Soviet colonel.

"There are some, but our own soldiers have a priority over these."

"Can't you at least release some nurses to provide them with some minimal care?"

"No, Comrade Oberst. My orders are to treat as many of our soldiers as possible. I must release some of my medical teams to move forward for the next push."

"I understand that, Colonel Gachev, but to spare a few nurses would have little impact on your ambitions."

The Soviet officer started to walk off, but was called back.

"What if I release some of my own medical staff to assist?"

The regimental commander looked him straight in the eye. "If you have spare resources, Oberst, then I suggest you release them to help our soldiers who have been fighting to free these people from the capitalistic yoke that hangs around their neck." With that, Gachev stormed off.

One of the civilians, a woman in her late seventies, a dirty, bloodied bandage wrapped around her face and covering one eye, peered at him with her good one. Recognising that he was speaking German, noting the uniform was different from the Soviet officer, she ascertained that he was with the *National Volksarmee*.

"Why are you doing this to us?"

The officer was caught off guard as the woman clutched at his sleeve, the single eye searching his face.

A middle-aged man also approached, pointing to a young boy slumped against a low wooden fence. The boy's upper chest was wrapped with what could only have been white bed sheets, torn into strips to act as a bandage. "He got hit by a stray bullet. We can't seem to stop the bleeding. Please help us. He will die if you don't do something."

"My daughter was hit by falling masonry," called out another. "She has a head wound. She keeps passing out. We have nowhere else to go. Have mercy on us. We didn't ask to be involved in this war."

The girl, probably no more than ten years old, was lying on a wooden door, either taken down, or blown down, to be used as a stretcher. Next to her, sitting cross-legged on the tarmac road, her brother stroked her arm.

Oberst Keller pulled away from the old woman who was now holding both sleeves, pleading for help. He walked ten paces back in the direction he had come from initially, and signalled to the driver of the Jeep that had brought him here. The driver, leaning against the side of the vehicle, quickly stubbed out his cigarette, jumped in the vehicle and drove towards the *National Volksarmee* Oberst's position.

"Get onto the 2nd Battalion," Oberst said to the radio operator sitting in the back of the vehicle. "I want their medical team here within the hour. Once they arrive, you are to direct them to assist these civilians. They are acting on my orders. No one is to prevent them. Understood?"

"Yes, sir."

"Thank you, thank you." The man with the wounded child

expressed his gratitude, and was quickly joined by others in the line.

With that, the Oberst left to rejoin the Soviet officer who had stopped about 100 metres down the road. When he was alongside, the Soviet officer barked. "Your Samaritan act will get you into trouble, Oberst."

"Had they been Soviet citizens, Herr Colonel, what would you have done?"

This time it was the German officer who stormed off.

Chapter 9

0920, 9 July 1984. B Squadron, Queen's Own Mercian Yeomanry.
West of Rehren, West Germany.
The Blue Effect -2 days

The Fox eased forward, poking its nose just outside the outskirts of the small village of Lindhorst. The vehicle commander called a halt, and a second armoured reconnaissance car joined him, pulling up alongside on his right. Ashford saw the 30mm RARDEN cannon swing right, the commander of that vehicle keeping a watch to the southeast. Ashford put the rubber cups of the binoculars to his eyes and did a quick search of the foreground, then further out. Above the ticking sound of the armoured car's Jaguar engine, he could hear a steady staccato of machine-gun fire, interspersed with the single cracks of SLRs and punctuated with the claps of explosions coming from somewhere west of Hanover. He had a good view of the open ground in front of them from here, except for a small wooded area to the north that was blocking his line of sight to the northeast.

He ordered his driver to pull forward, his intention to push east for a further two kilometres. The patrol first headed north, before turning east, passing through the southern tip of the forest that had blocked his view earlier. Once through, the view east was now clear. They pushed forward again, the second Fox following 100 metres behind as they crossed a narrow waterway called Rodenberger Aue. Ashford acknowledged the engineers that were preparing the small bridge for demolition. It wouldn't delay the enemy for long, such was the capability of the Soviet bridging and ferry units, but they had to slow the enemy's relentless advance somehow. This was the furthest east he would go for now.

After five minutes of patrolling the local area, the two Fox armoured cars returned to the bridge. The engineers had finished and, after a quick discussion, confirmed that the bridge was ready to blow and they would depart the area, two engineers staying behind to initiate the destruction of this crossing point. This section of Rodenberger Aue, between the canal to the north and Bad Nenndorf in the south, was under the watchful eye of a K-Company from the 1st Battalion, Yorkshire Volunteers. It was Lieutenant Ashford's job to watch for the enemy while the Territorial Army unit prepared its defences. He looked over his shoulder, his ears picking up the sound of four-tonners labouring under their heavy loads of infantry, equipment and as much ammunition as possible that could be packed on-board. It was time to cross the water again so he ordered his driver forward, and they tentatively made their way across the bridge, the second Fox fifty metres behind. This time, his two reconnaissance vehicles would need to move further east, acting as a screen for the battalion while they deployed, and informing them of any enemy threat. The Fox armoured cars crawled along the road, choosing stealth over speed. Ashford wasn't sure which was best: to dash along the road to the village of Haste and risk being ambushed on the way, but using speed to charge through it, or to try and spot any tell-tale signs and reverse out of danger quickly. He eventually chose to pick up speed, the growl of the two Jaguar engines intensifying as they sped at over fifty kilometres an hour along the metalled road.

They left Rehren to their south, passing through Nordbruch and the village of Wilhelmsdorf, the Mittellandkanal no more than a kilometre to their north. Following the edge of a small forest on their left-hand side, the two armoured cars eventually slowed down as they approached the first houses of the next village, Haste. Ashford's head moved from side to side, his neck straining to allow him visibility of as much of the area around them as possible. He admitted to being scared. He was a Lieutenant in the Queen's Own Mercian Yeomanry now, but two weeks ago he had been sitting comfortably in his office, part of a large accountancy firm, reading *The Times* while he sipped an Earl Grey tea. The news had been about the financial crisis, a countrywide moratorium on spending, a murder in the outskirts of Manchester, but nothing about a large planned annual exercise by the Soviet army. And certainly nothing about the impending invasion of West Germany. After eighteen months training in the Territorial Army as a troop commander, here he was now, in West Germany, going into battle for the first time in his life.

The driver slowed as they came to the junction, connecting the minor road they were on with the 442 that came from the north, from the direction of the Mittellandkanal to Bad Nenndorf in the south. A railway line also crossed their front.

Lieutenant Ashford ordered the driver to pull off to the left and to manoeuvre the Fox as best he could into the trees. Ashford twisted his shoulders and signalled for his other recce vehicle to move right and find a position amongst some scattered buildings on the southern side of the road. He ducked as a low-lying branch scraped across his face, nearly pulling his beret and headphones off. "Stop, stop."

The large wheels stopped turning.

"I'm going to the edge of the trees. Then I'll check out the village. I'll guide you forward."

He clambered down from the large turret and the Fox reconnaissance vehicle followed him slowly, stopping on Ashford's signal once it was positioned at the edge of the treeline. Checking his pistol in the canvas holster on his right hip, Ashford stepped out onto the road, ready to move towards the bridge over the railway line. His plan to walk as far as the outskirts of the town on the other side of the road and railway line, were not to be fulfilled as the Fox opposite exploded in a shower of flame and metal fragments. Ashford was stunned momentarily before regaining his senses and sprinting back to his Fox. His gunner, a bricklayer from the West Midlands, was on the alert; more out of fear of the position he found himself in on the frontline in West Germany than through professional training. He hit the firing button, and a burst of three 30mm rounds punched into the Soviet airborne troops he had seen assault his fellow soldiers, his friends, people he used to drink with after work.

The armour of the Fox rattled as small-arms fire spattered the turret, and the gunner heard Lieutenant Ashford screaming at him. "Behind you!"

The lieutenant was racing towards him, now within the trees, trunks splintering as the airborne troops across the road recovered and opened fire. Corporal Alfie Jarrett pulled himself up so his shoulders were out of the turret, and opened fire with his SMG, the 9mm rounds going wide but forcing the enemy who had been sneaking up to take cover. He quickly dropped back down and fired a burst from the coaxial machine gun at the first group of soldiers, pinning the airborne troops down, leaving Ashford safe to clamber on board.

"Harry, get us out of here, go right. Alfie, turret left as we go."

Harry Beale, the driver, didn't need a second telling. He was more than ready to carry out his orders and get out of the area, terror cutting into him like a knife. The four-litre engine screamed as he fumbled with the gears. Eventually, the Fox shot forward, a trail of mud and debris splayed out behind as he manoeuvred the vehicle sharply to the right, throwing the crew sideways. Ashford dropped down inside, on the left, pulling the hatch after him as the Fox was pummelled with bullets. Once the turret had turned to face the now burning second Fox, he banged the button and the two four-barrelled smoke dischargers fired, engulfing the area out to the front in a cloud of dense white smoke. Harry lost control, the Fox swerving left before he brought it back under control, an explosion behind them indicating that his accidental manoeuvre had put the airborne soldier who had just fired an RPG-16 off his aim.

Lieutenant Ashford looked back through the vision block to see Golf-One-Bravo on fire. The aluminium armour was capable of stopping 7.62mm rounds and artillery shrapnel, but not an anti-tank round from a rocket-propelled grenade launcher.

"Zero-Golf, this is Golf-One-Alpha. Contact. Soviet airborne. Golf-One-Bravo destroyed. Over."

"Zero-Golf. Roger that. Your location? Over."

"West of Haste, returning Rodenberger now."

"Roger. Friendlies in situ. Deploy and provide cover. Over."

"Understood. Deploy Aue."

"Golf-One-Charlie and Delta will join you. Out."

The driver had the Fox moving almost at top speed, barely able to avoid deep ruts on the edge of the road or to maintain track as he steered around the bends.

"Steady, Harry, steady. We'll be at the bridge in less than a minute. Then we can turn and fight."

The Fox slowed slightly, but mild panic ensured that the driver kept the reconnaissance vehicle moving at a steady pace.

They crossed the bridge and Lieutenant Ashford called a halt, shouting down to the Territorial Army infantry platoon that had moved in to defend the bridge. "They could be right behind us. Keep your eyes peeled."

"What is it?" responded the platoon commander, a Lieutenant, who up until a week ago had been a manager at a small warehouse.

"Airborne, Soviet airborne. Watch out for their BMDs."

"Are you staying?" asked the lieutenant, feeling exposed suddenly.

Thirty men in his command and two Carl-Gustavs as their defence against armour, the pressure was on.

"We'll keep an over-watch. I have two more units on the way."

"Thank God for that," the lieutenant replied, smiling. "I need to deploy my men."

0925, 9 July 1984. Elements of the 3rd Regiment Army Air Corps, 24th Airmobile Brigade. Kirchhorsten, West Germany.
The Blue Effect -2 days

The two Lynx helicopters hovered about 300 metres apart watching for signs of enemy movement that might interrupt the activity going on below. The TOW anti-tank missiles, two each side, were waiting to be unleashed should any Soviet armour appear. They were fully aware that a Soviet airborne regiment had parachuted in some fifteen kilometres away to the east, and the BMDs could prove to be a serious threat should they manage to evade the lookout posts deployed in the local area. If a small airborne force managed to bypass allied forces on the ground between their landing zone and Kirchhorsten, it would disrupt the groundwork going on below and delay the preparations for the defence of the Stop-Line Black Raven. Ahead, a Gazelle acted as a spotter. On the ground, elements of an airmobile company had been put into position. A rifle company, complete with eight Milan firing posts, deployed by Lynx helicopters earlier, was providing a security screen as the Forward Armament and Refuelling Point for the 24th Airmobile Brigade was being set up. They were in turn defended by elements of the Air Defence battery. A full AD section had been deployed, providing four Blowpipe teams to help defend the group from attack by the Warsaw Pact air force. High above, two Phantom Interceptors were providing a Combat Air Patrol, Higher Command recognising how vulnerable the airmobile brigade was during the initial stages of its deployment. Once the FARP was complete, stocked with pre-positioned ammunition, fuel and supplies, it would be available to support the next phase. Next would come more air defence and two of the Royal Artillery's gun batteries, with sixteen 105mm light guns. Artillery ammunition and more infantry would follow them. One kilometre away, the Gun Position Officer had already been dropped off and was in the process of measuring their planned positions, marking out the points where the Brigade's helicopters would drop the 105mm guns.

On a relatively open piece of ground, a Senior Non-Commissioned
Officer completed the final touches to his marking card, ensuring he
had made a note of the grid for the drop-off point and the pick-
up points where the helicopter would need to return to pick up the
rest of the platoon's stores. He checked that the information regarding
the current load, a machine-gun section, had the correct number of
personnel. There were no under-slung loads.

The platoon sergeant looked back to where the machine-gun
section of nine men was formed up behind him, waiting on his signal
to be called forward. The SNCO in command at the front, knelt
on one knee, his Self-Loading Rifle, SLR, resting on his left knee,
pointing forwards. Behind him, a soldier carried a General-Purpose
Machine Gun. The third soldier in the line was crouched down with
a tripod slung over his shoulder. Behind them, two more GPMGs
and two tripods were carried between the rest of the section. Once
in place, this fire support unit, with their weapons in a sustained-fire
format fitted with the C2 optical sight, could provide effective fire out
to 1,800 metres. They were just one of the elements of the airmobile
infantry battalion that were preparing to deploy. The majority would
first fly into the FARB, but this section would deploy straight to
their positions as part of the Aviation Company.

24th Infantry Brigade was highly mobile. With its two permanent
battalions – 2nd Battalion, the Royal Regiment of Fusiliers, and the
1st Battalion, the King's Own Royal Border Regiment – along with
the regularly attached 1st Parachute Battalion, it could pack a punch
that any attacking force would find difficult to counter. General
Cutler, commander of 1st British Corps, was depending on these
2,000-plus men to provide a blocking force from the Mittellandkanal
in the north, to the south of Stadthagen; hold a key part of Stop-Line
Black-Raven; put a halt to the rapidly advancing Soviet Operational
Manoeuvre Group that was threatening to outpace the general's
attempts to form a solid stop-line on the Weser; blunt the attack; and
hold while reinforcements continued to arrive on the Continent. Two
infantry battalions would be deployed initially, the parachute battalion
being held in reserve. The Paras could either be used to prevent a latent
breakthrough or, if it was feasible and the opportunity arose, to assist

in any counter-attack against the Soviet forces. This element of the Brigade, the RRF battalion of 700 men preparing to deploy, would first move to the FARB. But, one company, the Aviation Company, including a separate machine-gun section, would go directly to Nienbrugge, and dig in next to the southern bank of the canal. A Territorial company was out in front, providing a screen and waiting for elements of the retreating British units to pass through. The rest of the TA battalion was west of Niengraban, north of the canal.

The entire German frontline in the north was on the move as the Soviets slowly inched their way west. The Bundeswehr would only fall back as far as the Weser where they too had been ordered to dig in, along with 1 Netherlands Corps. Nienbrugge would be the northern anchor point. The rest of the battalion would be stationed along the road that ran south to Stadthagen. The KOBR Battalion was also preparing to move out. It was responsible for defending the southern side of Stadthagen down to the Forst Brandshof, north of the high ground of the Buckeberge.

0935, 9 July 1984. 662 Squadron, 3rd Regiment Army Air Corps.
Area of Stadthagen, West Germany.
The Blue Effect -2 days

The Gazelle reared up as the pilot brought the nose of the helicopter higher to ensure they cleared the tall, densely populated hedge line. The Gazelle dropped back down on the other side with a lurch, hugging the ground, the pilot banking it left and right to avoid obstacles. The engine strained as the pilot again jockeyed between the collective and cyclic, the craft shuddering as it whipped past a tree, the branches barely a metre below. The pilot dropped his craft again.

"Standby," he informed his passenger, an Intelligence Corps Sergeant who was conducting a reconnaissance of the area.

"Ready." Sergeant Tait clicked the toggle and responded, lifting his gyro-stabilised binoculars ready to do a complete scan of the area they had been tasked to recce. His stomach heaved slightly, and he very much wished he'd not eaten the egg-banjo thirty minutes before the flight. Had he known he was going on this flight, he would have been a little more selective about his choice of breakfast. The Gazelle, a five-seat helicopter and a scout from one of the aviation regiments from 24th Airmobile Brigade, vibrated heavily as the Army Air Corps pilot brought his craft into the hover, just behind what appeared to be a row of trees that crossed their front, lining each side of a minor road.

"Here we go." The pilot, Lieutenant Sheppard, manipulated the cyclic and the helicopter rose slowly up from behind the cover that was masking their presence. He took a quick sweep of the terrain ahead, searching the skies for any signs of enemy air activity, the glazed cockpit giving him a clear 180-degree field of view.

Tait placed the vibrating binoculars to his eyes, the gyro-stabiliser ensuring a clear and steady picture. He did a sweep left to right of the foreground before repeating the sweep further out. It appeared clear. He zoomed in to a couple of likely places where the enemy might be hiding, conducting a reconnaissance of their own, searching out the territory and route the advancing Soviet division would need to cross. Nothing. Not a sign of the Soviet airborne regiment they knew was on the ground not far from here, anything between three to five kilometres east. The road in front of them that ran from the canal in the north to the town of Stadthagen in the south was to be defended by the Royal Regiment of Fusiliers. Stop-line Black Raven had finally been decided upon as the only option if they were to hold the Soviet 12th Guards Division back long enough for 2nd Infantry Division to continue improving its defences along the River Weser. Black Raven continued to the south of Stadthagen, following a staggered line down to Hessich Oldendorf situated on the northern bank of the River Weser where a long stretch of the river ran from west to east.

Tait scrutinised the open ground where the Guards Division tanks would have to cross. *A good killing ground for the Milan teams,* he thought. *Where the hell is the Soviet airborne though?* That was the biggest worry. Well over 1,000 elite soldiers were out here somewhere, no doubt getting ready to cause havoc. The retreating British forces would have to fight their way through them if they were to get back to a safe area. But, first, they would be expected to hold the first stop-line, Red-Rook, that ran from the Mittellandkanal in the north, south to Barsinghausen, then further south again, spiking east to Springe, before turning back to Bad Munder and south to Hameln. The retreating regiments would need to try and consolidate along Red-Rook before they pulled further back. It was hoped that this could be achieved in good order, or the retreat could quickly turn into a rout. If that wasn't already the case.

Tait turned to the pilot and nodded, the action unsettling his stomach again. He had seen enough. Sheppard nodded back, smiling, recognising the sergeant's pale face and the reason for it. The Gazelle dropped back down, the pilot manoeuvring backwards before turning on the spot, heading north, steadily picking up speed before the hedge-hopping started all over again. They were to recce the locations where the 2nd Battalion, the Royal Regiment of Fusiliers, would be inserted. A second Gazelle was south of Stadthagen where two companies of the 1st Battalion of the King's Own Royal Border Regiment would be defending. A third Gazelle was conducting a recce of Haste, where a Territorial Army company would conduct a fighting withdrawal once the 3rd Battalion, the Queen's Regiment, had passed through.

Higher command had made a decision. The ground east of the River Weser had been lost, and they had no intention of frittering away the lives of British soldiers to defend a forlorn hope. Just hold the enemy back long enough to enable 1 British Corps to dig in.

1030, 9 July 1984. Aviation Company, 2nd Battalion, Royal Regiment of Fusiliers, 24th Airmobile Brigade. Northeast Stadthagen, West Germany.
The Blue Effect -2 days

A TOW-armed Mark 7 Lynx, along with its partner, hovered in the gap between Lindhorst in the south and the forest to the north. The Gazelle further east had reported the contact around Rehren where a Territorial battalion was providing a forward screen. South of Lindhorst, a second trio of helicopters were providing cover. West of Ludersfeld, four Lynx Mark 9s swooped down, each disgorging a section of infantry from A-Company, the Aviation Company, 2nd Battalion, RRF. Once their passengers had been offloaded, the Lynx helicopters surged forward and gained height as four more helicopters tilted their noses into the air, tail rotor dropping as the pilots brought their aircraft to a halt, depositing a second platoon. The first platoon was already running forward, skirmishing, until they found themselves up against the metalled road that ran north to south across their front. The road to the north connected with a crossing point for the Mittellandkanal and, to the south, swept southwest into Lindhorst.

The platoon commander, Lieutenant Oliver Thorpe, indicated where he wanted his sections deployed. He made his way through the line of trees, across the road and in between two houses. The entire road was an avenue of trees, scattered with houses of all shapes and sizes, wildly dispersed along its complete length. A-Company had to defend the line from Ludersfeld to the canal in the north. First-platoon were deploying close to the canal, by Niedernholz, a machine-gun section with them to help secure the northernmost anchor. Third-platoon would have Ludersfeld itself, plus out to 300 metres to the north. Second-platoon, Thorpe's platoon, would defend the centre. His platoon explored their positions whilst First-platoon pushed north to their area of responsibility.

Sergeant Cohen dropped down beside him. "The sections are in place, sir, but I've told them no digging in just yet."

"Agreed, Sarn't. We'll wait until the OC confirms this is our position. Just in case we have to change location. Make sure they keep their eyes peeled though."

"Sir." With that, Sergeant Cohen pushed himself up and went to check on each section, confirm their arcs of fire, and ensure they had found some decent cover. He was sure the lads wouldn't need reminding. They had witnessed some of the troops returning to the rear, loaded onto one-ton Land Rover ambulances and Samaritans, the ambulance version of the armoured CVRT, along with the wounded loaded onto supply trucks returning from the front. The wounded were swathed in bloodied and dirty bandages, some with horrific facial injuries and third-degree burns from blazing armoured vehicles. Limbs were missing as a consequence of artillery salvos or from heavy-calibre bullets fired by attack-helicopters or armoured infantry combat vehicles. They didn't need to be reminded of the necessity for good cover. But, he would remind them just the same. That was his job.

Lieutenant Thorpe eased himself forward, his SLR resting in the crook of his arm as he did a rough leopard-crawl until he was beyond the boundary of the house wall on his left and alongside the bole of a fairly old but thin trunk of a tree. He heard his runner and radio operator shuffle forward, so one was either side of him. Placing his SLR rifle on the ground in front of him, but within easy reach, he removed the binoculars from their case. "We're a bit out in the open here."

"Sorry, sir?" asked his signaller.

"Just muttering to myself, Pritchard."

They'll need to dig in to protect themselves from artillery and ground-to-air strikes, he thought, *but it's a good position from which to hit the enemy.* He scanned the area out to his front: wide open fields, out to two kilometres. Once his Milan firing post was set up, along with two additional Milan's provided by a detachment from the mobile anti-tank platoon, they could hit any armour that attempted to cross the open ground. A killing ground. The L445 road, 500 metres away, running to the northeast, had a water feature, the Ziegenbach, 200 metres this side of it – only a few metres across, so not a real obstacle for the enemy. But any crossing operation would have to occur under the guns of the lieutenant's platoon. He wasn't high enough to see the Mittellandkanal, but that was only 1500 metres to their north.

He picked up his SLR, slithered backwards and, once hidden from view, jumped up. "Pritchard, Barnes, with me. We'll have a better view from a two-storey house."

The trio moved along the outer wall of the house towards the front where it faced the road. The door was locked, but a quick boot by Pritchard and they gained entry.

"Barnes, you stay here and let Sergeant Cohen know where we are."

"Sir."

Lieutenant Thorpe made his way into the corridor, the stairs leading up to the second floor directly in front of him. The inside of the house was dark, the owner having closed all the wooden shutters. Many houses and flats in West Germany had a shutter system where they could enclose the windows in either wooden or metal shutters, providing additional insulation against the harsh German winters and also providing added security.

Thorpe took a left at the top, the clumping sound behind indicating that his radio operator was close behind. Once through the door on the left at the top of the stairs, he headed for the large window, a small crack of light showing him the way. He eased the shutter slightly, not wanting to expose himself behind the only unshuttered window in the house.

"Pritchard, open all the window shutters facing east, upstairs and down below, then back up here."

"Sir." With that, Pritchard went away to carry out his task.

Thorpe gave him a couple of minutes then pulled back both shutters, giving him a great view of the landscape out to his front. Hearing a clattering of boots on the stairs, he was soon joined by Sergeant Cohen.

"Good open country for the Milan's, sir."

"Yes, we can deploy them along this road. We need to keep a close eye on that road crossing our front. At least one firing point needs to be assigned to cover that. I'm sure they'll cross over it, but if they're stupid enough to travel down it, they will make a good target." Thorpe moved the binoculars to the left, the canal now visible. Two kilometres to the east was the forest north of Lindhorst. "At least the Army Air Corps are keeping a lookout for us," he said as he watched the hovering Lynx through his wavering binos. He passed the binos to his platoon sergeant.

"I want the sections dug in forward of the treeline. Let's have the houses and trees at our back. The Soviets will soon target the buildings, but they'll find it harder to spot us to the front, dug in. The houses can give us some cover when we need to pull back."

Cohen agreed, handing the binoculars back to his platoon commander.

"What about the spare Gympy?"

"Put it with Two-Section, and the mortar directly behind them. That way, they can both cover the entire platoon front."

"How long do you reckon we'll have to hold this place for, sir?"

"Anybody's guess, Sarn't Cohen. Our job is to hold for as long as possible, or at least until the last units have withdrawn to the river. Keep the Soviets away from 2-Div as long as possible. Give them every opportunity to establish well dug-in defences. Then we can pull back."

"Or get cut off."

"Exactly."

"We'll hold the river though, won't we?"

"We have to. We're running out of places to run."

The lieutenant twisted his shoulders to the right, zooming in to the village of Lindhorst. *A staging post for an attack*, he thought. *If only we had more men, it would be a good defensive position.* He saw movement on the road that ran west to east, from Ludersfeld to Lindhorst. It was a Fox, probably from the TA recce squadron that was providing a screen. *At least they will have some warning of the enemy's arrival.* "We have recce from the TA out to our front. Let the sections know," he said to his signaller who then moved away from the window, crouching down next to one of the internal walls, and contacted the sections of the platoon. "And remind them that there's a TA company out front and they, along with elements of 3 Queen's could come tearing through here at any time."

"Sir."

Oliver leant his elbows on the windowsill and tracked the open-topped Land Rover as it drove around the western outskirts of Lindhorst.

"The Weser is pretty wide, and we're building up a good defence."

"I know, but their bridging kit is pretty impressive. How about our reinforcements, sir?"

"We have an American Corps coming in to support NORTHAG, but it's not all arrived from the States yet. There's a division on the way though."

"That'll help, surely."

The officer turned to look at his platoon sergeant. "That depends on who gets first call. The Germans, Dutch, Belgians or us. Right, we need to get to work."

"I'll put two spotters from each section in some of the houses, sir. At least we'll have additional warning when the Soviets finally turn up."

"Yes, do that. The lads need to watch their backs as well. There could be Soviet airborne between us and the FARB. We know they've reached as far as Haste."

Before the sergeant could respond, they heard the *wop-wop, wop-wop, wop-wop* of rotor blades from a Chinook twin-engine helicopter as it suddenly descended low in front of the house, in between their position and the L445. The large helicopter spun in a southerly direction, backing up until the pilot was happy with their position. The ramp at the rear was down, and two white plastic pipes jutted out each side at an angle. Two Land Rovers careered across the open ground just as the engineers, sitting in the back of the Chinook, released L9 bar mines, anti-tank mines, sliding down the plastic tubes, laying two lines of these lethal weapons as the helicopter moved forward. Soldiers from the Field Squadron, Royal Engineers, jumped out of the open-topped Land Rovers and started to set the fuses, following the large helicopter as it discharged its lethal cargo.

"Thank God for that," uttered Lieutenant Thorpe.

"It will certainly slow the buggers down, sir."

"We can hit them as they try to cross the Ziegenbach, and again when they hit the minefield."

"What about our fallback positions, sir? We could do with checking them out."

The young officer stroked the light stubble on his face, making a mental note to shave as soon as time allowed. "Of course. If I leave you to settle the platoon in, I can take the FFR Land Rover and scout our positions."

"Shall I assign one of the sections to be the first to pull back?"

"Yes, make it the centre section. In fact I'll take Lance Corporal Jeffries from Two-Section with me."

When they abandoned this line, the platoon would have to move quickly on foot, with all their equipment, to the second defensive line. From there, they could hit the enemy again. Their final position would be behind the Holpe, another minor run of water that would act as a temporary barrier to the enemy. Once there, the helicopters of 24th Airmobile Brigade would swoop in behind them. As the Lynx Mark 7s of the Aviation Regiment provided cover, along with C-Company who were dug in along the road, the Lynx Mark 9s and Chinooks would pick them up and take them to wherever higher command dictated they would need to fight next.

Somewhere behind them, they could hear more helicopters, so they crossed to one of the rooms on the opposite side of the house to investigate. Pulling back the blinds, they could look through the line of trees out towards the open ground on the other side of the road. There was a flight of Chinooks, some carrying an internal load, either more troops or a Land Rover tucked inside. Slung beneath, several had a second Land Rover; others a net containing supplies and ammunition. Thorpe knew that at least one of the Chinooks would be carrying the Milan detachment, and the Land Rovers slung beneath would belong to them. This would enable his platoon to grab a ride, moving to their secondary positions much more quickly when required. Three Lynx hovered further to the south, dropping down on their skis, allowing the soldiers on-board to debus. B-Company was moving into position, their responsibility from Ludersfeld down to Stadthagen.

"Let's go then." With that, Lieutenant Thorpe headed for the stairs, closely followed by Sergeant Cohen and Pritchard.

"Pritchard, get onto Lance Corporal Jeffries and have him meet us here."

"Sir."

Once at the bottom of the stairs and out through the front door, they collected Barnes, Thorpe's runner, and waited for the second-in-command of Two-Section to join them. Barnes, in the meantime, collected the FFR, Fitted For Radio, Land Rover.

As soon as Jeffries arrived, the group mounted up and headed southwest. Once on a hard-packed lane, the driver steered south; then west along a narrow metalled road taking them a kilometre until passing through Lauenhagen and across the Hulse. Turning north, passing through the outskirts of the village and taking another metalled road to their half-left, they arrived at the location it had been agreed Second-Platoon would defend. The clatter of helicopters drowned out the sound of the Land Rover's engine as more troops arrived in the region. The build-up of the defence of Stop-Line Black Raven continued. Another Chinook touched down, and a Lynx not far away also connected with ground, an infantry section leaping out quickly, allowing the helicopter to return and pick up more soldiers. With the ramp of the Chinook down, a line of soldiers, hunched down with the weight of their loads, left the confines of the helicopter, moving down the loading ramp. Fifteen men were disgorged, a full mortar-section from the battalion's fire-support company. The men quickly dispersed. Nine of the men carried three mortar base plates, three barrels and three bipods, with sights, between them. Each item weighed over eleven kilograms, the sight coming in at thirteen and a half. They would need the remaining two Land Rovers and trailers that would be dropped within the hour to move about the battlefield. Once set up, the three 81mm mortars would provide additional firepower that A-Company could call upon when needed. With a range of five and a half kilometres, the section's mortars could pound the enemy in front of A-Company's lines with high-explosive bombs, and lay a barrier of smoke to cover them while they withdrew. The other two sections would no doubt support B and C Companies.

Lieutenant Thorpe, and the second-in-command of Two-Section, scouted the area, satisfying themselves where the section would deploy when they pulled back. He would send the section early, along with the two Milan FPs, giving them plenty of time to get their bearings and bring fire down on the Soviets as they crossed the open ground.

Corporal Prentice, commander of Two-Section, had passed out top in his Junior NCOs' cadre course eighteen months before and had proven to be an effective section commander and leader of men. Another eighteen months would potentially see him as a platoon sergeant. He had confidence that, supported by Sergeant Cohen, Two-Section would give a good account of themselves.

Thorpe and his men climbed back into the Land Rover as a second Chinook dropped a Land Rover and trailer that was slung beneath it before landing further afield and offloading more troops. The build-up continued. They headed back to the front line. Thorpe's men would need to prepare their defences if they were to be ready to have any impact on the juggernaut that was rolling towards them.

Chapter 10

1035, 9 July 1984. 1st Battalion (Cleveland), Yorkshire
Volunteers, 15th Infantry Brigade, 2nd Infantry Division.
East of Auhagen, Mittellandkanal, West Germany.
The Blue Effect -2 days

North of the Mittellandkanal, D and G Company, The Green Howards,
1st Battalion, Yorkshire Volunteers, Territorial Army, were digging in
along a two-kilometre stretch of the Rodenberger Aue, locking in with
K-Company, south of the canal. To their north, they tied in with the
1st Panzer Division of the 1st German Corps. The 3rd Panzer Brigade,
one of three brigades in the division, with their Leopard main battle
tanks, provided the German Corps with a strong right flank and would
help support the Territorial Army soldiers. The ugly-looking Saxon
armoured personnel carriers pulled up along the length of the five
to ten-metre wide water feature and disgorged the troops that would
defend this section of the Rodenberger Aue. Officers gave orders and
the NCOs made it happen. Sections were deployed to dig in, building
defensive positions on the west bank, making sure they had good
firing placements with overhead protection for the expected shelling
by Soviet artillery. Behind them, the ground was heavily forested; their
escape route should the enemy cross the water feature and force them
back. The unit was defending the northernmost boundary of the 1st
Armoured Division, within the area of operations corresponding to
the 3rd Battalion, the Queen's Regiment. All the Yorkshire Volunteers
had to do was hold this piece of ground long enough for the 3rd
Battalion, that was very much on the run, to pass through.

Lieutenant Colonel Delamere, Commander of 3 Queen's, had
been ordered to extract with all speed; conduct a fighting retreat,
but not get bogged down in trying to defend ground, ground that
was already lost to the enemy. The commanders of the 1st Armoured
Division and 1st British Corps needed to keep as much of the

95

battalion, along with the attached tanks from RTR, as intact as possible, to provide a force to block or even counter-attack the enemy wherever the Soviets managed to break through. 1 BR Corps had to hold the River Weser. Beyond that was Osnabruck and Bielefeld, Dortmund and the Rhein, then the Netherlands and, finally, the English Channel. If the Soviet Army managed to reach the Channel, they would split the NATO forces in Europe in two.

The battalion was expected to cross near Rehren. Although the bridge would be blown shortly to prevent the Soviet forces finding an easy crossing, Chieftain AVLBs (Armoured Vehicle-Launched Bridge) had been made available to dash forward, and in less than five minutes, two twenty-three-metre bridges would be laid across the Aue. Once 3 Queen's crossed, they had orders to race west as fast as possible; their responsibilities for defending that sector would cease. 2nd Infantry Division would take over full responsibility for the defence line from then on. The 2nd Division's stop-line was the River Weser, but while they prepared those defences, Territorial Army units allocated to them, along with the 24th Brigade, would be used to slow the enemy down. 1st and 3rd Armoured Divisions required a reprieve if they were to extract themselves from the battle and rest, resupply and rearm.

During periods of total war, the Territorial Army is incorporated by the Royal Prerogative into the Regular Service. They now came under the code of Military Law for the full duration of hostilities or until the situation was such that deactivation could be permitted.

"Mathew."

"Sir," responded Lieutenant Mathew Reynolds, running over to the Land Rover FFR where his company OC was standing talking into the radio.

"Roger that. Out." The Officer Commanding, Delta Company, 1st Battalion, YV, one of four rifle companies in this BAOR-assigned battalion, passed the handset back to his signaller. "Mathew, I've got a special task for you."

"Sounds ominous, sir."

"It is." The sandy-haired officer laughed. His freckled face stood out even through the streaked cam-cream that plastered his face. "See that concrete structure," he said, indicating the concrete mouth of the tunnel where the Rodenberger Aue passed under the Mittellandkanal, an amazing piece of German ingenuity. "I want your platoon to defend that. There are Soviet airborne all over the area, and they'll want to ensure the Soviet tank divisions have free passage."

Reynolds turned to his runner. "Get Sergeant Mason to move Three-Section up the top there. I'll join him shortly."

"Sir," responded the soldier, and ran off to carry out his orders.

"Have a Gympy facing down the canal itself, and I'll get a Milan FP over to you. I might send you a second FP, but the other three will be needed to support One and Two-Platoon."

"You think they might use the canal, sir?"

"Wouldn't you? Why try and cross it when you can send your troops along it. If they cross the Rodenberger that way, they'll get right behind us."

"I'll see to it, sir."

"Be quick, Mathew. That last radio message was telling us that the bridge at Rehren is about to be blown. 3rd Queen's are on their way with Soviet airborne harassing them every step of the way."

"They can't be that far away from us then."

"No, so make it quick. Two-Platoon will be on your left and Golf-Company will be on their left. I'll use One-Platoon to cover when we have to withdraw. Make sure your Saxons are close. Once they get across, or as soon as we get the order to move, we're out of here."

"Consider it done, sir."

"Good luck, Mathew." With that, the OC jumped into the Land Rover and was driven off. He would need to organise the disposition of the rest of his company.

Reynolds ran along the edge of the canal to his right, a tree-lined embankment above him, reaching the Saxon belonging to Three-Section, parked next to the concrete structure that was the start of the ten-metre wide tunnel.

Sergeant Mason was waiting for him. "There's a bloody great gap here, sir."

Reynolds looked at where his platoon sergeant was pointing. There was indeed a gap. Next to the canal, a hard-packed track ran parallel to it, straight across the top of the Rodenberger. In between the mouth of the tunnel and the canal, a twenty-metre stretch would allow the enemy easy access across the Aue. There was only him and his men that could stop them.

"Have you checked the tunnel?"

"It's blocked. They'll not get through it."

"What about the section?"

"Deployed, sir. I'll show you."

The sergeant moved off, his platoon commander, signaller and runner close behind. The first position they came across was the rifle-group. Four men, led by the section commander, were digging in on the left and right of the hard-packed track that crossed the gap between the tunnel head and the canal.

"Corporal."

"Sir," responded Corporal Brian Fletcher, the section commander. "I've got Roberts and Fraser digging in here. They can use this to protect their left flank," he said pointing to the concrete wall that stood two-metres high to the side of them, the mouth of the tunnel on the other side. "George and Jenkins are on the right. Above them is the gun-group."

Reynolds surveyed the positions, noting that the GPMG team of three men were at the top of the embankment, a spindly tree either side of their position. They were far enough back that they wouldn't receive incoming fire from the side; the wall of the tunnel mouth protected them as well.

"My worry is an attack from the canal." Reynolds frowned. "If the Soviets come at us from the direction canal and from the gap at the same time, the gun-group could find themselves in trouble."

Just then, a second Saxon pulled up in the tree line, next to the open mouth of the tunnel.

"I'm going to put Two-Section, less two men, next to the entrance of the tunnel mouth, along the western embankment of the Aue." Informed Sergeant Mason. "They'll have a view right across the other side, out to a couple of hundred metres with an arc of at least 180. The other two men, I suggest, sir, could set up on the edge of the canal itself. They can warn us of any movement on the water, and with One-Section in reserve, we can counter any assault from there, or along any of our area of responsibility for that matter."

"I like it, Sergeant Mason. When the Milan FP turns up, put it with Three-Section. If they send any armour to try and rout us out of our position, they'll probably use the track running along the canal."

"If they attempt a direct attack along that track, we'll be hard-pushed to stop them, sir. Half a dozen BMPs or airborne APCs charging down there would take some stopping. One Milan isn't going to make much difference."

The officer reflected on what his platoon sergeant was saying.

He trusted the man's judgement. He was a good senior NCO and an excellent soldier. "I'll get onto the OC immediately. This has got to be their first point of call."

"Can we have the mortar platoon give our fire-missions priority, sir?"

"Good idea. I'll try and get another Milan from the anti-tank platoon."

"What about some mines?"

"Anything else on your wish list, Sergeant?" Reynolds laughed. "I'll see what I can do."

"Sir, sir, its Company HQ."

Reynolds grabbed the handset off his signaller. "Zero-Delta, this is Delta-Three-Zero. Over."

"Zero-Delta. Friendlies starting to feed through numerous points, south of your water feature. They need figures two to four hours to withdraw through. We hold for as long as we can. Enemy spotted by heli-reconnaissance. They'll be on your doorstep in less than ten minutes. Over."

"Roger that, sir. We have a big gap here to cover. A likely focal point. Need immediate planned fire-missions and additional Milan FP. Over."

The Sergeant, having overheard the conversation, signalled that he would warn the rest of the platoon.

"On it already, Oliver. Send grids soonest."

"Roger that, sir. They'll be with you in one. Over."

"I'll join you shortly. Out."

Reynolds ran towards the concrete wall of the tunnel entrance, looked over at the two soldiers dug-in in front of him, and slumped with his back to the wall, pulling his map from his combat jacket pocket. Placing his SLR on the ground, his signaller crouching next to him, he called in the coordinates. *Three fire-missions should do it,* he thought.

A Land Rover raced up the bank towards the gap and pulled alongside the lieutenant.

"Sir, where do you want the Milan?" asked the lance corporal who was sitting in the passenger seat.

"Set up on the track, then dump your transport back the way you came up. You have Three-Section's gun-group on the high ground to your right, and you'll be in between them and the rifle-group. Understand?"

"Sir."

"Make it quick then. The enemy will be with us very shortly."

The driver reversed the vehicle, changed gear, turned right and pulled up next to the embankment. The two men manhandled the Milan anti-tank missile launcher out of the vehicle in order to take it to their allocated firing position.

Once Lieutenant Reynolds had finished transmitting the coordinates, he headed up the embankment.

Crump, crump, crump...crump, crump, crump.

Reynolds threw himself down alongside the gun-group as three mortar rounds erupted just north of the tunnel entrance, on the eastern bank of the Rodenberger Aue. Three more mortar bombs exploded, this time bracketing the tunnel entrance itself, one landing in the water, a fountain of spray plastering the structure with water.

"All call signs. Mask up, mask up," Reynolds ordered.

He knew there would be no chemical contaminants from the mortar shells, but he didn't know what else was lined up to hit them. He pulled on his own suffocating mask, checking that his runner, signaller and the gun-group were doing the same. Lance Corporal Marsh, second-in-command of the section and commander of the gun-group, nodded as if to say he was ready. Although nerves were eating at his gut, that simple contact with his platoon commander steadied his uneasiness.

Three more explosions. This time, more accurate, punching small craters in the hard-packed track, showering the Milan and rifle team in debris.

Crump, crump, crump...crump, crump, crump.

This time, the bombs landed on the west bank of the Aue, along the line where the soldiers of Two-Section were partially dug in. Reynolds doubted they had had time to prepare more than just shell-scrapes. More bombs hit the track below him. There were two mortar sections targeting his men, he surmised.

"Delta-Three-Two, Delta-Three-Zero. Report. Over."

After a delay of five or ten seconds, a muffled response came back. *"This is Delta-Three-Two...Hit hard...one killed...two...injured..."*

"Are you functional? Over."

"...Gympy intact. Over."

"Roger that. Hang in there. Will get you medical assistance soonest. Out to you. Hello, Zero-Delta, Delta-Three-Zero. Contact. Mortar fire. Two firing points. Need medical assistance to my location ASAP. Over."

"Zero-Delta. Acknowledged. Help on way. Pull your reserve section forward when needed, One-Platoon will plug the gap. Over."

Reynolds peeled his respirator off. "Can't communicate with this damn thing on. Roger that, sir. Standby for fire mission. Out."

"There, sir," called the GPMG gunner excitedly as he pulled the butt into his shoulder, straining to pick out the target through the round eyepieces of his S-6 respirator, and opened fire.

Sergeant Mason, on seeing his platoon commander mask less, pulled his own off and was quickly followed by the rest of the platoon who were in sight of him.

"Remember your training," responded Lance Corporal Marsh quite calmly as he stuffed his mask back in its haversack. A welder in Civvy Street, a section second-in-command in wartime. "Enemy contact, 500 metres, left of prominent tree." He then placed his cheek on the butt of his SLR, sighted an enemy soldier just as he dropped into position, and fired two rounds.

Brrrrrp…brrrrp…brrrrrp. The Gympy gunner fired controlled bursts, dust kicking up in and around the enemy, one soldier thrown sideways like a rag doll as two bullets smashed into him. The enemy returned fire. Flashes from AKs could be seen all along the line of trees opposite. The airborne troops were good, firing short, well-aimed bursts, unlike some of the TA soldiers who were firing wildly, an element of panic as they experienced their first action.

"All Delta-Three call signs. Place your shots, place your shots. Delta-Three-One, standby to come forward. Over."

"Delta-Three-One, roger. Ready to move."

Zero-Delta, this is Delta-Three-Zero. Fire Mission. Over."

"Send. Over."

"X-Ray-One, X-Ray-One. Enemy in treeline. Over."

"Roger that. Standby for ranging shot. Out."

"Standby for outgoing," Reynolds shouted to his platoon.

Zip…zip. Two rounds passed his face, so close he felt the draught on his skin.

"Get your bloody head down, sir, or you'll lose it," yelled Sergeant Mason.

Reynolds placed his helmet back on and called back. "I'm going to check on Three-Two. Keep me posted."

"Run low, sir, run low."

Reynolds nodded then shuffled back before getting up and sprinting north, his runner and radio operator close behind, dropping down the bank and passing behind the rifle-group and Milan FP, checking in on them as he passed. One soldier had a minor shrapnel wound, but all five soldiers were returning fire at the enemy. The Milan team waited patiently.

He ran round to the front of the concrete tunnel mouth and dropped down next to Two-Section. A medic was patching up the two wounded soldiers. Private Bailey lay still; a combat jacket had been thrown over his face. The cause of his death was obvious: the mangled lower part of his body, one leg missing, a bloody stump for the other, death would have come very quickly. The blood loss had been quick, his punctured abdomen adding to the steady loss of his life-giving fluids.

Corporal Walker, his wide eyes staring through his mask, looked at his platoon commander, almost pleading with him to help. But Reynolds was pleased with what he saw. The NCO had placed his men well, and they were returning fire, following his orders whenever he spotted a target. Once this was over, *if they get through it,* thought Oliver, the NCO would be the better for it.

Brrrrrp…brrrrp…brrrrp. The Gympy put rounds down on the enemy, and there was no sign of an assault yet. Two-Section was hurt, but OK. Three-One wasn't needed, just yet.

"You're doing a good job, Corporal Walker. Your section can remove their masks. If you see the Sovs putting their NBC kit on then get them back on quick."

The NCO peeled the mask off, and a deep breath of fresh air filled his lungs. "That feels better, sir."

"Good. I'm going back to Three-Three. Let me know the minute there's any change here. You're doing well. Just keep some steady fire going, but watch your ammunition. OK?"

"OK, sir."

"Sir, outgoing," informed his radio operator Simmons.

The mortar bomb travelled overhead, and they watched the trees part and splinter as the detonation tore a small section of the treeline apart.

The handset was quickly passed to Reynolds. "Zero-Delta, Delta-Three-Zero. Fire for effect, fire for effect. Over."

"On way. Out."

They only had to wait a mere five seconds before six more explosions erupted along the treeline as all three of the mortar sections opened fire. Then another six bombs battered the Soviet airborne troops who were on the verge of putting in an assault on the defenders. The Soviet mortar teams weren't left out either. A mortar-locating battery, using a Mark-1 mortar-locating radar, Cymbeline, had identified their location and long-range artillery was already pounding them into submission.

Corporal Walker smiled for the first time since the attack had started. "We're not on our own then, sir."

"No, we're not, Corporal, we're not."

More explosions burst deeper into the trees, pounding the airborne troops mercilessly.

"Zero-Delta, Delta-Three-Zero. On target. Adjust fifty metres right. Acknowledge. Over."

"Zero-Delta. Understood. Out."

"That should keep them quiet for a while. Keep me posted."

"Sir."

Reynolds and his small entourage returned by the same route, rejoining Three-Section.

"Just in time, sir," informed Sergeant Mason. "We have some definite movement out there. Once we stop the bombing, I reckon they'll come for us."

Reynolds turned to his signaller. "Warn the platoon and let Company HQ know."

He lifted the binoculars that were slung around his neck and surveyed the ground in front of him. It was suddenly quiet as the friendly mortar fire ceased. "What did you see?"

"It was Corporal Marsh; swears he saw a vehicle. He just had a glimpse, so it could be nothing."

Before they could debate the ifs and buts any further, the entire line of the Rodenberger Aue was engulfed in a hail of fiery, searing blasts and burning shrapnel. 122mm shells, fired by an artillery battery of the advance elements of a Regiment from 12th GTD or from the Soviet Airborne's D-30s, ripped up the meagre defences of Three-Platoon. 120mm mortar bombs were also lobbed onto the British troops from one of the surviving Soviet units. Even with decent foxholes or trenches, survival of the bombardment would have been difficult but, with shell-scrapes, they were at the mercy of the shelling.

"Gas, gas, gas," Reynolds yelled, hoping his men would follow suit all along the line as he refitted his respirator just in case.

"Delta-Three-Zero, Zero-Delta. Major push to our north. Bundeswehr

report major assault coming in. Expect strong push your sector. Over."

"Roger that, sir. Under heavy shelling."

Crump...crump...crump. Clouds of smoke enveloped the already battered, thin British line.

"Smoke, smoke." Yelled a soldier.

"Wait, Delta-Three-Zero." There was a pause on the airwaves. *"It's a big push. The line north of you has been penetrated. You have friendlies coming to you. They will cover your withdrawal. We've been ordered back. Soon as they arrive, pull back to Purple-One. Acknowledge. Over."*

Reynolds shouted into the handset, his voice drowned out by three explosions that bracketed the tunnel mouth, killing the Milan team and wounding two of the rifle-group below him. "Make it soon, sir, there won't be any of us left otherwise."

"Understood. Out."

"All Delta-Three call signs. Prepare to pull out. Three-One. Stay in situ and cover."

"Look, sir!" yelled Corporal Marsh, pointing at the BMDs, three of them powering through the smoke. The first one fired its 73mm gun, hitting nothing but causing the British soldiers to duck. The general-purpose machine gun rattled as the gunner poured a steady stream of bullets along the column of armour, but to no avail.

"Three-Three. Pull out, pull out now. Three-One, standby, standby."

"Grenade!" shouted Sergeant Mason as he threw a grenade towards the advancing enemy, the front BMD of the column now level with their line. The grenade exploded directly in front, but with no effect as the infantry combat vehicle maintained its speed.

"Watch for—"

Lieutenant Reynolds was unable to complete his warning as a round from a PKT, a coaxial machine gun mounted on the second vehicle, struck him square in the chest and he staggered sideways, Sergeant Mason catching him before he hit the ground. The staring eyes told the story, and the sergeant left him, calling to his men to pull back. There weren't many of Three-Section to hear the order. The rifle-group, bar one man, had been wiped out. Lance Corporal Marsh fell as he was covering his gun-group's withdrawal. Reynolds' radio operator was was giving the platoon commander's runner a fireman's lift, moving as quickly as he could for cover amongst the few trees that lined the embankment alongside the canal. The two soldiers from Two-Section, sent to guard the canal earlier, provided what cover they could, their SLRs barking as they each emptied a twenty-round magazine. Sergeant Mason ran with the gun-group, throwing themselves down on the grassy bank, and firing at whatever target they could see.

Airborne infantry were following the armour on foot, the last of the vehicles an ASU-85 self-propelled anti-tank gun. Mason saw two of the Soviets go down; then felt something pluck at his sleeve as the third BMD in the line had circled back, its coax PKT firing wildly as the vehicle bounced along the rough ground in between the hard-packed track and the embankment. He froze. In his head, it was all over. They had the enemy to their right and airborne armour to their left. He plucked a grenade from his webbing and was about to throw it when the BMD lifted at least two metres off the ground, the front dipping, the back flipping over, then skidding to a halt less than ten metres from their position. The ASU-85 fired at a target Sergeant Mason couldn't see, but it too erupted in a blaze, some of its crew screaming as they tried to escape the flames that were rapidly devouring them. A West German Marder, its distinctive zigzag pattern side-skirts, rocked to a halt in front of the stricken BMD destroyed earlier, its 20mm cannon pumping round after round towards the now retreating enemy. A second Marder moved along the track until level with the tunnel head, and six soldiers, sitting back to back in the troop compartment at the rear, dismounted. They were joined by a third, and Mason could see a Leopard 2, a Bundeswehr main battle tank, further back.

A Bundeswehr soldier, an Oberleutnant, a senior lieutenant, came running over to him at a crouch. "Where is your officer?"

"Dead, sir," yelled Mason as he peeled off his mask, his voice almost drowned out as a Marder fired a burst from its auto cannon.

"You get your men away. Now. You have *fünf Minuten*. Then we go."

"Have you seen the rest of my platoon?"

"There are some men back by the treeline to the rear. You have two vehicles. The enemy destroyed two. Now go."

With that, the German officer went to rejoin his men who were in a pitch battle with the Soviet troops. Mason called to the soldiers around him and led them west along the embankment. Once they could see the clearing and the two surviving Saxons, he took them west and rejoined the battered remains of the platoon. Before he did a check on the status of his surviving unit, he got onto HQ.

"Zero-Delta, this is Delta-Three-Zero-Alpha. Over."

"This is Zero-Delta. Good to hear from you. No time for a sitrep. Move your platoon immediately. Get them to Purple-One. Acknowledge. Over."

"Delta-Three-Zero-Alpha. Delta-Three to move to Purple-One. Over."

"Where is Delta-Three-Zero?"

"Down, sir."

"Roger. Move now. Out."

Chapter 11

1040, 9 July 1984. 5th Battalion, Royal Anglian Regiment (TA), 49th Infantry Brigade, 2nd Infantry Division.
Northeast of Rinteln, West Germany.
The Blue Effect -2 days

"I want your platoon on the eastern edge of the quarry." Major Dawson said, referring to the track that led to a large quarry that ran along the southern side of the E8 Autobahn, four kilometres northeast of Rinteln. "That way, you can cover a full 180-degree front. Two-Platoon will straddle the road north of you so; with you on the high ground, you can give them some cover. It's not high, but at 200 metres, you'll get a good view of any enemy approaching."

"Are we getting any mines, sir?" asked Lieutenant Gibson, commander of One-Platoon. "We need something to slow them down."

"Yes. Well, very soon anyway. There's a detachment of engineers joining us. You'll have Three-Platoon to your south. They'll cover your right flank."

"And the rest of the battalion, sir?"

The major turned and pointed. "Two-Company will cover from Bad Eilsen in the north to the forested high ground over there," he replied, indicating the high ground of Wesergebirge. "Three-Company are in reserve, covering our backs. Four-Company have been assigned as part of the Brigade reserve."

Gibson looked towards the tracks that ran up to the top and skirted the quarry and asked, "Do you think these will these make it, sir?" He pointed at the Saxon armoured personnel carriers. "It looks pretty rough, maybe better suited to tracked vehicles."

Major Dawson followed Gibson's gaze. "You should make it. Just ensure you stick to the tracks. If you get bogged down, there'll be no one to get you out."

Gibson laughed. "Added incentive then, sir."

"I doubt there's much cover up there, Michael, so make sure your men dig in well. We have to have a presence up there. When you extract, you need to move quickly." The major ran his finger along the map that was secured in a canvas case with a clear plastic front. "Looking at this, the southern slope of the quarry is out of the question. It's too steep to get the vehicles down. It's the same for the northern slope. You could get your platoon down, but without your vehicles. Anyway, that could take you straight into the arms of the Soviets. They'll more than likely use the road as their main axis of attack. So, you have to race back across the top, back along the route you'll use to get into position."

"We'll be pretty exposed to any air attack, sir."

"That's why speed is of the essence."

"Our RV?"

"We have to avoid Rinteln. So keep between the northern edge of the Autobahn and the high ground to the south. Three-Company will cover our withdrawal and our RV is Todenmann. That's where we'll have set up all over again. Oh, nearly forgot, you'll be joined by a section from the anti-tank platoon, with two Milan FPs."

They both turned as they heard the roar of diesel engines as four Saxon armoured personnel carriers of Two-Platoon passed them and swung off to the left onto the L442 and passed beneath the six-lane motorway above. Both officers' heads jerked upwards as two Spartan CVRTs came to a halt on the southern part of the Autobahn, directly above the platoon, as the last of the Saxons passed beneath. British soldiers quickly debussed and moved into position. A third Spartan, carrying more Royal Engineers, although invisible from the ground below, could be heard racing past their comrades, heading towards the far end of the flyover.

The Royal Engineers had two tasks: The first was to lay mines further along the motorway directly in front of Two-Platoon. The intention was to bring the enemy to an abrupt halt, giving the soldiers from the 5th Battalion, Royal Anglians, an opportunity to open fire on a disrupted enemy force. It wouldn't hold the enemy up for long as they would quickly attempt to outflank the defending force, calling in artillery and air strikes to dislodge them. The second task was to make life even more difficult for the enemy by blowing up the raised section of the Autobahn, forcing the Soviet army to bypass it, slowing down their advance. Any Soviet forces backing up as a consequence of this man-made traffic jam would then come to the attention of the NATO air forces and a battery of FH-70s, setting up further to the west to support the Royal Anglians.

The Territorial Army units, assigned to reinforce the British Army of the Rhine, and this particular battalion assigned to 2st Infantry Division, were being rushed to the front to help plug the gaps and slow the Warsaw Pact down, giving the retreating British Divisions some respite so they could recover, refuel, rearm and prepare themselves to be thrown back into the fight.

The 2nd Infantry Division, with the 15th (North-East) Brigade and the 49th (East) Brigade, along with additional Territorial Army battalions, were about to take the brunt of the massed army steamrollering towards them. Although well trained, they were not soldiers by profession. Only a week ago, their full-time profession was that of a clerk, bricklayer, accountant, hospital porter or a selection of many other trades and skills that provided them and their families with a living. Yes, they had all completed their annual two weeks of training for a small financial bounty, some of the exercises actually being held in Germany. The majority had also turned up regularly at the fortnightly weekend training sessions held at the various drill halls around the country, or weekends away on field training. But this was different; this was for real. Now they were full-time soldiers, about to come up against an aggressive, driven force of men and machines that had one purpose in mind: to crush them, destroy them, then pass through and continue with their relentless drive towards the English Channel.

"Who's covering them, sir?" Gibson said, pointing to the engineers already unloading some of the equipment they would need to use in order to prepare the flyover for destruction.

"They'll have to look after themselves, I'm afraid," the Company Commander responded with a smile. "I believe they've been bolstered to ensure they can protect each other. Anyway, the Soviets will need to get past us first."

They heard the roar of engines again. This time, it was Three-Platoon who passed them, to turn right and set up south of the quarry. They would drive southeast down Hamelner Strasse, turn left and dig in south of the quarry, protecting One-Platoon's right flank.

The lead vehicle pulled over. The large wheels locked and slid over the loose grit, and Lieutenant Shaw dismounted.

"Any change, sir? Hi, Mike," asked the officer, saluting, at the same time acknowledging his fellow platoon commander.

"No, Peter. As we discussed, we have no indication of their forward units. But get into position quickly. We've no idea how far away the Soviets are, or our friendly forces for that matter."

"Will do, sir. Good luck. You too, Mike."

"And you," responded both Lieutenant Gibson and Major Dawson.

The lieutenant climbed back into the Saxon armoured vehicle and sped off, closely followed by the rest of his platoon.

"Sir, sir, you're wanted," called Company Sergeant Major Webb, who had been keeping radio watch in the FFR Land Rover, waving the handset in the OC's direction.

"You had better be off as well, Michael. I'll come and check on your positions once I've established some fire support for us."

"Sir." With that, Lieutenant Gibson also went to rejoin his unit, First-Platoon, and climbed into the Saxon parked close by, joining his platoon sergeant, informing them where they were headed for. Gibson indicated for the driver to pull off and pointed in the direction he wanted him to take. "Through there. Don't stop. The gate looks flimsy enough."

The driver accelerated, and the powerful engine drove the ten-ton armoured personnel carrier forward, the prominent front of the vehicle making short work of the wooden gate that was designed to control access to the quarry.

"Make it fast. No stopping."

Once through, the driver, following the platoon commander's orders, turned right, following a narrow track through the trees. After five minutes, they left the thin covering of trees and were out in the open, rough scrub-covered ground either side of them. They looped back, almost to where they had started, before turning right and heading east along the escarpment, a stepped slope dropping down where large excavators had slowly extracted the minerals they sought from the quarry. They tracked along the rim. At one point, the wheels were centimetres from the edge, chunks of earth and rock dropping down disturbed by the armoured vehicles. The driver nudged the vehicle over, keeping as far to the right as possible. The track slowly led them northeast until they arrived at the far end of the quarry.

Lieutenant Gibson ordered a halt, and he and the sergeant surveyed the ground in front of them.

"Corporal Fletcher."

"Sir."

"Place your section over there," the Lieutenant ordered, pointing in the direction of the south-eastern edge of the slope. "Have your gun-group facing east, but have a couple of men watching south. You should be able to see Two-Platoon digging in below you any time soon."

"What about the vehicles, sir?"

Gibson turned towards his sergeant. "What do you think, Sarn't Newman?"

"Keep them within twenty metres, sir. That way, they can use the Gympy on top and make a quick getaway when needed."

"Agreed. Keep them near the track. When we move, it'll have to be quick. You sort them out. I'll deal with the rest."

"Roger that, sir."

The two men separated just as another Saxon troop carrier turned up, carrying a Milan team with two Milan firing points.

Lieutenant Gibson took control of the remaining two sections, positioning one on the left flank with the Milan's overlooking the Autobahn further down. The third section looked east, watching over the K-74 below. He wasn't entirely happy. There were at least 100 metres between each section. He prayed silently that the enemy wouldn't be coming this way.

Chapter 12

The Divisional Commander of the 12th Guards Tank Division threw the mug he had been holding across the other side of the farm building he was in. He lit one of his foul-smelling cigarettes directly from the one he had just smoked down to his fingertips. Frustration and anger were etched on his face. Even senior generals were suffering from the increasingly erratic logistical supplies getting through to the Soviet divisions on the front line. The Soviet air force was still holding its own, but that was all. As more and more American fighters arrived in theatre and with the floating airfield, the United Kingdom, far from subjugated, they were not getting it all their own way. But the Bear, Major-General Turbin, Commander of 12th Guards Tank Division, wasn't just dissatisfied with the Soviet resupply battalions: he was also extremely dissatisfied with his troops. What made it worse was that his deputy commander and political officer, Colonel Yolkin, had been bleating most of the morning: reminding him of his duty to his senior commanders and the Motherland. Their first attempts to shatter the forces defending a line between the Mittellandkanal and Stadthagen, and fulfil his division's role as an Operational Manoeuvre Group pushing deep into the enemy lines, had failed.

Turbin blew out a plume of smoke from the Belomorkanal cigarette, and it swirled around the officer standing before him. "Akim, Colonel Kharzin's 48th Tank Regiment crossed the Leine and pushed through the enemy force almost without a pause. To give him and his tank crews a well-deserved rest, all I asked you to do was cross a thinly held line and continue the fight and get us to the big prize: the River Weser."

The commander of the 200th Guards Motor Rifle Regiment

had flinched when the cup flew past him, but still stood stiffly to attention. "We need more artillery support, Comrade General."

"The first unit was made up of British reservists and you were supported by our airborne prima donnas!"

"Their Milan anti-tank missiles and helicopters have caused havoc with our armour, Comrade General."

"That's why we chose your infantry for the task, Colonel Yermakov," the chief of staff, Colonel Pyotr Usatov, added.

"I will not fail again, Comrade General, Comrade Colonel."

"I suggest you do not, Colonel. The consequences of failure will be far from pleasant," eluded the Deputy Commander of the division, Colonel Yolkin.

The Bear looked across at his skinny political officer, a uniform that wore him rather than the other way round. The meaning in the divisional commander's eyes was undisguised: *I will berate my officers, not you.*

"The Uman Division does not and will not fail. You will attempt a second breakthrough within the hour. I have secured two Hinds and ten Hips to support you. Allocate some men, find a place to set them down, and punch your way through their lines. Once you have broken them, release your tank battalion immediately to get as deep you can. Understood?"

"Yes, Comrade General, I will not fail you."

The Bear took a long draw on his cigarette, the red glow eating deep into the tobacco. He blew a steady stream in the air and moved closer to his junior, leaning in close, the scent of smoke and vodka almost choking the officer.

"The 12th Guards Tank Division, my division, is one of the best in the Soviet army. We were chosen especially for this mission to lead our armies to victory. We will not fail our Motherland, Comrade Colonel. You will get your artillery support and transport to fly in an assault-company. Use them and don't fail. Dismissed."

The colonel stiffened his body. "Sir." He saluted and left.

"You were too soft with him, Comrade General," alleged Colonel Yolkin.

The general shrugged his thickset shoulders and pointed a finger in the political officer's direction. "I have a suggestion, Comrade Colonel. Why don't you lead the airborne element behind the enemy's defences? You can lead the way and show us soldiers how it should really be done."

Colonel Usatov turned away so he could hide the smile that was breaking out.

"That will be all, Comrade Colonel."

The political officer shuffled out of the room, seething with anger inside, but not strong enough to challenge the Bear. Not yet, anyway.

"You need to step carefully with him, Comrade General."

The Bear waved a hand dismissively. "It will take someone bigger than him to frighten me."

"They say he has friends on high."

"Let's just focus on the war, shall we, Pyotr?"

"I see it has been agreed to bring elements of the 10th Division forward."

"Yes, I know Major-General Abramov well. He has volunteered his men to continue fighting."

"But once we're across the Weser and push the enemy either north or south, 20th Guards Army will do the rest."

The Bear pulled up a chair, sat down, pulled out a flask of vodka, and held it up. "Join me?"

"Of course," Pyotr responded, smiling. "Rather use your supplies than mine." The colonel picked up two shot glasses from one of the tables and brought them over. The Bear filled them up and they both drank the first one in silence.

"The 20th have been getting a hammering from the air. The bloody Americans have been getting in some deep strikes. The British Tornados are no better."

"Agreed, Comrade General, but they're easily at eighty per cent strength, if not more."

"I think our political masters are a little worried, my friend," the Bear whispered. "We have the East German and Polish armies playing a big role. Should they falter...having the 10th close by is just a little bit of insurance, I suspect."

The general refilled their glasses.

"They're also going to compete for our supplies. We've already had to give the Motor Rifle Regiment ammunition from the other regiments in the division."

"If Akim had broken through their lines by now, he wouldn't need any more!" Growled the Bear.

"Still, resupply is slowing down. The supply trucks are starting to break down in ever-greater numbers, and the spares for them just aren't available. Bring what's left of the 10th forward? Not only is there not enough room, making some great targets for the NATO bombers and artillery, but also they will need feeding. The distance from the Motherland gets ever longer."

"Now it is you that needs to tread carefully, my friend. Don't speak so openly when the rat is around. Eh?"

"Yes, yes, I know. Now, fill that up again if you please, Comrade General."

1500, 9 July 1984. Aviation-Company, 2nd Battalion, Royal Regiment of Fusiliers, 24th Airmobile Brigade.
West of Lindhorst, West Germany.
The Blue Effect -2 days

A freshly armed Mark-7 Lynx, hovering just behind the line of troops below, dropped down, moved left for 200 metres, and then popped back up again. The pilot had been back to the FARB to rearm and refuel and was now ready to give his support during the next attack. A Gazelle was conducting a reconnaissance further forward, trying to suss out the enemy's next intentions. As soon as the Gazelle pilot reported, he would take his Lynx further back and wait until needed.

Lieutenant Oliver Thorpe went from position to position, checking on his men. A-Company had to defend the line from Ludersfeld to the Mittellandkanal in the north. His platoon, Second-Platoon, would defend the centre of the Company's position. The entire road they were on was an avenue of trees, scattered with houses, some of which they occupied, not as defensive positions, but for observation purposes only. He had however moved one of the GPMGs onto the second floor of one of the houses, and was glad that he did. Once the Soviet troops had dismounted from their BMP-2s, the machine gun had caused havoc. Sergeant Cohen's suggestion that the gun-group change positions frequently, leaving stocks of ammunition in two other buildings, had also paid off. The men had been out of one particular house for only a couple of seconds when a Hind-D helicopter literally tore it apart with four of its S-5 rockets. They had held off the Soviet attack, but at a cost of one man dead and three wounded. When the Soviets attacked again, and he had been assured that they would, he was not sure they could keep the enemy at bay.

First-Platoon, deployed close to the canal by Niedernholz had been hit particularly hard. The Soviet troops had attacked in force, hoping to pry the canal away from the defending soldiers, allowing them to push their BMPs through and roll up the flank of the company. It was only because of the machine-gun section that had been deployed with them that they had been able to hold their position. The enemy paid a heavy price: three extra general-purpose machine guns, in the sustained-fire role, had been able to put down an overwhelming wall of fire. Soviet airborne troops, pushed into the attack by the 12th Guards Tank Division's commander, had lost over thirty men, killed or injured. Third-Platoon, defending Ludersfeld itself had got off lightly with two wounded men. One-Platoon, though, was down to seventy-five per cent of its strength, losing six men. The MG section was filling the gaps.

With his radio operator, Pritchard, and his runner, Barnes, behind him, Oliver made his way to the position, which held one of his three Milan anti-tank posts. Slinging his SLR over his shoulder, he dropped down into the firing position.

"Sir."

"See any movement?"

"No, sir," responded Corporal Gleeson. "We gave em a bit of a hiding, didn't we, sir?"

"We did that, Corporal. But they'll be back, so keep your men keen."

"The lads from Three-Queen's were in shit state, sir, and the TA lads didn't look any better."

"They've been fighting for a couple of days, Corporal. Most of 1st Armoured have been on the run since yesterday, in a fighting retreat. So, it's our turn now."

"Sir."

"Let's go."

All three clambered out of the position and moved back then north along the trees that lined the road, before going forward again to find the next firing position. The commander of Two-Section, Corporal Prentice, manned this.

"Any news, sir?"

"Nothing yet. But they're going to hit us hard. I want you to take your half-section to our fallback position, but leave your gun-group here."

"Still taking both Milan posts?"

The lieutenant thought for a moment before answering. "Yes, I think it will be the Gympy's that will be needed."

"When shall I move, sir?"

"Five minutes, make it five minutes. I'll be sending Sarn't Cohen back with you. We'll need you to cover us when we pull back, or they'll be all over us."

"Sir, incoming message," informed Partridge.

"Alpha-Two, this is Zero-Alpha. There is movement to your front. Watch out for returning air asset. Over."

"Roger that, sir. Moving elements of Alpha-Two-Two to Black-Jack-Two now. Over."

"Good move, Alpha-Two. They're going to hit us hard again. On the order 'Black-Jack fold', move the rest of your unit. Over."

"Wilco, sir."

"Good luck, Oliver. Out."

Oliver, along with his two shadows, moved further along the line, joining the second-in-command of Two-Section.

Lance Corporal Jeffries greeted his platoon commander. "Just heard from Two-Two, sir. They're in the Land Rover and on the way."

"Good. Is Sarn't Cohen with them?"

"Yes, sir. He said he'd radio in once in position."

"Right, you're down to just the gun-group, Corporal Jeffries, and one Milan, so watch yourselves."

"We likely to fall back pretty soon then, sir?"

"Wait one. Barnes."

"Sir."

"Get two men from Three-Section. I want them here."

"Will do, sir." Lieutenant Thorpe's runner left the firing-position and ran, at a crouch, back into the treeline before heading to find Three-Section.

"We'll wait for the order before we do, but I would expect it to be soon after the next attack."

"The OC, sir," informed Pritchard passing him the handset.

"Alpha-Two, go ahead. Over."

"Air-recce reporting movement, Oliver, so make sure your men are ready."

"Understood, sir."

"Zero-Alpha, out."

Two soldiers crashed down next to their platoon commander. "Where do you want us, sir?"

"Right of the Gympy, Two-Two-Alpha's old position. You join them, Barnes."

The three soldiers moved along the line and jumped into the vacated firing position previously occupied by the other half of Two-Section.

"Sir, radio."

Oliver took the handset from Pritchard again.

"Alpha-Two, this is Two-One-Alpha. Over."

"Alpha-Two. Go ahead."

The Observation Post, two men from One-Section he had earlier ordered to set up in the second storey of a house, reported in. *"We have movement, sir. Not sure, but it looks like an armoured unit, bit like one of our AVLBs. Over."*

"What's their location? Over."

"Two hundred metres west of the 445. Over."

"Roger that. As soon as it kicks off, you two get out of there. Out to you. Hello Zero-Alpha, this is Alpha-Two. Over."

"Go ahead."

"Definite movement Grid One-Seven-Eight-Zero-Three-Zero, probable MT-55."

A Gazelle helicopter sped overhead, drowning out the response from the Company OC.

"Zero-Alpha, say again. Over."

"Airborne recce has reported half a dozen TMMs. They'll be crossing the Ziegenbach at multiple locations. Over."

"Understood. Out."

Thud, thud, thud...thud, thud, thud.

"Smoke," yelled Jeffries.

All along the western bank of the Ziegenbach, clouds of smoke mushroomed, concealing the area from the British troops.

"Stand to! Stand to! Gas! Gas! Gas!" bellowed Lieutenant Thorpe, peeling his helmet off and exchanging it for his respirator. Hood of his NBC smock pulled over, helmet back on, he pressed down into the trench. He compressed his body as close to the floor of the trench as he was able, clutching his SLR to his chest. He knew what was coming next. And it arrived five seconds later.

The Bear had kept his promise. Over 1,000, 122mm rockets from 3rd Shock Army's BM-21 Brigade pounded the British lines from the canal north of Niedernholz to south of Ludersfeld. Lieutenant Thorpe felt thick clumps of earth hammering down onto his head and shoulders, and he had to clear it away from his face if he was to continuing breathing through his claustrophobic mask. The noise was incessant, thump after thump, the ground shaking with the violence of the bombardment.

To the rear of the main force of the RRF troops, four Elbrus surface-to-surface missiles (SSMs), from 12th Guards Tank Division's SCUD-B missile battalion, struck with deadly force. Preceded by a number of salvos from the divisional artillery group, the thickened VX nerve agent, odourless and tasteless, dispersed by the SSMs, carried out its deadly undertaking. Sergeant Cohen, and the section sent to act as a covering force for the rest of the platoon when it withdrew, were caught unawares prioritising the search for cover rather than NBC protection, paid the price in full. Sergeant Cohen was already slipping into a coma while other members of the section were in various stages, some with chests tightening and losing muscle control, others vomiting and defecating uncontrollably as they edged closer to death. Corporal Prentice, disorientated, his body suffering from myoclonic jerks, had crawled out of his trench only to be killed by a further salvo of 122mm shells.

Lieutenant Thorpe, forcing his body even lower as the Soviet Divisional Artillery Group switched its attention to the forward line of troops, wasn't to know that more of his men were dying behind him. Masonry clanged off his helmet as the last of the standing houses was demolished, and he prayed that the OP had made it to cover in time. He desperately needed to know the status of his small force, but the din was deafening and his head was pounded constantly by shock wave after shock wave as the Soviets maintained the pressure. Inside, he was worried. Worried for his men, but also worried how close the enemy were. He could hear the occasional whine of shells passing overhead, fired by his own supporting artillery, making life difficult for the motor rifle troops crossing the water to his east. As for his men, the one Milan FP left with them, had been completely destroyed. The OP team had made it back to their positions but their foxhole, with them in it, had been wiped out by a direct hit from a 152mm shell. Three-Section had been all but decimated. Of the gun-group, the gunner and assistant gunner were dead, and the rifle-group had one dead and two wounded, one of which was the young second-in-command, promoted to second-in-command only four weeks before the start of the war.

The firing stopped. Thorpe's ears hummed, and it took him a few moments to gather his thoughts.

"Stand to! Stand to!" he shouted as he lifted his head above the parapet, the sound muffled through his respirator. He rubbed off the coating of earth and dust and checked the detector-paper patches on his NBC suit: they were clear. He removed his mask.

"Sir! HQ," called his signaller.

He held the handset close to his mouth and ear. "Alpha-Two. Go ahead. Over."

"Zero-Alpha. Chemical attack to rear positions. Maintain NBC state. Out."

Oliver checked the patches again, they were clear. Either the droplets had missed him or they had escaped a chemical attack.

Brrrrp...Brrrrp...Brrrrp.

The Gympy was firing. He quickly got his bearings, glad that at least some of his platoon was on the ball.

"Target!" he yelled across to the next trench.

Lance Corporal Jeffries, standing to his right, opened up with his SLR. "Enemy on foot, west of the 445 road, 300 metres, junction water feature."

Oliver quickly focussed in on the area, trying to make out the enemy through the spewing debris and soil as the last of the British artillery salvo fell on his adversary. He heard the Gympy gunner bellow at the top of his voice, making himself heard through his rubber mask: "Armour, BMP, 11 o'clock, 300 metres."

He switched his view, hoping to God a Milan post had survived somewhere and the crew were switched-on.

He saw the streak as the Milan missile sped towards the BMP-2, now weaving from side to side after it had crossed one of the TMM bridges. But it was to no avail as the high-explosive anti-tank (HEAT) round met the armoured vehicle head-on, lifting the turret from the body of the BMP, then toppling sideways as the vehicle careered to a halt. At least two Soviet soldiers made it out of the back, but they were soon gunned down as the rate of fire from the recovering British soldiers increased.

But it wasn't his Milan that fired.

Between the front line and the second line that were still recovering from the devastating chemical attack, the fifteen men of the mortar-section from the battalion's Fire-Support Company quickly got into action. One of three mortar sections from the mortar platoon, they went into their well-rehearsed steps, firing rounds directed by the forward observers and the Mortar Fire Controller. It wasn't much in the scheme of things, but it was their own organic artillery support over which the Battalion and, in this case, the Aviation Company had direct control. Bombs left the three tubes one every four seconds, members of the team acquiring more bombs from the 'Greenies', twin plastic containers holding additional rounds. After ten rounds, they switched targets and fired ten more, but then it was time to move. The Soviets also had mortar-locating radar and would soon home in on the small unit.

While they loaded the base plates, tubes and sights onto two Land Rovers and trailers enabling them to move and set up elsewhere on the battlefield, another section would take up the fight, providing a continuous, devastating bombardment on top of the enemy. The Company's own mortar section was also pounding the enemy in front of A-Company's lines with high-explosive bombs.

Lieutenant Thorpe checked in with his platoon by radio, ordering fire-missions as he thought fit and at times leaving the decision to his NCOs who were performing well. He scanned the area out to his front, the wide-open fields now being torn apart by mortar bombs. The Milan firing posts, along the entire Company front, were hitting the enemy armour as it attempted to cross the open ground. A killing ground. The water feature to their front, no more than 300 metres away, was a mere couple of metres across and was proving to be no obstacle to the enemy. He looked on, frightened as an ever bigger force made its way onto the other side of the water, and BMP-2 mechanised infantry combat vehicles, carrying Soviet infantry inside, got ever closer. A Milan missile destroyed another BMP, lifting it off the ground, immobilising it. The Milan team shifted position before the Soviet mortars could home in on them.

Oliver ducked his head down as his position was showered with debris, a salvo of 120mm mortar bombs fired by a Soviet Company's mortar platoon, straddled the line. Artillery was deadly but, unless there was a direct hit, well dug-in soldiers could survive. Mortar bombs, lobbed from the enemy side of the battlefield, could drop straight onto a position and could prove crippling for the defending troops even if they were dug in.

More BMPs headed towards Thorpe and his men. One was stopped in its tracks by one of the surviving L9 bar-mines, the two lines of anti-tank mines laid earlier, lethal for the enemy armour. A burning T-80, with a mine plough attachment, was testament to Soviets last failed attempt to breach the minefield. Although some of the mines had been detonated by a carpet of artillery rockets and shells targeting them, some had still survived.

But the Soviets were better prepared this time. Two UR-77s had been quickly brought to the eastern bank of the water feature, emitting clouds of white smoke as a rocket was blasted from each of the twin launch ramps. The two rockets rose at an angle into the air, a twin high-explosive hose trailing behind it before slowly descending, the rocket bouncing along the ground towards Lieutenant Thorpe's position before coming to a halt no more than 150 metres away. The second one landed off to the left. The hoses detonated, erupting along a ninety-metre length, a cloud of dust obscuring parts of the battlefield as it cleared a path six metres wide through the minefield. Another rocket was launched from each UR-77 and the process was repeated. The Soviet motor rifle regiment to their front now had four clear paths directly towards the defending British soldiers. They took advantage of it quickly before the British came to terms with it.

Colonel Yermakov was determined not to fail. Even if his divisional commander didn't take action as a consequence of further failure, he knew that bastard of a political officer would see him relieved of his command and shot for cowardice. His plan was simple: committing a fresh battalion, one motor rifle company would attack left and one would attack right. They still had nearly sixteen BMPs between them. The weaker company, with only six of their armoured vehicles left, was already pouring through the two central gaps created in the British minefield. They were the bait. They would draw the sting from the British Milan's while, behind them, two companies from his tank battalion, now down to fourteen T-80s, would plough straight through the British lines then head southwest. The chemical attack on the troops to the rear had used a 'persistent nerve agent', making the British left-flank next to the canal difficult to defend. Once south of Lauenhagen, Yermakov's tanks would turn west where, joined by the remaining tank company, they were ordered not to stop until they reached north of Stadthagen. His third tank company, the strongest with eight tanks, would, once past Stadthagen, head north and cut off any British troops late in pulling back. His second motor rifle battalion had already received its orders to form up and follow immediately behind the advance force. He was confident they would swamp the British defences. He gave the final order and the Air Assault Company was on its way.

Clouds of smoke billowed up along the front of the British positions, hiding the Soviet armour as it crossed through the minefields. The menacing shapes suddenly appeared through the swirling smoke, and two of the Company's Milan teams were quick to respond, hitting both of the lead BMPs, those following having to veer round their stricken comrades.

"Tanks, tanks, sir!" yelled Pritchard.

Coming out of the smoke, two T-80s followed the last of the BMP-2s. There were now two Soviet motor rifle companies flanking left and right and main battle tanks followed BMP-2s coming straight towards Oliver's position, less than 200 metres away.

They heard the helicopters to the north, but couldn't see them. Oliver was sure they didn't belong to the Army Air Corps.

"Alpha-One and Alpha-Three, this is Zero-Alpha. Pull back, pull back. All your call signs pull back. Out to you. Hello Alpha-Two. Over."

The tank was 100 metres from Oliver's position and panic was welling up inside. *What the hell are the Milan's doing?* He screamed inside. Out of the five Milan FPs left with the company, two had been destroyed, one had run out of ammunition, one was on the move, and the fifth one was facing two BMP-2s heading straight for it.

The T-80, less than fifty metres away and spraying the trench with machine-gun fire, suddenly erupted into an inferno as the TOW missile, fired by one of the four Lynx helicopters sent in to cover the withdrawal, slammed into it. Not even its ERA blocks could save it from total destruction. Its sister tank, twenty metres north, met with the same fate as two TOW missiles delivered their justice. The first one, deflected by an ERA block doing its job, only managed to damage some of the optics; the second TOW missile ploughed into the front right track, derailing it, forcing the tank to a halt.

"Hello, Alpha-Two. What is your status? Over."

"Alpha-Two. Under heavy attack. BMPs and tanks are on our line. Over."

"Understood. You have a heli-assault to your north. You must hold for five, Oliver. Over."

"I doubt I have ten men left, sir!"

"Alpha One and Three are pulling back behind you. Give them a chance to set up midway and you can pull back through them."

"Wilco. Alpha-Two out."

"Are we pulling back, sir?"

"Not yet, Corporal. Pritchard, I want an update from the sections and tell them to prepare to move in four."

"Our fallback positions will stop them, sir?"

"Let's hope so. Well?" He acknowledged his signaller who was trying to gain his attention.

"One-Section down to five, sir, and Three-Section is not responding."

Oliver turned to Lance Corporal Jeffries as another Soviet tank poked its nose close to their position, another two TOW missiles saving the day. However, this was at a price as a Soviet SA-13 surface-to-air missile blasted one of the Lynx helicopters out of the air as it was shifting position.

"Two minutes and you pull back."

Brrrrrp, brrrrp, brrrrp. The Gympy kept on firing as Soviet troops, leaving their damaged vehicles, attempted to get closer to the British lines.

"You know the route. Meet up with One-Section, and I'll bring Three-Section with me. Got it?"

"Yes, sir."

"Minute and a half. Partridge, Barnes, with me."

He clambered out of the partly filled trench, his rubber gloves making it difficult to grip onto anything. With his SLR gripped by the carrying handle, he sprinted into the trees, moved south and past a pile of rubble that had once been a house.

They came across the first firing position belonging to Three-Section. It couldn't really be classed as a firing position. It was more like a conglomeration of craters. Continuing south, twenty metres away, what was once the gun-group was now a churned up mess of body parts and bits of wood and metal from the soldiers' GPMG and personal weapons. They eventually found the remnants of the section behind the rubble of a house next door. Two soldiers, one of them the section commander, were firing in the direction of the enemy. A third soldier was patching up a badly wounded colleague, the man's uniform covered in dark patches where blood had run freely from multiple wounds.

"Corporal Fletcher, I've been trying to contact you."

"Radio's knackered, sir," came the muffled response.

Oliver checked his watch. "We're pulling out. You and I will cover. Higgs and Franklin can carry Cliff. Pritchard, Barnes, take point. Let's go."

They were finally abandoning the line. What was left of his platoon would have to move quickly on foot with whatever equipment they could carry to the second defensive line. As they moved off, the mortar units supporting the battalion launched their last salvo, mixing the bombs with smoke and high explosive. The three Lynx helicopters were hovering just above tree height, conscious that ZSU-23/4s would soon be brought forward to swat them out of the sky. To a man, the Lynx pilots and crew feared the Shilka the most.

Lieutenant Thorpe took his men southwest, following a farmer's track that led through the fields. They were moving at a slow run, the injured man sitting on an SLR held between two of his fellow soldiers while he draped his arms around their necks. Progress was slow. The lieutenant was going to lead them southwest, take them through Lauenhagen; then across the Hulse. Once across this water feature, the covering force would give them some breathing space, but first he wanted to find the rest of his men. He looked to his left as he saw a BMP-2 come flying through the trees, taken out instantly by one of the Lynx aircraft covering them. But ammunition and fuel wouldn't last forever; the helicopters would need to pull back soon. Not too soon, he hoped.

He looked over his shoulder as he heard the growl of engines approaching from behind them, and stopped, ordering the section to continue moving. Two Land Rovers, plus trailers, pulled up alongside. The cabs, back and trailers were packed with pieces of the 81mm mortars, along with their crews.

"We can take your wounded man, sir," suggested the sergeant in command. "Possibly a couple more."

"Corporal Jeffries," Thorpe shouted loudly. "Get Cliff onto the vehicle now."

"Sir."

"Thank you, Sergeant, the rest of us will stick together."

"As you wish, sir."

They hauled the wounded man up into the back of the lead Land Rover. Then the mortar section left, on their way to set up again somewhere behind Lauenhagen.

Thorpe rallied his men, and after 400 metres they arrived at the track that would take them to the village of Lauenhagen.

One and Three-Platoon were defending a short stretch of ground, and the OC was there to meet him.

"Thank God, Oliver, we thought we'd lost you."

"Where's the rest of my platoon, sir?"

"I've sent them on ahead. Take one of those Land Rovers. The driver is waiting. Send him back when you cross the Hulse."

"They're right behind us, sir."

"I know, Oliver. Now, get going. We'll hold for another five minutes then we'll join you. We have help on the way. Get your respirators back on, it's heavily contaminated back there."

The lieutenant looked about him as he pulled on his respirator, and could pick out at least two Milan FPs. At least they had something to hit back with.

"Get going, Oliver."

"Sir."

He called to his men and they ran for the waiting vehicle. The last thing he saw as they pulled away was the positions they had just left enveloped by a storm of destruction as two Harriers, flying north to south, dropped eight bombs between them, each bomb containing over 100 sub munitions. Oliver knew, from his time at the Royal Military Academy at Sandhurst, that a single cluster bomb would discharge more than 200,000 fragments. He and his men were leaving a cauldron behind them.

The driver took them beyond the Hulse, turning right to head north, then northeast along an avenue of trees where they would conduct the next phase of the battle. From here, they hoped to hit the enemy again. The OC had confirmed that their final defensive position would be behind the Holpe, another minor run of water that would act as a slight barrier to the enemy. He wouldn't be sorry to get there, allowing the helicopters of the 24th Airmobile Brigade to pick them up and transport them to the rear where they could rest, regroup and rearm. A Lynx Mk 7 from the Aviation Regiment flew east, no doubt to cover the rest of the Aviation Company. The Land Rover ground to a halt and deposited its passengers before the driver returned to pick up more of the soldiers who were fighting a rearguard action. Now the lieutenant could be reunited with the rest of his platoon, the half section he had sent to prepare their defences for the next line of defence.

A Captain from the Support-Company called him over. "Oliver, you look like shit."

His face stretched into a smile behind his respirator. "I feel like it, sir. Do you know where Two-Two-Alpha are?"

"I'm sorry, Oliver," the Captain said, clasping the young officer's arm. "They didn't make it. We've had a pretty heavy artillery bombardment and some missile strikes. The area is heavily contaminated. We're pulling out. A flight of helicopters will be here in the next ten minutes. Make sure you and your men are on it. The rest of your platoon is over there." He pointed to the open ground. "Waiting for a lift. And I'm sorry about your men."

The Captain left, leaving the young platoon commander with his thoughts. He would find out how many men he had left, soon. He doubted it was a number he would be comfortable with. He had just experienced his first blooding, and he was not sure he had learnt any lessons from it. He called his men over and they headed off to find the rest of the platoon.

Chapter 13

1500, 9 July 1984. 73rd Locating Battery, 94th Locating Regiment,
Royal Artillery. Area of Rinteln, West Germany.
The Blue Effect -2 days

A technician, a Lance Bombardier serving with 73rd Locating Battery, 94th Locating Regiment, Royal Artillery, part of the British Army of the Rhine's Artillery Division, checked the launch mechanism of the Midge-Drone mounted on the Bedford three-ton truck.

Bombardier Armstrong stood below at the side of the truck and looked across at the hydrogen generator where Met-Troop had just launched a meteorological balloon. "Are we done?"

"Just," responded the technician who then climbed down off the platform of the Bedford truck.

"About bloody time." The bombardier smiled.

They both headed over to where the troop commander was waiting in a trench close by.

"All set, Bombardier?"

"Yes, sir."

"Met-Troop have just confirmed no change, sir," added the troop sergeant. "Div have also been on."

"Chasing again?"

"Yes, sir. Seems this is a pretty important flight."

"Let's get on with it then."

Under the control of the Royal Artillery, the Midge-Drone was operated by a troop of the divisional locating battery. The drone carried a single camera, loaded with black and white film. Set on a pre-programmed flight, it would conduct aerial photographic reconnaissance of a particular area of interest to 1 British Corps. This troop had two launchers, along with the necessary facilities to process and analyse the imagery on the drone's return. The artillery intelligence cell at Divisional HQ of 1st Armoured Division had tasked the troop. The primary use of this asset was to confirm suspected enemy locations, particularly enemy artillery. On this occasion, they had been given a task of extreme importance. The final preparations were made, and the group of four pulled their ear defenders down just before the booster rocket launched the drone. The turbojet then took over, and the reconnaissance drone started on its mission. Its target: the ground amid the gap between the town of Buckeberg and the high ground to the southeast. The two and a half metre rocket flew its course, a difficult target for the Soviets to see. Flying high, at subsonic speed and following its pre-programmed course, the camera switched on as it passed overhead a tank battalion, a line of T-80s camouflaged against the edge of a wooded area. Elsewhere, tanks and BMP-2s were secreted inside barns or spread through the outskirts of villages. Before the tank crews and motor rifle infantrymen had noticed the sound of the passing object, it had already done its job, photographing the positions of the enemy. It banked right, flew for a further three kilometres, banked right again, then flew towards its landing point. On reaching the recovery area, the drone's engine cut out, the parachute was deployed, and it swung as it was gently lowered to the ground, large inflatable landing bags cushioning it from any impact. The crew, followed by a Land Rover, ran out to it to recover the camera. Once acquired, the vehicle would race with the film to the Photographic Interpretation tent where the film would be developed.

1555, 9 July 1984. Photographic Interpretation Section, 94th Locating Regiment, Royal Artillery. West of Rinteln, West Germany. The Blue Effect -2 days

The Intelligence Corps Sergeant switched the light table on while the Corporal placed the recently developed roll of film on the glass surface. The lights flickered on, and the sergeant unravelled the first section, comparing each of the first few frames with the map until he got his bearings, matching up the black and white negative he was looking at with a map of the target area. He pulled the film across, frame by frame, until he found a good starting point. Then the analysis began. Using a loupe, he zoomed in to particular areas of interest.

"Got it. Alan, take a look at this."

The corporal took the loupe out of the sergeant's hand and stooped over the light table, studying the area pointed out. "I can't see anything."

"Look at those farm buildings, by the barn doors."

"Tracks, tank tracks!"

"Now, look at the woods behind it."

"I can see tracks, but they could be anything. Ah, I can see where the ground has been churned up. The tanks have spun round and reversed into the treeline."

"Let's try looking at it in stereo. I think we've found what HQ have been griping about."

"The Soviet advance regiment?"

"Exactly."

Chapter 14

1900, 9 July 1984. HMS Turbulent, SSN Task Force. Barents Sea.
The Blue Effect −2 days

Commander Walcott shifted in his seat, casting his eye over the repeater for the sonar systems before glancing towards the plotting table. Behind him were the two periscopes and mast of the nuclear-powered submarine, a Trafalgar Class SSN. It moved quietly as they barely made way. The submarine was coaxed along the bottom that was barely ten metres beneath the hull. The captain of the British SSN, HMS Turbulent, a nuclear-attack submarine that cost the taxpayer a quarter of a billion pounds, would rather have had a minimum of twenty metres beneath his submarine but, with potentially a Soviet fleet overhead, and only seventy metres above the sail, it was critical that they got close to their target without discovery.

The SSN held its depth as it crept forward at five knots across the Stor Bank. The deeper point, an average two kilometres deep under the Norwegian Sea, had been left far behind them, the shelf shallowing as it got closer to the shelf edge of the Barents Sea. Once it had left the safety of the deep, the submarine had tracked the Barents Trough, covering 400 kilometres before moving north across Stor Bank. Their target, a Soviet fleet, had left the vicinity of Murmansk where it had formed up ready for what NATO expected would be an assault on northern Norway. Commander Walcott and his accompanying submarines, a second Trafalgar class, HMS Trafalgar, and two older SSNs from the Swiftsure class, HMS Spartan and HMS Sovereign, intended to ensure the Soviet fleet didn't make it.

It had taken the submarine pack over three days to transit to their current position. They had left the North Sea, passing through the Greenland-Iceland United Kingdom Gap, known as the GIUK Gap, and into the Norwegian Sea, keeping Bear Island to their north. Now, they were in the Barents Sea, Svalbard to their northwest and the eastern tip of Norway to the south. Murmansk was less than 1,000 kilometres south southeast. British or US submarines tended not to work in packs, generally working in isolation. But, with a major Soviet Fleet on the move to launch an attack somewhere along the Norwegian or Swedish coast, perhaps in support of a second assault against Northern Germany or Denmark, a larger force was needed. Five hundred kilometres south, a second US submarine pack was making its way stealthily towards the approaching Soviet fleet. Behind them, protecting the GIUK Gap, a US Carrier Group, supported by a British anti-submarine fleet consisting of destroyers and frigates, was already doing battle against the enemy. Soviet SSNs were hunting the hunters, and both sides had lost ships and submarines. Two major assaults by the Soviet air force had sunk two US destroyers and crippled the British Aircraft Carrier HMS Invincible. The second of the British Invincible-class light aircraft carriers in the fleet, HMS Ark Royal, had its final stage of fitting-out accelerated and was rushed into service when the war against the Warsaw Pact seemed inevitable. It had assumed responsibility as the flagship for the British flotilla. Their sister ship, HMS Invincible, was helping defend the resupply route between the British Isles and the European Continent.

The GIUK Gap force had four key missions: help protect the airfield on Iceland, interdict Soviet SSNs attempting to go south to threaten NATO reinforcement and supply routes, and act as a blocking force for any major Soviet surface incursion into the Norwegian Sea. The last mission, jus as important, was tracking down and destroying Soviet SSBN ballistic missile carriers. It was likely that many of their Deltas and Typhoons were already attempting to secure their positions in preparation for a nuclear launch, should it be required. US and British SSN nuclear hunter-killer submarines would be tailing those that they were able, ready to destroy this element of the Soviet strategic nuclear arm should the threat worsen.

The Soviet Northern Fleet, the Red Banner Fleet was effectively responsible for the defence of north-western Russia, and was based at Severomorsk and in Kola Bay. The fleet was significantly larger than the entire British Royal Navy, with over 200 submarines at its disposal. The range started from the coastal diesel-electric (SS) attack submarines to the more powerful nuclear-attack submarines (SSN), along with the deadly strategic ballistic-missile submarines (SSBN). The armada that had assembled north of Murmansk was extremely powerful and a major threat to NATO's northern flank. The aircraft-carrier/cruiser Kiev carried vertical take-off and landing fighters as well as helicopters, and sported a sizeable array of weapons. It was supported by the nuclear-powered missile-cruisers Kirov and Frunze. Two Slava class guided-missile cruisers, the Slava and Marshal Ustinov, along with at least four Kresta-II class cruisers, backed up this powerful core of the fleet. Of particular interest to the British SSNs was an Anti-Submarine Division, consisting of a mix of Udaloy I and II class destroyers, whose primary mission was to provide an anti-submarine barrier and picket patrol. An element of this Soviet flotilla that was of particular interest to NATO high command was the 175th Independent Naval Brigade. This large military force could be used to threaten a number of NATO locations anywhere from the northern part of Norway to Iceland. A diversion had already been initiated on Zealand in Denmark, but the Danish forces had repulsed the attempted airborne assault and the snap landing by another Soviet Brigade.

Commander Walcott sipped at his coffee; his hand holding the mug seemed to tremble slightly. He swapped hands, holding the drink in his left, and straightened his right hand, flexing his fingers then clenching them into a fist. The fingers relaxed as he opened his hand again, and on further examination he could see it was perfectly still. He looked up and saw his XO watching and nodded, returning his coffee to the appropriate hand and finished his drink. It wasn't nerves or fear, he knew that. Just tiredness, bordering on fatigue. Operating in these conditions for an extended period of time would put a strain on the strongest man. His 130 crewmen had been in 'silent mode' for the last twenty-four hours. The standing order: if you don't have to move, don't. He would need to keep a close eye on his crew, perhaps a word with his XO later, although they appeared to be holding up well.

He slipped off his seat and went to check the plotter. The sub was on target. It wasn't the first time he, his crew and HMS Turbulent had entered these waters. During operations to acquire 'The Take', intelligence gathering that would enhance their knowledge of Soviet naval operations, he and his men had slipped past Soviet ships to spy on their exercises, fleet manoeuvres, being conducted by the perceived enemy. Now, though, they were a true enemy. But they must be close to the fringes of the enemy fleet by now. The outer anti-submarine defences would be the first of the barriers they needed to cross. Although, initially, they were part of a submarine pack, they would in fact operate independently as each submarine now had no idea where the other SSNs were since separating on leaving the Norwegian Sea. They would be aware of their respective allocated sectors of operation but beyond that, nothing.

"Sonar, contact bearing 124."

Walcott moved across the control room and into the sonar space where the operator was bent over his sonar stack, the first stack green, the bottom two white. The operator put his hand to the white cloth-covered headphones, a tattoo showing on his bicep under the rolle-up sleeve of his blue uniform shirt.

"What have you got, Roberts?"

"Still increasing in intensity, sir. Bearing now 125."

The chess game has started, thought Walcott.

"Any thoughts?"

"Small, sir, but I can't be certain."

"Distance?"

The sonar operator checked his stack. "Eleven thousand yards, sir."

The XO joined him.

"Udaloy?"

"Possibly."

"Ten thousand yards, bearing 125."

Walcott turned to the XO. "We'll maintain course, keep him to our starboard."

"New contact, bearing 086, 16,000 yards...a destroyer, I think, sir."

"Well done, Roberts. Keep on them."

"Their outer screen. What do you plan then, sir?"

The captain picked up the handset. "Left rudder, ten degrees."

"Ten degrees, left rudder, aye, sir," came the response from the helm.

"Need more of the picture, XO."

They both moved across to the board. Two pieces of the jigsaw were in place, but not enough to provide the bigger picture.

"We need to get a picture of his battle space, and two destroyers won't give us that," the captain continued.

What Commander Walcott needed to know was the formation of the Soviet fleet that was slowly heading in his direction.

"Well, at least we've spotted two of their pickets."

"Yes, and they are true submarine hunters. Those SS-N-14s have a range of up to fifty kilometres."

"So long as they have helicopters in the air to guide them."

"Oh, they will, XO. They'll be out there looking for us now. And, if they do find us, those destroyers can push up to thirty-five knots."

"Get past those, and we can get to grips with the high value targets."

"Sonar, Contact-One, identified Udaloy-1 destroyer, bearing 126, 9,000 yards."

"Contact-Two, Roberts?"

"Bearing 086, range 15,000 yards."

"Identification?"

"Nothing definite yet, sir, but I reckon it's a second Udaloy."

"Thank you."

"Helm, ahead ten knots."

"Ahead, ten knots, aye."

"We've got two of the pickets, XO, but what about the rest?"

"We must be on their starboard quarter. If we maintain this bearing, we'll pick them up, but we'll be right under the Udaloy that's coming straight at us."

"That's why we're going around them. Helm. Ten degrees port."

"Ten degrees port. Aye."

"Bill."

"Sir." Lieutenant Commander Bill Legge, weapons engineering officer, known as WEPs, made his way over.

"We're going to come in behind the Soviet fleet, Bill, so I want another check of weapons. If we can get amongst them, I want to hit them hard and then run. So make sure your team are on the ball."

"They won't let you down, sir."

"Good."

WEPs went to do another check on his team, those that would be responsible for loading and firing the submarine's torpedoes. The first contact had eventually moved behind them, and the second contact was now directly opposite their position but, as they were moving away on a ten-degree bearing, a gap of 11,000 yards had developed between them.

A Leading Hand brought a tray of sandwiches from the galley, and the captain, sitting on his green-backed seat, called him over. He and the XO grabbed some badly needed food. They both needed sleep as well. The six hours on duty, six hours off routine had fallen by the wayside as they were now so close to the enemy that an incident or attack could occur at any moment. Both had managed two hours sleep each in the last twelve, but it might be some time before they had that luxury again.

"Sonar. Contact. No, two...three contacts. Contact-Three bearing 155, 9,000 yards. Possible cruiser. Contact-Four, bearing 128, 10,000 yards. Contact-Five, bearing 127, 12,000 yards. It's big, sir, bloody big. It has to be her."

The XO picked up the handset and chastised the operator. "Get a grip, Roberts."

"Sorry, sir. Contact-Three and Four are likely cruisers, but Contact-Five is big."

The XO, standing next to the captain in the narrow corridor of 'track alley', spoke first. "The big one has to be either the Kirov or even the Kiev."

"A guided-missile cruiser. Now, taking that out would be a good start, eh XO? Helm, dead ahead."

"Dead ahead. Aye."

To the right of the captain's chair, the helm went through their manoeuvres to bring the eighty-four-metre boat back on course.

Commander Walcott reached across and grabbed the handset for the internal communications. "This is the Captain. We are currently tracking a Soviet fleet off to our starboard, but shortly we will be attempting to get right amongst them. Once we can track the elements making up the fleet and isolate the key targets, we will destroy as many of them as we can; then run and hide. I know you're all feeling a bit ragged, a bit tired, but stay focussed. All our lives depend on it. When we can get to a port or sea of safety, we can all catch up on lost sleep. This is the Captain. That is all."

He looked left towards 'fire-control alley' where the repeater station for the sonar systems sat along with the fire control technicians. He envisaged they would be busy very soon.

"Ten degrees starboard. Make for fifteen knots."

"Ten degrees starboard. Fifteen knots. Aye."

"This is it then, sir," said the XO.

The captain looked at his watch. "Fifteen minutes, then I want to go up and take a look."

"Is that wise, sir? There are bound to be submarines with the fleet. They'll have a good chance of hearing us."

"Unlikely, XO. They would have been at the head of the fleet, the fleet's first picket line, and they appear to have missed us. I want to make sure we haven't missed any contacts."

"Unless they're tracking us."

"This is not peacetime. We'd have been blown out of the water by now if a Soviet SSN had been following us."

After fifteen minutes, a period that seemed like a lifetime, the captain made his decision and picked up the comms handset. "Sonar. Update on contacts."

"Contact-Eight. Udaloy-1, bearing 268, 7,000 yards. No other contacts."

"Thank you. No sign of the big boys?"

"Negative, sir," responded the sonar officer, Lieutenant Powers.

"Periscope depth."

"Periscope depth, aye."

The captain bent down and placed his eyes against the search periscope as it slowly rose. He completed a quick 360-degree turn, but could pick out nothing, apart from a quick glimpse of a helicopter, probably on an anti-submarine mission. He zoomed in towards the direction of the fleet and could see dark shapes in the distance. Although it was unlikely that the search periscope would be spotted, as the water was choppy, he had it lowered before the feather from the periscope could be seen by an observant watch keeper; then he ordered the boat to dive.

"No transports yet, sir."

"No. Probably further behind, protected by a smaller force. Hard to starboard, steer 270, depth eighty metres."

"This is it, sir."

"That it is, XO."

The submarine sprinted at twenty-plus knots for ten minutes; then drifted while the sonar technicians reacquainted themselves with any contacts. They eventually caught up with the Udaloy-1, the picket ship at the rear of the fleet. The captain took the submarine down to a depth where he could take advantage of the thermocline, maintaining a speed of eighteen knots, closing in on the Soviet destroyer, eventually passing it using the ship's propellers to hide his boat. The fleet appeared to be in no hurry, maintaining a steady fourteen knots, so Commander Walcott was able to slowly gain on the bulk of the fleet. Once past the destroyer, they heard the propellers from a cruiser, a Sverdlov, an older class cruiser. On their port side was another Udaloy. They recognised this one. They had picked up the particular signature of this destroyer, Vice-Admiral Kulakov, on one of their 'Take' operations. It was one of the Soviet's latest anti-submarine warships. Commissioned only two years ago, with SS-N-14 anti-submarine missiles and two RBU-6000 anti-submarine rocket launchers capable of firing salvos of up to twelve rounds, then automatically reloading. If Turbulent came up against this ship in battle, being bombarded with 19.5kg shaped-charge warheads, to a depth of 1,000 metres, and actively being guided in the water...Walcott shuddered to think of the consequences.

They left the Sverdlov and Kulakov behind as they steadily crept deeper and deeper into the centre of the Soviet fleet.

"Sonar, contact. Contact-Nine, 6,000 yards bearing 267."

"The Kiev?" Uttered the XO, almost in a whisper. "God, if we could sink her..."

"Keep talking to me, Roberts."

"Sir. Contact-Nine, still on 267, 5,000 yards."

"What else?"

"Contact-Ten, bearing 186, 7,000 yards. Contact-Nine, 4,000 yards."

"Speed?"

"Contact-Nine, travelling at fourteen knots, sir."

"Maintain fifteen knots."

"Fifteen knots. Aye, sir." Responded the Helm.

'Contact-Nine, 3,000 yards. Can hear the screws loud and clear, sir."

"What have we above us?" asked the captain.

"Thirty metres, sir," responded the Coxswain.

"Take her up to twenty metres, XO."

"But we're getting close to the Kiev, sir. There won't be much clearance."

"There'll be enough, and the noise they're making will mask any sound we make."

"Take her up to twenty metres."

"Slowly."

"Slowly. Aye, sir."

The Turbulent moved up slowly, barely twenty metres between its fin and where the Kiev cut through the water.

"Contact-Nine, 2,000 yards."

It was good to maintain the reporting, but the captain knew how close they were. The throbbing of the Kiev's four propellers, less than 2,000 yards from his command, could be felt, let alone be heard throughout the boat.

"Contact-Nine, 1,000 yards, sir. But sensors overloaded. I can't pick up any other contacts or accurately identify Contact-Nine's location."

Walcott looked through the periscope, and could pick out the wash from the propellers. His concentration was total as Turbulent slowly slid in underneath. From top of the periscope, and the clean lines of the aircraft carrier, there would be little more than 3-4 metres. Walcott picked up the handset. "Just get what you can. Let me know when there's a change. I want any information we can get from the Kiev recorded, XO."

"I'll see to it, sir."

"Helm, fourteen knots. Watch your helm, we're right under her now." The captain looked up. There was 41,000 tons of ship above HMS Turbulent, eight times the displacement of his vessel. A steady throbbing indicated that the Soviet aircraft carrier's propellers were now over the stern of Turbulent. The main body of the 270-metre ship was directly above.

The XO looked at his captain in awe, as did the crew close by. Walcott had just taken a nuclear SSN submarine, their submarine, right into the centre of the core of the Soviet Red Banner Fleet, and was sitting directly beneath the country's capital ship. The thrashing of the four blades could be heard above, thrumming through the walls of the submarine. The captain looked at the two sailors at the helm. Sweat was pouring down their temples such was the level of concentration as they controlled the ship's depth and heading to match the behemoth overhead. The Planesman, in particular, had a tough task: over compensate and they would go too deep or, worse, lose depth and collide with the ship. He was their best, judging when the planes bit into the water after he had adjusted their angle. The Coxswain, sat behind the two helmsmen, caught the captain's eye as if to say: *We're pushing it, sir.*

The captain turned to his XO and weapons officer. "It's time."

They both nodded. "Standby for action. Down ten-metres. Make it thirteen knots."

"Down ten, thirteen knots, aye, sir."

"All tubes loaded with Tigerfish?"

"Yes, sir," responded WEPs.

"Start sonar contact reports."

"Aye, sir."

They heard and felt the noise and throb of Kiev's propellers pounding the water above them as they slowly lost ground, slipping behind the huge aircraft carrier. They must take out this ship first. Walcott wasn't worried about the twelve Yak fighter aircraft on board, but the twenty, Ka-25 anti-submarine helicopters would be deadly and would quickly hunt them down if discovered.

"Contact-Nine, dead ahead, 1,000 yards. Contact-Ten, 6,000 yards. There are contacts all around, sir."

Walcott picked up the handset. "Steady, lad, steady. Just monitor the others, and let me know if they get within 4,000 yards, but report on the carrier."

"Aye, sir. Contact-Nine, dead ahead, 2,000 yards."

"Helm. Turn slowly to port, ten degrees. Heading 190."

"Ten degree rudder, course 190. Aye, sir."

"From the side, sir?"

"Yes XO. But I also want give us some room so we can track the other ships. WEPs, standby for four solutions."

"We going for the nearest three, sir?"

"We are that. Depth fifty."

"Depth fifty, aye."

"They'll pick us up soon, sir."

"Once we fire, the entire fleet will know where we are."

The tension rose in the control room as the submarine settled at a depth of fifty metres.

"Sonar, where is Contact-Nine now?"

"Bearing 175, range 5,000 yards, speed fourteen knots. New contact..."

The captain and XO moved aft along track-alley to the plotting tables, the SNAPS tables.

"Christ, sir, we're in the middle of Hades."

They were practically in the centre of the Soviet fleet. Now Turbulent had settled on a steady, level course and was away from the thrashing blades of the Kiev's propellers, the passive, towed array sonar could do its job of picking up the movement and location of the Soviet fleet. The high value ships, the Kirov, a nuclear-powered missile cruiser, and the Kiev aircraft carrier were at the centre, and in the inner circle were three Kresta-I and one Kresta-II cruiser, and a Slava-class guided missile cruiser. For the pickets, on the outer-circle, they believed there be at least five Udaloy destroyers, at least one, the Kulakov. On top of that, there would be constant patrols by anti-submarine helicopters.

What the captain didn't know was how many Soviet SSNs, hunter-killer nuclear subs like his own, there were and, more importantly, their location. They would have a role on the picket line, far ahead of the fleet, sniffing out the enemy navy or any threats from SSNs. So far, they had failed. But Walcott's biggest fear was of a submarine closer to the centre of the fleet, looking for an enemy submarine doing exactly what he was up to.

It was time. The Captain and XO returned to the centre of the control room, the captain back on his chair.

"Are all targets designated, WEPs?"

"Yes, sir."

Further forward, down in the bomb shop, as the crew referred to the torpedo room on the third level, the men got ready to fire the four Tigerfish torpedoes. One torpedo would be fired at an individual target, but two for the big one. The captain's choice would have been two per target, the Tigerfish warhead was not the most powerful of weapons, but he had to settle for just two for the Kiev.

"Standby for engagement."

The fire control technicians stared at the red and amber plasma displays, concentration etched on their faces.

"Fire One."

"Fire One," mimicked the WEPs technician.

Very quickly, three more were fired and four torpedoes were away, the crew frantically reloading the next four.

The torpedoes were tracked and, at a speed of thirty-five knots, the first two fired would close on their target, the Kiev, in less than three minutes. For the Kirov and Sverdolov, the second two ships, it would take slightly longer.

"Talk to me."

"All four tracked, all four on target."

"The Soviet fleet?"

"No change, sir. Two minutes to impact."

"Let me know the minute they show any sign of alarm."

"One minute."

The captain and XO glanced at each other. Both were thinking: *This is going too well.*

"Kiev has powered up, sir! Course change, 080."

"Time to impact?"

"Fifteen seconds, sir."

"Speed?"

"She's up to twenty knots, sir. Ten seconds. Torpedoes gone active."

"Kirov?"

"Kirov picking up speed too, sir. Course now 115."

"Damn, XO."

"Five seconds."

They both heard and felt the explosions as the two Tigerfish exploded beneath the Soviet carrier.

"It's a hit, it's a hit," called out Roberts. The rest of the crew quickly picked up the excitement, fists thumped the air and grins spread across their faces.

"Silence!" Snapped the XO.

"Kirov?" asked the captain.

"Speed twenty-five knots, bearing 120. Time to target one minute."

"We're not going to get it, XO."

"Contact. Bearing 085, Udaloy, thirty knots."

"It's that destroyer we passed earlier, sir," suggested the XO.

"Damn. Time to dive and get out of here."

"Sir, sir. Explosions in the water. It's the Udaloy. It's been hit."

"It must be one of the others."

"Well then, XO, time to get out of here. Standby to dive the submarine. XO, take us down. One hundred metres."

"Sir.'

"We've got the Kiev. Let's go and hunt the Kirov."

Chapter 15

Wilf stirred the three sleeping soldiers and suggested they get some food down them, as they would be moving out in twenty minutes. While they were eating, Wilf did a quick scout of the area, circling their position out to fifty-metres, making sure there was nothing that would impact on their patrol once they left the hide. He sniffed the air which seemed quite fresh; just the occasional whiff of smoke coming from the many still burning hulks and buildings scattered around the countryside. He stopped for a moment, crouched down and listened. He could hear a steady drone of traffic moving along Route 3, a major road running south from Pattensen: reinforcements and supplies travelling south, with casualties and crippled vehicles heading in the opposite direction. Although, back in the UK the four men, as part of their remit, had studied the likely flow of Soviet logistical traffic and expected it to be heavy, even they had been astounded by the sheer volume. Apart from that, he could see or hear little else. He rose up from the ground, his thighs aching slightly, and continued his circuit. The previous day and night had been a heavy tab. After crossing the River Leine, Wilf's CPU had been tasked with moving at all speed west, with a specific target in mind. The speed of the advancing Soviet forces had outpaced the movement of the stay-behind forces. One of their patrols, allocated the area south of Hanover, had been diverted from the task Wilf and his team would now pick up. NATO electronic warfare units had picked up what could only have been a Soviet Army Headquarters, and their sister CPU had been re-tasked and given the HQ as their target. Wilf and his team would now have to replace that unit and carry out the task they had initially been ordered to complete. Wilf and his team had travelled at speed throughout the previous night, including early evening and late into the morning of the second day, until they had eventually crossed the river south of Hanover and made their way to a forest south of Hupede where they were now laid up. Going to ground in the trees at the most northern tip, the four men had eaten some of their rations, cold, then grabbed at least eight hours of sleep, taking it in turns to go on stag and watch the backs of their sleeping comrades. Wilf had taken the last watch, needing to think through the final plans for tonight. Soviet troops were everywhere and, on more than one occasion, the patrol had had to detour round them. Once, they were nearly hit by friendly aircraft fire as low-flying bombers came out of nowhere and strafed a Soviet column. Whenever they were able, reports of troop movements were radioed back to 1 BR Corps headquarters, their primary role still being that of reconnaissance. Now, however, they had been given two additional tasks: locate and report back the centre of mass of a missile regiment, probably belonging to either 3rd Shock Army or 20 Guards Army, and, once done, sabotage it to the best of their ability.

Wilf smiled as he remembered Badger's response to their orders. *"Yeah, let's take on half the Soviet army, why don't we?"*

Hacker and Tag had taken the mickey out of him for the rest of the day. But Badger would fight when called upon and not let any of them down, they knew that. And it could well become a major fight. They were glad they had all agreed to sacrifice some of their supplies so they could carry additional ammunition. Wilf completed his circuit and rejoined his team who were now ready. They knew the importance of speed, they still had a precarious route to travel, and they were in no doubt they were heading into a hornet's nest. They completed one last check of their kit then moved off. Tag took point, followed by Wilf, Badger and Hacker as tail-end Charlie. They headed southwest first, through the wood, avoiding a small engineer unit encamped amongst the trees to their south, not more than 600 metres away. The men then turned west again and patrolled until they came to the edge of the wood. There was a gap of about 300 metres they would need to cross before they could enter the much larger forest opposite. Tag and Hacker crossed first while Wilf and Badger covered them. Once safely across, and with no sounds indicating the two men had been compromised, Wilf and Badger joined them. They moved southwest, deeper into the forest, slowly climbing a hillock about 200 metres in height, weaving through the trees before turning south. Wilf wanted to intersect with a track. He could then get his bearings then head west along it until they reached the western edge of the forest. Finally they would be in the area where the Soviet unit, as a consequence of its poor communications security, had been located by an EW unit. It was not their first choice to use such obvious routes, likely points for a potential ambush, but speed was important. Time was running out for NATO, and, apart from providing good intelligence, the team were impatient to hit back at the enemy themselves. Hacker, who was now the lead, signalled that they were approaching the track. A steep bank dropped down towards the hard-packed route that would lead them to the edge of the forest. Hacker caught a flicker of white light below him. He turned to warn his colleagues when the mildew-covered soil gave way beneath his boot, his leg flying upwards, the second one following close behind as he crashed to the ground, his large heavyweight pack thumping him in the back as he plummeted down the slope, steadily gathering speed as he frantically attempted to dig his boots into the earth in order to slow his progress down the slope. He couldn't use his hands to try and get some purchase as they were gripping his weapon tightly, not wanting it lost or damaged. Wilf cottoned on to what had happened within a matter of seconds and pounded down the slope, bumping into trees to control his forward movement as he chased after Hacker. Hacker came to an abrupt halt at the bottom as his boots crashed into a Ural motorcycle, a dispatch rider's motorbike, toppling it off its stand, the weighty vehicle crashing down, clipping his shoulder as he slid past it and ground to a halt.

The startled dispatch rider, who earlier had been shining a small torch over his map in the vain hope he could get his bearings, all the while cursing in Russian, scrambled to get his AK-74 that had been resting on the fuel tank. His first thoughts were of an animal, but he caught sight of a moving body that looked more human than animal just in front of his bike. Before the Soviet bike rider's thoughts coalesced, Wilf shoulder-charged the man, knocking him sideways, but at the same time causing himself to lose balance, ending up sprawled on the floor. As the Soviet soldier pulled himself up onto one knee, then staggered to a half crouch, the butt of Badger's C-7 carbine collided with the side of the unfortunate soldier's head, a wet thud indicating a strike to the temple rather than the skull. The man dropped to his knees, poleaxed, as Badger struck him again in the same spot, knocking him to the ground. Tag, who had also arrived panting from his forced sprint down the slope, slipped the blade of his killing knife into the soft muscle of the dispatch rider's neck, in between the head and shoulder. Gripping the man's helmet, pulling it back hard so the strap, tight beneath his chin, forced the throat to arch, he cut deep into the oesophagus, sawing through the gristle before lowering the man to the ground.

The four men moved quickly, forming a circle around the motorcycle and body, each covering a compass point, steadying their breathing, listening, watching. Wilf slowly raised his body until on one knee, getting the image intensifier from its sack. The green glow lit up his eyes as he completed a full 360-degree sweep of the area. Nothing.

After a further ten minutes, they relaxed, or as much as was sensible. Wilf tapped Badger and Tag on the shoulder. They knew what had to be done: the soldier needed to disappear. While they carried the body away, Wilf and Hacker pushed the heavy dispatch bike into a dip about fifty metres off the track and, lying it on its side, pulled what dead branches they could find, supplemented by mulch, and covered it as best they could.

Regrouping, they moved off. Time was moving on. It was now 2036. They needed to be in position by at least 0200 the next morning so they could conduct their recce between then and 0330 when sleep would be dragging at the eyes of the sentries on duty, and any other soldier in their right mind would be getting as much sleep as possible. Another hour found them at the western boundary of the forest. Opposite them was the L422, running southwest towards the large village of Gestorf about a kilometre away. They would have to be quick and careful. They knew instinctively there were Soviet troops in the area. Just before the last battery of the image intensifier died, Wilf had spotted a vehicle a few hundred metres to their west, along with a small contingent of *Komendantskaya*, Soviet traffic controllers. They were camped on the opposite side of the L422, in a clump of trees a kilometre north of Gestorf. There was a steady stream of traffic moving along the road. Convoys travelling at about twenty kilometres per hour moved in both directions. Wilf led his men north, keeping just inside the treeline, out of sight of any prying eyes and of the Soviet traffic police. After 500 metres, the treeline veered sharply right and, after a few minutes observation, using binoculars and comparing what they could see with what was on the map, they concluded that they were at the western edge of a U-shaped opening in the centre of the forest. The U-shaped clearing was scattered with clumps of trees throughout. The U-shape was about 600 metres deep by 200 metres wide, completely open at the western edge. They were at the lower branch of the U-shape. Two dark shapes that could be seen off centre warranted further investigation. *Maybe we've found what we've been seeking*, thought Wilf, the purpose of the Soviet traffic police close by now evident.

"We need to get closer," hissed Wilf. "I want to recce across the other side of the road. The map shows a copse about 250 metres from the road. If this is what I think it is, there will be missile TELs scattered all around this area. I'll take Badger and we'll go east and do a full circuit of the open ground."

"Me and Hacker cross the road?"

"That's right, Tag. I thought you would appreciate the exercise."

"You mean Badger's too knackered," Tag responded with a smile.

"Fuck off, you two," grunted Badger. "Outrun you wankers any day."

"Yeah, being chased by a young girl's irate father."

"Stow it," snapped Wilf. He didn't mind the humour and knew it was just friendly banter but he needed to think, get his head around their mission. If these were what he thought they were, and headquarters for a change were correct, this was a high value target that needed taking out.

"Sorry, Wilfy," they chimed in unison.

"We meet on the corner there," he said, pointing to the northern branch of the U-shaped opening opposite.

"How long?" Asked Tag.

"How long do you need?" Responded Wilf.

Tag thought for a moment, calculating distances and timings. "The ground is wide open between here and the road. The soil of the field opposite the opening is too light. We'll go south for 100 metres then cross next to the field with cabbages, or whatever they are."

"Won't that bring you out close to the Soviet police?"

"Yeah. I'd prefer to go round the back of this lot and come at it from the north, but we ain't got the time."

Wilf nodded, knowing he was right. "How long?"

"We'll go for two hours."

"OK, shoot."

Tag and Hacker moved off south, and Wilf led Badger to the east. It took them eighty minutes to do a complete circuit, ending up at the rendezvous point. They had seen two TELs so suspected that Tag would find the other two across the road. After a twenty-minute wait, the pair were re-joined by Tag and Hacker.

"We found two," informed Hacker. "SS-23s would be my guess."

"Army?" suggested Tag.

"Yes but, according to HQ, these could be part of a GSFG SSM Brigade."

"Shit, that means there must be eighteen of the buggers around here."

"Wow, Badger, you listened to the briefings after all."

Badger humphed, not responding to Hacker's gibe.

"They have two brigades," Wilf reminded them. "We have two TELs as well. Badger and I will see to these two. I'm afraid it's back across the road for you, Tag. Did you see any movement?"

"Not a sausage apart from a couple of cops sat in canvas chairs on the roadside watching the traffic pass them by."

"Right, let's do it then. Tag and Hacker, take out the two across the road; me and Badger have these two. If you come across any resupply, sort them as well. RV here. The emergency RV is the southeast point of the Deister. We need to start moving west. OK...well, you know what to do. If you see any sentries, try and avoid them and target the vehicles. TELs first." He patted each one on the shoulder then patted Badger's arm twice. They would be working together. "Let's go."

Wilf and Badger moved off right while Tag and Hacker went left. They came across the first TEL, the NATO codename Spider, 200 metres from the base of the 'U' and settled down to watch.

"Great, there's no bloody guards," added Badger.

"They'll have some somewhere," whispered Wilf in response.

"Let's get on with it then, Wilfy," hissed Badger. "If they suddenly get a call to prep, we'll be stuffed."

The two TELs they were going for were spaced about 150 metres apart. Wilf peered into the darkness: only enough moonlight to pick out the lofty shapes of the bulky missile carriers. The nearest one, now within fifty-metres of their position, was heavily tarped, and camouflage netting had been stretched across it and tied to two trees on the one side making a canopy. The missile unit had chosen an area that was surrounded by trees, but the centre was open enough for the vehicles to move around freely and fire their rockets when required. This enabled the crews to hide their vehicles, but they had the ability to quickly prepare for a launch if called upon.

Wilf scanned the area with his binoculars, the batteries for the image intensifier having well and truly died. Handing them to Badger, he pointed to the bundles that lay beneath the man-made canopy, next to the nearest TEL. Badger handed the binoculars back and Wilf secreted them in his small pack, the larger pack hidden next to a tree trunk to be collected when they had completed their mission. If they were unable to pick it up as a consequence of being discovered, their supplies of food, water and ammunition would be severely limited.

Wilf indicated they move, and the two men, like ghosts, flitted from tree to tree, constantly on the lookout for a sentry on guard duty. As they found themselves in the vicinity of the tail end of the TEL, Badger grabbed Wilf's arm and pointed towards the boat-shaped front end of the amphibious Transporter Erector Launcher. Wilf stared but saw nothing. He was about to shrug his shoulders and ask Badger what he was on about when he saw the windows of the missile carrier's cab light up. Ten seconds later, it occurred again.

"Got him," Wilf whispered in Badger's ear.

They moved off again until they were directly opposite the tail end of the vehicle and then made a beeline for the TEL, stopping as they came up against the back end. Although similar in some respects to the SCUD-B, this was a very much later model. It still had four pairs of wheels, two at each end, but the missile was hidden inside the TEL; not exposed like that of the Scud-B.

Badger peered around the one side, checking on the sleeping bundles next to the centre of the TEL, while Wilf looked along the opposite side, which also looked clear. They immediately got to work. Badger prepared some Plastic Explosive to attach close to the launching mechanism of the TEL while Wilf walked at a crouch beneath the much lower canopy of netting, stretched out from the vehicle and pinned to the ground. He arrived at the point where he was close to the cab, the three side windows just above him. He needed to place the PE as close to the warhead as possible, which would be difficult as the missile was shielded. A sudden glow indicated that the occupant, probably the sentry, was still partaking in a smoke. At any moment, the guard could exit the cab and discover the intruders, so Wilf got on with his mission. His task was to place a charge that would destroy the warhead, making it and the rocket section unusable. Once he crimped the detonator, they would have three hours to get out of the area. It wasn't just the likelihood of discovery, or even the potential explosion if the missile was ignited along with the fuel, that worried him. He, along with the rest of his team, suspected that these could be tactical nuclear warheads, probably 100 kiloton in size. Although the explosion of the PE would not cause a nuclear detonation, it could certainly create a 'dirty bomb'. To a man, they feared the effects of nuclear radiation.

His dilemma was how to get up there. The top of the vehicle was three metres high. He couldn't use the step next to the cab for fear of alerting the occupant. He placed his boot carefully and quietly on the wheel nuts and levered himself up so he was able to stand on the metre-tall tyre. He moulded the PE onto the missile cover, crimped the detonator, and lowered himself down. Wilf headed back to Badger who was peering at him around the corner. They conferred and then moved further into the centre of the 'U' shaped clearing to where they found a second TEL. Two more PE packages were deposited.

Wilf checked his watch and whispered to Badger, "We'll have time to do the resupply vehicles."

Badger agreed, and they crept back into the forest and transited across the base of the 'U' where they had spotted two resupply vehicles, each one carrying a reload for the SS-23s. Next to them was a transporter loader, also carrying a spare missile. They had to be quick. Time was running out.

As they drifted back into the trees, crossing a track that ran along the edge of the treeline, the silence was shattered by the sound of a vehicle engine tearing along the track. They saw a flicker of lights to the east and threw themselves to the ground, closing their eyes to protect their night vision as it raced past. It didn't stop, and once they were sure it was long gone, they moved to the RV with fifty minutes to spare. Tag and Hacker were already there, having only had two TELS to target.

"We need to split, Wilfy. We have about fifty minutes."

"Agreed. Soon as we can, I need to radio in and confirm this location. HQ will want to organise a much heavier strike from the air. Hacker, you lead, Tag you're the last man."

They recovered their Bergen's and moved northwest, sticking with the treeline until they reached the point where the forest butted up against the road. A steady stream of logistics vehicles, with only convoy lights showing, drove past in both directions.

Thirty minutes.

As soon as there was a break in the traffic, the four men scooted across, and Hacker led them at an angle, across an open field for about 300 metres until they were safe amongst the trees again.

Twenty minutes.

The troopers crossed open ground to a smaller copse; then headed west to a minor road, crossing the Roter Bach, an irrigation ditch, turning north using the trees next to the road that ran alongside for cover.

Fifteen minutes.

A fast march had turned into a double march, as they were desperate to get away from the exposed road. The CPU came across a small copse with a pool of water at its centre. Wilf knew where he wanted to get to and urged his men on.

Ten minutes.

The patrol crossed a further road, which ran west from Hupede, until they approached the ditch on the opposite side, the place Wilf had been heading for. Two hundred metres to their right was the L422, traffic still moving along it and, just under a kilometre to their north, the L402 where they could also hear the steady drone of traffic, that likewise ran west from the village. The Soviet's logistic force was ever on the move, feeding and resupplying their front line troops.

Five minutes.

They tabbed along the edge of the ditch, often slipping into its cold waters, trees and foliage lining each side giving them some cover. They moved quickly, much faster than they would have wished, but they knew that, once the explosives were detonated, the Soviets would be out for revenge. There was also an element of mild panic. Yes, they were Special Forces, trained for this type of operation. But, up until now, none of them had done it for real.

Thump...thump...thump.

They threw themselves to the bank, seeing white flashes lighting up the dark skies.

Thump...thump. The explosive charges ripped into the SS-23s, wrenching apart the launch mechanisms of the TELs and destroying the missiles. Neither the TELs nor the missiles, or even the resupply and loading vehicles, would be used in anger in this war. Two more explosions shattered the silence of the night as more TELs or resupply vehicles were destroyed.

Whoompf...whoompf. The fuel from the TELs and possibly the rocket propellant was adding to the destruction. Many of the Soviet rocket troops would be killed, and Wilf and his team knew that the Soviets would be baying for blood.

Thump...thump.

Fourteen major explosions were counted, plus numerous secondary explosions, meaning that every PE package that had been placed had done its job. The four men took a few minutes to congratulate each other before Wilf quickly drove them on, and they continued slopping along the edge of the ditch, Wilf wanting to get them to the Deister, the forested high ground, where they could rest up and hide. If they could make it that far without getting caught, they had a chance of survival. He also knew that it was a hollow victory. If it were indeed one of the two missile brigades of GSFG, there would still be over thirty of these tactical ballistic missiles left to rain nuclear warheads down on NATO troops. He picked up speed, urging his men to do likewise. Time was against them. They needed to skirt the village of Bennigsen to the south, using the ditch as cover.

After two hours, Wilf called a halt on a piece of high ground next to a road. Now they were closer to their own lines, he hoped they could make contact with 1 BR Corps.

"Have you managed to get through?" asked Tag impatiently.

"Eventually," responded Wilf. "We can still get a good signal from them, but our transmission to them is shite."

"Fuckers keep pulling back," growled Badger.

"Stop whinging. What did they say?"

"A code word: Yellow Jack."

"Any numbers?" asked Tag.

"Yes," responded Wilf as he pulled out a map and spread in on the ground in front of them.

"Yellow Jack is the word for a tactical nuclear strike. The numbers are telling us six locations. That means we've got fourteen hours to get out of range."

"What do you suggest?"

"Yellow Jack is targeted here, here and here. Bad Nenndorf is the closest. So if we stay on the southern edge of the Deister, we should be safe." He looked up at Tag who was scratching the dark stubble on his chin.

Before Tag could respond, Hacker interjected. "I can hear something."

"What?" Challenged Wilf.

"I don't know...it's a chopper, a bloody chopper."

"There's more than one," added Badger. "Look, there are four of them."

"They're looking for us," suggested Tag. "We need to take cover, or run."

Chapter 16

2000, 9 July 1984. 2nd US Division, US III Corps. West Germany.
The Blue Effect -22 hours

The General climbed up onto the glacis of an M1 main battle tank and surveyed the officers gathered around below his position. "At last, we've got our orders from on high, men. Central Army Command have stopped dithering and 7th US Army have finally made a decision."

The assembled officers smiled, used to the general bitching about higher command. The man's uniform was immaculate, his boots a deep gloss shine, his uniform almost more starch than material. God help any officer he came across who didn't meet his exacting standards. At only five foot five, with a crew cut that nearly went to the bone, and a bristled moustache, his head gave the impression of being too big for his body. But he was a good soldier, highly respected by his men.

"As you all know, III Corps' task is to reinforce the Northern Army Group of Forces. Well, they can't expect to fight the war without us now, can they?"

Another chuckle from the assembled officers.

"Well, can they?!"

"No, sir!" responded the jubilant soldiers, the odd whoop in the background.

"Now that we have finally got our equipment issued and sorted, we can fulfil that mission. But, we've had a further delay. Who do we support? Where do they need some real muscle to help knock those red bastards right back to where they belong in Moscow?"

This time, the grins were broader and supported by more laughter and whooping from the group.

"It has been decided, against my better judgement I might add…" More laughter. He held his hand up for silence. "It has been decided that the Corps is going to be split. The 1st Cavalry Division, along with the 5th Infantry Division, are going north, to support the Dutch and Germans. The Germans are doing OK, but the Dutch are in a bit of a mess. They were late getting to the party, and the Soviets took advantage of that landing an air assault brigade behind them and kicking ass. There's also a Polish army pushing hard up against them. Higher command believe that the Warsaw Pact are ready for a big push, so we have to get these two formations ready to blunt that attack. Otherwise, the northern flank will collapse, and we'll have reds running all over us."

"What about us then, sir?" called one of the Brigade commanders.

"Patience has never been one of your strengths, has it, Brigadier Daniels? Your Fort Benning report said you were too smart for your own good."

Laughter ensued, and some of his fellow commanders backslapped the Brigadier.

"Just want to get into the fight, now we're ready, sir."

The US III Corps had flown all the way from the United States. The 1st US Cavalry Division headquarters was based in Fort Hood, Texas, and the 5th US Infantry Division in Fort Polk with the 2nd US Division, consisting of three brigades, an aviation brigade and an artillery regiment, also from Fort Hood in Texas. The 2nd US Division had been in country for twenty-four hours. The soldiers, flown in by civilian airliners, had gone straight to their respective POMCUS sites in Monchengladbach and Straelen, West Germany, to be reunited with their equipment, stored in Germany for this very event. The 1st Cavalry and the 5th had also collected their heavy equipment, M1s, M2s, etc to be ready for battle. Their respective POMCUS sites were based in Belgium and the Netherlands.

"A fight I can promise you, Teddy. Your Brigade has the honour of leading the way."

"Hey, now you've done it, Teddy. Do you want to borrow my map?" Heckled one of the officers in attendance.

The General calmed his officers down again. He encouraged their high spirits, not always welcomed by the senior officers of the Corps. But it was him and his men that would have to fight. They might as well do it with some style.

He lowered his voice. "We have two missions. The first is to get as close to the Weser as possible. We have been tasked with supporting the Brits."

He saw their heads nodding. They had done field exercises

with British units during various Reforger exercises, and although they thought the British food was lousy and they never seemed to have enough equipment, they held their fighting capabilities in high regard. The one message he did give to his men in regard to the Brits was: don't get into a drinking competition with them. You will lose.

"Once there, especially for you, Teddy, 2nd Brigade will take part in a multi-force counter-attack." There was a broad grin across Brigadier Daniels' mouth, but a groan from the other senior officers.

"Now, now, boys, you know I wouldn't leave the rest of you out. Once the 2nd Brigade, along with a Brit Division and a possible Bundeswehr Brigade, have punched a hole in the Soviet front line, 1st and 3rd Brigades can help push them all the way back to the Inner German Border. To start with, anyway. Eventually, we'll have a drink together in the Kremlin."

More cheers from the assembled officers.

"Teddy, I want you boys on the move within the hour. The remaining two Brigades will follow later tonight, early tomorrow. Let's go and give those red sons of bitches a boot up the ass."

Chapter 17

0100, 10 July 1984. 25th Tank Division, 20th Guards Army.
Staging areas, Wunstorf, Garbsen and Kolenfeld, West Germany.
The Blue Effect -17 hours

The commander of the 25th Tank Division was far from happy. His division had been allocated a staging area that was less than satisfactory. There just wasn't enough room to deploy his force. 32nd Guards Tank Division was on his left flank, and the 90th Guards Tank Division and the 35th Motor Rifle Division were behind him. Ahead, he had the 12th Guards Tank Division, from 3rd Shock Army, which was in the process of preparing for an assault river crossing. He was expected to exploit the breakthrough. On top of that, the remnants of 10th GTD were camping on his doorstep. One of his tank regiments was attempting to use south of Haste as a staging area, using the forested area south of the Mittellandkanal, but elements of the 12th were still moving out. A second regiment was dispersed through the town of Wunstorf. His motor rifle regiment had been allocated south-east of Dedensen with the third tank regiment amongst the battered buildings of Garbsen, while his senior officers competed for space to accommodate his artillery, engineers and resupply. 20th Guards Army high command was in complete chaos. A recent attack by British bombers on the forward headquarters had seriously impacted on the command and control of this huge army, with in excess of 900 tanks at its disposal. Although still some thirty kilometres away from the Forward Line of Enemy Troops to the west and twenty to thirty kilometres to the south-west, the risk of NATO air strikes had significantly increased. His Soviet commanders from on high continued to push them to move ever faster, which conflicted with the General's desire to move more slowly, leapfrogging, keeping his air defence assets available and in a position to defend the units from fast-moving ground attack aircraft.

The division, split into three independent columns, had marched along three separate, parallel routes in the region of six to eight kilometres apart, eventually reaching Salzgitter. They were allowed very little time for rest before being ordered to move yet further west. The width of the march-sector the division required was in the region of thirty-five kilometres. Such was the mass of Soviet forces in such a small area, their march-sector had been reduced to as little as twenty kilometres wide and they often found themselves up against the flanking divisions fighting for space. This mass concentration of men and armour only encouraged the West to initiate further attacks, and the Soviet air force was hard-pressed to defend the forces under their protection. NATO had initiated deep strikes in order to disrupt the Soviet flow of reinforcements, and both the division and 20th Guards Army as a whole had suffered losses. More and more US aircraft were joining in the fray and, with France joining in the fight, a greater number of West German and US aircraft had been released from a defence posture, to one further forward, interdicting the Soviet air-to-ground attack missions.

As for the British, although they had been kicked out of many of the bases in West Germany, they could still operate from the United Kingdom. General Yashkin, even before arriving at his staging areas, had been forced to put one of his tank regiments in reserve until they were able to consolidate after being hit by US B-52 bombers. Nine aircraft, flying from RAF Fairford in the United Kingdom, had dropped close to 500 bombs over an area of two square kilometres. Seventeen tanks and other armoured vehicles had been destroyed or damaged; not forgetting the devastation caused to the communication routes. Also, a complete tank battalion, late getting to its assembly area, such was the mayhem on the congested roads, moving in a column formation, had been caught out in the open. It had paid a heavy price. The exposed target, the location and details radioed in by a stay-behind force, was hit by a joint British and American strike. Thirty aircraft, a mixture of Tornadoes, Jaguars and US F111s, protected by US F-15 Eagles, destroyed eleven T-64s and damaged eight before they had been driven off by the SAMs and the Soviet air force. Although the local air defence forces had destroyed one of the planes and Soviet fighters another two before the force escaped back across their own lines, it had the effect of making the commanders of the advancing units extremely nervous.

Once they reached their final departure line, orders had been passed down almost immediately. His division was to exploit the river crossing, once 12th Guards Tank Division had secured a decent bridgehead, and smash the British forces once and for all. His commander ordered him to then to be prepared to go either northwest or southwest, dependent on where the British Corps was at its weakest. In the meantime, he and his men would have to deal with the British long-range artillery and missiles raining down on his stagnant forces.

0200, 10 July 1984. 8th Guards Tank Division, 5th Guards Tank Army.
Belorussian Military District, southwest of Gotha, East Germany.
The Blue Effect -16 hours

The destruction of the railroad and road-bridge at Torun, Poland had created major problems for the 5th Guards Army in getting to its staging area from whence it could be brought into the fight against the NATO forces. It was a race. The western Allies were also bringing their reserves into the battle. The Soviet 2nd Strategic Echelon was on the verge of committing fresh, powerful forces that would surely finally crush the enemy divisions stacked up against them. Using as many ferries as could be commandeered, adding pontoons and makeshift platforms that could float troops and armour across the river, the 5th Guards Tank Army had finally been able to board transport trains and continue its journey. By the time the 7th Guards Tank Army had arrived in theatre, the bridge had been rebuilt and the Soviet Railway Construction Brigade had laid a new railway line across it. As a consequence, the second group of the Belorussian Military District forces was able to continue its journey with little disruption, apart from the continuing congestion all the advancing Warsaw Pact forces were experiencing. Behind these two armies, the BMD had released the 28th Combined Arms Army along with the 1st Tank Corps. In total, the BMD would add over 300,000 troops and 4,000 tanks to the battle, their target, the Central Army Group, CENTAG, and the two American and two German Corps, and mitigate the French forces joining in the fight.

Chapter 18

0310, 10 July 1984. Synthetic Aperture Radar (SAR) flight.
West of Minden, West Germany.
The Blue Effect -15 hours

The wings of the Platypus, a twin-engine Islander, wobbled slightly as turbulence caught the aircraft's squared-off wings. The pilot steadied the controls and continued on his track flying north to south along a line between Petershagen and west of Rinteln.

"Two minutes," the pilot informed the two crew sitting in the back of what was once a civilian passenger aircraft. But it had been converted for the special purpose to which it was now dedicated.

One of the crew looked up from his workstation. "She's tracking nicely. Recording in nine-zero seconds."

The second crewman adjusted a couple of dials and the screen in front of him brightened slightly. The feed from the multi-mode all-weather radar, tucked away in the aircraft's long, circular, flattened nose, hence its nickname Platypus, was coming through fairly clearly.

"Sixty seconds," informed crewman 1.

"Acknowledged," responded the pilot.

Somewhere above, two West German Phantom Interceptors flew with them, providing cover for their vulnerable charge below. The operator turned the equipment up to full power, and the antenna illuminated its target, the microwave being transmitted obliquely at right angles to the direction of the aircraft's flight. The swathe, the footprint being illuminated, covered an area where tanks of the 197th Guards Tank Regiment of the 47th Guards Tank Division of 3rd Shock Army were assembling en masse, waiting to follow through the gap that 7th Guards Tank Division had created. The short pulse width and the intra-pulse modulation were helping to enhance the picture being created, providing a resolution fine enough to pick out the armoured vehicles and the folds in the ground where they were hiding or on the move. This all-weather system would back up the intelligence already provided by the drones that had been flown the previous day. This next piece of the jigsaw would confirm the early morning positions of the massed forces. The information, once transmitted back to base, would help guide the defence that was slowly being mounted against these fresh troops that were threatening the defence of the entire front of the Northern Army Group.

The aircraft was again buffeted by a pocket of turbulence, a slight blip in the radar tracking but not enough to jeopardise the mission. The pictures were being transmitted to a receiver station, set up as close as possible to the aircraft's line of flight. Imagery analysts would soon be pouring over the product, putting their expertise to use, pointing out the various armoured formations but, more importantly, the location of each one.

"Ugly Duckling, this is Top-Cover. We are about to get a visit. ET your mission end? Over."

The pilot of the Platypus called back over his shoulder. "We've got company. How much more time do you need, guys?"

Crewman 1 responded, "Thirty seconds. Just keep us steady for thirty seconds."

"Roger that. Hello, Top-Cover, this is Ugly Duckling. We're nearly done. Another three-zero seconds. Over."

"Top-Cover. We hear you. We have unfriendly units on route to us. We'll leave you in ten seconds to head them off. Once you've completed, bank hard right and run. I repeat, once complete, bank hard right and run. Good luck. Out."

The pilot was nervous now. The BN-2T Islander, a high-wing cantilever monoplane, was not cut out for military operations. It was normally only used as a light troop transport or for minor support operations, not to be right up in the front line.

"How long?" he asked again, his nervousness reflected in his voice.

"Fifteen," responded crewman 2.

The pilot did the countdown inside his head, his co-pilot readying himself for the sharp turn.

"Five."

The pilot got ready.

"We're done."

"Hold tight. This is going to be a tight one."

The pilot pulled on the stick and banked hard right, the airframe juddering slightly as the g-force kicked in. Once he had made the ninety-degree turn, the throttles of the two engines were pushed forward, power from engines building up as their speed steadily increased to its maximum of 270 kilometres an hour. Whatever happened now, they had done their job. The information had been passed back; the Soviet tank units preparing to assault had been located. It was up to the more conventional means now to confirm the details. Reconnaissance aircraft would now have to take their turn.

Chapter 19

0320, 10 July 1984. Romeo-One-One, 1st Avro-Vulcan bomber
flight, 13,000 metres above Spain.
The Blue Effect –15 hours

The three Vulcans, Avro Vulcans, officially known as Hawker Siddeley
Vulcans, banked left slowly. Flying at a height of 13,000 metres, they
were now bearing north high above southern Europe. Although the
Warsaw Pact still threatened Southern Europe, to date they had made
no moves to invade Italy, Spain or Switzerland, choosing to coax
those countries to withdraw their support from NATO and declare
their neutrality. The Soviets were advocating that they only wished to
remove the threat of West Germany from their borders, and had no
axe to grind with what they referred to as *friendly countries*. In truth,
the fight in the central and northern regions of Europe was going
so well, they didn't feel the need to attack NATOs southern flank.
The decision had been made by Stavka, the Soviet High Command,
to focus resources, including ammunition, fuel and supplies, on the
Group of Soviet Forces Germany, with the Northern Group of Soviet
Forces attacking Schleswig-Holstein and Denmark, and the Southern
Group of Soviet Forces pushing into Southern Germany and Austria,
in order to maintain the forward momentum they had achieved so far.

"Romeo-One-One, this is Tango-One. Over."

"This is Romeo-One-One, ETA. Over."

"Figures five. Dropping to zero, nine, zero."

"Acknowledged."

There was no more that needed to be said. This had been
rehearsed, theoretically and in practice, back at RAF Waddington.
The Vulcan had a range of 4,000 kilometres. Their journey so far had
taken up nearly three quarters of their fuel. A top-up was necessary
if they were to hit their target and return safely – Soviet air force
permitting that was.

The pilot reduced power, taking them from their cruising speed of just under 900kph to the speed required if they were to be refuelled successfully by an equally ageing Handley-Page Victor tanker, an ex V-bomber, part of Britain's earlier nuclear deterrent.

The Vulcan was also an ageing V-bomber, and had in effect been stood down from active duty. Operationally disbanded two years earlier, the Vulcans were once again going to be used in anger. Their most recent operation had been during the Falklands War, when single Vulcans flew to the Falkland Islands in order to bomb the runway at Port Stanley and prevent its use by the occupying Argentine forces. But now, only eighteen of the aged Vulcans were serviceable, barely. In order to have enough aircraft available to make a significant contribution to the war effort, additional servicing and maintenance work had been required. Engines and spares were generally plentiful, although some spare parts had been scavenged from every possible source, even reusing items on display in museums throughout the world. Sometimes, it meant cannibalising other Vulcan and Victor aircraft in order to provide enough bombers to participate in the forthcoming action. With engineers working around the clock, the RAF was finally able to wheel out twelve Vulcans that were capable of fulfilling the mission that higher command had lined up for them. There was a mixture of squadrons used: some aircraft and crews were from No 50 Squadron and No 101 Squadron; others were from No 44 Squadron. The question had been asked in many quarters: why? Why use an aircraft that was over twenty-five years old, practically obsolete. Although the Tornado and Sepecat Jaguar ground-attack aircraft were effective in conducting air-to-ground strikes, the number of missions assigned to those squadrons to provide close-air support to the army was ever increasing and far more than there were aircraft and pilots available. Attacks on NATO bases by Soviet bombers, Spetsnaz sleepers and fresh groups parachuted in to bring the battle to the heart of the Western defences, caused major disruption. Also, the consequential loss of airbases as NATO forces withdrew applied more and more pressure to the overstretched air force. With further disruption to desperately needed supplies, the RAF was being pushed to the limit. On top of that, fighting almost continuously for five days, the pilots were on their chinstraps. A solution had to be found. The Warsaw Pact was continuing their advance and they seemed to be unstoppable. The troops on the ground would welcome anything that would slow the Soviet juggernaut down, slow their relentless push west, enabling the allies to catch their breath and regroup.

Unlike the attack on the Falklands, three years earlier, where they had flown distances well in excess of 12,000 kilometres, the shorter European distances would place fewer demands on the aircraft's airframe, and the number of refuelling top-ups would be significantly less. The navigation requirements were also very different.

"There he is," pointed out the co-pilot, peering through the three, slanted, very small central cockpit windows, the large V-shaped tail of the Victor tanker visible.

"I see it," responded the squadron leader and aircraft captain, Ted Merritt.

Probably the most dangerous part of the mission was about to start as the Vulcan bomber slowly gained on the large Victor tanker flying ahead. The pilot of the Victor tanker held the craft steady, although it rocked occasionally when buffeted by a crosswind, but he skilfully kept the large aircraft in place. Merritt steadied the Vulcan bomber, and applied a small amount of thrust, creeping forward until they were in the wake of the Victor. The wavering fuel hose and drogue, at times flickering like a demented snake, was now closer to the cockpit, the tail of the tanker less than seven metres away. The slightest of errors could see an air collision that would cripple both aircraft and put the lives of the crews, and the mission, in jeopardy.

"Steady, steady, steady," the pilot whispered to himself as probe and drogue got closer and closer, slowly merging as one until the final connection. The red lights on the hose turned to green and the 9,000-gallon tanks of the Vulcan were slowly topped up. Once complete, the two aircraft separated, and it was the turn of the next aircraft in the flight.

"Tango-One, Romeo-One-One. Dropping back, you are clear to receive."

"Roger, Romeo-One-One. Good flight. Out."

That was it; the physical and communication connections between the two aircraft were broken, the tanker pilot needing to focus on the next bomber that required his services and already moving forward into position. One Vulcan aircraft, from the third flight back, was already returning to base. The connections linking the probe and drogue had shattered, allowing tons of fuel to wash over the cockpit of the bomber. With an extremely restricted view, and the pilot unable to clear the fuel from the window, along with a flameout in one of the engines, the bomber broke off immediately before the problem was exasperated further, and the aircraft and crew were lost. Four attempts later, the engine was reignited. Disappointed, but alive, they had headed back to RAF Waddington.

Merritt would hold a steady course at the same speed until all three aircraft had been topped-up. Once ready, the flight would climb back up to their cruising height and continue as planned. Within the hour, mid-air refuelling was complete, and the three aircraft climbed back to their optimum cruising altitude of 13,000 metres.

"*Romeo-One-One, Juliet-One. Over.*"

"This is Romeo-One-One. Go ahead. Over."

"*Ugly Duckling positive. I repeat, Ugly Duckling positive. Over.*"

"Roger, Juliet-One. Out."

"Is that it?" asked the co-pilot.

"Yes, it's a go."

The Platypus in the skies over West Germany had done its job, and HQ had just informed the Vulcan captain that the enemy had been sighted and were on the move. The mission was a go.

The navigator plotter, who was sitting behind the pilot and co-pilot in a separate area facing rearwards, spoke to Merritt on the internal comms.

"Stay on course zero, four, nine. Three hundred kilometres, twenty-one minutes."

"Roger. Do we still have company?"

"Yes," responded the navigator radar. "Both are with us."

The three crewmen were sitting in a line, on rearward-facing, green, metal, bucket-like seats, the yellow steel-rung ladder that led to the cockpit behind them.

"What's below us?" asked the pilot.

The nav-plotter adjusted the flexible lamp that shone down on his charts.

"Bilbao will be coming up on our left; then open sea. The Bay of Biscay will be below us in two minutes."

"Roger." Merritt turned to his co-pilot. "Adam, if you reach back, there's a flask in my bag. Should still be warm."

His co-pilot reached behind and in between the large ejector seats. It was difficult to move in the cramped confines of the cockpit, perched on the nose of the thirty two-metre long aircraft. He fumbled in the bag and extracted the flask. On opening the top, a spiral of steam drifted upwards, only their facemasks preventing the aroma from tantalising their nostrils. He poured the hot liquid into the screw-top container he had removed from the flask top and passed it to the pilot who removed his mask, sniffed the coffee before taking a drink, then handed it back. The smell of the coffee was a significant improvement on the other smells: of sweaty bodies, electronics and worn leather seats. The mug did the rounds of all the crew. The fifth member in the back of the cockpit, the airborne electronics officer, the AEO, finished it off. In the dark hole of the rear cabin, the AEO then placed a pan on an electric heater. The contents were tomato soup, the smell mixing with stale sweat and fumes; a small treat they would allow themselves. The Vulcan carried a crew of five: the captain, who was also the pilot of the aircraft; the co-pilot, assisting the pilot in the control of the aircraft, but also responsible for control of the fuel supply and communications with the outside world. Further back, there were three additional crew with equally important roles to play: the AEO had numerous responsibilities on-board. His key role was the operation of the Electronics Warfare suite. If required, the AEO could use Electronic Counter Measures such as initiating active jamming of the enemy's radar, detecting enemy fighters, controlling the launch of anti-radar missiles, and the launching of defensive countermeasures such as 'chaff', hopefully confusing any inbound enemy missiles. The navigator plotter, sitting on the right side of the plane, was in charge of getting them onto the target and back home again. Although he would spend hours preparing the flight plan before he took off, he would be kept busy throughout the entire flight ready to plot any changes that were forced upon them due to weather or enemy activity. The last, but not the least, was the navigator radar. Control of the bombing fell to this officer. He would also assist the nav-plotter with his navigation of the aircraft.

This flight had three Vulcan B2s. Behind those were three more flights. Up until 1970, the Vulcan had carried the Blue Steel nuclear standoff missile, until the British Polaris submarines took over that strategic role, leaving the Vulcan to carry the WE.177B, a half-kiloton nuclear bomb, in a tactical nuclear strike role in support of NATO. The Squadron on this occasion though, was not carrying nuclear bombs, but each aircraft carried twenty-one 450-kilogram conventional free fall bombs.

Between the twelve aircraft assigned to this mission, they could drop 85,000 kilograms of conventional bombs on their intended target. Unfortunately, one of their number was on the way back to the UK.

Tactical nuclear strikes were now the provenance of 50 Missile Regiment, Royal Artillery, using the nuclear tipped Lance missile. The RAF Sepecat Jaguar and Tornado aircraft could also be used to deliver tactical nuclear bombs if called upon. After taking off from RAF Waddington, the Vulcans had flown southwest, knowing that Soviet spies would be monitoring all of Britain's key airfields. The intention was to convince the Warsaw Pact that the aircraft were flying to RAF Akrotiri in Cyprus, a base that had housed two squadrons of these V-bombers up until 1975. Activity at the RAF base was already being accelerated, giving the impression that these aircraft were indeed heading back to their old base. Three other Vulcan bombers were already flying towards RAF Akrotiri. These three remaining aircraft were in no condition to go into battle. Therefore, they were being used for an equally important role: one of deception. There was even some concern that these three, most well over twenty years old and the least airworthy of the aircraft available, might not even make the flight. But it was a gamble that was considered worthwhile.

After an uninterrupted flight, Merritt's trio of bombers headed further to the east, planning on circumnavigating the outskirts of Paris. The French Government had been reluctant to allow nuclear capable aircraft to fly through their airspace, concerned that, if picked up by the Soviets, they would respond with a pre-emptive nuclear strike of their own. But the British, along with other NATO countries, had convinced them that the subterfuge would work. A raft of distractions and misdirection had been set in motion. Only time would tell if they worked.

The AEO monitored his equipment closely. Should the equipment detect radar lighting the aircraft up, he could not only inform the pilot of that danger, but also let him know which quadrant the radars were in. The pilot could then simply veer away on to a new course. Their biggest threat would be the Soviet fighters with a look-down/shoot-down capability. One of the latest Soviet fighters, the Mig-29 Fulcrum, would be out hunting for NATO bombers of all types. Finding the Vulcans would be the icing on the cake for the enemy. At high level, each Vulcan's electronic countermeasures supported each other, but down in the weeds, the Vulcan bomber and its crew would be isolated, on their own. One of the weaknesses of the Vulcan when low-flying had been their lack of ability to jam. With height, the footprint of their electronic jamming was wide enough to be effective, but at low level, it would be no greater than the radius of the aircraft. In fact, it would serve to highlight the bomber, not protect it. But lessons had been learnt from the attack on the runway at Port Stanley in the Falklands. In preparation for the bombing of the runway at Port Stanley, the Vulcan had been given a hotchpotch of add-ons to improve its defence. The ALQ-101 electronic countermeasures pod was one of them, taken from a Buccaneer aircraft. Now, they had a chance. When the time came, their ability to jam the enemy radar, such as the Soviet surface-to-air missiles like the SA-2 and SA-3, drop chaff and manoeuvre out of trouble ensured the crew had a good chance of coming out of this alive. They even stood a chance against the Shilka, the dreaded ZSU 23/4.

"Nav, I can see the Forest of Fontainebleau, ninety degrees left." The pilot passed back a visual fix for the navigator.

"Montereau?"

There was a moment's pause. "Dead ahead."

The reading off the triple offset radar was made, confirmed by the pilot's sightings. With three points confirmed, the bomb aimer had the necessary information to ensure they were on target. They had to get this right. Once past Paris, through Belgium, into the Netherlands, they would bank right west of Nijmegen and then fly an easterly course until they crossed the British front line.

Chapter 20

0430, 10 July 1984. 15th Missile Battery, 50th Missile Regiment,
Royal Artillery. Area of Wagenfeld, West Germany.
The Blue Effect -14 hours

The tracks of the M113 chassis churned up the ground as it was jockeyed into position. This transporter was somewhat different from the standard M113. It didn't transport troops, as did its cousin, the M113 armoured personnel carrier. This one, an M752, transported something much more deadly.

The British Government, along with the other NATO members, had agreed that there was a need to strike back at the Warsaw Pact who were currently bombarding the allied forces in West Germany with a mix of blister and nerve agent toxins. Although the Western forces were well protected and reasonably well trained, it was inevitable that casualties would mount. The soldiers were operating in a hostile chemical environment and, even with their best endeavours, the shield sometimes failed: incorrectly fitted respirators, torn or damaged NBC suits as a consequence of shrapnel or a bullet entry point, would expose the soldiers' skin to the deadly poisons.

50th Missile Regiment, Royal Artillery, part of the British army's long-range artillery and the core of the country's tactical nuclear strike force, under orders from the Prime Minister herself, were about to hit back in earnest.

One of the greatest fears of Western governments was a war of escalation: starting out as a conventional war, but then the introduction of biological and chemical warfare by the Warsaw Pact tipping the balance, with the NATO forces responding in kind. The West, at the outset of any conventional war, had always advocated the non-use of chemical weapons, although they had the stocks available and their armies were trained in their use. But NATO had always worked on the premise that, should the Warsaw Pact decide to use chemical weapons, their response should be nuclear. For all that, governments had dithered. However, with civilian and military casualties mounting, and front lines being pushed back, it forced a far-reaching debate amongst NATO government heads. They had eventually agreed that the US, Great Britain and West Germany would launch a tactical nuclear strike. Once the go-ahead had been given to launch a strike against the Soviet forces that were advancing relentlessly along the entire NATO front in West Germany, the American Government had released the nuclear warheads to their allies.

It had also been agreed that the Soviet Politburo would be notified of the launches within minutes of the missiles leaving their launchers, with a message that stated the following:

Although not wishing to trigger a tactical nuclear exchange on the battlefields of Western Europe, or even escalating to a full strategic nuclear exchange with devastating consequences for both NATO and the Warsaw Pact countries, the United States of America, Great Britain and the Federal Republic of Germany would do so if there was a continuance in the indiscriminate use of Chemical Weapons, which was not only killing soldiers, but thousands of defenceless civilians. These six tactical nuclear strikes will not be replicated, should the Soviet Union, and its allies, cease using these inhumane weapons.

Three countries would participate: Great Britain, West Germany and the United States. Two missile launches would be initiated by each country, targeting predetermined Warsaw Pact targets. It was a gamble. There would be German civilian casualties, but not on the same scale should chemical warfare continue. It was possible that the Soviet Union would initiate their own tactical nuclear strike against the West. The risk of an escalation to a strategic nuclear exchange could still be very much on the cards.

The driver, sitting in the small cab on the front left side of the M752, signalled by his guide, brought the vehicle to a halt, in between two small trees with decent canopies to provide overhead cover. Three hundred metres away, a second vehicle, an M688, with two missile reloads and a loading hoist, reversed amongst some scattered trees, the driver and another soldier quickly draping a camouflage net over it ensuring it was hidden from any prying eyes above. The MGM-52 Lance, was a tactical, surface-to-surface missile. It could be configured to carry both conventional and nuclear warheads in order to provide support for some of the NATO countries, in particular the British, Dutch, Belgian, US and West German armies.

The 15th Missile Battery from 50th Missile Regiment, Royal Artillery, had been given their initial orders and the Lance missiles were now armed with the W70-3 warhead. Using a yield of one kiloton, the neutron bombs, with an enhanced radiation feature, would inflict severe damage on the enemy regiments. 15th Missile Battery had three self-propelled launchers. Two of those would be active very soon. Elsewhere, the three remaining missile batteries were getting ready to support the ground forces in a conventional role.

Chapter 21

0500, 10 July 1984. Romeo-One-One, 1st Avro-Vulcan bomber
flight, 1,000 metres above the Netherlands.
The Blue Effect -13 hours

Four hundred kilometres from the target, the three Vulcans dropped
to less than 1,000 metres above the ground, using the River Waal as
a landmark.

Merritt peered through the cockpit window. There was
approximately fifty per cent cloud cover, but through the fleeting
gaps he could pick out the occasional feature. The Vulcan dropped
lower, levelling out at 600 metres, the pilot wanting to stay beneath
any Soviet radars. This was the earliest the aircraft could drop
down to this level, as too much low-level flight would have burnt
extra fuel.

The crew were tense now, knowing they were getting close
to enemy territory, waiting for enemy flak or missiles to come
their way. They would be at the drop point very soon. The River
Waal turned south, but the flight of Vulcans continued east towards
Munster. West of Munster they turned north, skirting Osnabruck to
the south. One hundred kilometres out, they made a gentle descent
down to 100 metres. The nav-radar, Flight Lieutenant Bell, turned
on the Vulcan's HS2 radar which had been kept silent up until now,
not wanting the transmissions to alert the enemy to their presence.
At 320 knots, they would be on the target in about ten minutes.
Then, all being well, they would catch the Soviets completely by
surprise. The pilot now had to focus hard as he prepared to fly nap-
of-the-earth. No longer at their cruising ceiling of 13,000 metres, or
even a safer height of 1,000 metres, the terrain following radar was
needed to aid the pilot in the control of the eighty-ton aircraft. The
safety of the aircraft and crew were dependent on it. Pilots referred
to it as being 'down in the weeds'.

The nav-radar officer spoke to the pilot. "Standby for height demand, coming up on Melle."

"Roger."

One of the consequences of the bomber's poor manoeuvrability at low-level was a delay in the controls responding to an NOE demand. The pilot was always given a warning of when the aircraft needed to be pulled up or dropped down.

The nav-plotter adjusted his body until comfortable, lying prone in his position at the lower part of the cockpit from where he would release the bombs. The ground raced past beneath him, the Vulcan barely 100 metres above ground level.

The aircraft captain looked across at his co-pilot and nodded. Nothing needed saying. The AEO would warn them of any SAM radars scanning the skies. The aircraft's variegated pattern of greys and greens making it difficult for the higher-flying Soviet fighters to see them. Hopefully the land clutter would interfere with their lookdown radars. Soon, the rapidly retreating British forces would be beneath the bomb bays of the Vulcan bombers. Release too soon and the attack bombers would devastate an already battered force. Release too late and they would miss their target, the advancing Soviet army that smelt the blood of victory as they howled after their withdrawing enemy.

Chapter 22

0505, 10 July 1984. 662 Squadron, 3rd Regiment Army Air Corps.
South of Porta Westfalica, West Germany.
The Blue Effect -13 hours

The four Lynx Mark 7 helicopters, flying at low level in pairs, followed two Gazelle helicopters that would act as spotters, one for each pair. The pairs separated, moving towards their starting points. Once there, they would wait. The Gazelles, ahead of the TOW armed helicopters, maintaining radio silence, drifted apart, ready to cover a front of two or three kilometres. Their job was to watch and wait. Higher command would have to assume that the Helarm was in position. The helicopters would remain where they were until they received the coded signal to move to their firing positions and unleash their anti-tank weapons.

0505, 10 July 1984. 27th Field Regiment, Royal Artillery.
Southwest of Minden, West Germany.
The Blue Effect -13 hours

On receiving the relevant code word from divisional headquarters, the twenty-four M109s of the three batteries of the 27th Field Regiment, Royal Artillery, pulled out of the wooded areas they had been hiding in. The forest tracks were churned up as the twenty-seven-ton self-propelled artillery came out into the clearings that had already been recce'd, positions for each battery marked out and ready. Then they had to wait for the order from higher headquarters. Timing was critical. The 155mm cannons would soon be firing dual-purpose, improved conventional munitions, DPICMs, onto the enemy, the aim to cripple their advance as they chased after the retreating British unit. This regiment was part of the 4th Armoured Division. They were rested and rearmed after fulfilling their role as the covering force for 1 British Corps. Once the 27th had completed their task, the 47th Field

Regiment, their sister unit, would lay a carpet of scatterable mines, FASCAMs, across the route any remaining enemy tanks would take. All they could do now though, was wait. Wait for the next code word authorising their fire mission.

0505, 10 July 1984. 197th Guards Tank Regiment, 47th Guards Tank Division, 3rd Shock Army. Area of Buchholz, West Germany. The Blue Effect -13 hours

The BMP-2s bounced across the open ground. The motor rifle troops in the cramped troop compartments at the rear tensed their bodies yet allowed themselves to be rocked from side to side rather than fighting against the motion. The vanguard of tanks from the 1st Tank Battalion, having crushed the British defenders, a Territorial Army unit, forcing them to flee towards their last bastion, the River Weser, pushed west. A motor rifle company, following two companies of T-80, raced after the enemy forces, their masters pushing them hard, willing them to catch up with the battered British unit and destroy it before it could get to safety on the western bank of this next natural barrier. The Royal Royal Anglian battalion, a Territorial Army unit, hadn't stood a chance: practically pounded into submission after repeated artillery and air-to-ground strikes. On the other hand, the tank battalion of over twenty T-80 main battle tanks, supported by a motor rifle company from the regiment's motor rifle battalion, had suffered minor casualties, losing only three tanks and two BMPs. One of the tanks had been halted due to a lost track, attempting to negotiate around the collapsed flyover east of Rinteln, destroyed by British engineers. Soviet engineers in turn had been pushed forward to clear a route. Once past the blockage, west of a large quarry south of the Autobahn, they could press on. The Soviet tank crews had exhibited no signs of pretence that they were advancing carefully. Engines raced, powering the forty-two ton giants as they crashed through treelines and crushed wooden fences, and even a small barn was partly demolished in their haste to close the gap. The whip had been cracked, and an entire battalion, along with additional supporting forces, was racing for the gap created by the retreating army.

Yes, they suspected a trap. Their regimental and divisional headquarters expected a trap. But they were confident that there were too few enemy troops to make much of an impact, particularly as they were reserve troops, civilians in uniform, they had been told by their political officers. They would be no match for the forces of the Motherland. The defence put up by the British had surprised the Soviet vanguard. Despite being hit by a forty-minute artillery and missile barrage, followed up with an attack by ground-attack aircraft, the soldiers of the Royal Anglians had still given the Soviets a bloody nose, but had suffered heavy casualties themselves. It was questionable as to whether or not they could have survived a second assault of that magnitude, but they were never asked to find out.

The Soviets were walking into a trap, but not one they were expecting. The British TA unit had withdrawn at precisely the right time: at a time when a second, probably stronger, assault by the Soviet forces was expected.

Colonel Barbolin, commander of 197th GTR, ordered his advance battalion, along with the motor rifle company, to push forward, follow the autobahn and cross the gap over the Wesergebirge, then head west for Lohfeld. His second battalion and the motor rifle company, which he was leading, the battalion commander killed earlier, would follow. Once through the gap, they would target Mollbergen and his third battalion, with the remaining motor rifle company, would secure Eisbergen to the south. His regiment would then be within four to five kilometres of the River Weser to the west.

26th Tank Regiment had a different mission. Close behind, once the way was clear, they would follow across the high ground of the Wesergebirge, using the A2 Autobahn, and head straight for Porta Westfalica. 47th Guards Tank Division's mission was not to attempt to cross the Weser but to go through the motions of preparing to do so between Porta Westfalica in the north and Vlotho in the south. The purpose was to increase the pressure on the British forces. Should a crossing prove possible, and higher command allowed it, the division could project its forces across the river.

Barbolin contacted his forward battalion, keen to ensure that he and the second battalion weren't dropping too far behind. "One-Zero, this is Zero-Alpha. What is your position? Over."

There was a five-second delay before any response.

"One-Zero...crackle...north Luhden...Crossroad's a mess...suggest you...north Buchholz....Over."

"Engineers at location? Over."

"Yes, but...crackle...need time. Over."

"Hold north of Todenmann and wait. Out."

Barbolin cursed at the delay and indicated for his driver to head northwest towards Buchholz. He then contacted the rest of his formation to do the same. He pushed his shoulders through the hatch, checking the ground ahead as they crossed an open field. He kept his forces moving forward at speed, suspecting, yet unsuspecting; comfortable that nothing could stop them now. In fact, he was confident the division could reach the River Weser without stopping. The British didn't have a unit this side of the river that was actually capable of stopping the regiment's seventy-plus tanks and additional BMP-2s. He believed that there was nothing between his unit and the river.

0520, 10 July 1984. 1st Battalion, 197th Guards Tank Regiment, 47th Guards Tank Division, 3rd Shock Army.
Northwest of Todenmann, West Germany.
The Blue Effect -13 hours

Lieutenant-Colonel Kovrov, commander of the 1st Tank Battalion, ordered his driver to ease the T-80K forward another metre, the barrel of the 125mm gun poking through the other side of the line of trees. Once across the high ground, he had moved his unit off the Autobahn, where they would be sitting ducks if they remained. Out to his front-right, he could see an uncultivated field, and to his front-left a field with row upon row of what looked like the green foliage of a root vegetable. The German farmer wouldn't be harvesting any of it this year that was for certain. Kovrov had just been informed that his regimental commander, along with the 2nd Tank Battalion, had skirted north of the E8/A2 crossroads and was preparing to move along the Autobahn behind him. The artillery battalion, with its twelve 122mm self-propelled howitzers, would form up east of Buchholz, ready to support the regiment when called upon. One platoon of six guns had been lost as a consequence of some effective counter-battery fire from the British. Their 175mm M107s, although not the most accurate of weapons, had a range of nearly forty kilometres. The platoon of Soviet 2S1s had been too slow in relocating after firing and was destroyed by the heavyweight shells.

Kovrov's headphones crackled, and he received orders to move out, protecting the right flank of the regiment's advance. He ordered 1st Company to go right, in formation with a platoon of BMP-2s, and he would lead the 2nd Company across the field of root vegetables with the 3rd Company following as the reserve. He felt the edge of the hatch dig into his back as the T-80K powered forward.

"Hawk-One and Two, this is Buzzard-One. You have business coming your way. Over."

"Hawk-One. Roger."

"Hawk-Two. Acknowledged."

"Hawk-One, Hawk-Two. Three, Tango-Eight-Zero. Two thousand metres Red-Bravo."

"Hawk-One. Understood."

"Hawk-Two. Roger."

The two hovering Lynx helicopters now knew the enemy tanks were north of Eisbergen, and it was time for them to go into action. The Helarm had been initiated as a last resort, to blunt the attack of the massed line of tanks that were steadily rolling towards the Weser. Another pair of Lynx was positioned further north, and one pair was covering the road that ran parallel with the northern bank of the River Weser to the south. Hawk-One and Two, in the hover, slowly rose above the treeline that had been concealing them. The co-pilot, using the roof-mounted sights, zoomed in on the armour heading towards them, the tanks weaving around dips and potential barriers as they advanced, turrets swivelling as the gunner's turned their main guns towards where a potential threat could be waiting to ambush them.

"Hawk-Two, Hawk-One. I'll take right."

"Roger, Hawk-One."

Staff-Sergeant Hill, the gunner sitting in the left seat of Hawk-One, looked at the pilot. They were both ready. They were going into battle for the first time since the war started. Up until this moment, they had been held back in reserve. But now a Helarm had been requested, and they would get the chance to make their contribution and let the Soviet armour know the tables were about to be turned. He turned back to the weapon sights and prepared to fire. Once the target crossed the 1,500-metre line, the TOW missile was launched.

Kovrov flinched as to his right one of his tanks flared up, flashes and sparks thrown up and out into the air, followed by billowing black, oily smoke as the T-80 skewed to the right before labouring to a halt. The shock wave of the explosion reached him, taking his breath away. His head snapped left as a second tank was struck by a TOW missile's extended probe. The 5.9kg warhead detonated, the shaped-charge jet-formed and, at hypersonic speed, twenty-five times the speed of sound, the stream of heated material penetrated the armour, killing the crew inside. Two more missiles were launched from the pair of helicopters. Once clear of the launch tubes, the four short wings sprang out, and the tail controls to the rear sprung open. The two gunners, using a small joystick, kept the crosshairs on their respective target and, five seconds later, two more tanks were hit. This time, though, the TOWs were less successful, the explosive reactive armour fulfilling its intended role. On one, the outward explosion deformed the jet enough to prevent it penetrating through the turret. On the second, although one of the ERA plates did its job, the molten jet still managed to damage the turret ring enough to lock it in place. The crew survived, but the T-80 would need to be recovered and repaired.

"One-Zero call signs weave, weave for God's sake. Weave. Six-One-Zero and Six-Two-Zero, this is One-Zero. Contact, contact. Where the hell are you?"

"*One-Zero, Six-One-Zero. Six-One-One hit. Moving forward.*"

"Hurry. Six-Two-Zero, report!"

"*One-Zero, Six-Two-One engaging now.*"

Far off to the right, where his flanking company was on the move, a flash caught his eye as another tank was hit. Kovrov cursed, angry that he hadn't brought his air defence forward sooner. He had just lost one of his ZSU 23/4s. Another lost the previous day; he desperately hoped the remaining two could do something. The three SA-9 mounted BRDM-2s were also moving forward to give cover. He nearly slipped down into the turret as the driver swerved the tank violently to the right, doing his best to make them as difficult a target as possible. Kovrov pulled himself back into position as a blurred object shot by, striking the tank just behind to his left. The missile had detonated, but the reactive armour again defeated its effect, the tank surviving to fight another day.

0535, 10 July 1984. 662 Squadron, 3rd Regiment Army Air Corps. South of Porta Westfalica, West Germany.
The Blue Effect -12.5 hours

"Hawk-Two, Hawk-One. Moving."

Hawk-One dropped back down behind the trees just as the

Gazelle, Buzzard, took up a position 200 metres to the right, ready to plot the movement of the armour as the two Lynx moved further back to new positions. Two missiles fired. It was time to relocate.

A flash of light swamped the gunner's view, overpowering the sight of his left eye as Hawk-Two, struck by a surface-to-air missile, fired by an SA-9 Gaskin, erupted into a multi-coloured, glowing cloud, as the explosion tore it apart. The two-and-half kilogram Frag-He warhead had struck the Lynx directly at the point where the fuel tanks were positioned.

"Christ!" Shouted Staff-Sergeant Hill as he watched the Lynx plummet to the ground, a much larger explosion engulfing the helicopter's body as over 300 litres of fuel exploded, a tower of flame and smoke pirouetting upwards. There would be no survivors. The pilot couldn't look. His focus had to be on getting them away and into their next location.

"Calling Hawk-One, Hawk-Two, this is Hawk-Three. We have troops dismounting with shoulder-launched missiles. Over."

"Hawk-One. Roger that. Hawk-Two is down. Out."

0540, 10 July 1984. 47th Guards Tank Division, 3rd Shock Army.
West of Buchholz, West Germany.
The Blue Effect -12.5 hours

"Zero-Alpha, this is Zero-Echo. Zero-Bravo is pushing hard and is right behind you. You have to make headway. Over."

"Understood, sir. Helicopters have withdrawn. But One-Zero has taken casualties. Over."

"Just keep moving, Nikolay. I have ordered more air defence assets forward."

"Understood, sir."

"No stopping. Out."

General Arsenyev, commander of the 47th Guards Tank Division had made it clear: Colonel Nikolay Barbolin had to keep his tanks moving before his regiment caused a roadblock, with tanks backing up making a perfect target for enemy air assets and artillery.

The order was passed down the line, and Kovrov continued to move his 1st Battalion forward. The 2nd and 3rd battalions close behind. And behind them another tank regiment was powering west.

"One-One-Zero. This is One-Zero. Leave any crippled vehicles and keep moving. Acknowledge."

"One-One-Zero. Understood. Units advancing."

"One-Four-Zero, support One-One-Zero. Out."

The commander of 1st Company, the right flanking company, with his remaining eight tanks, continued across the fields heading for a position north of Lohfeld, the motor rifle company moving to join them.

"One-Three-Zero, left flank, take up position south of Lohfeld."

"Moving now."

3rd Company picked up speed, bypassing their battalion commander.

"One-Two-Zero, hold position. Move in two minutes. Out."

The units of Kovrov's 1st Battalion picked up speed again, and he could see his 1st Company off to the far right. 3rd Company started to pass to his left, two platoons up front and the third at the rear. On his orders, the driver drove the T-80K forward and he closed his eyes and mouth for a moment as they drove through a cloud of choking black smoke, flames still licking at the turret of the T-80. No surviving crew could be seen. There were two more burning hulks that 2nd Company, when it moved, would leave behind. He twisted in the turret, clouds of dust in the pale light indicating that 2nd and 3rd Battalion were joining the attack, making space for the regiment not far behind them.

0545, 10 July 1984. 662 Squadron, 3rd Regiment Army Air Corps.
West of Lohfeld, West Germany.
The Blue Effect -12.5 hours

"Hawk-One, this is Buzzard. Four Tango-Eight-Zeros and one Bravo-Mike-Papa-Two. Approaching your previous location. Moving your location now. Standby."

"Roger that, Buzzard."

"Hawk-One, this is Hawk-Three. Engaging."

Another TOW anti-tank missile left its pod, streaking towards its target, this time a BMP-2, the gunner concerned that it could well be carrying Soviet troops from the anti-aircraft platoon and carrying shoulder-launched surface-to-air missiles. If they managed to get close enough, the three launchers carried could prove deadly. There was a satisfying blast as the mechanised infantry combat vehicle was

181

literally engulfed in an inferno. The turret was torn asunder, thrown up and sideways, and the ammunition ignited ensuring that not a living soul left the confines of its now flaming hull. For a fraction of a second, both the gunner and pilot felt some empathy towards the men who were experiencing a horrific death, but quickly focussed their thoughts back on the mission.

Another TOW missile left the rail, striking a T-80, but failing to cripple it. Again, they flew to an alternative position to start all over again. This time, a main battle tank was destroyed. Then the call came through.

"All Hawk and Buzzard call signs, this is Hotel-Zero. Romeo, Tango, Bravo. Acknowledge. Over."

"Hawk-One. Romeo-Bravo-Tango."

There was no call for Hawk-Two, who would not be responding to the call to return to base. The aircraft and its crew were still burning in a rapidly diminishing pyre on the ground. Two further Lynx helicopters did not respond to the call, but they had given the Soviet tank unit something to reflect on: nine T-80s had been destroyed, along with four damaged, and four BMP-2s, along with the troops that rode in them, had also been taken out of the fight. The Helarm had done what was asked of it.

The Soviets were adjusting their line, ready to push west again. The second tank regiment, still unable to push south-west, was going to ground until the traffic jam up ahead had cleared. The Soviet troops were about to feel the wrath of the retreating British Army for the second time that morning.

0550, 10 July 1984. 27th Field Regiment, Royal Artillery.
Southwest of Minden, West Germany.
The Blue Effect -12.5 hours

The three artillery batteries, now lined up in their appropriate formations, were taking up the positions allocated to them by their officers. They had plenty of room to manoeuvre. Pre-planned fire missions had been laid down, the location of the Soviet forces had been confirmed by the Midge drone and the Platypus's SAR, updated by a recce flight earlier. The crews waited nervously, aware of the task they had been assigned, higher command wanting them to know how crucial their mission was if they were to give the retreating battalion a chance of survival and be available to continue the fight once they had rested and rearmed. On top of that, their mission was to cripple the advancing Soviet unit. Commands were given, and the first of the 155mm howitzers rocked back on their torsion-bar suspension.

0600, 10 July 1984. Romeo-One-One, 1st Avro-Vulcan bomber flight.
Southwest of Porta Westfalica, forty kilometres from target.
The Blue Effect -12 hours

The Vulcan pilots and their crews made their final checks. They were not afraid, but apprehensive, conscious that Soviet fighters could jump them at any minute.

Ten minutes out. Timing was crucial. They'd even been forced to do a circuit further back to ensure that they arrived exactly on the scheduled time. Too soon and they would have interfered with the Helarm and the artillery strike. Soon, they could deliver their bombs, and do their bit to contribute to the destruction of the enemy forces that seemed to have had it all their own way so far.

0605, 10 July 1984. 1st Battalion, 197th Guards Tank Regiment.
South of Porta Westfalica, West Germany.
The Blue Effect -12 hours

Lieutenant-Colonel Kovrov was still smarting from the comms he had just received. Colonel Barbolin, his regimental commander, normally of a calm disposition had actually ranted over the radio. Clearly, he had been berated by General Arsenyev. Soviet high command was impatient. The battle along the entire Soviet front had gone well so far, advancing around 150 kilometres in only five days. Stavka sensed victory, smelt the British army's defeat and drove their soldiers to thrust the knife deep in a killing blow. Kovrov looked across to his right: a platoon of three T-80s, and behind those a platoon of BMPs. On his left was the same. The scenery changed slightly as his command tank crashed through a wire fence, and the force he was in line with moved from one cultivated field to another. Looking back, he could just make out a company of tanks from the 2nd Battalion rushing forward to take advantage of the ground taken. 3rd Battalion was moving up on the left, eventually taking over, allowing his battered unit to rest.

His vision was suddenly interrupted as a myriad of explosions straddled the force of armour to the fore. Instinctively, he dropped down and closed the turret hatch as explosions buffeted his own tank. He peered through the vision blocks.

"Faster," he ordered his driver.

The tank picked up speed, the driver pulling hard on the left stick as he veered around a crippled tank. Kovrov's tank rocked again as another barrage of improvised munitions straddled the platoon he was with. The DPICM sub munitions that landed on top of the thinner armour of both the tanks and the mechanised infantry combat vehicles cut their way through. Some were deflected by the ERAs, but this defensive coating as a matter of course was slowly being stripped away. More bomblets battered the advancing lines of tanks as the British artillery threw down a carpet of destruction. Kovrov cracked his elbow as the tank rocked violently, the front slewing to the right as his driver lost control, the damaged track peeling off its bogie wheels. More explosions battered the advancing Soviet armour. Multiple explosions could be heard in all directions.

Clang. A piece of shrapnel struck the turret, causing his Gunner to shrink down towards the floor of the fighting compartment. Kovrov had told the driver and gunner to remain inside but to keep their eyes peeled for any advancing British armour. They couldn't move, but they could still fight. Leaving the protection of their armoured shell to check for damage at this moment in time would be suicidal as a torrent of anti-personnel munitions engulfed the ground around them. The bombardment continued, Kovrov unable to pierce the haze of dust and debris thrown up by the myriad of explosions. The chatter between regiment and battalion confirmed that all three of the regiment's battalions had been hit.

"One-One-Zero. What is your situation?"

"One-Zero…brought to a halt…engineers."

"Understood. Fixed mines?"

"Negative…sir…dropped…the last salvo."

"Your location?"

"Lo…n…xzxy."

"Hold position until mine clearance. Out. Zero-Alpha. One-Zero. Need urgent mine clearance. Location west Lohfeld."

"Will send. What is your situation, Colonel? You need to move. Elements bogged down behind you."

"Zero-Alpha. Wait. One-One-Zero, this is One-Zero. Where are you? Over."

"One-Zero. This is One-One-two. Comrade Major Yagalin is dead. We have three units destroyed, two damaged and stranded on the

minefield, and no contact with our infantry. Over."

"Understood. Hold position. One-Three-Zero. Stop, stop, stop. Report."

"We have hit the same minefield, Comrade Colonel. One-Three-Three is stuck, two tanks damaged. No contact with One-Three-One and Two."

He was unable to make contact with his other company or any of his Infantry.

"All One-Zero call signs. Consolidate your positions and await orders. Out. Zero-Alpha. Waiting confirmation, but estimate minimum additional twelve units disabled. Over."

There was a pause, and Kovrov could picture his regimental commander grinding his teeth, dreading passing the information back up the line to the divisional commander. His lead battalion was down to less than ten fighting units, the infantry had been scattered, and his remaining two battalions had also lost seven T-80s between them.

"One-Zero. Hold your current line. Two and Three-Zero will continue to flank you left and right. Zero-Bravo will move your location. Mine-clearing units on the way. Out."

Kovrov slumped in his uncomfortable seat, no longer worrying about the tactical situation. That had been taken out of his hands. For the moment, his battalion had effectively been withdrawn from the fight. Despite the odds against him, his inability to make progress would be seen as a failure. His future now would be in the hands of his seniors. His only hope, if given a second chance, would be to commit his battalion to fight, as dictated by his leaders, and succeed at whatever the price. Thinking that, he doubted he could even pull together a company, let alone a battalion. Before his thoughts could return to his current predicament, sat in the middle of a battlefield, the ground shook, as if a seismic event had just been triggered.

0607, 10 July 1984. Romeo-One-One, 1st Avro-Vulcan bomber flight, on target.
The Blue Effect -12 hours

Romeo-One-Two, on the far right of the flight of three bombers, moved slightly ahead of its two sister planes and was the first to fire its anti-radar missiles, the AGM-54A Shrike, from its twin-launcher. At first, the AEO of the aircraft was unable to pick up any enemy radar. One was switched on briefly, but turned off again just as quickly. Just as he was about to focus on their primary mission, two radars suddenly

185

lit up, searching the skies for any NATO aircraft in the vicinity. This created an immediate threat to the Vulcan bombers. One Shrike was fired and, after a slight adjustment to the flight line, the second one followed. The crew had no idea if the missiles were successful, destroying the ground radar that would feed target information to the SAM missiles. But the radar signatures disappeared. Once the bombing started, and the enemy were fully aware of what was occurring, the follow-on flights would certainly have plenty of radar targets to go at.

Back in Romeo-One-One.

"Nav, Radar. We're on track."

"Roger."

"Two minutes till release."

"Acknowledged," responded the pilot.

Fifteen kilometres from the target, another check was made on their position, and the bomb-bay doors were finally opened. The pilot and co-pilot looked at each other again, both thinking the same thing. Where was the enemy flak and missile fire? It seemed to be going well so far, perhaps too well. Both wished for their good fortune to continue. The AEO had picked up a couple of high-pitched shrieks from a Straight Flush, the fire-control radar for a Soviet SA-6 surface-to-air missile, on his warning receiver, but they disappeared. He placed a hand on his headphones pressing them close to his left ear. Nothing. Perhaps one of the Shrike anti-radar missiles had put it out of its misery.

Speed was now 300 knots and the computer responsible for the timing, signalled it was time for the bomb release. The first group of bombs left the bomb bay. Within seconds, a retardation chute opened at the end of each one, slowing the fall of the bomb, allowing the delivery aircraft time to leave the area before the bombs exploded, showering a rain of death over its target.

One second.

The speed of bombs fall dropped, slowed down as the drogues released from the tail end did their job.

Two seconds.

Squadron Leader Merritt maintained his course as five more 450kg bombs left the bomb bay.

Three seconds.

He heard the shriek himself before the AEO warned him. "Shilka, twenty degrees port."

"Roger." He glanced left, knowing he would see nothing unless it was the bright flare of a missile or the flare of tracer rounds. He kept the aircraft's flight line steady, the dropping of their bomb load the priority.

Four seconds.

Another five bombs had been released.

The aircraft continued on its level course, the pilot gripping the control stick tightly. He had no option if they were to drop their deadly load effectively, and lay waste to the unsuspecting Soviet troops below.

"Chaff fired," informed the AEO.

Five seconds.

The last of the bombs tumbled from the aircraft. Squadron Leader Merritt could now manoeuvre, taking them away from the ever-increasing number of threats from the many fire-control radars that were lighting up below.

It took twenty seconds for the bombs to touch down, hitting the ground at quarter-second intervals. But when they did, they caused widespread destruction. Flanked by two other Vulcan bombers, Romeo-One-Two and Romeo-One-Three, sixty-three 450kg bombs blanketed the area beneath them. Through the sidewall of the cockpit and above the noise of the engines, they could hear the staccato crump as the bombs detonated. Behind them, eight more bombers would be dropping their bomb loads on the unsuspecting armour and infantry targets below.

Merritt pulled on the controls, pushing the engine throttles forward, powering the engines, taking the aircraft into a full power climb, banking round to the right, inwardly wincing, waiting for a response from someone down below.

"Hotel-Zero. Romeo-One-One. Red light, red light."

The code word for the strike had now been sent. Now it was time to head for home, picking up a refuelling Victor on the way back, and then a plate of bacon and eggs.

0609, 10 July 1984. 47th Guards Tank Division, remnants of 7th Guards Tank Division, 3rd Shock Army. Stretched from Mollbergen to Rinteln, West Germany.
The Blue Effect -12 hours

The forty-ton T-80 flipped over, the blast from the 450kg bomb making light work of brushing the behemoth aside. Although shaken badly, with the driver suffering a broken leg, the crew actually survived, their only hope a rescue by their comrades at some point in the future. A second T-80 was torn asunder, the turret ripped from the turret ring, the crew's bodies also rent apart.

Kovrov could only listen over the radio, the screams of his tankers calling for help, help he was unable to provide. Nearly 30,000 kilograms of bombs had carpeted Kovrov's battalion and the two behind it, destroying yet even more of his formation.

"All One-Zero call signs. Status? Over."

He was met with just the crackle of his radio along with a background of unsquelched noise.

"Zero-Alpha, Zero-Alpha. One-Zero. Over."

"Zero-Alpha...report...under...heavy...air...attack."

"One-Zero call signs have not responded. Orders. Over."

"Cx...yx...Alpha...."

Contact with his regiment had been lost. Unknown to Kovrov, a second flight of Vulcans had dropped their bombs right on top of the 3rd Battalion, destroying eleven armoured vehicles, wiping out Barbolin's T-80K. 197th GTR was rapidly being depleted, and it was questionable as to whether there would be enough time for it to ever recover and reform to become an effective fighting unit again. The forward regiment was then given a reprieve as the last three Vulcans deposited their deadly cargo on the second tank regiment. The regiment that was closing in on the stalled Soviet forward unit, pushed on by its leaders, was not to escape the onslaught. The 450kg bombs landed amongst the compacted force. More T-80s met the same fate as those up front, a tank and Infantry Company all but destroyed. As the closeness of the funnelled tanks and BMPs prevented individual vehicles from racing away from the area of destruction, a flight of German Tornadoes and British Jaguars picked off tank after tank. Allied fighter aircraft overhead had a run-in with the Soviet air force racing to the defence of their stricken comrades below. It was a short-lived fight, the British fighters having to withdraw after losing three of their aircraft. But the ground-attack aircraft, joined by six Harriers, had caused havoc amongst the targets they had been given before they too, losing only two planes, had withdrawn from the fight, leaving the two major elements of 47th Guards Tank Division to lick their wounds.

The Vulcans, taking advantage of the distraction created, left the area. Only one aircraft was lost, that due to mechanical failure, the crew parachuting to safety behind their own lines. A second was to be lost over the English Channel, taking a Victor tanker with it after a collision caused by a lack of concentration for a few seconds by one of the weary pilots.

Kovrov pushed open the hatch. A sea of destruction as far as his eye could see surrounded him. Burning hulks lay strewn across what was once arable farmland. The food being grown to feed the German population was now burnt, tainted and blackened. The silence was overpowering after the constant hammer of anti-tank missiles, artillery shells, and now the bombers had finished their run. There was little sound, other than the occasional crackling of small-calibre rounds set off by the white-hot heat as the T-80s burned. His gunner joined him in the turret, his eyes wide as he took in the scene. One minute, he was part of an effective powerful battalion, an element of a much larger and more powerful force; then he was in the centre of a scrapyard, the might of the Soviet army immobile, many of the crew dead or dying.

"What do we do, sir?"

"We need to assess the damage, see if we can get back on the road," Kovrov said, tapping the armour of the tank. "We'll be needed much sooner than we think." His thoughts, dark and clouded earlier, brightened, despite the destruction that surrounded him. Blame could not be pinned on him for this. Perhaps he would get away from being a scapegoat after all.

Six kilometres away, the remnants of the TA battalion, keeping ahead of the now battered juggernaut, had a clear run to the Weser. They knew they had done a good job, but would be pleased to get to the relative safety across the fast-flowing waters. They were to find out later the consequence of their actions: the destruction of a major Soviet formation.

Chapter 23

What do you do if a Nuclear War occurs?
RED WARNING – There is an imminent danger of attack. This will be of a siren, consisting of a rising and falling note. If you are outside or driving a car, then park off the road as soon as possible. But do not park where you may obstruct emergency vehicles. Take cover in a building close by, or find a depression in the ground, or a ditch. If you are at home, turn off the gas, turn off any fuel oil and disconnect any electric heaters. Shut the windows and go to your fall-out room.
GREY WARNING – Fall-out expected within an hour. This will be a siren with an interrupted pitch, a continuous sound. If there is no siren nearby, you may hear the sound of church bells. If you are at home, complete any last-minute preparations, such as turning off the gas, fuel oil, water supply at the stopcock, and tie up the ballcock in the WC cistern. If outdoors, get home if possible. If not, seek safer surroundings before the fall-out comes down.
BLACK WARNING – Imminent danger of fall-out. Maroon flare, gong or whistle sounding a morse code 'D'. Dash…Dot…Dot. If you are at home, you must go immediately to your fall-out shelter. If you are outdoors and away from your home, you must immediately seek the best cover available. If there is no warning, the first thing you will experience is a blinding flash of light and heat lasting up to twenty seconds. This will be followed by the blast wave. Do not look at the flash and fling yourself down immediately and take cover.

Protect your Family – Handbook 3

0600, 10 July 1984. Prime Minister, United Kingdom.
The Blue Effect -12 hours

The lead vehicle turned onto the main road, the Prime Minister's Jaguar following suit. Behind her, a second vehicle with the rest of her close protection team followed. The convoy drove at speed.

The country was at war, and there had already been an attempted assassination on the Home Secretary and a senior army general. Fortunately, both attempts had failed, but the Spetsnaz sleeper teams had come very close. There was a real concern for the security of Prime Minister and the Secretary of State for Defence. Military Intelligence Department 5, commonly known as MI5, had warned that they couldn't guarantee that all sleeper teams within the country had been accounted for. They were certain that some groups had been landed, probably covertly by Soviet submarine, on the mainland, and were waiting for the appropriate opportunity to strike again. Both MI5 and the Ministry of Defence had insisted the PM had additional security, but she had resisted, advocating that too much security would only draw attention to her location. With very little choice, they had climbed down, but her close protection team had been increased to six officers.

She spoke to the Defence Secretary, sitting on her right in the rear of the Jaguar. "Lawrence, you're not happy with the final decision."

He shrugged his shoulders, defeated. "Any use of nuclear weapons, whether strategic or tactical can only lead to an all-out nuclear escalation."

"Not necessarily so," responded the PM, leaning forward, turning her head towards him. "We will issue them with notice of our intention and the reasons why we've had to resort to such measures."

"But only minutes prior to the strike, Prime Minister," he responded, frustration clear in his voice.

She leant her head back against the cream leather headrest. "What do you suggest we do? Resort to chemical weapons? Thousands of German civilians already lie dead in the streets or are clogging up civilian and military hospitals, victims of blister gas and nerve agents. If we respond in kind, it will just add to the misery and is unlikely to prevent the flood of troops swamping our front line."

"It is a big risk for just a ruse, Prime Minister."

"Of course it's a risk," she responded, leaning forward again and fixing him with a stare. "And, yes, it's a ruse. The Americans are hanging on by the skin of their teeth, and in the north it's about as fragile as it can get. How long do you think the Dutch army is going to hold up, or the Belgians for that matter?"

"But the French—"

"Lawrence, you've seen the latest estimates of the enemy's strength. At least three Soviet Military Districts have been mobilised and are on their way. How many troops is that? I'm led to believe tens of thousands."

"Over half a million, Prime Minister."

"Be it so. And what about the rest? Yes, it's a ruse. Hit them with six tactical nuclear strikes followed up with a counter-attack and we can do them some real damage."

"And casualties?"

"Yes, Lawrence, casualties. As many as if we started to use chemical weapons? I doubt it. Another thing. And please don't try and tell me otherwise, I'm not naive. Yes, we train for fighting in a chemical and nuclear environment, but have we done enough? It is the right thing to do."

"And the Soviet response?"

"That's up to them. But if we don't so something drastic then a strategic nuclear exchange may be the only option left open to us. Unless you want to join the Communist Party…"

0700, 10 July 1984. Ballistic Missile Early Warning System
station, Flyingdales, United Kingdom.
The Blue Effect -11 hours

The Specialist-four operator called to the duty officer, Major Dixon, and pointed at the circular screen in the centre of his consul. The information was being passed down from the three radomes above.

"What have you got, Specialist?"

"We have an incoming, sir. Signal seems a bit weird, but there is definitely something there."

"Trajectory?"

"Picking it up from 2.5 and 5 degrees, sir."

"Pass the phone. We'd better make the call."

"Sir." The operator reached down to the phone console, took the black telephone suspended low down on the left-hand table leg of the situation display and passed it to the officer.

Major Dixon pressed the bottom right button marked 'MOD' and informed RAF Strike Command at RAF High Wycombe. Once the message had been passed, he pressed the top right button and contacted the United Kingdom Warning and Monitoring Organisation (UKWMO) at Preston.

0710, 10 July 1984. United Kingdom Warning and Monitoring
Organisation (UKWMO), Cowley, Oxfordshire.
The Blue Effect -11 hours

The lamp illuminated, and the incoming message was slowly perforated
onto a reel of white paper tape. The operator got up from her chair
and walked over to the tape-perforator, hovering while she waited for
it to complete its task. Once the clacking of the machine had stopped,
the message complete, she tore the tape from the punch and checked
the header. It was routine. She transferred the paper tape. The strip of
message tape used a 5-bit baudot code to punch a five-hole code for
each character in a straight line across the width of paper strip. The tape
was then inserted into the reader, and the teleprinter started to tap out
the message onto a much wider roll of paper. Once complete, she tore
the sheet from the machine and walked over to the desk of the duty
officer who read it and then picked up the phone.

0720, 10 July 1984. Royal Observer Corps, Eleven-Post, Horsham,
United Kingdom.
The Blue Effect -11 hours

Charlie Watts clattered down the steel rung ladder in a vertical shaft
taking him to an underground chamber seven metres below ground
level. Showing above was a raised mound covered in turf, with only the
green painted vents, sensors and entrance showing. He stepped off the
last rung into the chamber below, and passed the WC compartment
with its chemical toilet. The sound from above was excluded, replaced
by the steady hum of the fans powered by a 12-volt battery, circulating
the air through two grilled ventilators. The chamber was far from
big, a mere five by two metres and, being just over two metres in
height, there was very little headroom. Watts called to his fellow Royal
Observer Corps volunteer.

"Well, Bill, is this it or another bloody exercise?"

"You know as much as I do, but it doesn't matter. We have to
take them all seriously in case this is the big one."

"If it is, Bill, it will be bigger than we would like, that's for sure.
Have you heard from Group HQ yet?"

"Nah, only the standby warning. The wife's made a flask of tea
by the way. Help yourself."

"Yeah, but what about the butterfly cakes?"

"Hey, she spoils me, not you. But there are some ginger biscuits in the tub. Freshly baked."

William Jackson sat at a small metal table; more of a metal shelf bolted to the wall with two legs supporting it, and pushed the Tupperware container of biscuits towards his fellow observer. They were one of over 700 observer teams called out on the basis that there was the potential for a nuclear attack on the United Kingdom. Although a uniformed force that came under the command of the Royal Air Force, they reported operationally to the United Kingdom Warning and Monitoring Organisation.

"Have you done a kit check?"

"Somebody had to do it while you took your time getting here. You need to countersign though."

Charlie picked up the list of kit they had to ensure was on hand, and was needed to fulfil their role as observers. The HANDEL receiver was next to Bill, the handle, used for the hand-operated siren, the pyrotechnic-maroon, a means through which they could warn the local population of an imminent attack. The maroon would explode in the air: *bang, bang-bang* – the Morse code letter 'D'. They both turned towards the carrier-receiver as it issued the start of a six-second alert signal. Even in the poorly lit chamber, anyone looking would have seen the two men's faces pale.

"Oh God, no," uttered Charlie.

Once the initial alarm was finished, the carrier-receiver transmitted the alarm signal for a further six seconds.

Neither man moved as the following words were emitted from the speaker. *"Attack warning red, attack warning red, attack warning red."*

They both stared at the speaker as a high-pitched, uninterrupted tone sounded for four seconds, followed by a lower-pitched tone lasting a full minute, interrupted every four seconds. The entire sequence was repeated, and only then did the two men move, their thoughts disturbed by the arrival of observer three.

"Sorry I'm late," the third member of the team shouted down the shaft. They heard the ringing bell of a Green Goddess as it roared past on the road above.

"You've just made in time. Did you hear the alert as you came down the ladder?" Bill asked the new arrival.

Alfie Rose dropped to the concrete floor from the last two rungs of the ladder. "Yes, I did. Police and Civil Defence teams are running about like headless chickens up there."

"If you'd left it any later," responded Bill, the leader and observer one, rather sarcastically. "You'd be a headless chicken yourself, but fried. Right, Charlie, you man the loudspeaker telephone."

As Charlie made his way to the telephone, a message was transmitted from the post display plotter. *"Horsham, ten, eleven, twelve posts. Standby for message. Over."*

Horsham Ten-Post responded. Then it was Charlie's turn. "Horsham-Eleven Post. Over."

"Attack warning red. Message ends. Over."

"Horsham-Twelve, thank you. Out."

In the meantime, Alfie, observer three, switched on the fixed survey meter (FSM) and confirmed that the check sequence read zero-zero.

"Confirmed zero-zero, Charlie."

"Horsham Eleven-Post. Over." Observer two transmitted to the post display plotter.

"Horsham Eleven-Post. Over."

"FSM on. Over."

"FSM on. Out."

The team of three men would now commence and maintain a continuous watch on the bomb power indicator.

Bill sat on one of the bunk beds up against the wall at the opposite end to the entrance shaft. "Buggers have done it," he moaned.

"We'll know soon enough," added Alfie.

"Come on, you two, it's not definite," suggested Charlie.

"Horsham Eleven-Post. This was an exercise. Stand down. Over."

"Horsham Eleven-Post. Thank you. Over."

"Horsham Eleven-Post. Out."

"Bastards," growled Alfie. "Playing games at a time like this."

Bill patted both his fellow observers on their shoulders. "Hey, let's be thankful. It wasn't for real this time round."

"Yes. This time round..." added Charlie.

Chapter 24

The tracks of the erector launcher were locked and the straps securing the missile removed. The rear platform was lowered, and two soldiers, dressed in their NBC suits, ran forward and proceeded to attach the four fins. Gunner Boyes cranked the launcher, raising it enough to allow Bombardier Jones access to the panel. The NCO loosened two screws before removing a small oval panel, tucking it beneath his armpit. He armed the nuclear-tipped missile; then replaced the cover. Joining Boyes, he helped the soldier lift off the protective cover from the MGM-52 lance missile. Sergeant Lawson, in the meantime, sighted the missile before entering the parameters for the warhead. Once the men had completed their respective tasks, the six-metre missile was slowly raised until it was in the correct azimuth with the nuclear warhead pointing east in the direction of a part of West Germany that would be the target of its deadly load. It was not the standard nuclear warhead that could be carried by this messenger of death. The standard would be between a ten-kiloton and 100-kiloton nuclear warhead. This one was special, a W70-3. This was seen as more of an anti-personnel weapon rather than an anti-infrastructure destroyer and killer of civilians. The W70-3 was a neutron warhead, with an enhanced radiation capability. Once the missile was ready to launch, two of the gunners sprinted back to the firing point where the weapon launch would be controlled. The remaining two soldiers carried the remote launching unit, unwinding the firing cable behind them as they went.

The officer in command got the nod from the two men that their task was complete. "Standby then. Ensure safe."

"Ready here, sir," confirmed the corporal at the control box. "On safe."

"Minus one minute," added the sergeant next to him.

The officer crouched down next to them. "Arm."

"Minus three-zero," the sergeant, listening to the comms, informed him. He then flipped the cover that allowed him to arm the weapon.

"Minus thirty," confirmed the captain in command. "Standby, standby."

The sergeant flipped the red cover up, exposing the firing switch. "Minus two-zero."

"Minus twenty," added the captain.

The sergeant's gloved finger hovered over the switch as he counted down. "Ten, nine, eight, seven, six, five, four, three, two, one, zero."

"Fire!" ordered the captain, and the switch was depressed.

One hundred metres away, two jets of black gas shot out from vents halfway up the missile, quickly followed by the white-hot flame discharged from the rocket motor, engulfing the launch platform in a thick black cloud, punctuated by the hot white and yellow flame as the burning liquid propellant thrust downwards, forcing the projectile to leave the launcher. In less than a second, the missile left the rail and climbed at a sixty-degree angle higher and higher, leaving a black trail behind it, marking its progress as it flew towards its prey. The sound of the launch was like the din of a heavy airliner blasting off from a runway, slowly diminishing until it merely sounded like an aircraft flying overhead at high altitude. Eventually, there was just a faint glow from its tail as it rapidly disappeared from view; ultimately only the swirl of a contrail evidence of its journey. A further 700 metres to their north, a second lance missile streaked across the sky as it too flew towards a very different target. Elsewhere, an American unit fired two lance missiles carrying the same deadly warhead. The last pair to blast off were launched by a West German missile unit.

Chapter 25

1803, 10 July 1984. 12th Mechanised Division, 1st Polish Army.
East of Bremen, West Germany.
The Blue Effect

Colonel Bajeck's view of the landscape in front of him suddenly disappeared, replaced by a blinding white light. He, along with twenty or more tank crews of the Polish tank battalion, was about to experience the effects of flash-blindness. They had just witnessed the detonation of a West German neutron warhead exploding 200 metres in the air above one of their sister tank units, T-72s moving into position ready for an attack the following day.

"I can't see! I can't see!" Shrieked a sergeant close by. Shouts could be heard from other soldiers of Colonel Bajeck's tank battalion. Flash-blindness, an effect of the initial brilliant flash of light produced by the nuclear detonation, is harmful to the human eye. The retina, unable to tolerate the high levels of light focussed by its lens, caused the visual pigments to bleach. Unknown to the panicking tank crewmen, some injuring themselves as they blundered around their environment, the effects would only be temporary, perhaps gaining some level of returning vision within the hour. For some of their comrades, directly beneath the detonation, the suffering was far worse.

Lieutenant Sawicki, sitting cross-legged on the glacis of his T-72 tank directly beneath the blast wave, was flung against the armour of the adjacent tank. His body was incinerated a second later. Any tank crews sat, stood or sleeping outside of their vehicles, suffered a similar fate.

Further afield, Corporal Zawadzki, adjusting a cam-net at the time of the detonation, was not only blinded but his exposed skin experienced third-degree burns, and the flesh on his hands and face smouldered along with his uniform clothing. He felt no pain. There were no nerves alive within his flesh to send signals to his brain of the terrible damage that had been inflicted upon his body. His comrade, sitting next to his T-72 tank, screamed as he dropped the mug of hot soup onto his lap. The sensation of the burning liquid soon unfelt as the nerves of his seared hands and face overloaded his nervous system, blocking out all pain. Many of their fellow soldiers were not so lucky, and screamed in agony, some passing into unconsciousness, such was the level of torture they were experiencing. Even further away from the centre point of the detonation, the tank crews didn't escape as they were bombarded by a lethal dose of neutrons and gamma rays.

1803, 10 July 1984. Motor-Schutz Regiment, 8th Motor-Schutz Division, 5th German Army. Area of Tellingstedt, West Germany. The Blue Effect

The tank crews, fulfilling some of the maintenance requirements to keep their T-72Ms functional for the forthcoming battle they knew would be a tough one, saw and heard the blast of a nuclear warhead as it struck one of their battalions half kilometre away. Although shocked by the power of the blast and the intensity of the light generated, those in and around the tanks that had guessed what had occurred, felt lucky that they had survived.

Immediately beneath the Enhanced Radiation weapon, and out to a radius of 100 metres, houses, buildings, fencing, trees and people were first flattened then engulfed in a conflagration with an intensity that could not be envisaged, only experienced. As per its design, the casing of the neutron bomb was made of chromium and nickel rather than uranium and lead. With the addition of tritium adding to the cocktail, the neutron yield was ten times that of a conventional nuclear bomb. With a greater focus on the transmission of radiation rather than that of blast and thermal radiation, this 'clean kill' weapon increased the gamma and neutron intensity.

The crews congregated, seeking an explanation and orders from their officers and NCOs. They discussed the event they had just witnessed and listened to their fellow soldiers, those who recognised what had just occurred. There was a sense of relief in their survival, but a concern for those that may have not survived. The men within the tanks, or under cover, had felt the blast, but at a distance of half a kilometre, all they had experienced was a jarring of their vehicle or hide. However, unbeknown to them, their bodies had been bombarded with a lethal cocktail of strontium, neutron and gamma radiation.

The neutron radiation transmuted the surrounding area rendering it radioactive, as it would remain so for many years to come. The armour of the crews' combat vehicles, tanks, trenches with overhead cover, and box-body vehicles was no barrier to the high, acute radiation dose the hundreds of East German soldiers' bodies were now absorbing. The ionising radiation went to work immediately, damaging bone marrow and the intestinal lining. Acute radiation sickness would soon follow. Those men that experienced the highest levels of absorbed doses would experience nausea, loss of appetite, vomiting and severe abdominal pain within a matter of hours. This would be indicative of a fatal dose that without major treatment such as a bone marrow transplant meant that death was inevitable.

Corporal Eberhardt, who had been sitting in the fighting compartment of his T-72 at the time of the detonation, had felt the ferocity of the blast, but felt protected, deep inside the thick armour of the main battle tank. But, unknowingly, he had received the full vehemence of the emitted radiation.

As he patted his *Kameraden* on the shoulder, although sad for the other *Kameraden* that would have no doubt been killed, he was overjoyed about his and his friend's own survival. But, inside his head, he had already started to feel twinges of pain. In just over an hour, the pain became more severe. Along with other invisible damage, his bodily functions would shut down and he would be dead in less than two days.

Most of the crews of the tank battalion would be incapacitated within a matter of hours and dead within fourteen days. Ironically, the majority of the T-72 main battle tanks would still be serviceable.

1803, 10 July 1984. 25th Tank Division, 20th Guards Army.
Bad Nenndorf, East Germany.
The Blue Effect

As Lieutenant Colonel Belochkin staggered out of his command tent, his sickly-looking second-in-command handed him a radio handset.

"It's divisional headquarters, sir."

"This is Belochkin. Over."

"Belochkin, we've lost contact with your regimental headquarters. What the hell is going on down there?"

Colonel Belochkin lowered the mouthpiece and retched, dropping to his knees, his legs shaky and his face as white as a sheet.

He heaved; a gush of vomit spattered the ground beneath him. He recovered slightly, wiping the streaks of puke from his mouth and nose with his sleeve.

"We're in a bad way, sir. Need help."

"Who am I talking to?"

"Colonel Belochkin, sir. 2nd Battalion."

"Get a grip, Colonel Belochkin. I need an update. We know you've been hit, but you need to get moving, now. Why can't we raise your regiment? We even had trouble getting through to your battalion for that matter."

The Colonel breathed deeply, still on his knees, bending at the waist as he thought he was going to be sick again. But this time it was at the other end as a foul smell reached his nostrils. Warm, sticky diarrhoea ran down his legs, his stomach groaning and his legs trembling uncontrollably.

"We are not...in a position to move...Comrade General. I don't know...where my regimental commander is. One company alone has twenty men with serious injuries, and many are sick.

There was silence at the other end. Soviet high command had received the warning from NATO representatives. The warning came with a caveat: *Continue to use chemical weapons, and NATO will escalate to a tactical nuclear conflict, the consequences of which will be unknown to all.*

"You must get your battalion ready to fight Colonel. Do you hear me? Colonel?"

The handset fell from the Colonel's hand and he slumped to the ground, pulling his legs up to his chin as the pain lanced through his innards.

1803, 10 July 1984. 62nd Guards Tank Regiment and elements of 20th Guards Army. Northeast of Bad Nenndorf, West Germany. The Blue Effect

Although Colonel Trusov's tanks had been able to stand up to the significant amount of blast and heat from the nuclear explosion detonated close to his regiment, the lethal dose of radiation emitted by the ER weapon just passed through the armour, eroding the crews inside. Whereas a dose of six Gy would be considered lethal, killing half of those exposed to it, the symptoms taking some hours or days to appear, Trusov's men had received between seventy and eighty Gy.

A lethal dose had blanketed his men, out to a radius of half a kilometre.

Trusov clambered out of the turret of his T-80K, nausea causing him to feel faint and unsteady on his feet. He gagged and heaved, bringing up the food he had eaten earlier in the day. He saw other tank crews, wandering around in a state of shock. He went to call out to them, order them back to their vehicles, to be ready if called upon to do battle. All he succeeded in doing was to trigger a new bout of queasiness. His ashen-faced driver, Kokorev, and Barsukov, his gunner, joined him. Both collapsed to the floor.

"What's happened, sir?" Kokorev appealed to him, followed with a bout of retching, finally vomiting the foul-smelling contents of his stomach onto the ground.

"The West has detonated a nuclear bomb. You had better prepare for the worst."

Barsukov moved closer to his regimental commander as the officer dry-heaved but brought up nothing.

"Do you think we've had a bad dose, Comrade Colonel?"

"The worst kind. Make yourselves as comfortable as you can. We're going nowhere. I need to contact HQ."

He climbed back onto his T-80K command tank, not realising that the armour would be exposing him to radiation for at least another forty-eight hours. After another short bout of retching, bringing up only bile, he dropped into the turret and picked up the handset of the radio. Before he could transmit, still holding the mouthpiece, he pressed both hands to his temples as a sudden thumping migraine racked his skull. He released his head and stared at the handset. He could see clumps of his hair clutched there as well.

Trusov dropped the handset, slumped in his seat and ran his fingers through his hair only to find more tufts sticking to his sweaty hands. He rested his still pounding head against the contaminated armour, closed his eyes and wept.

Chapter 26

1930, 10 July 1984. Combat Team Bravo, 14/20th King's Hussars,
22nd Armoured Brigade, 1st Armoured Division.
East of Espelkamp, West Germany.
The Blue Effect +1.5 hours

Major Lewis, commander of B-Squadron, 14/20th King's Hussars,
took the mug of hot, sweet tea passed to him by one of the troopers
from Bravo-Troop. A second mug was handed to Lieutenant Alex
Wesley-Jones, the troop commander.

"Thank you, Corporal Patterson." Alex thanked his gunner.

"Sir."

"How are your repairs going, Alex?" asked Major Lewis.

Alex looked out of the open flap of the penthouse tent attached
to the back of the OC's Land Rover. He could hear the revving
engine of a FV434 as it manoeuvred closer to the rear of his own
tank. Suspended from the crane boom of the 434 was a power pack,
badly needed to replace the faulty one that was now on the ground
alongside the tracks of the tank. Whilst the remnants of the 14/20th
had been in their recovery area, the Royal Electrical and Mechanical
Engineers Light Aid Detachment, had been kept busy, repairing,
and in some cases, replacing key elements of the Chieftain tank's
systems. This was the second power pack for Alex's tank, the initial
replacement having acquired a fault as they moved to this final locale.
Although many of the reliability problems of the Chieftains had been
resolved over the years, they still proved to be troublesome. Here,
the regiment was conducting its final preparations so they would
be ready to carry out the next stage of higher command's plan to
hold off the advancing enemy. The Battle Group had lain up in
a small forest about four kilometres east of Espelkamp, roughly
twenty kilometres northwest of Minden.

"Now I've got a new power pack, we should be pretty much

there, sir. Two-Two-Charlie is fully functional. How are the rest of the squadron, and the regiment for that matter?"

"Well, Alex, A and C Squadron were down to nine tanks between them, and D squadron had six. But with replacements from the mainland, and consolidating units, all three squadrons now have three troops each."

"And us, sir?"

"You're the lucky one, along with Two-One. You both have a full troop, but Two-Three and Two-Four only have two tanks each. But we are the strongest squadron in the regiment, although we have lost the second-in-command's tank. Which brings me on to another subject." The major placed his now empty mug on a small table in the corner next to the rear tailgate of the vehicle. He turned in his collapsible seat and looked at Alex. The young officer from Cardiff raised his eyebrows slightly, curious as to the look of concentration on his Officer Commanding's face.

"I am promoting you to Captain, Alex. It has been approved by Colonel Clark."

"But, sir—"

"No buts. You are the most…I was about to say most experienced officer. That really applies to us all now," he said with a laugh. "But you have been well and truly in the thick of it, and you and your men have performed extremely well."

"Thank you, sir."

"Although in rank, you will be my new second-in-command, I need you to remain with your troop. But, should anything happen to me…you will take command. Understood?"

"Understood, sir."

The major picked up a wax pencil from the small table and pointed at the map suspended from the side of the tent. "We must be ready to move as soon as the Soviets cross the Weser. They will be allowed to advance at least eight to ten kilometres before the counter-attack commences."

"Can't we just hold them, sir, stop them from crossing? Our regiment is recovering, and so must some of the other units."

"Yes, we could hold them for a little while longer, but there is another full Soviet army coming in behind Three-Shock." The major sighed. "Not forgetting the Soviet 5th Guards Tank Army, one of many units under the command of the Belorussian Military District that has arrived in theatre. Do they continue towards CENTAG or turn towards us? We don't yet know. And, to make matters worse, the Carpathian and Baltic Military Districts will also be lining up to hit the front line from Hamburg down to Austria. Once 20th Guards Army puts its full weight against our defences along the river, we'll never hold them. So, we have to lull them into a false sense of security, get them to cross, isolate those forces, and cripple them as best we can, followed up by a counter-attack across the river. I know we have only Territorial troops reinforcing us, but their numbers are growing daily. We also have to strike while they're still recovering from those tactical nuke strikes."

"When do we pull the regiment together, sir? We're pretty widely dispersed."

"We have no choice, Alex. The risk of a counter-nuclear strike is still very real."

They were interrupted by the sound of vehicular movement outside. A Foden, a low-mobility tanker, carrying in the region of 12,000 litres of fuel, made its way to a refuelling point where the tanks of the squadron could top-up. It was closely followed by a tarpaulin-covered, six-wheeled Stalwart, bringing in more supplies of ammunition, preparing the tank regiment to go back into battle. The war for 22nd Armoured Brigade and the rest of 1st Armoured Division was far from over.

They both faced the map again.

"Once the 12th Brigade come at the neck of the bulge from the north and the Americans from the south, our Battle Group, followed by the RGJ and 2RTR, will be the first to cross. Your troop will be the first over the river."

"Can't wait, sir." The young, now captain laughed.

"Our squadron has the task of punching as far into the enemy's rear area as possible. Get deep into their lines; disrupt any attempts at stopping the crossings. The rest of the Regiment will be close behind us, consolidating our position."

"Is our crossing point still the same, sir?"

"Yes, here," the major responded tapping the map. "Just south of the Heisterholz. But that depends on the ground we've secured and what's available should the Soviets leave any of their crossing points intact. Our pre-emptive air and artillery strike will avoid those targets, other than troops on the eastern bank."

"12th Armoured, sir?"

"Just south of Todtenhausen. But, like us, they will take any opportunity to use any abandoned Soviet bridging points."

"It's going to be a tough one, sir."

"As if it hasn't been tough already, Alex." The OC started to rise up from his seat. Alex followed suit. "There will be a final briefing tomorrow. In the meantime, make sure your men are ready and your tanks are topped and rearmed. And for God's sake, keep your troop well camouflaged. The forest provides us with some cover, but the Soviet air force and the military will be looking for us, and these forests will be likely hiding places."

"Understood, sir."

The OC shook his hand. "Congratulations, Alex."

"Thank you, sir."

They both left the tent and walked over to Alex's tank. The engine had been lowered into its compartment, and REME were going over the final connections, linking the power pack to the components that would get the tank mobile again.

"Ah, Corporal Patterson." Patsy drew himself up to attention, arms by his sides. "Thank you for the tea."

"Sir."

"Now, I think Captain Wesley-Jones would like a word with you all."

He turned to Alex. "Let me know the minute you have any equipment failures. We need to know what we've got available at all times."

"Understood, sir."

With that, Major Lewis left.

"Did he say captain, sir?"

"Yes, he did, Corporal Patterson. Now, gather the troop together. I want to talk to them."

With a grin across his face, Patsy sped off, calling for the tank crews to form up. The REME LAD had finished for now, so the troop assembled next to Two-Alpha. The tank although now fully functional, at least once they'd done a road test with the new power pack, was still wearing its battle scars. Two-Charlie was in a similar state. Two-Bravo, on the other hand, was practically brand new, straight out of a workshop back in the United Kingdom. The new tank's crew, apart from Trooper Lowe who was still the driver, and Trooper Wilson, the loader, were new, survivors from other elements of the regiment. Their tank had been destroyed, but they themselves had survived. Sergeant Andrews, platoon sergeant, with a head injury and a hand that had been badly crushed, was now back in the UK. Although still recovering from his injuries, he was still capable of training new replacements, allowing the healthy instructors to be assigned to units at the front. However, Lance Corporal Owen, the gunner, would not be fighting any more wars. He had been killed during the first artillery bombardment experienced by the Regiment in Gronau. The two new members of the troop had also lost their tank, loader and senior NCO, to a Soviet T-80.

The crews shuffled into position, finding somewhere to sit, either on the stump of a felled tree, a camping chair or pallet of supplies not yet broken down.

Alex looked at the expectant faces of his men. Some showed weariness and a little fear; some determination; others he couldn't read. To a man, they were looking to him to lead them through the horrors that were going on around them, keep them safe and get them home to their families.

Alex's crew were chatting, grins plastered across their faces, occasionally flicking their eyes in his direction. No doubt Corporal Patterson had filled the rest of the crew, Lance Corporal Mark Ellis, his loader, and the driver, Trooper 'Mackey' Mackinson, in on their troop commander's promotion. He and his crew had bonded well during their recent battles, and the Chieftain Mark 5/3C had truly become their home.

Captain Wesley-Jones looked across at Acting-Sergeant Simpson. All were sipping mugs of tea that had miraculously arrived from somewhere. There was no doubt: the Boiling Vessel, BV, had a positive impact on the tank crews' morale. This could possibly be their last hot drink for some time.

Alex shuffled his backside onto one of the track guard stowage bins, the foliage used for camouflage crackling beneath his weight, his booted feet dangling over the edge.

To his right was his crew. Sitting along the track guard of the tank opposite was Acting-Sergeant Simpson, tank commander of call sign Two-Bravo and the troop's second-in-command; sitting alongside him his crew: Lance Corporal Wilson, newly promoted, his gunner, Trooper Wallis, new to the squadron, his loader, and Trooper Lowe, his driver. To his left was the newly promoted Corporal Moore, commander of call sign Two-Charlie, with his gunner Trooper Gregory, another replacement, loader Trooper Robinson and driver, Trooper Carter. These twelve men made up the crews for Bravo-

Troop, B-Squadron of the 14th/20th King's Hussars Regiment.

Before the captain could speak, Acting-Sergeant Simpson piped up. "On behalf of the troop, sir, we just want to congratulate you on your promotion."

Alex blushed slightly, not yet used to his raised profile within the squadron. "And you, Sarn't Simpson," he responded. "We have finally received our orders, and our troop has a key role to play."

He looked over their faces, not sure what he was seeing. Was it disappointment at having to fight again, or were they glad they would have an opportunity to hit back at the enemy?

He dropped down off the tank and unrolled a map that had been tucked under his arm. "Corporal Moore, grab that board we've been using as a table and bring it over."

"Sir."

"Wallis, Lowe, the small table next to the penthouse, bring it over," ordered Moore.

The table was cleared, upended, and wedged up against the side of the Chieftain tank, resting at an angle where Alex could pin the map.

"Right, gather round before we lose the last of our light, and I'll take you through what's in store for us."

The troop either dropped down from their tanks or shuffled in closer. It was very different from an exercise where there was feigned interest, just looking forward to ENDEX when they could get home for a shit, shave and shower, and sex if they were on talking terms with their wife or girlfriend, and then a drink with their buddies. But now, it was important that they listened and understood what was being asked of them. Otherwise, the consequences could be far-reaching.

"The time has come for us to hit back."

"About time we give em some...make them pay for Owen," came back some one of the comments.

The troop commander pinned up a BAOR road map, marked with sweeping red lines.

"We're here, near Espelkamp, along with the rest of our Brigade. 12th Brigade is here to the north, west of Warmsen, and 7th Brigade here, Lubecke. Our American cousins have a brigade moving in southwest of Minden. On top of that, we have a Bundeswehr Brigade in reserve. The enemy, our friends from 3rd Shock Army, in particular 12th Guards Tank Division, are already at the River Weser, north of Minden. Intelligence tells us that the 12th Guards will try and force a crossing either between Minden and Petershagen or Petershagen and Stolzenau. Or both."

"Aren't 3-Shock feeling the pinch a bit now, sir?" asked Acting-Sergeant Simpson.

"They probably are, but the 12th and 47th Guards Tank Division will be using their second-echelon regiments, and they are pretty powerful. But, beyond them, there is a second army, 20th Guards, who haven't been committed yet."

"Are they close, sir?" Corporal Moore asked.

"Their headquarters have been plotted in the area of Bad Nenndorf, so I would imagine at least two of their divisions will be pushing forward. Our guess is that the 12th cross the river, push as deep as they can, and a division from the 20th exploit it."

"Shit," one of the troopers exclaimed.

"But this is where we come in, Gregory. We're going to be the ones that stop them. You have all listened to rumour control and heard—"

"And felt, sir," added Sergeant Simpson.

"...and felt the nuclear strikes. The Polish and East German armies have been hit in the north with 20th Guards in our sector. The Americans have also struck back at the Soviet reserves in their area."

"Is that why we're so widely dispersed?" asked Sergeant Simpson.

"Yes it is. But we did inform the Soviet Politburo of the strike and the reasons behind it, as I briefed you earlier. It is hoped that they will see sense. As to the bigger picture for us, 4th Armoured Division, now recovered, rearmed and reinforced, will hit the enemy from the south, pushing up through and around Rehren, striking for Bad Nenndorf."

"That'll give their HQ a headache, sir, no doubt about that," someone piped up.

"Button it," ordered Sergeant Simpson. "We'll know sod all if you lot keep interrupting the captain."

There was a red face in the group, but lots of smiles from the rest.

"Thank you, Sarn't, you saved me the trouble. With 4-Div hitting them hard from the south, Special Forces sabotaging the enemy, and airborne troops acting as a blocking force from Bad Nenndorf to Wunstorf, here," he pointed at the map. "The enemy will be unable for a short period of time to move either east or west easily."

He tapped the map around Minden. "Now, to our role. We're

going to allow the enemy to cross the Weser."

There were lots of passing looks amongst the men. A mixture of concern and puzzlement.

"It's in our best interests. With some resistance, we allow the enemy to form a bridgehead, and knowing their desire to get as deep into our rear area as possible, let a bulge form, drawing their forces from the river. Then we strike. 12th Brigade will come in from the north and a US Brigade from the south."

"Thank God for the Spams," someone muttered.

"7th Armoured will blunt the attack from the west. Our Regiment will be the first to exploit any weakness and push through to the river. Our troop will be first across the bridge."

"Christ, sir," uttered Acting-Sergeant Simpson. "Into the mouth of the lion."

Alex laughed. "A bit like that, Sarn't Simpson. But, there will be some prepping before that. There will be arty strikes on the eastern bank, followed by air strikes. The west bank of the Weser will also receive some attention. Then arty will drop FASCAM mines behind the enemy, preventing them from pulling back to the river."

"We'll need to pass through those mines, sir," added Corporal Patterson.

"They will be laid in such a way that there will be a passage for us to pass through. We'll have some engineers leading the way."

"It's going to be mayhem out there, sir. So many units in such a small area. It'll be Christmas for the Sov air force," suggested Corporal Moore.

"It will, but most of NORTHAG's air assets will be in support."

"Grunts, sir?"

"Yes, Sarn't. We'll have infantry with us again."

"Good, they put up quite a fight at Gronau."

"They did that. They've received some replacements as well."

"Kick-off time the same, sir?"

"Yes. So, I want everyone to go over his vehicle one more time. Mackinson, you need to test the new engine on Two-Alpha."

"Sir."

"I want tank commanders and Corporal Patterson to remain behind so we can go through the movements for tonight and tomorrow."

This time when the captain examined their faces, he was sure he saw an element of excitement. His men were ready. He just hoped the rest were.

Lieutenant Baty was crouched on top of the front deck of his Scorpion; Sergeant Gough sat on the edge of the tank. They were going over the route the troop would need to take only hours from now. A sheet of canvas had been pinned down along the side of the small reconnaissance tank, then pegged to the ground below, acting as a tent to cover the two sleeping crewmen, Thomas, his driver, and Lance Corporal Alan Reid, his gunner. He'd managed to catch a couple of hours himself, but his two crewmen had been working like Trojans getting their vehicle fit for battle. Maintenance, refuelling, rearming – it was never-ending. Once finished, and only then, did they manage to get some food down them and a hot drink, but their eyes were closing even as the last dry Tac biscuit made its way down. They had even turned down the offer of some fruit cake, generously offered by a local who had stumbled into the British camp, past the sentries unseen, suddenly to appear alongside the lieutenant's tank with his offering. After thanking him graciously and ordering Thomas to guide the civilian back out of the camp, Baty proceeded to track down the sentries on duty and gave them the bollocking of their lives.

"It's our bloody minefields that worry me, sir." Gough pointed at the 1:50,000 map, barely legible under the pale glow of the last fading light. "They've marked where the two routes through the mines will be, but all it takes is a couple of those bloody sub munitions to go astray and we're fucked. The planks can't map read to save their lives."

"That's why we've got some engineers with us. They will be call sign Two-One-Golf."

"Is that their Spartan at the entrance to the Laager?"

"Yes, we'll go and have a chat with them shortly."

"Scrounge a brew, eh, sir? My driver makes shit tea."

They both chuckled.

"This is the route I think is best." The lieutenant got back on track. "We're forming up north of Mindenerwald. Then its east along the 770, turning north as we get to the outskirts of Petershagen. Then we go where we're advised."

"I concur with that, sir. When will we know our final objective?"

"Last minute, I would imagine. If air recce can give us a steer, that would be good. Otherwise, they will be depending on us to

211

tell them if any of the Soviet bridges are still intact."

"So, we either find a ready-made crossing point, or move to where we will be preparing our own."

"That about sums it up."

"It could be a complete fuck-up, sir."

"Why so negative, Sergeant?"

"Look, sir. Going up against the river, finding a ready-made bridge, calling the combat team forward to secure it. It is still Bravo with the grunts from RGJ, isn't it?"

"Yes."

"That's all fine. But if that is a no-go and we head north or south to link up with our own engineers throwing a bridge across, we will probably be coming up against retreating Soviets and then into the guns of our own tanks. You know what trigger-happy bastards 12th Brigade are."

"It's a dilemma, that's for certain. They know they have to look out for us."

"That's even worse, sir." The sergeant laughed. "They'll be gunning for us."

"We'll be fine. Let's go and scrounge a brew from our engineer friends."

1930, 10 July 1984. Two-Section, Three-Company, 1st Battalion, Royal Green Jackets. Espelkamp, West Germany.
The Blue Effect +1.5 hours

"Aren't those sausages ready yet, Finch?" complained Corporal Carter to Rifleman Michael Finch who was hovering over a hexe-burner, warming up a tin of compo sausages. Next to him, Conroy was warming soup over a home-made stove: two large stones with burning diesel mixed in with churned-up soil, and a waterproof propped up with a stick at an angle over the top to hide the flicker of the flames.

"Two ticks, Corp, this bloody hexe's gone out."

"Well, stick another one on then, you prat," demanded Alan Berry.

"You focus on the tea. Leave me to do my bit."

"Do you two buggers ever stop fighting?" Chided Lance Corporal William Graham, the section second-in-command.

"Hey, Conroy, stick a bit of Marmite in that soup and tart it up, will you?"

"Yes, Corporal," replied one of the new recruits to the section.

The section had three new faces in total. Conroy, Jesson and Kent had been flown over from the UK by Hercules along with other reinforcements, and then driven in convoy to the front. Up until two days ago, they were part of 5th Battalion (V) Royal Green Jackets, a battalion that had been assigned a Home Defence role. But, such was the need for reinforcements; some of the Home Defence battalions were being stripped of soldiers to reinforce the regular infantry units in 1 Br Corps. Conroy and Jesson had come from A-Company, whose recruitment patch was High Wycombe, whereas Kent was from E-Company based in Milton Keynes.

The section had lost four men in total. The gun-group of three men had been wiped out entirely. The youngest member of the unit, Ashley, had his body peppered with shrapnel from one of the Soviet grenades launched from a Plamya, an AGS-17 grenade launcher, by Soviet motor rifle troops. Many others on the front line with Corporal Carter's section had also died: the forward observers spotting for the mortar section and a Milan-FP team. A German unit sent to reinforce them had also suffered horrendous casualties, many of them as a consequence of a chemical strike. Carter didn't think he would ever be able to shake off the look of the German officer's face as the chemical agent did its stuff. The blisters forming on the man's face, thrashing his body from side to side, arms flailing as he tried to breathe, but his lungs continued to fill up with his own fluids, eventually killing him. Now, he had three new soldiers to look after. He'd decided to put Finch and Berry on the GPMG, under the command of Graham, and he would have the three new ones, along with Price, as the rifle-group.

"Sausages are ready."

"About bloody time," moaned Finch.

"Do you want yours, tosser?" responded Berry.

"Pack it in, both of you," ordered Carter. "Right, lads, gather round while we eat. Kent, get out of your maggot and get over here."

"Corporal."

Two-Section gathered around their section commander, and a mess tin of hot, sweet tea was passed around while Finch forked sausages out of the two tins, slapping one in each mess tin that was wavering in front of him. They were using their mugs for soup, which was doled out by Graham, the section second-in-command.

After the tea did its first round, and the soup had been tasted, complained about and had burnt a few tongues, Graham talked to his men.

"You new boys, when we go into action tomorrow, you need to keep it tight. Listen for orders and, for God's sake, keep your safeties on until I give the word."

"Yeah, I don't want a bullet up my arse," moaned Finch through a mouthful of soup and sausage.

"Take your lead from Price and, if need be, I might assign one of you to support the Gympy team. Got it?"

They all responded positively, in awe of their section commander who was not only a regular but had seen some real action.

"We'll be with the armour again."

"At least we'll have some muscle," suggested Graham.

"And it's with Bravo-Troop."

"Good, that Lieutenant Wesley-Jones is alright for a Rupert," added Finch.

"He lost a tank though, didn't he?" Elaborated Price.

"If it had been one of the other Ruperts, he'd have probably lost all three," grumbled Berry.

"Will we definitely get some real fighting in then?" blurted Jesson.

Finch and Berry looked at each other and smirked.

"It's likely, but we won't know that until it all kicks off. But don't go wishing for it," advised Carter.

"Final briefing, Corporal Carter?" interrupted Lieutenant Chandler, their platoon commander, who had appeared out of nowhere.

The section scrambled to get up.

"As you were," ordered Chandler as he crouched down next to them. Platoon Sergeant Bob Thomas was next to him.

"Brew, sir?" Asked Corporal Graham. "I've just warmed up another full mess tin."

"Why not."

"You too, Sarge?"

"Sure." The sergeant handed over his and the platoon commander's mugs. Once filled they were handed back.

"Your section up to speed then, Corporal Carter?"

"Yes, sir. We've stowed the extra ammo and a couple of extra missiles for the Milan section."

"Rations?"

"Yes, Sarge. The QM issued us with three days worth. Is that how long the op will last for, sir?"

"If successful, it should be less than that."

"And if it goes to rat shit, sir?" Asked Graham.

"Then I'll hold you personally responsible," growled Thomas.

"The plan looks good. We're rested and rearmed, our forces are in position, and the enemy have stretched their axis of attack. When they cross the Weser in the morning, we'll make them pay for that overconfidence."

"Sounds good to me, sir," agreed Carter.

The lieutenant and sergeant stood up.

"We'll have a five-minute briefing at 0200, just before we move off, so make sure your section is ready."

"Sir," responded Carter.

The sergeant looked at his watch. "You'll need to provide two men on stag, between 2100 and 2200."

"Jesson and Conroy, Sarge."

The lieutenant and sergeant smiled at each other, both thinking the same: the new guys were at the bottom of the pecking order.

"Make sure they're not late and know the password."

"Sarge."

"Let's go and check on One-Section then, sir."

1930, 10 July 1984. Combat Team Delta, Royal Hussars, 7th Armoured Brigade, 1st Armoured Division. Area of Lubecke, West Germany. The Blue Effect +1.5 hours

The Scammell Commander tank transporters finally turned up, and not a moment too soon. The drivers manoeuvred the Scammells into position, and the crews of D-Squadron quickly got to work offloading the badly needed tanks. Out of a squadron of fourteen tanks, five from Delta-Squadron had survived the battles around the Rossing and later west of Pattensen: two from the squadron HQ, one damaged tank that had crossed the river early on in the battle, while three others had escaped, one being destroyed before the unit was able to make it to safety.

These replacements were badly needed. The regiment as a whole had lost over forty per cent of its strength, far more than high command had hoped. Along with fresh crews, D-Squadron was to receive nine of the replacement sixty-ton main battle tanks. This would take their total squadron numbers up to thirteen, nearly at full strength. The rest of the regiment had received twelve tanks to allocate to the remaining three squadrons. A-Squadron and

B-Squadron now had a force of ten each, three troops of three and one for the squadron HQ. C-Squadron also had thirteen and, like D-Squadron, would field four troops of three and one for HQ. Some of the tanks brought across had been from repair shops in the UK, training tanks from regimental depots, and some direct from the Royal Ordnance factories. But these were the last. If lost, it would be a long time before there were anymore more replacements.

Once the Challengers were offloaded from the semi-trailers, the Scammells started on their 470-kilometre journey back to the coast. With two drivers, the vehicles would move almost non-stop, taking seriously damaged armoured vehicles to repair shops well to the rear. And, if any could be repaired, they could eventually find themselves back at the front. But then it would probably be too late. The new tanks were very much needed, as the Royal Hussars Battle Group was yet again to consist of all tanks, not being diluted with mechanised infantry. High manoeuvrability would be key if they were to hit an unsuspecting enemy hard.

Once the offloading of the new tanks was complete, Lieutenant Barrett gathered his men around his troop tank. "Well, first of all, welcome to the new members of our troop. Have the crews been assigned, Sarn't Glover?"

The troop sergeant had been injured during their last fight at Ditterke, west of Pattensen, after they had escaped a trap forming in between the enemy crossing the Leine and airborne troops to their rear. Although his shoulder was still painful and there was a slight limp when he walked, he had insisted on remaining with the unit. They were so short of experienced tank crews, it was difficult for higher command not to approve it. "Yes, sir. Your crew will remain as is, with Corporal Farre as your gunner, Lance Corporal Coleman loader, and Trooper Field as your driver."

Barrett nodded, pleased that his crew had survived the battle with him.

"I will keep Four-Bravo with Lance Corporal Tompkins and Trooper Woodford, but I've transferred Lance Corporal Frith to Four-Charlie and taken one of the new boys, Trooper Lockhart. Corporal Mason not only has a new tank but needs to replace Trooper Mann and Trooper Deacon, who has been promoted and transferred to C-Squadron."

"They're welcome to him, Sarge," broke in Corporal Mason, jokingly.

"Deacon a Lance Corporal? God help us, Sarge," added Lance Corporal Frith.

"Belt up, you two, or I'll have you both transferred to the cookhouse."

"Sarge."

"Sarn't."

"Sorry about that, sir. We're obviously not working them hard enough."

"We could always make good on that, Sergeant Glover," responded Lieutenant Barrett, smiling.

"If I can be allowed to finish. So, I've got Trooper Bellamy as my new loader."

"Thank you, Sarn't Glover. Welcome to the troop, you two," the lieutenant said, referring to Lockhart and Bellamy. "We know we've got a tough fight ahead. I won't run through the plans again. We all know our jobs. I suggest you get as much rest a possible. Just make sure everything is up to scratch. You will need to have a thorough check of Four-Charlie, Corporal Mason."

"Looks fine, sir, but I'll run through some checks."

"I'll give him a hand," volunteered Farre.

"Cheers, mate."

"Questions?"

"Trooper Mann, sir. Any news?" Woodford asked after their friend who was hit when the enemy near Ditterke bounced them, the same time as the sergeant received his injuries.

"Nothing new, Woodford. But the OC has told me that he's well on his way back to the coast. He'll soon be on a boat for home, I'm sure." He looked around at his men. They looked tired, but in good spirits. "Nothing? Right. We move out at 0200. Dismissed."

Chapter 27

1930, 10 July 1984. 4th Armoured Division.
Area of Kalletal, West Germany.
The Blue Effect +1.5 hours

The REME LAD section lowered the replacement power pack into the main battle tank's engine compartment. A few hours' work would see the engine connected and the tank belonging to the commander of C-Squadron, 3rd Royal Tank Regiment, 3RTR, ready for combat again. Although they had been badly mauled during their role as part of 1 British Corps' covering force, delaying the Soviet advance until the 1st and 3rd Armoured Divisions were in position to take the brunt of the attack, the regiment, along with the rest of the 4th Armoured Division, were preparing to go into the fray yet again.

The strongest of the brigades in the division, 33rd Armoured, with the Royal Scots Dragoon Guards Tank Regiment, the 1st Battalion Royal Highland Fusiliers and the 1st Battalion the Black Watch, were preparing for the planned counter attack. They had also been allocated a new battalion, the 1st Battalion, the 52nd Lowland Volunteers, a Territorial Army battalion fresh from Britain. The 11th and 20th Brigades had suffered the most in their role as a covering force, having to hold at bay two of the Group of Soviet Forces Germany, most powerful divisions: the 10th Guards Tank Division and the 7th.

They too had been reinforced. 20th Brigade had been allocated the 5th Battalion, the Queen's Regiment along with the 3rd Battalion, the Royal Regiment of Fusiliers. The 1st Battalion, 51st Highland Volunteers, had reinforced 11th Armoured Brigade. The 11th Brigade, consisting of 3RTR, the 2nd Battalion RGJ and the 1st Battalion RRF, was also preparing to go into battle again. 1RRF, reinforced with troops from Britain, now stood at about seventy per cent strength; but still down to less than 400 men. 3RTR and

2RGJ were in a slightly better position. 3RTR had received nine replacement Chieftains. The regiment's strength now consisting of four squadrons with A and B Squadrons fielding ten main battle tanks each, and C and D Squadrons with eleven each. Including all headquarters Chieftains that gave the unit forty-two tanks. 2RGJ, also reinforced, could now put 480 men into the fight. They had received their initial orders. 33rd Armoured Brigade would lead the attack in the south, followed closely by 11th Armoured, ready to exploit any breakthrough. The RRF and Highland Volunteers would follow on, ready to deploy and hold ground should the forward brigades be pushed back and have to withdraw. It was now a case of just standing by, waiting for the Soviet army to cross the Weser to the north, and attempt to break through and race for the Rhine. Then, it would be time to counter-attack from the south.

1930, 10 July 1984. 2nd Battalion, Royal Green Jackets, 11th Armoured
Brigade, 4th Armoured Division. Area of Almena, West Germany.
The Blue Effect +1.5 hours

Major Andy Phillips, the commander of A Company, the 2nd Battalion, the Royal Green Jackets, chatted to his Company Sergeant Major, CSM Tobi Saunders. The CSM wore a patch over his left eye, the consequence of hot splinters from a grenade burning the surrounding area of his eye socket. He was a lucky man: partially sheltered by a building, squinting to peer into the twilight, his eye had been missed. But now he had to protect the lacerations from infection, and it had earned him the nickname of Bluebeard, behind his back, naturally. Even the OC had found it difficult to stifle a smile when he overheard the soldiers, thinking no one was within earshot, refer to his new nickname.

"Let's get the show on the road, CSM."

Although a senior non-commissioned officer, a SNCO, the CSM carried a tremendous amount of authority within the organisation of the Company unit. To the soldiers within the unit, he was next to God, the OC being the top man. Even the young lieutenants deferred to him on a regular basis. Having served sixteen years with the Battalion, it was expected that he would assume the mantle of Regimental Sergeant Major, RSM, when the current incumbent retired in a year's time. If the CSM was God, the RSM was a deity in his own right.

"Let's be having you," the CSM bellowed, bringing the gathering to order.

The three-metre by three-metre tent, erected alongside the OCs command 432, was tight for space, and warm. But the flaps had to remain secure for fear of light escaping and flagging to any Soviet recce planes overhead that 2RGJ were in the vicinity. The soldiers moved themselves until they formed a semi-circle around a board that had been hung from the frame of the tent. On it was a map of the area of Lauenau, east of the A2 Autobahn, and two photographs. In the semi-circle was Lieutenant Dean Russell, commander of One-Platoon. It was far from his original unit. With the death of both Lieutenant Ward and Sergeant Holland at the outset of the war, killed by the Soviet initial artillery and missile barrage, Three-Platoon had not only been left leaderless but had also suffered other casualties, as had One-Platoon. So the OC had amalgamated the two platoons into one, commanded by Dean. The young lieutenant, only fifteen months out of the RMA Sandhurst officer academy, had then found himself embroiled in a second battle around Coppenbrugge, where he and his men had excelled, earning themselves a reputation throughout the battalion. Standing next to him was Colour Sergeant Rose, his platoon sergeant and second-in-command. Also in the group was Lieutenant Dunmore, commander of Two-Platoon, and his platoon sergeant, Robert Macintyre. In addition, there was Captain Lucas Banks, responsible for the Battalion's Anti-Tank Platoon, Corporal Bernard 'Bernie' Cooke, commander of the mobile anti-tank section, and Corporal Len Ward, commander of a second anti-tank section, this one not mobile. On the far left, seconded specifically for this operation, was Sergeant Dave Kirby who would command the three Scimitars from the Recce-Platoon, allocated to A-Company and, finally, Corporal Burford who would command the mobile mortar teams. It would have been a full house except they were missing a platoon. Three-Platoon was being reformed, with reserves brought in from the UK, using experienced soldiers to supplement the recruits. The OC, in agreement with the commanding officer, had decided to leave the platoon out of the initial phase of the forthcoming action. They would reinforce A-Company twenty-four hours after the main bulk of the unit were in position.

Captain Brian Haworth, the Adjutant, started the brief. "You all know that the big show is to kick off tomorrow, so this is the final briefing. Just to reiterate, I will go over the big picture, before the OC goes over your individual missions."

He ran his pointer along the A2 that ran northwest from Rinteln to Bad Nenndorf, in between the 300-metre-high Buckeberge to the west, and the Suntel and the Deister to the east. "This is the route 33rd Armoured Brigade will take. Their primary objective is Bad Nenndorf. Along the route, Special Forces and volunteers from 24th Airborne Brigade, will carry out sabotage missions and act as blocking forces. We have a Bundeswehr territorial battalion, attached to the Division that will dig in around Hessisch Oldendorf to protect the Brigade's right flank. For the left flank, the 4th Parachute Battalion has been attached to 4 Div and will secure Rinteln and Buchholz. The Brigade, once they make their way across the Weser, using two crossing points west and east of Rinteln, will charge up the A2 at speed. The Royal Highland Fusiliers will hold Apelern and Lauenau while the 1st Battalion Black Watch secure Bad Nenndorf. As for the Royal Scots, what they do will be very dependent on the enemy reaction and the success of the attack."

"They will have the option of pushing through to Wunstorf, attacking the Soviet units withdrawing from the area of Petershagen, or even head for Hanover, coming up against 20th Guards Army forces," added the OC.

The adjutant continued. "Now, closer to our sector of interest. 11th Brigade will cross here." He pointed to two crossing points, one in between Hameln and Fischbeck, the second near Tundern. "Once across, 1st Battalion Royal Regiment Fusiliers (1RRF) will pass through Fischbeck, then swing east, skirting the high ground, passing through Hofingen and Potzen, travelling south-east until they reach the 217 before going north towards Bad Munder. The 3rd Royal Tank Regiment (3RTR) will head at all speed for Springe. Sir?" The Adjutant looked at the OC who took over the briefing.

"Our battalion's role, although piecemeal, is critical to the success of the mission. B-Company will seize and hold Coppenbrugge, C-Company, with Support-Company and the Battalion HQ, will hold the crossroads at Hachmuhlen, while we have been given Bisperode. We can't work on the assumption that the Soviets will just roll over and die," he admitted with a smile. "We first have to push through; then be prepared for any counter-attack. Our Brigade has been reinforced by the 4th (V) Battalion, The Royal Irish Rangers. They will be our reserve. Depending on the success of the initial attacks, 20th Armoured Brigade will be committed along whichever axis is proving to be the most productive, the idea being to cut deep into the enemy forces and disrupt their formations. If we can confuse them enough, we may be able to build on that attack. Another Brigade is being formed as we speak, using Territorial units from the UK. The 8th Queen's Fusiliers, 5th Battalion, The Royal Anglian Regiment, from 49th Brigade, who now have the 6th Battalion as a replacement. 4th Battalion, The Queen's Lancashire Regiment and the 3rd (V) Battalion, The Royal Regiment of Wales." He paused for a moment.

"A bit of a mouthful, I know," he smiled. "They will help shore up 3 Div, which will allow them to release 4th Armoured Brigade should an opportunity to press further attacks arise. The 5th Airborne Brigade is also on standby. The situation is not as dire as it was yesterday."

He moved aside slightly so he wasn't obscuring the two photographs pinned on the board.

"I managed to acquire these from the PI boys, taken by a flight of our Harriers yesterday. You can spend some time familiarising yourself with them later, but for now come in as close as you can."

The soldiers shuffled as close they could, some peering between the heads of others. Two large black and white aerial photographs showed the village of Bisperode and the surrounding area.

"Bisperode. Sounds like it's right out of a spaghetti western."

The assembled group laughed at the OC's joke.

"There aren't many of us," he continued. "So how we allocate our forces is crucial to defending our sector. We'll have the Hasselburg to our right. It's—"

"Two hundred and ninety metres, sir."

"Thank you, Brian. On our left, we have another piece of high ground, nearer 400 metres in some areas. Between the village and the high ground, on both sides, it's open space, agricultural fields – a gap of about 1,500 metres to the west and 750 to the east. About two kilometres to the south, there's a crossroads. The 425, west to east, crosses the two sections of high ground, and the 588 passes through Bisperode, south to Halle. I want eyes on that crossroads, not only to give us a warning if the enemy is on its way, but we can also warn the rest of the Division if the enemy moves south-west. Then there are tracks over the high ground each side of us."

He turned and locked eyes with Sergeant Kirby. "I will use your three Scimitars for that. Any problems with that, Sarn't Kirby?"

"None, sir, my boys are ready," responded the tall SNCO, his hair giving the impression it had a life of its own.

"Don't they have barbers in the recce platoon, Sergeant?" Asked the CSM, but he was smiling as he said it.

"The Russians kind of cancelled my appointment, sir."

The group laughed.

"I'm sure we can find you a pair of scissors when this is over," added the CSM.

"Sir."

"I'll leave the deployment of the units to you, but if the enemy head north or south, you need to cover our right and left flanks and cover the Milan units deployed there. I know you're used to your vehicles working in pairs, but we're all spread pretty thin. We may get two 438s in support. To be confirmed."

"Understood, sir. What if we spot the enemy using the heights?"

"Good question Sarn't Kirby. I will have a Two-Platoon dug in and One-Platoon acting as a QRF."

"That will leave only one Scimitar to cover the Milan's, sir."

"Yes, I know. Well, that gives you a clue as to where I want one of your anti-tank sections, Captain Banks."

The captain moved closer to the larger of the two photographs. "There's a ditch here, sir, fed by water that flows off the Hasselburg. It runs right across the gap on our right flank. We're not sure of its depth or width, but if it causes the enemy a delay, my mobile team can take advantage of that and pick off any armour."

"Why the mobile section, Captain?"

"If they're in danger of being overrun, they can at least reposition themselves quickly. Corporal Ward's section, sir, I suggest, is deployed close to and around the village."

"That makes sense," responded the major. "Lieutenant Russell."

"Sir."

"You will be our Quick Reaction Force. In fact, I want one of your sections at the southern crossroads, with the other two in the village on five minutes notice to move."

"They'll be ready, sir."

"The new men settling in OK?" asked the CSM.

"Yes, Sarn't Major. I've put the new ones with Corporal Stubbings. He's my most experienced section commander."

The OC turned to Lieutenant Dunmore. "We'll go through the deployments in detail when we're in position, but I want one section at the southern edge of the village, one section covering the mobile Milan section, and a third along the strip of forest that links the east of the village with the forest. That will protect our left flank and cover any infiltration along the edge of the forest. We're thin on the ground, but once Three-Section get here, we can double up on the defence of the village. In the meantime, we'll have to make do. Questions?"

Dean was in first. "We're not a big force if we have to fight our way there, sir."

"We're not. We are very much dependent on 1RRF and 3RTR to smash any enemy forces aside. That's not to say our passage will be easy."

"What is the Intel on the Soviet forces in the area, sir?" Captain Banks asked.

"Brian, you take this one."

"Sir," responded the adjutant. "The Soviet focus seems to be further north, around Minden, Petershagen, and even further north in 1 German Corps' sector. In our sector, we have 47th Guards Tank Division that got badly beaten recently. We have Intel that says reinforcements are moving up, but 20th Guards Army have been sent further north. They were on the receiving end of one of our tactical nuclear strikes. The biggest worries are the Military District Forces moving up. We don't know yet where they'll end up. Which is why the counter-attack has to go ahead in the morning."

"Have the nuke strikes had much of an impact?"

"Yes, they have."

"But no response yet?"

"No, Captain," the OC interrupted. "But that's not to say there won't be. So, make sure your soldiers have their NBC kit on and masks close throughout. They've been issued with fresh canisters. Make sure they have them and their respirators close at hand at all times. Right, we move out at 0200. The Adjutant will take us through the running order and timings. Brian?"

2000, 10 July 1984. 23rd Amphibious Squadron, 28th Armoured Amphibious Engineer Regiment. West of Hameln, West Germany. The Blue Effect +2 hours

The Ferret Scout Car manoeuvred alongside the command vehicle. A sergeant climbed down and across the engine deck to be met by a major who appeared from the tent at the back of the Spartan.

"They've arrived, sir."

"About bloody time. What are they like?"

"Shit state, but they'll do."

"Let's go and take a look."

About a hundred metres down a track, through the forest, three twenty-one and a half ton M2 Ferry Systems were lined up beneath a canopy of trees. Four Sappers were in the process of pulling camouflage netting over them.

"So long as they work, Sarn't Draper, we'll now have a full set."

"I'll get the lads checking them over straightaway, sir."

"Yes, do. We expect to move out at 0200."

"I'm on it, sir."

"Good, I'll leave you to it. Oh, let me know if there are any problems."

"Sir."

The squadron commander left and the Royal Engineers sergeant went over to the engineers working on the netting.

"Seen anything to worry about, Billy?"

"Looks OK to me, Sarge. The factory done all the repairs alright; just ain't tarted them up."

"Do a thorough check, eh?"

"Will do, Sarge."

"We'll need those buggers tomorrow. Let me know as soon as you're done. The OC's wanting an update."

"On it."

The sergeant took a step back. He had confidence in Billy, one of the rig drivers. He loved the old M2s, but they were a pig at times for breaking down. These three had been back at the factory where they were originally made, the only place that could fulfil the repairs that had been needed. They had been flown in; then transported here as a matter of urgency. It was all going to kick off tomorrow. The Squadron had two troops, with five sections in each, giving them fifteen M2s per troop. His troop would provide a crossing point around Hameln, while Second-Troop would be further east. The Bundeswehr were also providing engineer support. With two bridges in operation, they could get across over 100 vehicles an hour; meaning one of the weakened Brigades could cross in four. The 64th Amphibious Engineer Squadron was way up north, with 1st Armoured Division.

But that was their problem. He just had to worry about his troop.

Chapter 28

2010, 10 July 1984. Ministerium fur Staatssicherheit, MfS state prison, Hohenschonhausen, East Berlin.
The Blue Effect +2 hours

Drip...drip...drip.

Bradley's head ached. He had no idea how long he had been in this position. But what he did know was the constant impact on his forehead from regularly descending drops of water. It felt like a hole was being slowly bored into his forehead.

Drip...drip...drip.

He wanted to scream but had bitten back the urge so far. Not that he could have had he tried. When attempting to utter a sound, in order to counter his isolation, his dry throat and puffed up tongue had only allowed a croak to emanate from his cracked lips.

Drip...drip...drip.

He looked up and back for the umpteenth time, his eyes trying to peer through his eyelids, but he was unable to see the drops of water as they poised to descend then drop down onto his now pressured, forehead.

Drip...drip...drip.

The darkness prevented him anyway, from seeing either the droplets of water, or the apparatus that they came from. Apart from the pressure from the droplets, the only other sense was that of the dark and damp, with a musty smell that invaded his nostrils.

Drip...drip...drip.

He had no idea of the time, or even if it was night or day. His mind was unfocussed and wandering. Even the most recent of focussed thoughts, of hunger and thirst, had subsided. The occasional droplet splashing on his bare forehead would send a minute cascade onto his upper lip, his tongue reaching out to moisten his dry lips.

Drip...drip...drip.

His first thoughts when he had first woken up were those of confusion. He remembered being in the interrogation room, questioned by the officer assigned to him. Then he took a drink of water. Was it water? Yes, it was water. But that was all he remembered. He didn't remember slumping down in his chair or being dragged out by two MfS guards. After what seemed like only a few moments, coming round from his drugged state, he had established that he was lying down, at a slight angle, his bare feet lower than his head, but his body was tightly strapped to some form of bed or bench. He was unable to move his body or his arms. They, together with his legs, were secured rigidly, his arms strapped to his sides. A metal frame gripped his head, securing it slightly back, forcing his face to look upwards where the incessant drip of water was slowly driving him mad. At first, he had counted the drips, about one every second, using it as some form of clock. After five minutes, he had panicked, sensing a hole forming in the centre of his skull, trying to wrench his head from side to side to escape. All that achieved was to create even more panic, the relentless compressing force of the water seeming to increase tenfold.

Drip...drip...drip.

He groaned.

Drip...drip...drip.

His next strategy was to try and enjoy it, to take pleasure from, the refreshing splashes. But that had lasted a mere few minutes, the hole in his forehead seemingly getting bigger and bigger, deeper and deeper. It was incessant. *Is that water I can feel on my head, or is it blood?* He thought. It just got worse. His mind screaming, unable to focus on family, friends, his job or even the outside world.

Drip...drip...drip.

He went through another bout of panic, the blood vessels in his arms and face pronounced as he tried to wrench his body free.

Drip...drip...drip.

Then the tears came, causing him to blink rapidly, the salt stinging his eyes, his eye sockets filling up until they overflowed, trickling down the side of his face. He shivered. Still in his barrack-dress trousers and No. 2 shirt, although both were soiled and damp, the dark, dank cell was sucking away any warmth from his body, adding to his discomfort. Bradley groaned and closed his stinging eyes, hoping that sleep would provide some relief, but that just enhanced the drilling sensation, the hole getting bigger, deeper.

Drip...drip...drip...drip...drip...drip.

Chapter 29

2020, 10 July 1984. Corps Patrol Unit. North of Gestorf, West Germany.
The Blue Effect +2.5 hours

Wilf fired off a burst from his M-16 and had the satisfaction of seeing one of the NKVD soldiers go down.

"Ready," yelled Badger, ten metres behind him.

Tag, in a prone position on the edge of a dip alongside Wilf, heaved a grenade in the direction of the enemy troops. "Go!"

Tag and Wilf picked themselves up and sprinted towards where Badger and Hacker were waiting to provide cover. The grenade exploded, distracting the enemy for a moment as they sprinted past their friends. They ran a further ten metres and then threw themselves down behind another shallow dip in the ground, reloaded their weapons, and got ready.

"Go!" called out Wilf.

Their roles were now reversed as Tag and Wilf put down covering fire while Badger and Hacker dashed past them to go through the same process all over again.

It was about half an hour until dusk. They had to keep moving, keep their distance from the pursuing troops, and then, in darkness, slip away. They weren't on their chinstraps yet, but it was getting close. They were also eating into their ammunition far too quickly. The anger of the Soviet Army commander towards the Special Forces operating behind his lines was being taken out on Wilf's small patrol. He reckoned there was an entire motor rifle battalion on their tail along with Soviet *Ministerstva Vnutrennikh Del* (*MVD*) internal security troops, on their tail. Sent to assist in the subjugation of the civilian population, they had been reassigned to hunt down the enemy saboteurs. On the run for over eighteen hours, the CPU's only respite had been at the time of the tactical nuclear explosions a couple of hours ago, which seemed to have knocked their pursuers off their stride.

But now they were back and the chase was on. Bergen's had been dumped, and all the food, water and ammunition they could carry had been packed into their fighting order, but they were eating into their ammunition at a phenomenal rate. They'd broken contact once, but the enemy had persuaded a Soviet Army General to release two Mi-2 Hoplites, small helicopters, to help in tracking the enemy saboteurs down, and their trail had been picked up again. The four men had been on the run again since dawn and were now just trying to hang on until darkness would provide them with some sort of shield. But the enemy had an advantage: speed. Once Wilf's CPU had been located, trucks of soldiers could be driven to a point behind them, cutting off their retreat, forcing Wilf to switch his direction of withdrawal. Just as he thought they had broken contact yet again, they would hear the *whop, whop* of rotor blades as their airborne hunter returned to the scene.

Badger and Hacker started to put down fire as Tag threw the last of his grenades, and he and Wilf sprinted for cover yet again. Wilf paled as he heard a yelp from Tag as a bullet struck his friend's leg, causing him to spin sideways, landing in a pile on the floor.

"Man down! Man down! Cover me!" Wilf screamed.

Badger fired the last of his grenades from the under slung launcher on his M-16, and Hacker threw the last of their smoke grenades, one they had been saving for this very moment they feared might happen: one of them going down.

Tag screamed as Wilf heaved him up off the ground, finding strength from deep down inside, throwing his friend over his shoulder in a fireman's lift. Smoke billowed out behind them, providing momentary cover, as he collapsed in a heap alongside Hacker and Badger. The two men continued to put down fire while Wilf cut away at Tag's combats. Tag groaned in pain, and Wilf could see why. The round had shattered the soldier's lower leg. White pieces of his tibia were poking through the muscle. Even patched up, there was no way he could run with them now.

Tag reached out and gripped Wilf's jacket, pulling him close. "You need to go Wilfy. I'm fucked. I'm going nowhere with this."

"We'll find a way."

"Bollocks! I won't get anywhere with this."

"I'll carry you. We can take it in turns."

"Don't be fucking stupid, Wilfy. Even Badger could only carry me for a short distance. They'll be all over us."

Hacker crouched down. "We're low on ammo, Wilfy. They look like they're getting ready for a push."

"Tell him, Hacker. I can cover you. Give you a chance."

Hacker looked at Tag, saw the blood-soaked leg of his combats and a piece of white bone protruding through the blood. He nodded.

"Shit!" Exclaimed Wilf, knowing they were both right.

"Turn me over on my front, guys. Get me in a good position."

Wilf went to inject Tag's with morphine, but Tag objected. "No, I need my wits about me. Leave it here. If I get the chance I'll use it before they get to me."

Tag bit back a scream as they helped him get into a firing position.

Hacker pressed his shoulder. "See you, mate." On Wilf's orders, Hacker ran to a new position, fifty metres west. Badger, who had been keeping in touch with the their situation and that of the enemy, said his goodbyes to his mate; then threw his last grenade, the last the team had, and ran to join Hacker.

Wilf ruffled Tag's hair; nothing needed saying really. "Thanks, Tag."

"Fuck off, Wilfy, before they get you too." But Tag said it with a smile. Wilfy returned the smile and shot off to join the other two.

The three men ran at a crouch as fast as they could, taking advantage of the opportunity given to them by the injured member of the team. They heard burst after burst of gunfire as Tag emptied three magazines off towards the advancing security troops, having the satisfaction of seeing at least two go down. The sound of gunfire receded the further Hacker, Wilf and Badger were from the fight until there was only silence. Should they survive, beat the clock, they would have a few drinks for their friend. But, for now, they would run until their legs collapsed beneath them.

Chapter 30

2030, 10 July 1984. Elements of 2nd Spetsnaz Brigade.
Rodinghausen, West Germany.
The Blue Effect +2.5 hours

A member of the crew spoke into the microphone of the internal communications system, informing the team leader they were five minutes away from the landing zone. The team leader tapped the shoulder of the man next to him, holding up five fingers, and he, in turn, tapped the soldier next in line, repeating the warning until all eight of the soldiers, sitting in the back of the shaking helicopter, were aware that they were only five minutes out. This was the cue to check their weapons yet again, even though they knew implicitly that everything was perfect and well prepared for the operation ahead. The majority carried an AKS-74U, a stripped down version of the AK-74, the standard Soviet assault rifle. Each man also had a spade, the preferred weapon of choice for a Spetsnaz soldier. In fact, it was the only weapon they trained with at the start of their training, and they quickly learnt to use it with deadly effect. One of the team favoured a VSS sniper rifle, and two carried a PSS, a silenced pistol. It only had an effective range of twenty-five metres, but it would assist their covert operation until it went loud. All in all, they could give a good account of themselves when required.

Next came the two-minute warning, then one. The Mi-8 Hip shuddered and vibrated as the pilot pulled back on the stick, banking hard left, throwing his passengers violently against each other as he brought the helicopter round, pointing in the direction from which they had just flown. Pulling back on the controls again, he brought the Mi-8 to a hover as the crewman in the back pulled the door open. A blast of air whipped around the cabin, and the eight Spetsnaz operators stood up. Two went forward, pushing eight packs out of the aircraft to land on the ground below. The lead man then launched himself from the helicopter, dropped a metre to the ground as the pilot kept the helicopter from landing on the deck, holding it in a steady hover. The first man to drop ran, hunched down. Then, at twenty metres' distance, he threw himself to the ground, his assault rifle up into his shoulder, ready in case they had been discovered. He heard the grass rustle to his left as one of his colleagues joined him, followed by five more.

The team leader took one last look around the cabin, making sure nothing had been left behind. He signalled the crewman then leapt out to join his team. The cockpit of the MI-8, seeming to dip down, was, within seconds of the last man leaving, moving, the pilot powering the helicopter, flying it forwards and up in one swift movement.

The team of eight men then just lay in place, adjusting senses, particularly their hearing, to the environment they were now in. They had been dropped in a clearing, a meadow, west of a path, the Wittekindsweg, that ran along the southern edge of the lengthy Wiehengebirge, north of Rodinghausen. It was twenty minutes before the team leader felt it safe to move, and he led his men to the edge of the meadow. They waited again until a red light, no more than 100 metres away, flashed four times. The leader responded twice with his own red-screened torch and relaxed a little when the other party returned two flashes. His men spread out to provide cover as a shadowy figure ran to join them.

"Gregor?" asked the shadowy figure.

"Who else?"

"I thought I recognised the squashed nose."

They both laughed quietly as they gripped each other's shoulders.

"All clear, Andrei?" Gregor, the team leader, asked as they crouched down.

"Yes, I've been here for three hours. Nothing. How about you?"

"No problems. We came in with two Rooks. They've been attacking a few enemy positions, and the helicopter slipped through their lines as the British were keeping their heads down. We came in nice and low. The pilot knew what he was doing, although he scared the shit out of me at times."

"I've not heard any alerts going off around here."

"Good. Have you found a good route for us?"

"Of course. Couldn't depend on you to find your own way." His grin stood out in the dark.

"Vadim," he then hissed, and another Spetsnaz soldier joined them. "This is Vadim. Meet Gregor, our contact and guide." The two men shook hands.

Andrei pulled a map out of a pocket in his black waterproof jacket and unfolded it. Then, taking a cape from a small rucksack on his back, he pulled it over their heads as the three men crouched down together, heads touching as Gregor played a smaller white torch over the map.

"We go north for about two and a half kilometres; then east for about 500 metres. The first part is a dip between two pieces of high ground. We just need to stay in the treeline. When we hit the northern edge, we follow it round towards the east, and the British unit is about 500 metres away."

"What have they got?"

"Standard comms vehicles, but the company defending it has those boxy-looking armoured vehicles."

"Saxons?"

"They're the ones."

"Size?"

"I'm pretty certain it's a Brigade Headquarters."

"Good," added Vadim. "That will be the one controlling the battalions defending the river and the troops further back."

Andrei looked at his notebook. "15th Brigade. It's a reservist unit. We need to go. Lead on, Gregor."

Andrei packed the cape away as the rest of the group were briefed. They were less than two kilometres as the crow flies from their objective, but had about a three-kilometre march ahead of them. All they had to do was move silently, ensure they were undetected, and then strike the enemy hard. This was just one small mission, part of a much larger operation right across the NATO front. The aim was to stun the enemy, blind them, and confuse them. Two thousand Spetsnaz soldiers, operating in teams from as few as four men to as large as twenty, would be a thorn in NATO's side from as far north as Bremen and south to Kassel. A few teams had been flown in by helicopter, the sparse number of NATO troops along the front line making it easier than anticipated. Others were parachuted close to their targets, but far enough away to ensure stealth. Many teams had been in West Germany for the past two months; sharing homes or other accommodation with sleepers that had been living in the West for anything up to twenty years. A small core of GRU assets had been living in West Berlin and West Germany since the Cold War began almost immediately after the end of the Second World War.

After just over two kilometres of threading their way through the trees, the team arrived at an empty building. Two Special Forces soldiers approached the small farmhouse, waiting for thirty minutes as they watched the main entrance but, after no sign of movement, they moved in closer, peering discreetly through windows, the blinds purposefully left open, no sign of life visible. The sergeant signalled to his comrade, and they moved to the front door. As had been agreed, the door was unlocked, and they entered slowly. After a quick check of the rooms downstairs and upstairs, clearing all the rooms and wardrobes, or anywhere someone could be secreted, they were satisfied the property was empty.

The sergeant sent Stepan to fetch the rest of the detachment. Within ten minutes, two of the nine men were on sentry duty outside while the remainder sorted through the supplies and equipment that had been placed there by one of the GRU agents who had come across four weeks earlier as a member of the crew on an Aeroflot aircraft. The supplies had been smuggled across the border in one of the thousands of lorries that transited between East and West Germany. The driver, also a GRU operative, coordinated with the agent, Gregor, and the supplies were deposited in the farmhouse that belonged to yet another Spetsnaz sleeper. The cache contained additional ammunition, two RPG-16s, a Strela-2 shoulder-launched surface-to-air missile, landmines and plastic explosives.

The sleeper wouldn't be in attendance: another task had been assigned to him in order to keep the pressure on the already overburdened NATO forces.

"Yulian, Dmitry, sort the mines out. Ilia, Marat, I want a patrol out to 100 metres."

Acknowledging their orders, two men went to pick up a handful of small landmines that would be placed at strategic points around the building. On their return to this location to restock with ammunition and supplies, should they need them, the detonated mines would alert them to the location being compromised. The two other Spetsnaz operators would complete a 360-degree circuit of the building.

On their return, and with the mines prepared and armed, the lieutenant ordered his men to move.

After consulting the map one last time, the detachment commander was satisfied it would take them no more than two hours to get to the site where they would find their target.

Ninety minutes later found them skirting the edge of a small complex, the patrol moving more slowly the closer they got to the target. Signalling his men to halt, he was sure that the British brigade headquarters was close.

They lined up along a shallow embankment, just inside the trees, keeping their heads down while some military trucks drove along the road in the centre of the complex. There was silence once the last vehicles left the compound, somewhere to the north. The Soviet EW unit that had been tracking the radio transmissions of NATO headquarters' scattered across West Germany had done well in identifying this particular headquarters. Someone had been careless, too loose with their communications, allowing the Soviet army to find them.

Gregor signalled his team forward, and the group passed from tree to tree, dropping down the gentle slope, keeping their eyes peeled now, looking for signs of sentries.

Lieutenant Gregor Antonovich dropped to one knee, signalling back to his men to do the same, although the order was not needed: the second in the file had been watching the point man closely. They could now hear the generators running, needed to power the lights and the vast array of communications equipment required by a brigade headquarters to control its subordinate units and keep in touch with higher command. The sound could never be completely muffled, even using dips in the ground or other vehicles to try and mask it. The throb of the motors could be heard for some distance.

Gregor's men lined up and split into two teams of four. Andrei would remain there and cover their withdrawal.

"Let's go," uttered Gregor, and the men moved forward silently. Gregor's eyes darted everywhere, looking for a sentry, or sentries. *They will have at least a dozen men on guard at any one time*, he thought. His PSS pistol moved from side to side as he edged around one of the buildings. Three hundred metres away, across an open piece of ground, he could see at least six single-storey buildings interspersed amongst an array of trees. He picked out at least two of the ugly Saxon vehicles facing him and could hear at least a couple of generators.

To his left, 200 metres away, was another building, the one he would make for. He signalled to Yulian, Dmitry and Marat to follow him, and ran at a crouch towards the single-storey building.

Halfway across, he was suddenly dazzled by the lights of the

Saxons opposite, holding up his left hand to shield his eyes as more and more headlight beams banished the darkness. He saw a different sort of light, a flash from amongst the trees, as he was spun round, the sound of a heavy machine quickly following. Two more bullets thudded into his body as he dropped to the ground, his pistol falling from his lifeless fingers. One Spetsnaz soldier managed to fire a burst as he too went down, but it was all over. All eight men were killed, some struck by a dozen or more bullets, such was the ferocity of the fire launched at them.

Andrei look on disbelievingly. Then he gathered his senses and sprinted up the shallow bank, running smack into a British patrol that was closing the trap that had been set for the unsuspecting Soviet Special Forces. Three GRU agents, under scrutiny for the last three weeks, had been caught in the last two days, but they had continued to operate, on pain of death, leaving Soviet high command convinced all was well.

Chapter 31

0110, 11 July 1984. Corps Patrol Unit Southeast of Bad Nenndorf, West Germany.
The Blue Effect +7 hours

The SAS trooper eased himself forwards on his elbows until he was ten metres from the sleeping sentry. It would be difficult to take this one out. Not because he was alert; on the contrary, he was sitting on the rear step of a Zil-131 box-body vehicle, his feet on the ground with his forehead slowly dropping towards his knees. When his helmetless head got to a point where he would topple forwards, or sideways, his body would rear up and, still asleep, the young soldier would again rest the back of his head against the door that was situated above the steps. Then, the process would start all over again.

The trooper rose up and moved quietly across the open ground until he was alongside the main body of the vehicle. Edging along the flat side of the truck, he reached the back end seconds before the soldier would again go through his familiar routine. As the man's head dropped, Trooper Glover made his move. He whipped around the corner at speed and, as the soldier's head reared up, as he anticipated it would, wrapped his left arm around the man's face, clamping his mouth with his hand, jerking the soldier's head around to the left sharply before he forced the knife deep into the man's exposed neck. Slicing backwards through the jugular, the blood gushing out as he hugged the man's head tight into his chest, pulling the struggling body around to the side of the truck where Trooper Mathers' joined him in subduing and ensuring the death of the Soviet guard. They dragged the soldier's body across to the trees while their two companions kept watch. Now they could move deeper into the camp, the inner confines of the headquarters of the Soviet 20th Guards Army. They knew it was an Army headquarters by its sheer size.

After hiding the body as best they could, placing his body in the centre of a clump of shrubs, the four soldiers continued with their probe of the headquarters. This particular box-body was of no importance, so they needed to move deeper into the complex. The four soldiers moved slowly and quietly. Their Bergen's were hidden, to be picked up on the extraction route. The four SAS troopers wore only their belt kit, but still carried a bag of explosives each, to take out any key pieces of equipment they came across.

They passed two further box-bodied vehicles, all on Ural-375 chassis, before coming across the major assembly area they were looking for: Galenberg Park. At the south-eastern edge of Bad Nenndorf, the outskirts in this part of the town was scattered with trees. With the liberal use of camouflage, it made an ideal vehicle park. All vehicles were covered in netting and ranged from UAZ-469 jeeps, UAZ-452s, Gaz-66s and a mix of other utility vehicles – in particular, one with a tropospheric scatter array. There were also a number of armoured command vehicles, such as ACRVs, MTLBs and BMP command vehicles from the four divisions of the army units, plus all the supporting elements that came under the command of a Soviet Army. They weren't sure where the main area of operations was housed, but they had enough here to make a start. The four men were amazed at the lack of security; such was the confidence of the Soviet Army.

Time was against them though. It was time to split, choose a number of comms vehicles, or other high-value targets, attach the explosives, meet up again, and then disappear as silently as they had arrived.

0115, 11 July 1984. Elements of the 3rd Regiment Army Air Corps and 24th Airmobile Brigade. Area southwest of Beckedorf, West Germany. The Blue Effect +7 hours

The Lynx Mark 9 quivered as a gust of wind whipped across the rotor blades, jolting the passengers in the rear. The pilot fought with the controls as the wind was funnelled in between the high ground of Buckeberge to his left and the Deister and Suntel to his right. On top of that, he was flying low, almost at treetop height, with only the light of a pale moon to guide him. Flying in a straight line was near impossible but, if he didn't, he would fly his helicopter into the trees that towered above him to his left as they climbed the slopes of the Buckeberge.

Keeping low and close to the treeline may be risky but, if they flew down the centre of the valley, closer to the Autobahn, Soviet troops scattered all around the valley floor would spot them. He had no doubt they would have a mixture of ZSUs, SA-13s, and SA-6s and their associated radars would be intermittently searching for any aircraft that could threaten the soldiers on the ground. At this very moment, on the opposite side of the valley, four Harriers were conducting harassing attacks as a distraction. Behind Zulu-One, three other helicopters had followed their leader along the same route. Zulu-One's passengers, a team of eight men from 2RRF, had two missions to perform, critical to the success of the forthcoming attack by the NORTHAG forces.

His co-pilot spoke. "Twenty seconds, treble-four."

"Roger," the pilot responded.

The countdown was spot on as they flew across the L444, a minor road that ran east west, crossing over the Buckeberge.

"We are five minutes out," he then informed his passengers.

The craft jerked again, and Captain Farrell quickly regained control as a gust threatened to drive the helicopter into the trees on his left. In the back, the soldiers from 2RRF went through their last-minute checks. Once the Lynx was brought into the hover, they would have less than thirty seconds to debus.

The pilot and co-pilot discussed their position and agreed their location, difficult to do with the ground racing beneath them at over 100 kilometres per hour.

Behind them, the number two helicopter dropped their passengers as close to the L444 as they dared, while numbers three and four banked right, and flew across the E30, picking a gap between the convoys of traffic moving north and south. The crossing was successful, and they both turned back on their original northerly heading. On arrival at the waypoint, both aircraft would fly over the high ground of the Deister. Once on the other side, they would split: Zulu-Three would fly to Kolenfeld whilst Zulu-Four headed for Haste.

Each eight-man team had two missions. Half the team were made up of engineers who carried as many mines as could be carried in their packs. Their task was to mine major routes such as Route 65 between Rinteln and Bad Nenndorf and roads west to east. The other half of the respective team would act as pathfinders, identifying, and later highlighting, the dropping zones for the paratroopers who would be landing later that morning.

Captain Farrell manoeuvred the Lynx into a flare the same time as he pivoted the craft around so he was facing away from the high ground for when he would need to power up and fly back to base. The pilot brought the Lynx into a hover, about a metre off the ground, and the eight men in the passenger section pushed out their heavy Bergen's that dropped to the grassy earth below with a thud. Once completed, the eight followed them out, forming a circle facing outwards as the Lynx built up power and flew east before banking right and heading back down the valley.

The eight men waited thirty minutes until they were satisfied their landing had gone undiscovered. The two groups quickly conferred as to their location, and both team leaders agreed they were within 100 metres of their chosen landing zone. They metaphorically took their hats off to the pilot and co-pilot who had got them here safely. The two teams, made up of volunteers, split from each other. Lieutenant Forde led his pathfinders north towards Lindhorst while Sergeant Jackson led the three Royal Engineers west. The four engineers moved into the trees, happier once they were under cover. They had only five hours until dawn, so needed to keep out of view and move quickly.

Their packs were heavy. Each man carried Hunting Engineering IMP lightweight anti-tank mines. Sergeant Jackson led, and Corporal Simmonds was tail-end Charlie sandwiching the two sappers in the centre. They kept the spacing tight as the trees cut out what little light there was. Jackson would have welcomed an image intensifier, but the few that were available had been allocated to the pathfinder teams, as their role was considered more critical. They had the lives of hundreds of paratroopers to consider.

The first part of the climb was quite steep as they ascended to 150 metres, and Sergeant Jackson soon had a film of sweat beneath his gear. The heavy packs didn't help. After an hour, they had reached the roof of the ridge and found the going easier on the way down as they headed west, although the weight of the Bergen's caused their knees to jar every time a boot was put on the sloping ground. It was either that or losing control of their descent and crashing down to the bottom. Ninety minutes later found them moving along a strip of forested land that led them right up to Hannoversche Strasse, Route 65, their target.

While they had not come across any Soviet forces so far, that was all about to change. A mere 400 metres from the major road and the engineers came across a large farm off to the left, seen through the trees. It seemed fairly quiet and was certainly darkened but, as Jackson led his team closer to it, it became obvious from the silhouettes of camouflaged vehicles that an enemy unit were using it as an arbour, taking advantage of the large barns and, no doubt, the farmhouse. On arrival at the kerbside of the road. A steady flow of logistical vehicles moved left and right.

The men dropped their packs, and Sergeant Jackson and Corporal Simmons crept forward to the very edge of the road, which was tree-lined on both sides for at least a kilometre in each direction. Jackson checked his watch, triggering Simmons to do likewise. It was 0330. They had sixty minutes to prepare for their mission.

Jackson signalled his number two to remain where he was and keep watch while he withdrew back into the trees to start the process of bringing the anti-tank mines forward. Between the three of them, the Bergen's were brought to the edge of the road, just inside the trees, out of sight of the vehicles trundling east probably on their way to pick up fresh supplies and ammunition having deposited their precious loads at the front, resupplying and rearming the front-line locations.

The attack on the road would take three forms. First, two anti-tank LAW, off-route mines, a hollow-charge weapon, would be set up opposite each of the two wide lanes. The two each side would be 100 metres apart. At the last minute, during a reasonable gap in the traffic, all four would run across, two from each side, and deposit anti-tank and anti-personnel mines in a staggered formation across the tarmac lanes. And finally, anti-personnel mines would be laid either side of the verge, to thwart any attempt by the Soviet soldiers to pass safely around the danger area. The mines had been painted a colour to match that of the road and it was hoped that with convoy lights and driven by tired soldiers, they would be seen too late for the drivers to react.

The team split up. Corporals Simmons and Perry went west, and Sergeant Jackson, followed by Vaughan, headed east. Each had one of the Bergen's. Once in position, and during a gap in traffic, they raced across both carriageways and prepared their trap on the northern kerbside, then return and set up on the southern edge of the road. The anti-tank off-route mines would be fired manually. The mines lain across the road would be detonated by the pressure plate being activated, as would those on the verge.

The four men arrived back at their starting point on the southern side, panting, their faces running with sweat. Yet all four were smiling. They were doing what Royal Engineers were good at, apart from building things: getting ready to blow things up. They grabbed a drink of water from their canteens, prepared the last of the mines, watched the vehicle packets pass by, and waited for the appointed hour.

0145, 11 July 1984. SAS Troop, 22 Special Air Services Regiment.
Southwest of Wundstorf, West Germany.
The Blue Effect +8 hours

The SAS team of eight men, inserted into the area the previous day, went about the task that had been appointed to them. Troopers one and two kept watch over the Soviet guards that were patrolling the bridge that spanned the water below them. This was a bridge erected by Soviet engineers after the retreating NATO forces had destroyed the original bridge. The majority of significant crossing points across the length and breadth of West Germany had either been destroyed during the retreat or later attacked by NATO ground-attack aircraft to deny the enemy an easy passage. Over wider rivers, the Soviet pontoon bridging system, PMP, had been particularly successful in keeping the advance moving. But, for the higher crossing points with much higher riverbanks, girder bridges had been thrown across by Soviet Engineers. Beneath this structure, under the very noses of the sleepy, casual Soviet sentries, six men from 22 Special Air Service Regiment, were clambering over the supporting structure, laying explosives that would soon remove this facility, denying the enemy the ability to move troops, tanks, ammunition or supplies across. Situated in a prime location where the Soviet army could cross if they needed to pull back, or bring reinforcements forward when needed, it was high up on 1 British Corps' target list, bringing disruption to the Soviet forces, increasing the chances of the counter-attack being a success.

Trooper three, suspended beneath the bridge by his arms and legs, looked down at the black surface of the Mittellandkanal, the weight of the charges in his bag, over nine kilograms each, pulling him down. He turned his head upwards as he heard the footsteps of the sentry clattering overhead. They had considered removing the sentries to enable them to work faster, but that would have just created an additional problem once their comrades missed them. This

242

way was best. He continued his task, setting up a Charge Demolition Necklace. The No 14 Mark 1s, were wedge-shaped hollow charges and he placed two, one each side of a selected girder, and clipped them together. A third and fourth were placed by the side of the first two. Now, four shaped-charges faced the girder. The five other troopers were going through the same process, placing more of the 'Hayrick' charges on selected girders of the Soviet bridge. Trooper four had completed his set of charges, and now started to attach the detonation cord to the housing at the top.

Even working as quickly, and as quietly, as possible, and taking risks at times as they clambered like monkeys in between the supporting girders, it took the six men two hours to finish the job. They were exhausted, but they still had to extract themselves from the bridge, taking the linked detonation cord with them. Just as the six men reached the southern end of the bridge, they froze as the roar of tracked vehicles came out of the blue, the bridge playing its own tune as the armoured vehicles, MTLBs towing T-12 anti-tank guns, rattled across. The SAS troopers looked at the shaking charges, and secretly prayed that they had secured them well.

The column seemed endless as eighteen sets crossed over, led by a BRDM2 and followed by a BRDM1. Eventually, the crossing was completed, and relative silence returned as the troopers lowered themselves to the ground, trailing the det-cord behind them. Troopers One and Two covered their fellow soldiers while they moved through the long grass to the area they had chosen as the firing point. They needn't have worried about the sentries. Once the convoy had gone, they reverted to type. Two of the four sentries, as agreed amongst themselves, went back to a small hut on the northern end of the bridge and went back to sleep. The sergeant-in-command hadn't even bothered to leave the building, kicking the two sleeping sentries out when the convoy had turned up. After another ten minutes, the full SAS patrol was reunited and, as agreed, the six grabbed some kip while two kept watch. All they had to do now was wait.

Chapter 32

The clamshell doors of the IL-76 transport opened slowly; ready to allow the waiting paratroopers to board. The airborne soldiers were in two lines outside, and turned to the left and right on the orders of their officers. On a second order, the two lines of men shuffled forward, the dark interior of the transport aircraft eventually swallowing up the 125 heavily armed paratroopers. These were part of the Soviet Union's elite, the *Vozdushno-Desantnaya Voyska*, the Soviet's air assault force. Behind them, Gaz-66 utility trucks pulled D-30 122mm howitzers, preparing to be dropped as part of a second wave. Further afield, BMD-1s, the paratroopers' Airborne Mechanised Infantry Combat Vehicles, were either going through a final check or through the last stages of being loaded onto a transport aircraft. The AIMCV, once on the ground, would be the regiment's primary mobile weapon: a weapon that was not only capable of carrying the troops into battle, but also packing a punch with its 30mm gun when the soldiers came up against their enemy, the soldiers of NATO. The Soviet army were pioneers in the use of heavy platforms for dropping equipment. The majority of the equipment for this airborne regiment had already been placed on-board the aircraft that would deliver them to the drop zone. An aircraft roared down the runway as the first of the troops headed west, to pile on the pressure on the beleaguered British forces.

The air was forced from his lungs as he struck the ground hard, jarring his shoulder badly, the explosion having flung his body violently sideways. His ears buzzed, and he urgently tried to focus his mind as other explosions erupted nearby, showering his helmet with a deluge of earth and debris. Corporal Barker panicked suddenly, scrabbling for his respirator, the warnings from the platoon commander just before they disembarked from the private roll-on/roll-off ferry, seconded to the military, ringing in his ears. *Remember, if you get shelled or attacked from the air, it could be a gas attack. Hold your breath and get your respirator on quickly.* He yanked it out of the square green case, holding his breath, but letting it out again realising he had been panting and breathing air in and out of his lungs for at least a minute. He pulled it over his face, emitting a cry as he jerked his injured shoulder. The respirator was adjusted until comfortable and he had a good seal. *Too late,* he thought, *too fucking late. But better safe than sorry if the gas is still heading my way.*

Realising he was still exposed as more rockets landed less than 100 metres away, he scrambled on all fours, throwing himself into the trench head first, his boots kicking his masked comrade in the face.

"For fuck's sake, Kev," a muffled voice cried out. "You nearly took my bloody head off then."

"Yeah, yeah. We're under fire, in case you haven't noticed."

Corporal Kevin Barker peered over the trench, seeing his SLR less than ten metres away. He left his shelter again and quickly retrieved it, dropping back down to the bottom of the trench as two bombs bracketed their position, lifting one end of their defensive position and almost engulfing them in a heap of earth.

"God, Corp, what the hell's going on? Where's it coming from? We're not at the front, for God's sake!"

"Keep your bloody head down, Parr. It'll be over soon."

They stared at each other through the goggle eyes of their gas masks, eyes almost as wide as the lens in the rubber. Two jets, one after the other, flew low overhead, and a furrow appeared along the front of the trench as 30mm-calibre shells tore up the ground.

Corporal Barker heard an unmuffled shriek from someone in severe pain to his left. Pushing his way past Parr, he made his way to the second slit trench, his heart pumping as a second scream, unblocked by the confines of a respirator, let rip. The screams were getting louder and more panicky the closer he got to the source of the sound.

"It's Powell, Corp, he's a mess," shouted Miller through his mask.

Barker saw the infantryman slumped on the firing step, mask off, his face white even through his cam cream, rivulets of sweat leaving streaks down his blackened face. Another green-smocked soldier tore at Powell's NBC suit, cutting it away as best he could.

Barker knelt down. "Easy, easy. Slow down, Dan. Cut it straight down the front, and we can peel it apart."

The soldier calmed down and complied, and after making a jagged cut down the centre of the front of the chemical smock, they could get to his combat jacket.

Corporal Barker could see quite clearly that the dark pattern on the combat jacket beneath was not only the disruptive pattern of his camouflage jacket but also a large black patch that covered the entire front of the casualty's chest.

Powell's body started to jerk violently, blood ejecting from his mouth, spraying them all in a frothy pink cloud. He screamed as they lay him down. Someone was yelling for a medic for a second and third time. The call went unheard above the din of rockets and bombs that continued to rain down around them.

"Get on the radio, Woody, but keep your bloody head down. It's not over yet."

Lance Corporal Woods, the section second-in-command, keyed the radio and called for assistance. It would be some time before they got help. The medical resources of the Company, and Battalion for that matter were sorely stretched as the casualty rate mounted. Whiskey Company, 6th Battalion Royal Regiment of Fusiliers, 6RRF, was receiving their first taste of battle. It was unpleasant and bitter. The soldiers would have to do the best they could in the meantime.

Once they had cleared Powell's jacket and cut away his shirt, the extent of his injury became apparent. A large fragment from a 30mm shell, from the cannon of a Soviet Frogfoot, a ground-attack aircraft, had plunged straight through his upper left chest, leaving a five-centimetre hole at the front and a mangled mess at the rear. One lung had more than likely been severely lacerated; the second, punctured in places, was far from adequate to do its job. Powell's gasps got louder and more violent as Dan placed a first-aid dressing on the wound covering the ragged bloody hole. Corporal Barker pushed a bandage beneath the casualty's upper back, Powell spitting blood as he panted trying to get the oxygen his body demanded. He cried out as Corporal Barker lifted the bandage at the front, placing a piece of plastic carrier bag, he had used to wrap some food in to keep it dry, over the wound. It was far from perfect, but it might at least seal the sucking wound until they could get him some more professional help. The bandage was placed back on the wound, and ties were passed under the soldier's body until they were in a position so it could be secured tightly.

Powell's cry of pain was suddenly very loud, the silence around them ominous now that the Soviet ground-attack aircraft had fled, one shot down by a Rapier missile, a second and third destroyed by German and British Phantoms. The rest had bolted for home, back to their base, where they could refuel, rearm and come back to hammer the British again.

Corporal Barker peeled his S-6 respirator off his head and face and called out for his radio operator. "Get onto platoon again. We need a bloody medic here now!"

He took one last look at Powell, before he left to check on the rest of his section. Powell's breathing was becoming more laboured. He didn't hold out much hope.

"Corp, platoon for you."

He grabbed the handset. "Whiskey-Two, this is Whiskey-Two-Two. Over."

"*Whiskey-Two. Sitrep. Over.*"

"One man badly injured. Powell. The rest shaken, but OK. Over."

"*Roger Whiskey-Two-Two. Stretcher party on way to you. We have reports of slow-moving aircraft heading our direction. Over.*"

"Do we know what they are, sir? Over."

"*Negative. Keep your heads down and I'll keep you posted. Oh, and, Corporal Barker, check all your firing positions. I'll be with you as soon as I can. Out.*"

Barker handed the handset back. "Ripper, pass the word: slow-moving aircraft heading our way. Make sure the lads keep their heads down and get their NBC kit sorted in case we need it. We had a lucky break last time."

"Apart from Powell."

"I know. But we ain't finished yet, so get on with it."

"Will do, Corp."

It suddenly dawned on him that he was no longer just a part-time NCO; someone who went away for the occasional weekend to practise soldierly skills and have a laugh and a joke with his mates.

He was in charge. In charge of these men, and they were looking to him to lead the way. The responsibility thrust upon him suddenly felt heavy on his shoulders. He shook himself metaphorically and moved back down the trench just as the stretcher party turned up to take Powell away. Eight of them now left.

"Corp, Corp, its HQ again."

"Whiskey-Two, this is Whiskey-Two-Two. Over."

Before his platoon commander could respond, he saw the reason for the call. White fluttering packages were falling from either side of a large aircraft. He could now hear the drone of their engines. Three of the large transport planes were coming directly for him, a trail of parachutes leaving the three troop carriers as they lumbered closer and closer.

"Stand to! Stand to! Soviet airborne. Stand to!" Barker yelled.

"*Whiskey-Two. You've got company, over.*"

"I see them, sir."

"*Hold your fire until your men have a clear target, understood?*"

"Roger, sir."

"*Good luck. Whiskey-Two out.*"

"Stand to, stand to!" Barker yelled again, more out of a need to do something than giving any clear orders.

He darted along the firing points, checking on his men. As he stuffed his respirator back into its bag, he doubted it would be needed now with Soviet paratroopers about to descend.

"Get ready. Check your arcs. Hold your fire."

He, along with the rest of his men, watched as the three aircraft passed overhead, paratroopers still leaving. Further back, Soviet airborne soldiers were swaying from their parachute harnesses, the canopies above billowing, catching the flow of air, slowing them down, lowering them to the earth and into battle.

Barker laid his SLR on top of the sandbags that lined the front of the trench. There hadn't been time to sort out top cover. The priority had been to provide one for the gun-group and the attached Milan FP.

He zeroed in on the nearest paratrooper, probably 500 metres away, and seconds away from hitting the deck. But the closer the planes travelled towards them, the closer the enemy, tumbling out of their transports, would land near to the British positions. "Standby, standby. Gun-group, only when I give the order."

The first of the enemy hit the deck. Some of them fired a few rounds, but knew they were too far away to have much of an impact.

But, as more of the Soviet airborne troops, those that had jumped later in the stick, started to land, the closer they were to the soldiers waiting for them.

"Corp."

Barker grabbed the handset from Ripper.

"Go ahead."

"Whiskey-Two. Outgoing. Out."

"Mortar fire on its way," he hollered to his men.

Crump...crump...crump.

Crump...crump...crump.

Small mushroom clouds erupted amongst the Soviet soldiers, killing several as they tried to shake off their harnesses. Others threw themselves to the ground with their parachutes still attached to their bodies, but too late for some as bomb after bomb tore into the assembling paratroopers. Parachutes fluttered 300 metres away as more of the enemy airborne touched down.

"Gun-group, controlled bursts, 300 metres, open fire."

The Lance Corporal in command of the gun-group didn't need telling twice. He had been holding back Jenkins, the gunner, who was gripping the GPMG so hard his knuckles were white. But now, released, he pulled the trigger, the belt of 7.62mm rounds flying through the assistant gunner's fingers as he guided the belt into the breech mechanism. Firing controlled bursts of roughly five to ten rounds, every fifth round a tracer, bullets thudded into the ground close to the nearest Soviet paratroopers, particles of dirt propelled up in front of them. A slight adjustment of his aim and Jenkins was on target: the enemy started to fall as round after round tore into their ranks. More and more parachutes fluttered to the ground: 200 metres, 150 metres, and 100 metres.

"Rifle-group, 100 metres, ten rounds, rapid fire!"

The SLR rifles cracked as 7.62mm bullets were launched at the enemy. The thuds as they penetrated flesh and bone of those nearest could almost be heard as they hit the soldiers, piercing their fragile bodies. One airborne soldier literally had his arm ripped from his shoulder, only sinews and his uniform keeping it attached. Another was hit in the hip; the bullet deflected vertically, travelling almost the full length of his body, exiting at his shoulder blade. Both men went down and didn't get up again.

Some returned fire with their AKS-74 assault rifles, and bullets zipped past Corporal Barker and his men. Barker snapped off two rounds himself before checking on his men.

"Fire at will, fire at will," ordered Barker.

A billowing white cloud of a parachute suddenly impeded his view as a paratrooper landed less than fifty metres away. He fired off a shot into the mass, hoping to hit the hidden enemy. Luck was with his adversary that day: the round winging overhead as the soldier dropped to the ground. The airborne warrior recovered quickly, pushing the parachute silk aside, releasing the harness, and firing off a burst that flew over the heads of the dug in soldiers.

Crack. A shot from Ripper hit the soldier full on in the chest as he raised his body to return fire again, knocking him back, his AKS dropping from his grip. He was still alive when he slumped to the floor. But, without treatment, he would be dead within the hour.

"They're fucking behind us!" screamed a soldier off to the right. Coming from Three-Section.

Corporal Barker called out, "Ripper, Miller, watch our backs, watch our backs!"

Bullet strikes flicked up bits of debris and some of the sandbags shook as more and more rounds came their way. The Soviets were starting to regroup, a light machine gun, a PKM, was putting down fire. Bullets stitched a line along the top of the sandbags making it more difficult for the TA soldiers to respond.

Lieutenant Cox crashed down into the trench. "Corporal Barker, One-Section is about to be overrun. You and two men, with me. Let's go."

Without waiting for a response, the young lieutenant clambered out of the hole and ran towards One-Section's position.

"Ripper, Miller, with me! Let's go. Now!" yelled Barker as he too clambered out of the trench, his SLR held out in front of him. "Woody, enemy to our rear. We have it. Watch your front," the section commander yelled to his second-in-command. He heard pounding boots behind him: Ripper and Miller were following.

He reached around behind him and pulled out his bayonet, fumbling slightly as he fixed it to his rifle. "Fix bayonets!"

Within another twenty strides, he was at the nearest edge of One-Section's trench, partially obscured by smoke drifting across it from the bombs exploding to the rear, grenades thrown by the Soviets, and small arms fire.

A soldier, wearing a Soviet airborne smock, the blue and white striped T-shirt barely visible beneath, fired a burst of automatic fire into the trench, two rounds killing the lance corporal who was already wounded from grenade shrapnel.

Barker swung his SLR left and fired a round into the enemy. Struck in his right shoulder, the soldier was spun round, his AK flying from his hand. Before the paratrooper could recover, Barker had leapt across the width of the trench and thrust the steel bayonet into his guts with such force that the NCO almost lost his balance. Driven half mad by fear, anger and frustration, Barker was nearly pulled down on top of the Soviet as the man collapsed, but the Corporal quickly recovered. With a boot on the body, he withdrew the bayonet just as Ripper ran past firing round after round into three more airborne soldiers who had just appeared. To his left, he saw the Browning pistol jump in the lieutenant's hand as he emptied a magazine into the advancing enemy soldiers. Suddenly, half a dozen soldiers came from the left: more reinforcements, led by Sergeant Fox, screaming, firing wildly into the paratroopers who fell back, many of them wounded or dying.

"Get the Gympy on line," ordered Sergeant Fox.

He had brought the gun-group from One-Section, who was on the right flank of the platoon's line, just in time. Within a matter of seconds, the Gympy was firing and, along with fire from SLRs, heavy fire was sent down range, decimating the dozen airborne soldiers that had been about to join their comrades in attacking the rear of One-Section, who were in turn responsible for protecting the platoon's rear.

"Corporal Barker."

"Sir."

"Get your men back. We'll hold here now."

"Sir. Ripper, Miller. On me."

The two men rejoined their section commander and sprinted back to their own trenches, and not a moment too soon. Fear crawled up Corporal Barker's spine as the ominous silence of the Gympy boded ill. Kennedy lay dead in the bottom of the slit trench as Barnes, standing over him, threw a grenade into the midst of the Soviet airborne troops who were skirmishing towards them.

"Thank God, Corp, I thought we were fucked."

"Go right," Barker ordered Miller and Barnes as he made his way, with Ripper, along to the location of the gun-group.

"What the fuck, Woody?"

"Stoppage…" The working parts of Lance Corporal Wood's

SLR clattered in between each word as he maintained a steady rate of fire towards the enemy who seemed to be growing in strength as more and more paratroopers descended. "Jenks…" *clunk* "…is…." *clunk* "…sorting it…" *clunk*.

Corporal Barker also opened fire, as did the two soldiers manning the Milan firing post.

Brrrrrp…Brrrrrp…Br. "Shit!" Jenkins cursed as the Gympy jammed for a second time.

"For fuck's sake, get it sorted, Jenks. We're dead men walking here."

"Take it easy, Woody. Don't panic him. He'll sort it."

Ripper, his lungs heaving, came alongside the two NCOs. "Look," he said, pointing at another flight of aircraft flying low towards them. About 700 metres away, six large aircraft flew in formation, large packages being pulled out of the rear of the planes by a drogue chute. Once clear of the aircraft, the armoured vehicles, mounted on large wooden platforms, started to drop towards the ground, half a dozen smaller parachutes forming above them, in turn drawing out much larger parachutes, controlling the descent of the BMD MICVs as they were delivered to the troops waiting on the ground below.

"Oh Christ," Barker groaned. "Your radio."

Woody passed the handset across. "Hello, Whiskey-Two. This is Whiskey-Two-Two. Over."

"Whiskey-Two…go ahead."

"Whiskey-Two-Two. We have armour dropping to our front. Seven hundred metres approx. Over."

There was a pause as Lieutenant Cox took in the information passed to him. *"Understood. We are secure here. Sitrep. Over."*

"Whiskey-Two-Two. One dead and one wounded." *Brrrrrp….
Brrrrrp.* "Problem with the Gympy, but up and running now."

"Ammo?"

"Will get back to you on that, sir. Over."

"Milan FP?"

"Secure, sir. Over."

"Roger that. You and One-Section are secure. Three-Section down to four men, but holding. Soviets regrouping. Will likely attack from rear and front. Over."

"Understood, sir. We getting help? Over."

"Yes, Whiskey-Two-Two. Help on way. Just hold firm. Out."

Crump…crump…crump.
Crump…crump…crump.

Barker saw the explosions 200 metres out to the front, then moving out to 800 metres, where it was hoped the salvos of mortar bombs would disrupt the enemy. The Soviet paratroopers would no doubt be preparing for a second assault.

He completed a quick check of his men and did an ammo count. They were low and would need a resupply pretty soon. Powell was out of the fight now. He must ask after him on his next comms call. His second-in-command, Lance Corporal 'Woody' Woods, and Jenkins were still in the fight, as was Barnes. Kennedy was dead, but Miller and 'Ripper' Reid were still fit and well. His radio operator, Blackie, a blacksmith in Civvy Street, a Geordie from the outskirts of Newcastle, was standing next to him. So, including himself, he had a section of seven men.

"Corp, look." Blackie was pointing east in the direction of Hartum.

Barker swapped his SLR for binoculars and scanned the area out to his front. A shaky image flickered in his lens. Lodging his elbows on the edge of the sandbags, he focussed in on the moving target again. This time, an armoured vehicle shimmered into view.

"Stand to, stand to," he warned his men. "Blackie, radio."

He clicked the handset and transmitted. "Hello, Whiskey-Two, this is Whiskey-Two-Two. Movement 800 metres east of my location, enemy armour. Two, I repeat two Bravo Mike Deltas. Over."

He turned to Reid. "Ripper, make sure the Milan team are ready."

"Corporal." With that, the soldier clambered out of the slit trench, bypassing the next two until he arrived at the Milan FP, passing on his section commander's warning.

"Hello Whiskey-Two-Two, this is Whiskey-Two. Acknowledge your last. Keep me informed. With you in figures ten. Out."

Barker checked the horizon again. Out to their front was nothing but a patchwork of fields. Flat, open ground. *If only we had some bloody Chieftain tanks,* he thought. He checked the activity out there again, but they had not made any progress. However, he could now see at least four BMDs lining up for an attack. *Where will they strike?* He wondered. *Would they go for another part of the line?* Barker's company, Whiskey Company, recruited from the area of Alnwick and Berwick-upon-Tweed, was defending Sudhemmern, blocking the L766 that ran through the village, running parallel with the Mittellandkanal to the south. 2nd Platoon of Whiskey Company was dug in north of the Village of Sudhemmern. X-Ray Company, made up of mainly Geordies from Newcastle and recruits from Hexham, had the defence of Nordhemmern, a kilometre north. They blocked the K-14. Yankee-Company held the crossroads at Holzhauser Damm, with Zulu Company, HQ and Support-Company positioned around Hille to the west as the Battalion's reserve. The bulk of 15th Infantry Brigade was defending the River Weser. 2nd Battalion, the Yorkshire Volunteers, had been given a three-kilometre stretch north of Minden. German home defence units would defend the town itself. The 4th Battalion (Volunteers), the Parachute Regiment, would defend up as far as Petershagen. The 1st Battalion, the Yorkshire Volunteers and the 7th Battalion, the Light Infantry were now the divisional reserve, resting in Lubecke and Rahden. The two battalions had taken a beating whilst defending the earlier stop-lines, quickly pushed back by a far more powerful force. They were functional, but badly mauled.

A sprinkling of stones and dirt clattered on the lengths of wood on the floor of the firing position, used to give the soldiers a solid footing while fighting. Lieutenant Cox's boots weren't far behind as he dropped alongside Corporal Barker, his platoon runner close behind him.

"Shit. You scared me then, sir."

"Sorry, Corporal Barker, I was in a bit of a rush to get out of the open," his platoon commander responded with a smile. "What's happening out there?"

"I can see movement. At least half a dozen armoured vehicles, sir."

"Radio."

His runner passed over the handset.

"Whiskey-Two-Three, this is Whiskey-Two. Over."

"This is Whiskey-Two-Three. Go ahead, sir. Over."

"What can you see to your front? Over."

"Same as Two-Two have been reporting, sir. BMDs. We think figures six. Over."

"Roger that. Have your men stand to. They'll be coming at us soon. Out to you. Hello Whiskey-Two-Alpha, this is Whiskey-Two. Over."

"Whiskey-Two-Alpha. With Whiskey-Two-One sir. Over." Sergeant Fox, the platoon sergeant responded.

"Stay with them. Elements of Whiskey-One at your location yet? Over."

"Negative. But Three-Three-Alpha inform with us in three. Roger so far? Over."

"Roger."

"Resupply, your location figures five. Over."

Cox turned to Corporal Barker. "The CSM will resupply us in five." Then he spoke to Sergeant Fox again. "Acknowledged. Request a section from Whiskey-One on standby to reinforce us here. Over."

"Wilco, sir."

"Out to you. Hello Zero-Whiskey. This is Whiskey-Two, have sitrep. Over." He turned towards his NCO. "Corporal Barker."

"Sir?"

"Make sure your ammo is redistributed until resupply gets here."

"Sir."

"Oh, and make sure grenades are at hand. I think we'll be needing them."

"Sir."

"Whiskey-Two. What have you got for me, Edward."

"We have at least six Bravo Mike Deltas forming up to our front. Seven hundred metres out. Over."

"You will have to hold, Edward. There has been a second airborne assault on Black-Diamond. They are prepping for a river crossing. Over."

"Hell, sir, we have one Milan post. Isn't there any more help?"

"No. I will use Whiskey-One to plug any gaps if they breach yours or Whiskey-Three's locations. The battalion will deal with the airborne building up to our rear, but you have to hold the element to our front. Do you understand that, Edward? Over."

Lieutenant Cox lowered his handset, watched as Corporal Barker weaved his way back, nodding his head to indicate that he had carried out his platoon commander's orders.

"We'll hold, sir."

"I've just been informed that we have elements of the recce platoon. I'll send you and Whiskey-Three one unit each and keep two in reserve. The mobile Milan section will also respond where needed, but they have a large area to cover."

"Understood, sir. We'll do it."

"I know, Ed. Good luck. Out."

"We getting help then, sir?" Asked Barker.

"No, Kevin, we're not."

Corporal Barker looked up at his platoon commander. He had

a lot of respect for the man. A senior engineer with a medium-sized construction company, he had learnt the art of managing men of all types of character and differing levels of education. Unlike a regular army unit, the relationship between officer and the soldiers was on a different footing. They may have been under full military discipline whilst on drill weekends and training exercises, but once completed, the men or women would return to their day-to-day jobs. Kevin was a trainee engineer at a major hospital in Newcastle, so he and the lieutenant had often had debates about how the NHS could improve the mechanical side of their operation, particularly in the operation of coal and gas-fired boilers that provided the hospitals with heating, hot water and the sterilisation of surgical instruments.

"They'll not get past us, sir."

"We'll see. We have a Fox armoured car joining us. When it turns up, guide them to the hedge line left of our position."

"The intersection between us and Three-Platoon?"

"Yes, it's our weakest point. Then get on to One-Section. I want yours and their Saxons brought up to the hedge line as well."

"Use their Gympys?"

"And there's extra ammo."

"I'll get onto it now then, sir."

Cox turned to his runner. "Chase the CSM up on that resupply."

"Sir."

The lieutenant rested his elbows on the sandbags along the eastern edge of the firing position. It was quiet in the local area, although he was sure he could hear the occasional rumble of an engine as the Soviet BMDs got into position to make an assault on their location. He was sure there were more than the six that had been spotted. And now it seemed Soviet airborne were attacking the troops along the River Weser. That was no more than seven kilometres away. If the Soviets secured a bridgehead, and an armoured spearhead managed to cross the river, there wouldn't be much of 2nd Division left in this area to stop them.

His OC, Major Brooks, had hinted at there being a bigger picture. He remembered seeing Chieftain tanks further to the rear when he had been to the Brigade headquarters for a briefing. Some were undergoing repairs, and others rearming and refuelling. For the second part of the briefing, the commander of 15th Infantry Brigade had dismissed them, allowing only battalion commanders and above to remain behind. One other incident had stuck in his mind. An

American officer had been attached to the Brigade as a liaison officer. But, there were no American units in the area, or so he thought.

He looked behind him as he heard the growl of the Fox's Jaguar engine. The sergeant in command of this vehicle, and another like it attaching itself to Two-Platoon, would give them a little more firepower. With the 30mm RARDEN cannon, along with the machine guns from the Saxons, they would give the Soviets a run for their money. The BMDs would also have to face the two Milan firing posts attached to One and Two-Sections, along with two more with One-Platoon. Behind them, one of the batteries from the 101st Northumbria Field Artillery Regiment would also be preparing their shells to give the advancing enemy some more to think about.

Chapter 33

The team waited patiently for a gap in the traffic. At one point, the convoys going west had been almost stationary – it was moving that slowly. They appeared to be fuel tankers and ammunition carriers in the main. *A fantastic target*, thought Sergeant Jackson. He was slightly worried. Dawn was rapidly approaching, and daylight would make it easier for the drivers to see the deadly blobs laid across the road. Keeping out of sight, he looked down both directions of the road and could see a gap about to appear. He ordered the team to split. Sergeant Jackson and Corporal Simmons gathered their deadly packages and, on his command, after the last vehicle driving west had passed them, sprinted across. Sergeant Jackson headed for the other side of the dual carriageway while Corporal Simmons laid his mines on the southern stretch. Vaughan headed east and Perry west to get to prepare to set off the LAW off-route mines. The ambush was set. Hannoversche Strasse, Route 65, had now become a death trap for the enemy.

Their final preparations complete, Jackson went west to join Perry, avoiding the anti-personnel mines that had been set, and Simmons went east to wait with Vaughan.

They didn't have to wait long as vehicles from both directions, having a free road ahead of them, drove at a speed of sixty kilometres per hour and ploughed straight into the mines. The front of the first, a Zil-131, was lifted off the ground and flipped over, its momentum forcing it to continue on its journey, the vehicle sliding down the bank 100 metres further on. Behind it, a second Zil, attempting to avoid the vehicle in front of it before it careered off the road, turned right to pass it, hitting another one of the explosive traps. The driver of the vehicle behind, failing to follow the requirement of keeping a fifty-metre gap between convoy vehicles, stood on the brakes, but only succeeded in slowing the inevitable collision with the vehicle in front. On the opposite lane, a similar event was occurring, but one of the trucks was carrying aviation fuel for the Soviet helicopters and erupted in a ball of flame. As the convoys on both sides of the road ground to a halt, the four men unleashed the off-route mines, destroying an armoured BRDM-2 and two further trucks. The fourth failed to fire. But it would be some time before the Soviets sorted out the mess.

It was time to go.

0430, 11 July 1984. SAS Troop, 22 Special Air Services Regiment. Southwest of Wundstorf, West Germany.
The Blue Effect +10.5 hours

The eight men from 22 Special Air Service Regiment watched from their place of concealment as a small convoy of trucks approached the bridge from the west. They were Ural-375 fuel bowsers, needed to feed the ever-hungry armoured units of the Soviet Army. The trucks going east were empty, but their destruction would still be missed. They were badly needed to pick up more supplies to feed the fuel-hungry Soviet divisions.

The charge demolition necklace was in place. It was time. The team leader pointed at his watch and hit the detonation switch. Seconds later, the wedge-shaped hollow charges that had been placed each side of a selected girder and clipped together, exploded. The hot force of the 'Hayrick' charges cut through the steel of the girders as if they were butter. The centre of the bridge lifted, flinging vehicles into the kerb and up against the railings, before dropping back down and collapsing, falling to the depths below, taking vehicles and some of the sentries with it. Another thorn had just been pierced in the enemy's side.

The eight men pulled out, their job done, but their work was far from complete. They had a second mission to perform.

It was time to hit back a second time.

0530, 11 July 1984. 1 British Corps counter-attack. Petershagen, Rinteln and Hameln, West Germany.
The Blue Effect +11.5 hours

The six missiles, launched moments earlier from the British 50th Missile Regiment, flew through the air at a speed greater than Mach 3. Six missiles, each one carrying an M251 warhead loaded with high-explosive sub munitions, struck the advanced elements of the attacking forces when they were less than three-kilometres from 2nd Infantry Division's second line of defence. The Soviet 12th Guards Tank Division, urged on by their masters, had gone for a narrow front, hitting the seven-kilometre gap between Minden and Petershagen. The Soviets had bombarded the 2nd Battalion, Yorkshire Volunteers, who had been given a three-kilometre stretch north of Minden to defend, with a forty-five-minute deluge of high explosives, and a significant air-to-ground strike. Following it up with an entire air assault battalion landing directly behind them. Although the 4th Battalion (Volunteers), the Parachute Regiment, defending the line north of the Yorkshire volunteers, had managed to release a company to send in support of the beleaguered battalion, it was soon mauled by Soviet Hind and Hip attack helicopters and went to ground. By then, it was too late and, within an hour, Soviet amphibious vehicles, K-61s carrying troops and heavy amphibious pontoons, along with GSPs carrying armoured vehicles, 12th Guards Division crossed the Weser. The minute a bridgehead was secured, the Soviet bridging units with their PMP pontoons were rushed forward under an umbrella of Soviet fighter aircraft. The speed at which the floating bridge was erected defied all records, and from the first pontoon unfolding in a splash into the waters and the first BMP-2 crossing to the other side, only forty minutes had passed.

The Bear, far from being a patient taskmaster, drove his commanders and his soldiers relentlessly. The Territorial Battalion to his front just crumbled, and the tough paratroopers to the north, although they fought bravely and at times almost fanatically, were no match for the ever increasing number of infantry combat vehicles and tanks. They were quickly rolled up as more and more troops poured across. The Bear knew that there was a third British battalion ahead of him, but he'd received reports that, under attack from Soviet airborne troops from the front and back, they were being withdrawn, probably before they were completely surrounded and overrun. He was surprised at the state of the British defence. *Where was their armour? Where was the American unit that was designated as a NORTHAG reserve? Had it been sent to support the Dutch and Germans to the north?* The Bear had raised it with his superiors, but he had been slapped down and told, in no uncertain terms, that his division was to do what it had been selected for: take advantage of a weakness in the enemy's defence, exploit it and push for the coast. They had reminded him that units of the 20th Guards Army were close behind him, and as soon as a fresh unit could bypass their advance division, recovering from the consequences of a tactical nuclear strike, he would have the reinforcements he needed. Before he could respond, reminding them that it was becoming a traffic jam back there, he was reminded of his mission and the connection was broken.

Now, up to six kilometres west of the river, one of his battalions was pushing west, and another northwest, smashing through the remnants of 6RRF when the British artillery struck. With two MTLB command vehicles back to back, a tent covering the gap in between, the Bear screamed down the radio at his commanders.

"Dorokhin, I don't care if you're being shelled, just keep moving. You have to take Diepenau."

"We are moving, sir, but we're being hit regularly by their artillery."

"If you keep on the move, get close to their lines. They will have to stop."

Colonel Dorokhin, commander of the 353rd Guards Tank Regiment, paused before responding. *"We have been struck by NATO missiles. The sub munitions have crippled one of my companies. I am moving around them now. Over."*

"Just take Diepenau. I'm sure you don't want me to replace you with another officer, or even come down there and take command myself. Out. Tsaryov, Tsaryov, where are you? Report. Over."

"Sir. Just hit a British headquarters pulling out of Hille. Finishing them off. Over."

"Tsaryov, don't you listen to your orders? Leave them. Get your tanks moving. I want you in Frotheim by midday and Espelkamp occupied soon after. Do you understand? Over."

"Yes, sir...we are being...hit by heavy..."

"Come in, Tsaryov. Over."

"Sorry, sir. The British are throwing everything at us."

"Understood. You have your orders. Out."

The political officer and deputy commander, Colonel Yolkin, popped his head through the tent flap.

"I've been listening to the transmissions, Comrade General. They don't seem capable of giving us the victory our Politburo is demanding."

The Bear lit up a cigarette and turned to his deputy. "Well, you'll get a chance to find out for yourself. I'm going further forward and you're coming in with me."

"But…but—"

"No buts, Yolkin, that's an order." The Bear spat out a piece of tobacco. "You are, believe it or not, a Soviet officer and you will obey my orders. If you don't, I'll have you shot. We leave in thirty minutes. Now, get out!"

The political officer paled before withdrawing his head from the flap and leaving to prepare for his excursion to the front. He was shaking.

More salvos descended in the area, and the Bear looked up, as a rolling barrage appeared to be less than a kilometre from his position. Taking another pull on his cigarette, he reflected on the situation. He knew he would need to contact headquarters again soon, and it wouldn't be pleasant. Something was worrying him, though. The NATO forces' artillery bombardment was proving ferocious. His bridgehead was clogged with logistics vehicles bringing forward ammunition and fuel. His forward units had to get to grips with the enemy so he could start prioritising his own artillery strikes. At the moment, they were firing blind. He had screamed at his engineers to put more bridges across, and the GSPs were working flat out to bring more and more armour across. His two forward regiments still weren't up to full strength. It was taking over an hour to get a battalion across, and he needed more crossing points if he was to bring forward his other two regiments. Although they were the weaker units, having been fighting almost constantly for days, he would feel happier having his entire division across the water. He didn't have a lot of faith in the follow-up forces getting here quickly. Also, if the British shifted their fire to his bridgehead and river crossings, it could prove problematic. He needed to get to the front.

Chapter 34

0535, 11 July 1984. 3rd Panzer Brigade, 1st Panzer Division, 1st German Corps. Southwest of Verden, West Germany.
The Blue Effect +11.5 hours

The Leopard tank, a fifty-five-ton Leopard 2, powered by its liquid-cooled 47.6 litre V-12 engine, hummed as the driver eased it forward into the brush ahead of him. It rocked forward gently as the driver made some minor changes to the tank's position, guided by his tank commander. The glacis of the German main battle tank barely poked its nose through the hedge line, some of the shrubs slightly higher than the top of the turret. The commander still had a good view overlooking the River Weser and the road, the 215 that ran north to south, less than 500 metres on the other side. Hauptmann Faeber ordered his crew to camouflage the tank well, using some of the foliage close by. To their left, fifty metres away, a second tank pulled into position. Although this stretch of the river had been defended over a number of days, the previous occupants had been pulled back after being battered by Soviet heavy artillery and air strikes. Decent defences had been dug, and they would move to those once an assault river crossing started. In the meantime, they would remain mobile, mitigating in some small way the threat of a regular pounding from the Soviet artillery. The Soviets were bringing more and heavier artillery forward, such as 203mm self-propelled artillery and 240mm mortars. He made a note to get the engineers forward all the same, and dig some new berms along the length of his patch, so at least they would have some ready-made positions close by to drive into.

He dropped down from turret, onto the engine deck, and descended onto the remnants of a cornfield that bordered the hedge line.

The gunner moved the turret left and right, checking that the barrel of the 120mm smoothbore main gun was clear to move in a full arc. One final sweep and he was happy that nothing would get in the way should they need to fire.

A DKW Munga F 91/8 Jeep pulled up alongside, and a Bundeswehr officer stepped out, calling Hauptmann Faeber over. The driver of the Jeep also got out and crossed over to the tank to talk with the crew and perhaps acquire a cigarette, his having been lost during the last retreat.

"Herr Major."

"Klaus, I have an update for you." The Bundeswehr major placed a map on the bonnet of the Jeep. "The large manoeuvres planned by NORTHAG are in progress."

Hauptmann Faeber leant over and followed his senior officer's pointing finger.

"There's a major artillery strike on the enemy here," he held his finger over a length of the River Weser from Porta Westfalica to Petershagen, "along with two major air-to-ground strikes. They are in support of a major counter-attack, consisting of a British Division and a US Brigade."

"Not using our reserve Brigade, then?"

"No, not now the Americans have got here."

"Any more intelligence on the tactical nuke strikes, Herr Major?"

"They have done their job, Klaus, but we're waiting for the Soviets to retaliate. If they are going to then it will definitely be during the counter-attack. We've been ordered keep our forces well dispersed. You are to take your platoon to this location."

Hauptmann Faeber looked at the major quizzically. "What if they use their strikes as an opportunity to launch an attack against us?"

"If we get hit by tactical nuclear missiles, and we're not in some decent cover and widely dispersed, we won't have a battalion left."

While they had been talking, an eight-wheeled Luchs, an armoured reconnaissance vehicle with a 20mm gun mounted in its turret, sped past. Following behind were four Marder armoured infantry fighting vehicles (AIFVs), mounted with their deadly remote-controlled machine gun along with the Milan anti-tank guided missile system. They drove quickly, not wanting to draw fire from any Soviet unit on the opposite bank. The growl of engines slowly diminished as they left the Leopard tank and the two officers behind. One swung right, heading for the hedge line overlooking the road, the other continued on. The mechanised infantry platoon would reinforce the tanks already here; providing the tanks with cover should they experience an assault by enemy infantry.

"The Infantry will be pulled back as well at the appointed time," the Major informed Faeber.

"Are we leaving anybody to watch the river?"

"Of course, Klaus. If they want to cross here, they can soon land an airborne assault. If they hold it long enough, they could very quickly ferry more troops across and then they have the beginnings of a bridgehead. We'll leave some reconnaissance troops all along the riverbank and, should they make that attempt, you will be ordered forward."

Klaus looked at the map. "From these deep protection positions, we could be back here within fifteen minutes."

"We have a quick reaction force from the rest of the battalion, who could be here in ten. There's also a company of Fallschirmjager, within a ten-minute helicopter flight, on standby."

"Swapping parachutes for helicopters." Klaus smiled.

"It doesn't make them any less crazy," laughed the major.

"Are we expecting them to attack along this stretch, sir?"

"Again, I am only surmising. The British are already advancing from their staging areas around the west of Minden and Petershagen." He spun the map around so Klaus could see where he was pointing. "The Soviets are already across the Weser. It's possible they may also attack furhter north."

"Hit the Dutch."

"Maybe. With the Soviet army crossing between Minden and Petershagen, they'll want to put some pressure elsewhere along the front. There is as good a place as any."

"Then why don't we do the same?"

"Do what?"

"Counter-attack. Take the bloody fight to them."

The major clapped him on the back. "Hauptmann Klaus," he laughed. "We'll make a battalion commander of you yet."

"We've been either digging in or running. It's about time we did what we've been trained to do: fire and manoeuvre."

0535, 11 July 1984. 45th Paantserinfanterie Battalion, 42nd
Pantserinfantriebrigade, 4e Divisie, 1 Netherlands Corp.
Outskirts of Bremen, West Germany.
The Blue Effect +11.5 hours

Lieutenant Dahlman ordered the soldier to open fire, and the 25mm cannon blasted the upper windows of the building opposite. After about twenty rounds, the YPR-765 armoured infantry fighting vehicle quickly reversed back down the street, just as a rocket-propelled grenade (RPG) struck the building they were next to, sending a deluge of bricks and mortar crashing down onto the street. The battalion, responsible for this section of the River Weser, had been playing cat and mouse with the troops opposite for the last couple of days. The Soviets had been probing, looking for opportunities to get soldiers across to the other side of the river that transited through this major West German city. It was proving wearing for both sides and the 42nd *Pantserinfantriebrigade* had been sent in to replace the Canadian Brigade that had initially been responsible for the city's defence. The 1st Netherlands Corps was recovering from the brunt of the attack by the 1st Polish Army, and expected a renewed attack by either the Polish or elements of the Soviet Guards Army at any moment. The Polish army had been very quiet, parts of it still recovering from the tactical nuclear strike. They were aware of the nuclear strikes, and that the Dutch Government had agreed to them as their own troops had suffered badly as a consequence of the chemical attacks.

All they could do now was wait: wait for the outcome of NORTHAG's counter-attack; wait for the Warsaw Pact's response.

Chapter 35

0535, 11 July 1984. Combat Team Delta, Royal Hussars,
7th Armoured Brigade, 1st Armoured Division.
Northeast of Lubbecke, West Germany.
The Blue Effect +11.5 hours

Corporal Farre, the gunner for Four-Alpha, was sitting right of the breech of the Challenger's 120mm gun; behind him, the legs of his platoon commander, Lieutenant Barrett. Farre looked through his periscope tank laser sight, the distance displayed for both the gunner and commander showing 2,100 metres as the first of the Soviet T-80s appeared between the villages of Diekerort and Isenstedt to the south. Two troops of Challengers were just inside the trees of the wooded area south of Espelkamp. The Regiment's Scorpions had probed the area ahead of the slowly advancing forces and had managed to escape unseen. They were able to report the enemy movement.

Barrett did a quick 180-degree search, looking for any sign of the Soviet's dreaded Hinds. That was the one weapon he feared, having seen the destruction they were capable of delivering whilst his unit defended the River Leine. There was a Tracked Rapier unit somewhere behind and, closer, two or three units with Blowpipe, the shoulder-launched surface-to-air missile. But he knew that the attack-helicopters would be hard to hit and, more importantly, hard to bring down. What he wasn't to know was that the Soviet battalion commander, lashed by his divisional and regimental commanders in turn, had urged his men forward, but had lost his bearings. As a consequence, he was sending a company of tanks forward south of where four Hind-Ds were heading for; to provide the much-needed support for the Soviet troops that were in danger of being encircled.

"Four-Four call signs. Hold until they're all out in the open."

"Two thousand metres. They're picking up speed," informed Farre.

"Roger."

Farre watched his target move, it had already been agreed which one they would target first, along with the second and third if they got the chance. The computerised sighting system assimilated the information from the laser rangefinder with that of the moving target, calculating and setting the lay of the main gun.

"Get ready," advised the commander.

"One thousand, nine hundred metres." Farre made a final quick adjustment. "On."

"All Four-Four call signs. Engage!"

"Firing."

After Farre pressed the firing switch, the tank rocked as the sabot round left the barrel.

"Hit!" Barrett called. "Target left, 1800."

"On."

"Fire."

"Firing."

A second round left the Challenger. This time, the penetrator failed, deflected by one of the ERA blocks. But the Soviet tank wasn't to escape the onslaught as a second sabot round, fired by Four-Bravo, collided with it, stopping it dead in its tracks. Seven Soviet main battle tanks were left immobilised on the battlefield as the survivors fired off their smoke grenades, placing a carpet of smoke in front of them, the drivers hitting full power as they reversed back away from the killing field.

Two things happened then. Firstly, a switched-on forward observer brought down a barrage of artillery fire on top of the Soviet positions, timing it well, immersing the retreating unit in a salvo of high explosives. Secondly, using the Soviets' own smokescreen as cover, Delta-Squadron advanced, intent on keeping up the pressure on the Soviet forces that, all across the NATO northern front, were finding the tables turning.

0715, 11 July 1984. Combat Team Bravo, 14/20th King's Hussars,
22nd Armoured Brigade, 1st Armoured Division.
South of Petershagen, West Germany.
The Blue Effect +13 hours

The embankment of the River Weser came alive as tanks of C-Squadron moved up to provide cover. In the meantime, the US low-profile M88 amphibious bridging vehicles lumbered out of hiding from the

Heisterholz Forest, making their way down to the riverbank and into the water. A cloud of smoke, mixed in with high explosives, erupted on the opposite side, blinding the few enemy units in place. Close behind the barrage, ninety men from 24th Brigade were helicoptered in to secure the area. US M163 Vulcan air-defence systems searched the skies, looking for any Soviet ground-attack aircraft bent on interfering with the activities in progress. Once in the water, the amphibious bridging vehicles, MFAB/Fs, pushed out towards the centre of the river, their bridging sections pivoting until they were at right angles to the length of the transporter. One vehicle, nearest to the edge of the river, unfolded its ramp, lowering it onto the western riverbank, providing a route onto the bridge for the vehicles waiting to cross. Its sister vehicle manoeuvred alongside it, and the two sections connected. More of the vehicles linked up until at least a dozen provided a crossing for the forces waiting. Once the last amphibious vehicle had lowered its ramp on the opposite bank, a British Scorpion, commanded by Lieutenant Baty, crossed quickly. Once it was confirmed that the bridge was working effectively, two more Scorpions followed, fanning out to link up with the soldiers from 24th Brigade and secure the other side of the river.

It had gone exceptionally well. The initial plan to drive through the centre of the combat area had been cancelled. Aerial reconnaissance had shown that the Soviets had dismantled the bridges north and south, and held two centre ones with a strong force, a battalion for each at least. The Soviets had pushed so far west, and stretched their forces so thin along a ten-kilometre-wide corridor as far as Frotheim in the south and Diepenau in the north, pushing to split the NATO forces in the region, that the US Brigade attacking from the south and 12th Armoured Brigade from the north had very few forces to prevent them. 7th Armoured, acting as a blocking force, prevented the Soviet forces moving further west, while 22nd Armoured, using the 239, headed north, then east, passing through elements of the 12th that had secured the western bank of the River Weser. Further north, Chieftain AVLBs had laid single-piece No 9 bridging units, along with the No 8 scissors bridge, to ensure fast movement by the advancing British Brigades. Barbarians, specialist Chieftain AVREs carrying Maxi Pipe Fascines, dropped their cargoes into tank ditches, dug as part of the defence against the Soviet attack. Now the British needed to cross them to press home their counter-attack.

The tracks of Alex's Chieftain rattled across the floating bridge.

Behind him, his troop, a platoon of infantry in their 432s and, behind them, would come the rest of B-Squadron, followed by the rest of the regiment.

"Left stick," he ordered his driver Mackey. "Left, left...forward." He heard the rattle of gunfire through the swirl of smoke as the reconnaissance unit and the airborne infantry got to grips with the enemy.

Corporal Patterson kept the turret and main gun facing in the direction of travel, while Sergeant Simpson's Two-Two-Bravo covered right. Behind him, Two-Two-Charlie, commanded by Corporal Moore, covered their rear quarter.

"Scorpion up ahead, sir," called Patsy.

"I see it. Stick with him, Mackinson."

"Sir."

The Scorpion roared off, and Alex knew he was to follow. Ahead, there would be two other Scorpions recceing their route ahead. After 500 metres, the Scorpion spun right, and Alex instructed Mackinson, his driver, to follow. They passed between the village of Weiterscheim and Auf dem Sande, keeping the road, the 482, on their left.

"*Two-Two call signs, stop, stop, stop,*" ordered Lieutenant Baty in the lead Scorpion.

"Stop, stop, stop," ordered Alex. Patsy turned the turret, covering a ninety-degree arc to their front.

The infantry call sign pulled over and dismounted from their 432s.

"*Two-Two call signs, this is Tango-One. Standby. Friendly outgoing south your location. Out.*"

The lead Scorpion had just informed them of friendly fire. All they could do now was wait. Alex felt uncomfortable: they were sitting ducks here. He hoped the other two recce vehicles were close by, keeping watch.

"*Two-Two-Alpha, this is Zero Bravo. Over.*"

"Go ahead. Over."

"*We're forming up behind you. As soon as strike over move in.*"

"Roger, sir. Out."

Ahead of Bravo-Troop, a Soviet motor rifle company, supported by a platoon of three tanks, was preparing to respond to reports of an assault river crossing by the enemy further north. They had received a call for help from one of their units attacked by soldiers from the 24th Brigade, and were preparing to mount their vehicles when the DPICMs struck. The dual-purpose improved conventional munitions, filled with small grenades, detonated in the air, a rain of lethal shrapnel spraying over the crouching soldiers below. Looking at it from afar, the ground became submerged in a grey cloud of dust, debris and shrapnel, and the air above it was like a concentrated fireworks display, blue-white sparks of light filling the air as far as the eye could see. The soldiers dived for cover, pressing their hands to their ears, some praying for this hell to end before it drove them mad. During a period of time, that lasted less than a minute, but for the soldiers exposed to it seeming like an hour, the effects were crippling as shrapnel tore into their fragile bodies, destroying their weapons and equipment. Tracks were torn from their armoured vehicles, armour was pierced and red-hot flames consumed the ammunition. The larger main battle tanks suffered extensive damage; aerials ripped off and the sighting systems shattered. The explosions stopped abruptly.

"Two-Two call signs, Two-two-Alpha. Advance in line of attack, right flanking. Two-Two-Delta, follow on."

The rest of Alex's troop acknowledged and Two-Two-Bravo and Charlie moved up on his right, the infantry platoon lining up behind as Alex ordered his small force forward. The Scorpion veered off to the left, ready to cover their flanks as the Chieftain tanks powered forward. The tanks advanced in line, the pointing 120mm barrels staggered left and right, covering all arcs of a potential attack.

"Target," yelled Patsy.

A yellow flash erupted from the end of Two-Two-Alpha's barrel as the tank gun fired, followed by a pale grey plume of smoke. A controlled explosion accelerated the round, a short flight at 1,000 metres per second, and it rocketed the projectile towards its victim, a surviving Soviet MICV. The BMP-2 lurched on its tracks as a yellow cloud encased the armoured troop carrier. The wading plate, attached to the front for use during a river crossing, shot forward as the yellow blast turned to orange. On hitting the front of the vehicle it was immediately ricocheted back, slamming against the engine cover before repeating the cycle all over again. Black and orange plumes swamped the stricken vehicle. The infantry carrier had been torn apart, along with the troops within.

"*Two-Two-Alpha, Zero Bravo. Go left, go left. Tango-One will lead. Over.*"

"Roger that. All Two-Two call signs. Left, left, left. Form up left flanking. Over."

"Two-Bravo. Roger."

"Two-Charlie, on your left."

"Left stick," he called to Mackey down in the fridge, although his Noddy suit and the fear of battle were keeping him well and truly warm.

The Chieftain turned on its tracks, and Alex pushed his way through the hatch, turning the cupola left as Patsy swung the turret right. He looked across as the rest of his troop caught up and drew alongside. Behind them, the four 432s of Two-Delta followed.

"Zero-Bravo, Two-Two-Alpha. In position. Over."

"Charlie will be on your right, Delta your left and Alpha in reserve. Out."

That's a relief, he thought. Although the artillery attack had been devastating, there were always survivors. More and more of 1 Div troops would be crossing. 12th Brigade and the US Brigade would secure the area west of the river where a battle with the Soviet Division was still in progress. Battered by ceaseless artillery and air strikes, the Bear had pulled some of his forces back to attempt to form a line and get control of the situation, only to have his tanks run into the last of the British FASCAM reserves. Seven tanks had been crippled, along with five BMPs. His force was slowly being whittled down. A counter-attack would have been the right move. Split the two British Brigades to his front and left flank; let the 20th worry about the Americans. But one of his officers, in a panic, had sent his forward battalion, down to fourteen tanks, in the wrong direction, straight into 7th Armoured Brigade's Challenger tanks. Fourteen quickly became seven. He would now have to hold, consolidate and wait.

Alex's troop continued to advance, accelerating up the banks of the 482 Autobahn, through a thick layer of trees running along it, crashing through half a dozen soft-skinned resupply vehicles, Patsy spraying the panicking Soviet soldiers with the coaxial machine gun. They crossed the central reservation, brushing aside two more Zil trucks. Ellis loaded a HESH round, and Patsy put it to good use, as an ammunition carrier ripped itself apart.

"Two-Two-Alpha, Tango-One. Platoon, Tango-Eight-Zeros, 2,000 metres west of 482. Sitting ducks. Over."

"Roger. Out to you. Two-Delta, watch our six. Over."

"Two-Two-Delta. We have it. Over."

"Out to you. Two-Bravo, Two-Charlie. Three targets, twelve o'clock, 2,000 metres. Forward slowly."

"Roger."

"Roger."

"Watch the bank, Mackinson."

"Got it, sir."

Mackey manoeuvred the tank through the trees on the other side of the dual carriageway, stopping just before the bank dropped down on the other side.

The 432s of Two-Two-Delta climbed to the top of the bank, the drivers halting while still in the trees on the hard shoulder of the road. Infantry piled out of the back and ran forward while the two battle taxis with their peak engineering turrets opened fire on the milling Soviet drivers and soldiers that had been sent along with the convoy to defend it.

This is a turkey shoot, thought Corporal Graham as he threw himself down alongside his section.

Finch and Berry knew what they were doing and soon had rounds going out, punching through cab doors, piercing the canvas sides of the trucks and mowing down soldiers who were leaping down from trucks just arriving, or backing up in the melee.

After assessing the situation, Lieutenant Chandler knew what he needed to do: cover the back of Bravo-Troop and clear a safe passage for the rest of the squadron that would not be far behind. His turreted 432s and gun-groups received their orders, and he took the rest of his platoon, fourteen men, through the trees, just below the bank, until he was opposite the latest Soviet arrivals. The fire-support team let rip, spraying round after round into the still bewildered enemy who thought their Army was across the other side of the Weser and winning. The last thing they expected was to be facing NATO soldiers on this side of the river.

"Go! Go! Go!" Chandler bellowed.

The infantry soldiers rose up as one, skirmishing forwards. Their NBC roll packs, water bottles and kidney pouches bouncing on their hips, the 58-pattern ammunition pouches bulging with loaded spare magazines for their SLR rifles, they closed in on the enemy's position. Three Gympys poured hundreds of rounds into the Soviet infantry right up until the last minute. A BMP suddenly appeared out of the smoke of the burning trucks, its 30mm gun blasting one of the gun-groups, killing all three men.

"Two-Alpha, Two-Delta. BMP right behind you!"

"Roger Two-Delta. Heads down."

"Hit the deck!" Chandler yelled to his men as the BMP spun round to face him, disgorging soldiers from its troop compartment at the rear.

But that was all it did. It lifted off the ground and flipped onto its side as a HESH destroyed it and the troops with it. The fuel tanks in the rear doors fuelled the flames, and a black plume of smoke quickly formed as the BMP was engulfed in a conflagration, the popping of burning ammunition even putting New Year's Eve fireworks to shame.

The lieutenant didn't waste a moment and, leaving the burning BMP behind them, now of little use to the enemy, his platoon quickly routed the opponent in their immediate vicinity.

Alex and Patsy peered through their scopes: their view out of the front was clear. Open fields were laid out in front of them as far as the eye could see. The only object blocking their vision to the southeast was the heavily forested high ground north of the Mittellandkanal. But, directly in front, a trail of dust following behind, a second platoon of Soviet T-80s headed their way. Directly behind them were another two tanks. Off to the left, they could see two more, being reported by Lieutenant Baty's troop, as a full tank company, no doubt stragglers from 12th Guards Tank Division rushing to the rescue of their parent unit.

Alex passed his orders to his troop; then to Corporal Patterson who was more than happy to oblige.

"T-80, 1,500 metres, sabot."

"Up," shouted Ellis.

"Fire," Alex ordered.

Patsy pressed the firing button, and the deadly package left the barrel of the tank.

"T-80, one o'clock, 1,500 metres, sabot."

The first round struck the far front right T-80, catching it on its front right guard, smashing through the front road wheel and dislodging the track, forcing it to slew to the left.

"Up."

"Fire. First target. Damaged T-80, 1,500 metres, sabot."

"Up."

"Fire."

"T-80, second line, twelve o'clock, 1,600 metres, sabot."

"Up."

"Fire."

"Zero-Bravo, Tango-One. Tango-Eight-Zeros, company strength, 2,000 metres east my location. Over."

"This is Zero-Bravo, acknowledged. Two-Three and Two-Four. Engage."

The rest of the squadron was up on the road now and joined in the slaughter.

The turret of Two-Alpha filled with fumes, and sweat poured down the faces, necks and backs of the crew as they worked almost mechanically, intuitively, firing round after round into the enemy until the fields out to their front were strewn with burning hulks, pillars of black and white smoke like columns appearing to hold up the rapidly clearing sky. A covered position on high ground, an unsuspecting enemy, and the pinpoint accuracy thanks to the Chieftain's fire control system and professional crews had just routed the best part of a weakened Soviet tank battalion. But, now, they needed to move before the deadly Hinds turned up, or artillery and Soviet aircraft zoned in on their position.

Alex took his tanks back on the road, went south for 200 metres, shooting up more soft-skinned vehicles, crushing men and machines that got in the way, before dropping down the eastern bank of the road, followed closely by a jubilant infantry platoon. He pushed east again, leading the rest of Bravo-Squadron to their objective.

0820, 11 July 1984. 4th Armoured Division, 1st British Corps.
Between Rinteln and Hameln, West Germany.
The Blue Effect +14 hours

The Soviet attack plan had been simple, on paper at least. 12th Guards Division had crossed the River Weser in 1st Armoured Division's sector, and troops had poured across in their hundreds. The Soviet plan, dependent on the success after the crossing, was to either push north, hitting the flank of the Bundeswehr, getting in behind them and cutting them off, or to skirt Minden and swing south, following along the fifty-kilometre stretch of the Wiehengebirg, a 300-metre high, heavily forested feature than ran from west of Porta Westfalica to just short of Osnabruck. The border with the Netherlands would be less than eighty kilometres west. Here, the Soviets would be well and truly behind the British lines. Using small detachments of Spetsnaz and heliborne motor rifle troops to act as the division's southern flank screen, their orders were to move without stopping, bypassing

275

strongholds where they were able, and split the two major NATO forces in Europe, NORTHAG and CENTAG, in two. Once able, they were to attack the rear of the Belgian forces and strike out for the Rhine. Advance divisions of 20th Guards Army would follow the OMG of 3rd Shock Army and exploit the weaknesses that the forward division would create. 20th Guards Army could then become an army level OMG in its own right. But, things weren't going to plan.

For 4th Armoured Division, their first attempts had ended badly when their counter-attack had been pre-empted by an attack by the Soviet 47th Guards Tank Division, closely followed by forces from 7th Guards Tank Division who, like the 10th, had been badly mauled and had been pulled out of the line, exhausted but still available. The 47th were also recovering from a failed attempt to reach Porta Westfalica in strength and force a river crossing to push south, their objective, the gap between Herford and Bad Salzuflen with the final objective, Bielefeld. Although elements had reached west of Rinteln, they had been partially broken by a heavy bombardment from the air by a small Vulcan bomber force. Along with ground-attack aircraft, a concentrated artillery bombardment and meeting repeated defensive positions set up by a brave but now battered Territorial battalion, they had eventually run out of steam. 49th Infantry Brigade, 2nd Infantry Division, had put up a strong fight. All along the River Weser, down to the border with 1st Belgian Corps, 3rd Armoured Division on 2nd Infantry Division's right flank were digging in, securing 1st and 4th Armoured Divisions' right flank. The day for the 47th and 7th was about to get worse.

Two British brigades led the attack from the south. 11th Brigade was already crossing the Weser near Hameln, punching into the thinly spread Soviet forces. Major General Walsh, commander of 4th Armoured Division, knew that Soviet reserves were on their way. Although suffering from the consequences of two tactical nuclear strikes, the Soviets would soon recover, and push forces forward to attempt to blunt his counter-attack and continue their advance west. Therefore, speed was crucial. A two-pronged attack was initiated, one striking north-east between Bad Munder and Coppenbrugge, the target Springe, a second pushing along the A2, the target Bad Nenndorf and beyond. Elements of a battalion from 24th Brigade had already been flown in and positioned along the route of the A2 to act as a flank guard and conduct sabotage missions wherever possible. SAS forces had also been dropped behind enemy lines to disrupt the enemy's flow of supplies and reinforcements. Paratroopers, guided in by Pathfinders taken behind enemy lines the previous night, were on their way to add to the Soviets' rapidly growing misery. Two Brigades were not a large force but, well focussed, they could hurt the enemy badly.

But, then, the entire operation was a gamble. 1st Armoured Division had crossed their sector of the Weser with 22nd Armoured Brigade, restricting the enemy's space to manoeuvre, retaking ground they had recently defended. Two brigades had closed in behind the tail end of 12GTD, blocking their retreat and interdicting their supplies of fuel and ammunition, and preventing 20th Guards Army coming to the rescue. Another gamble. Eventually an entire British division and a US Brigade would be advancing on Hanover. Another gamble.

0830, 11 July 1984. 2nd Battalion, Royal Green Jackets,
11th Armoured Brigade, 4th Armoured Division.
Southeast of Hameln, West Germany.
The Blue Effect +14.5 hours

Lieutenant Dean Russell's platoon followed the troop of tanks across the bridge. Dean listened to the roar of jet aircraft above the sound of rattling tracks and the growl of engines. His temptation was to drop down inside the 432, seeking protection from within its armoured cocoon. As thin as it was, it was better than nothing. Combat Team Alpha had been rested and reinforced from soldiers sent across the English Channel from mainland Britain, and were on their way to do battle with the enemy yet again. A Fulcrum flew low over the man-made bridge as Russell's platoon rattled across.

The commander of the tank in front swung the cupola round, firing a burst of 7.62mm rounds from the turret-mounted Gympy. The Corporal knew it was fruitless, but it made him feel better.

Dean ducked his head as two plumes of water shot up either side, soaking him and the surface of the flat-topped 432 as gravity brought the water back down to river level. Streaks of tracer filled the skies as two Bundeswehr Gepard anti-aircraft guns created an umbrella of lethal 35mm AA rounds. They had been brought in with the German Jaeger unit that would protect the crossing point on the southern side of the Weser should the Soviet forces find themselves able to throw the British back and counter-attack themselves. Rapier missiles raced high in the sky, chasing the Soviet aircraft as they desperately tried to plug the gaps that were forming along their entire front. Radio chatter on the Soviet military network had intensified. Orders and counter-orders, demands for reinforcements, air and artillery support were constant. One Soviet air-to-ground attack squadron had been ordered to hit this particular crossing point; then had it countermanded to target the 24th Brigade's airmobile units behind their lines. On receiving a third set of orders, the sixteen aircraft had returned to their base as their fuel tanks began to run dry, only to find a British Corps Patrol Unit (CPU) had sabotaged their localised fuel dump and armaments.

The 1 BR Corps' commander had taken another gamble. Using the 16th Air Defence Regiment to defend his artillery brigade and the 105th (Volunteers) Air Defence Regiment, Royal Artillery, shipped over from Edinburgh, to support 2nd Infantry Division, he had released as many of his Rapier air-defence units as possible. Moving them into positions where they could defend the crossing points, the Soviet air force suddenly found themselves confronted by the latest in the British army's air-defence armoury. Fresh stocks of artillery shells from the UK, hoarded by the British gunners, were now being used freely, with the Soviet troops along the entire northern bank of the Weser between Rinteln and Hameln feeling the effects. It wasn't without consequences, with Soviet long-range counter-battery fire hitting the British artillery units at every possible opportunity, forcing commanders to frequently switch position of their self-propelled guns. Soviet bombers did their best to hunt them down. As large as the Soviet air force was, it was being stretched. Harrier GR3s, protected by Phantoms, flew mission after mission until exhausted and running low on ammunition and fuel, laying waste to the defending motor rifle and tank troops.

Recognising how critical this counter-attack was to the entire defence of not only NORTHAG but also the entire Allied Forces Central, AFCENT, front line, two squadrons of A-10 Warthogs had been assigned. Although both squadrons were down from eighteen to fewer than eleven aircraft each, using a stretch of the Autobahn east of Bielefeld as their runway, they inflicted devastation on any enemy armour that dared to show its face. To prevent retaliation by Soviet fighters, US fighters had been sent to provide combat air patrols. Deep strikes were also sanctioned. Two squadrons of Tornado GR1s, sixteen aircraft in total, struck at the 20th Guards Army positions, adding to the disruption caused by the recent tactical nuclear strikes. They paid a heavy price though: four were lost through the ever-increasing umbrella of surface-to-air missiles being thrown forward by the Soviet Stavka. But more attacks followed, maintaining the pressure on the Soviet ground forces.

The 432 jolted and shook as it clattered down the slope of the bridge on the northern bank of the Weser, the engine labouring as the driver changed down to climb the steep bank once the armoured personnel carrier left the bridge. Dean was glad that his driver had survived, not just because he was one of his soldiers, but because he had been with the lieutenant during the battles around Coppenbrugge, so had been blooded like him. One of his sections had a new driver fresh out of training, replacing Rifleman Daly, killed during a chemical attack. In fact, the soldier's training had been cut short, and he had only driven the battle taxi for a matter of a few hours. Prior to that, as a reservist with a home defence battalion, he had not even driven a Saxon, but was moved around in four-ton lorries. He would learn, and learn quickly.

Dean looked back; checking the rest of his platoon was sticking with him. The new driver, with Two-Section, was the third vehicle back, penned in the middle so, if he had problems, he wouldn't be the last in the file and potentially get detached from the unit. Also, the front two sections would be required to react quickly should they come under fire. Dean cracked his side against the hatch opening as the 432 slewed to the left as it dipped into a shell crater. *One of ours or one of theirs*, thought Dean. It didn't matter: both sides had been pounding each other for the last twenty-four hours.

Coming up out of the hole, the driver pulled on the left stick, applied some power, and caught up with the Chieftain forging ahead in front. Combat Team Alpha although reinforced were still below full strength. In fact, they were down to only eighty per cent of their original strength. The 2RGJ Battle Group had one key mission assigned to it: to protect the right flank of the line of attack as the 3rd Royal Tank Regiment Battle Group battled its way north-east. The crash of tank guns could be heard occasionally as 3RTR Chieftains came up against the T-80s of the 47th Guards Tank Division. The enemy had been caught completely on the hop.

Hercules aircraft flew overhead, flying as low as possible until the last minute, protected by a force of British and German Phantoms and British Hawk fighters. Once over their target, they would climb to the right altitude and release their cargo, 600 men of the British 1st Parachute Battalion, the reserve force of 24th Airmobile Brigade. Up until now, it had been the goal of the Soviet army to keep NATO forces on the hop, dropping multiple airborne units on and behind the lines, using Spetsnaz forces to create mayhem and disruption behind the NATO lines. Now it was the British army's turn to give them a taste of their own medicine. The men of the parachute battalion would be dropped east of Wichtringhausen. Here, they could threaten the crossroads where the A2 crossed the 65; more disruption of Soviet reinforcements moving west, and a thorn in the side of 20th Guards Army.

3RTR continued to fight its way towards Springe, bowling over unit after unit, taking the local military commanders completely by surprise. The Soviet airwaves were awash with panic, calls for help and assistance. Over-reporting the strength of the enemy to compensate for their failures, the unit commanders added to the confusion that was overloading their divisional headquarters who in turn passed their concerns and confusion to army headquarters and so on. Although the Soviet army had modernised somewhat, they were still generally dependent, on set-piece manoeuvres; only the OMGs having a longer leash. But, for the follow-on forces from the 20th Guards Army and the Military Districts, the leash was much tighter. With the map covered in flashes where small actions were being fought, arrows showing large movements of enemy troops, circles where parachutists, heliborne landings and acts of sabotage had been reported, Stavka were at a loss. Many of the actions reported were out of date as the British forces had long gone, but back in the depths of the concrete bunkers, the maps of the commander of the Group of Soviet Forces Germany, looked more like a mosaic. As a consequence, reinforcements were diverted, but often to the wrong locations, supplies were delayed or redirected, and the picture grew more ambiguous.

Having spilt up, a squadron from 3RTR led 2RGJ through the gap between the high ground of Eichberg and Shecken, the retreating Soviets leaving a trail of dust as they ran. An ambush took out one of the accompanying Scimitars and two of their Chieftains, but an attack by B-Company, 2RGJ, cleared the way. On arrival at the crossroads south of Behrensen, the 3RTR squadron sped north to link up with its regiment. Here at Behrensen, HQ, Support-Company and C-Company went about the business of digging in, while B-Company headed east to Coppenbrugge and A-Company south to Bisperode. The remaining two reconnaissance tanks were despatched east and west of their location, very much searching for a needle in a haystack.

Two-Platoon started their preparations to defend the small village, and the Milan teams were deployed along with the 438s. The OC stood next to Dean's 432.

"Dean, I'm making some changes. If you take a look at our position." The OC scraped some patterns in the soil. "Three-Platoon will be with us first thing in the morning, whether they're ready or not. We need more men."

Dean looked around at the high ground each side of them and the vast open space of farmed fields to their south. "Makes sense, sir. A battalion would be better though."

"I know, Dean, but we don't have a battalion. If 20th Armoured Brigade are released, they will take over and push south and east."

"What's the trigger for their release, sir?"

"Success, Dean, success. A bit of a catch-22. They are in position just in case the counter-attack is a failure, which I understand. Yet, if they were in the fight now, we'd have a much better chance. Anyway." The OC scraped some more lines in the dust patch. "Losing that Scimitar has left us blind, so I'm changing your platoon's role." He tapped the two extended oval markings either side the long stretch that represented the road. "I've already contacted the recce, and they will hold for you. I want one of your sections with each Scimitar, and they are to pass along the entire length of the high ground. Once they are opposite Route 425, they can hold. The recce boys can then complete some roving patrols. The same thing the other side. Here." He tapped the crossroads to the south. "This is where I want you, and one of your sections. That way, you will have some control over the sections that will be either side of your position. But you are not to hold. It's not a defensive position. I just need a warning of any enemy movement. Clear?"

"Clear, sir."

"You'd better get moving."

"Sir."

Within fifteen minutes, One-Section, under the command of Corporal Reid, his rank now substantive, were heading back the way they had come, before turning south, weaving along the centre track on the high ground, following behind the Scimitar leading.

Colour Sergeant Rose was with him. Corporal Stubbings, his most experienced Junior NCO, with Two-Section, headed north along the 588. The NCO sighed with relief when he met up with the second Scimitar, Sergeant Kirby in command, who led them east to climb the Krullbrink.

Dean's command 432, along with Three-Section, commanded by Acting-Corporal Cole, set off for the crossroads. Dean's vehicle led, and they were soon travelling in excess of forty kilometres per hour. It was a good metalled road; potted with trees either side, but not too many that would obscure their view. The road weaved gently; then angled left and right. He sniffed the air: it felt fresh. To his right, yellow fields that had once perhaps been wheat or cornfields; on his left, green root vegetables, maybe cabbages or potatoes. They were approaching a large farm on the right, and Dean ordered his driver to slow down. He was looking at the tracks that had torn up the ground north of the farm. *Used as a lager for armoured vehicles at some point,* he thought. It was his last thought as the high explosive anti-tank warhead of the 9M124 Kobra missile struck his 432. At hypersonic speed, twenty-five times the speed of sound, the jet of molten metal penetrated the front of Dean's vehicle, the spall stripping the flesh from his legs, his driver dead as the battle taxi swerved off the road, only to be hit a second time by a kinetic penetrator shot from a second T-80, fired from off the road. This struck the 432 on its slabbed side, knocking it over, the pressure wave and deadly particle spray inside killing the men within and blowing the rear door open. The same fate met Three-Section.

Some elements of 20th Guards Army were very much functional and ready for a fight.

Chapter 36

1200, 11 July 1984. 12th Guards Tank Division, 3 Shock Army.
West of Minden, West Germany.
The Blue Effect +18 hours

The Bear, Major General Turbin, commander of the 12th Guards Tank Division, leant on the collapsible wooden table in front of him, his head hanging between his shoulders. He lifted his head as an explosion shook the foundations of the house he had occupied as his temporary headquarters. In anticipation of a quick push west, his main headquarters had been set-up on the west bank of the river, and he had just been informed that it had been hit hard, and the majority of his senior staff had been either killed or captured. *Why didn't I foresee this?*

He swept the maps off the table in rage, his anger building up. *Why had higher command authorised this when the British still had a powerful force available, and 20th Guards Army were still whining over a glass of vodka?*

The door to the room put aside for him creaked as it was opened. "Get out!"

The deputy commander and political officer, Colonel Yolkin, continued on into the room. "Headquarters are wanting an update, Comrade General. They are insisting that we counter the British attack and push west. We have special forces creating opportunities for us."

"There will be no counter-attack, Comrade Colonel."

"You have your orders, Comrade General."

"The last set of orders were pointless. We launched our attack too soon. So why should these later ones be any better?"

"Then I will...have to relieve you of command, Comrade General," the political officer blurted out, his voice shaky.

The general lifted his hands off the table and raised his body to its full height, still facing away from the colonel. "And you will lead

283

my men to victory? What will you use? Political speeches?"

"I'm sorry, Comrade General, but I must ask you to step down. I shall report your behaviour to my superiors."

Yolkin turned and headed for the door at the same time the Bear turned to face him. "Colonel Yolkin."

The man turned back round to face his commander and felt his body jerk at the same time the Makarov pistol, held out in front of the Bear, barked twice.

"You'll be reporting to no one."

Chapter 37

1300, 11 July 1984. 4th Battalion, 67th Armoured Regiment,
3rd Brigade, 3rd Armoured Division, US V Corps.
Stop-Line Colorado, area of Steinau an der Strasse, West Germany.
The Blue Effect +19 hours

With only three tanks left in his platoon, leaving two behind on Stop-Line Dallas, Lieutenant Dardenne waited for the enemy to appear for a second time that day. He knew that, if they could blunt the next attack, a counter-attack would be launched, and he and his men would get some desperately needed respite.

"Tango-One-One. Standby for outgoing. Out."

Artillery at last. Artillery, he knew, with its immense destructive power, was one of the key assets in the forthcoming battle. His history studies had informed him that, during World War 2, artillery fire was responsible for nearly seventy per cent of casualties. He prayed that, in this more modern war, they would inflict a similar level of casualties on the Soviet forces. The gunners would not be able see their target. They would have to rely on mathematical calculations, using computers, to hit enemy targets many kilometres away. The forward observer team to his left was under his protection. As an armoured company, his unit had one M981. Its crew consisted of a lieutenant, a non-commissioned officer, and two soldiers. They would be advising the company commander on fire support issues.

The fire direction centre command post, the M577 FDC, located nearby, was a hive of activity. Numerous platoons of US M109s, in staggered lines, waited for orders from the brains of the artillery. To ensure they didn't become an easy target themselves, the howitzers were scattered over a wide area. Weather and meteorological data was fed into the complex systems of the FDC. SP4 Gorman tapped the keys of the consul as he stared at the red numerals lighting up as he fed in the required information.

The ground out to 2,000 metres in front of Dardenne's platoon seemed to boil; a cauldron of hot explosives and splinters engulfed the Soviet advanced unit. But there was more to come.

The pilot, after receiving his orders via radio, banked left; coming out of the circuit he and his wingman had just flown. The two aircraft had been loitering for ten minutes, waiting for confirmation from base via the ground forces below that their targets were approaching the killing ground. North of the two aircraft, another pair of tank busters also manoeuvred, ready to follow in behind their fellow pilots. On receiving instructions from the lead plane, the four Warthog A-10As flew east, keeping no more than 300 metres above the ground. Flying at a steady speed of 480 kilometres per hour, they would be on target in less than four minutes. The four aircraft had left their base twenty minutes earlier; a base that consisted of a dozen soft-skinned vehicles and part of a German Autobahn as a runway. Their original airfield at Spangdahlem was undergoing repairs after yet another attack by Soviet bombers, missiles from Soviet SCUD-B launchers, and an attack by Spetsnaz sleepers. The SCUD missile had been the most disruptive, one landing directly on the airbase, dispersing a lethal nerve agent. The chemical agent used was a persistent agent, and the base required extensive decontamination before it would be fully functional again. Other aircraft, flown over from RAF Bentwaters and RAF Alconbury in Great Britain, were also getting in position to attack. Despite the tactical nuclear strike, one on the 8th Guards Army and one on the 3rd German Army, NVA, the Soviets were determined to strike for the heart of Frankfurt: disrupt the US army's supply lines, destroy its stockpiles of ammunition, and overrun bases and airfields. The commander of US V Corps was about to hit back. After being hit hard by artillery bombardments and air strikes, forces on the ground had pulled back a further five kilometres, Colorado their latest defence line. The Soviet commanders, sensing victory, had lunged at the retreating enemy. Pushing forward a full tank regiment of over eighty T-64 tanks. Although finding the terrain difficult to negotiate, the damage caused by the numerous nuclear ADMS, used to break up the ground they would have to cross, they had succeeded in pulling together a spearhead that drove right through the centre of the defending forces around Schluchtern.

The US command had been patient. Resisting demands to throw in reinforcements earlier, conscious that hundreds of soldiers on the ground were dying, they had kept their nerve. But now was the time to release their surprise. Four tactical fighter squadrons were launched: two from tactical fighter wings stationed in Great Britain, and two squadrons from West Germany. There was also the additional and unexpected support from a US navy carrier that was in the process of launching yet another strike.

The ground raced beneath Major Tuckey as he flew his aircraft, at times below 200 metres, at speed towards the enemy. Behind him, three others were strung out. He just caught a glimpse of US forces below, getting into position again after their withdrawal; digging in ready to hold the Soviet breakthrough. Behind them was a fresh, fully armed US armoured brigade, one of three forming up after arriving from the US, waiting their turn to hit the enemy, payback for all their buddies that had been lost since the start of the war.

"Two minutes," came the warning over his headset. The American big guns, M107s, M110s, M109s, with their 175mm and 155mm shells pounded the Soviet force's rear area, destroying some of the surface-to-air missile launchers. Other ground-attack aircraft had launched ARM missiles, the explosive packages seeking out the Soviet SAM missile radars. Fighter aircraft were providing a CAP overhead and a small mixed force, fighters and bombers, had secretly penetrated deep into the Soviet lines to pop up and provide the Soviet fighters with an alternative distraction.

"One minute," Major Tuckey informed the flight he was leading.

He dropped his speed, the other three as practised doing the same. They then climbed up to 1,200 metres, enabling them to have a better view of the battlefield and the targets they sought. Their main armament was best suited to a slant range of 1,200 metres with the A-10 in a thirty-degree dive.

There, he said to himself as he spotted a line of tanks moving at speed west. But he had another target in his sights first. He saw the four barrels of the ZSU-23/4 swing towards him as he depressed the trigger. His A-10 shook as a 23mm round clipped his cockpit, but the titanium-armoured shell, the 'Bathtub', protected him and his aircraft.

The GAU-8/A Avenger Gatling-type cannon fixed beneath was at speed in less than a second and, within one second, it had fired fifty, 30mm depleted-uranium armour-piercing rounds, sixty per cent of them hitting the ZSU Shilka along with its comrade fifty metres behind. The furthest was immediately disabled; the second, the closest, was torn apart.

Tuckey banked right, jinking occasionally, then banked left as a line of three T-64s came into view, a trail of dust thrown up behind each one as they travelled at speed. Once in his sights, they received a long burst. A full second, now the gun was at full speed, resulted in seventy rounds targeting the three main battle tanks. Thirty-two of them struck home, the majority punching through the thinner top armour. Major Tuckey didn't see the end result as he pulled into a steep climb, banking hard left, seeking out more tanks or tracked ground-to-air weapons systems. The three others were doing the same with only two minutes left on target. Suddenly, one of their party pulled out, limping back to base. A huge chunk of the left wing had disappeared, the fuel tank had been punctured, and the main body had been peppered with 23mm shells from a third Shilka. The self-sealing fuel tank, protected by fire-retardant foam, had done its job and, using one of the triple-redundancy flight systems, the pilot would get back in one piece. The remaining three picked their targets, each one knowing where the other was looking, and launched their second weapons system. Major Tuckey fired his first Maverick anti-tank missile. Two seconds later, it connected with a T-64 on the left top of its fighting compartment, a ring of flame and smoke ejecting from the turret ring as it lifted the turret two metres into the air, the crew dead, the tank finished as a weapon of war. This time, he banked right, pulling up and round, setting his position for one last attack. A huge flash pricked his eye as an SA-6 SAM missile, followed by an SA-9 missile, struck an A-10 so accurately and with such force that with all its armour and fail-safe systems it was literally destroyed in mid-air. He cursed under his breath, came in again at 1,200 metres, and let rip with the 30mm cannon, catching two BMP-1s swerving left and right, doing whatever they could to avoid the airborne tank busters above them. Further back, eight more of the tank busters were on the way, lined up for a further attack. And behind them, two more squadrons. Once the devastation of the tank regiment was complete, the Soviets would have to face a second major counter attack.

Chapter 38

1900, 11 July 1984. Combat Team Bravo, 14/20th King's Hussars, 22nd Armoured Brigade, 1st Armoured Division. Haste, West Germany. The Blue Effect +1 day

Having lost five in the last thirteen hours, what were left of the tanks of Combat Team Bravo had dispersed along the edge of the wooded area east of Haste. It was late in the day, and they were low on fuel and ammunition. Fuel bowsers had been promised, but ground-attack aircraft had hit them as the Soviet air force sought revenge for the counter-attack that came out of the blue, catching the Soviet forces completely off guard. But, until they received a resupply, it would be madness to go any further forward. They had also been promised that the US 2nd Brigade and 7th Armoured Brigade were on their way to bolster the attack that would continue the next day.

"Sir, sir."

"What? What?" answered Alex as he jolted his body upwards, having fallen asleep slumped over the turret hatch. "Corporal Patterson...what's up?"

"Thought you might feel better for a tea, sir."

Captain Alex Wesley-Jones rubbed his eyes, took the hot, sweet drink and felt its positive effect within a matter of moments. His body felt drained. If he didn't know better, he would have considered himself to be suffering from a severe dose of flu.

"Thank you, Corporal."

"You're welcome, sir."

"Where are Mackinson and Ellis?"

"Asleep, sir. I've just relieved Ellis on stag. Thought a brew would go down well. Didn't mean to wake you."

"That's OK. You lads did well today."

"Gave the Sovs a kicking, and that's no mistake, sir."

"We did, but it's not over yet."

"Do you think we might actually win, sir? I just want to go home."

"Thinking of your wife and daughter, Patsy?"

Patsy smiled at the use of his nickname. "Yes, when I'm not shitting myself. What the hell is that?" Exclaimed Patsy looking skyward.

Dusk suddenly turned to daylight. Alex thrust Patsy's head down and tucked his own into his chest as the sky got brighter and brighter. The flare eventually died down, and both looked back through the gap in the trees behind them. The ground shook, and the noise of the detonation eventually reached them. Towards the west, a glowing plume was slowly rising higher and higher; a plume they both recognised, something they had seen in history books, magazines and on TV documentaries. They never ever thought they would see one at first-hand.

"Oh God," Alex groaned. "Gas! Gas! Gas!"

1900, 11 July 1984. Combat Team Delta, Royal Hussars,
7th Armoured Brigade, 1st Armoured Division.
South of Rehburg-Loccum, West Germany.
The Blue Effect +1 day

The tanks of Combat Team Delta were dispersed around the small forest south of Locum. They couldn't go any further east until they had refuelled and rearmed. They had enough of both to defend their current position, but not enough to advance any further. They had met stiff resistance while fighting against the encircled Soviet division, who fought ferociously. It was only the enemy running out of ammunition and fuel before the 7th Armoured and 2nd US Brigade did that secured the allies a victory. But now across the Weser, they would have to wait before they could move any further forward in support of 22nd Armoured.

They would never know what happened next. Positioned 100 metres from the centre of the nuclear air burst, the crews outside and inside their tanks, along with the ordnance and equipment, out to a radius of 300 metres were instantly vaporised as temperatures reached 6,000 degrees. The trees that had been providing them with cover from the enemy swayed away from the direction of the blast, stripped, their foliage vaporised, before springing back, some crashing to the ground in flames. The tarnished tree trunks that remained were blackened, smouldering stalks, like rotten, broken teeth. Light armoured vehicles were flipped over; soft-skinned vehicles likewise, quickly bursting into flames.

★

The corporal, zipping up his fly as he returned to his tank twenty metres away, just inside the edge of the forest, looked at the flash, the sky, the air, the space in front of him losing all colour: just white, blindingly white. But only for a fraction of a second as the rapidly increasing fireball engulfed him, vaporising skin, flesh and then bone. He felt nothing. He just didn't exist any more. A modern-day crematorium furnace generates a heat of 1,000 degrees Centigrade to burn a body and ensure the disintegration of a corpse. The bodies of soldiers and civilians engulfed in the nuclear fireball didn't just disintegrate: in the 6,000-degree temperatures, they were vaporised.

Out to a kilometre, the air blast demolished most buildings, destroyed soft-skinned vehicles and killed all those that weren't protected by solid cover. Even out to three kilometres, soldiers and civilians alike suffered injuries that in many cases were fatal. If the fireball and blast hadn't killed Lieutenant Barrett and his crew, the rest of his squadron and elements of his regiment, the 70 Gy radiation dose would soon see to it, within hours or, at the most, a couple of weeks.

Three kilometres away, a unit of men from the Royal Signals, setting up a new relay station to ensure communication could be maintained for the Brigade to initiate its next advance, did not escape. A captain ran as fast as he could towards the large paddock alongside the farmhouse, his NBC suit smouldering, diving onto the grass, rolling his body over and over, smothering any potential flames. He put his red-blistered hand to his face and screamed as swollen flesh met swollen flesh. The other soldiers caught out in the open also suffered. A sergeant, his body facing the arc of the blast, his chest and legs saved by his Noddy-suit, felt the flesh on his hands and face begin to break down. He felt no pain; there were no nerves left to feel the pain with. Even those three and a half kilometres away, suffered third-degree burns. If there was one positive, as a consequence of it being an airburst, the level of fallout would be a minimised.

But 1,000 soldiers and civilians had just died, with the estimated number of casualties in the region of over 6,000. The Royal Hussars Regiment, along with its logistics support, signallers, drivers, military police, gunners, ceased to exist as a fighting force.

Civilians who were away from shelter, without the protection of NBC suits, had no chance. Their blackened bodies could be seen lying around the area for days. Those that survived would be collected, eventually, but the facilities just didn't exist to treat so many people.

2000, 11 July 1984. HQ, 2nd Battalion, Royal Green Jackets, 11th Armoured Brigade, 4th Armoured Division. Behrensen, West Germany. The Blue Effect +1 day

"You wanted me, sir?" the CSM asked as he stood at the entrance to the OC's penthouse tagged on the back of the OC's 432.

"Yes, come in, CSM."

He handed Tobi Saunders the sheet of paper with the notes the company signaller had made.

> *Battle Group RGJ.*
> *CO and OC eyes only.*
> *Six 50-kiloton tactical nuclear strikes occurred at the following locations:*
> > *Bassum*
> > *Asendorf*
> > *Rehburg-Loccum*
> > *Brakel*
> > *Schloss Steinau*
> > *Schlotten*
> *Units to disperse. Prepare for additional strikes.*

"The flashes and noise were a bit of a giveaway, sir. Same number of strikes we launched. What the hell happens now?"

"Only God can answer that one, CSM. But we need to get the Company dispersed and dug in deep."

"Any news on Lieutenant Russell sir?"

"Nothing. And air-recce tells us the Soviets hold the crossroads.

Chapter 39

0830, 12 July 1984. 12th Mechanised Division, 1st Polish Armee.
Tostedt, West Germany.
The Blue Effect +2 days

Gunter Keortig pulled his wife close to him as they gazed through
the bedroom window of their house on Bremer Strasse. For the last
twelve hours, there had been a steady stream of Polish soldiers moving
east through the town of Tostedt. It reminded him of the war, the
Second World War, when he as part of the Wehrmacht had traipsed
along roads in a similar manner to this. Not defeated, but on the run.
The Polish army was using as many vehicles as it could acquire in
order to get their men back home. The baker across the road had been
forced to surrender his small van. It was then used to carry wounded
soldiers. Keortig and his wife had watched as the van was loaded with
the injured, their faces and bodies covered with horrific burns. Others
they had seen looked to be well, in that there were no visible wounds,
but they would suddenly collapse onto the road, heaving their guts up
until there was nothing left, then retching some more.

On one occasion, there had been a confrontation right outside
the house. A Soviet unit, the maroon flashes indicating Soviet
Internal Security, MVD, had clashed with a Polish unit. A Polish
captain and Soviet major, along with half a dozen men, had been
killed, the Soviet unit withdrawing after being threatened by an ever
increasing number of Polish infantry supported by a T-54 tank. After
the clash, the column continued its move east.

0915, 12 July 1984. Motor-Schutz Regiment, 8th Motor-Schutz
Division, 5th German Army. Area of Schalkolz, West Germany.
The Blue Effect +2 days

"What is wrong with your men, Oberst Keller? We had the enemy on the run, and a crossing of the River Eider was wide open to us. Now, we are having to get ready to defend what we've already taken!"

"My orders, Colonel Gachev, are to hold position until further notice. In the meantime, my men will assist our *Kameraden* who were hit by the nuclear strike."

Colonel Gachev slammed his fist on the bonnet of the UAZ Jeep causing his driver to jerk awake. "Some of my men were caught in it as well, Comrade Oberst. We've hit back, and now is the time to finish them off."

"I'm sorry, I have my orders."

"You are under the command of the Northern Group of Forces, as am I."

"I take my orders from Generalmajor Urner, Colonel."

"*Chush' sobach'ya!* You take your orders from the Motherland!"

Oberst Keller stared into the eyes of the Soviet officer. "That is about to change, Comrade Colonel," he said under his breath. "I take orders from my General."

With that, the Oberst stormed off, his orders to assist with the repatriation of as many wounded as possible. Many of them were suffering from major trauma injuries, third-degree burns and radiation sickness. One thing he hadn't informed the Soviet colonel about was the second set of orders he'd received, and were tucked away in his pocket.

Top Secret
To: Oberst Keller
Command: 8th Motor-Schutz Regiment
From: Generalmajor Urner
Command: 8th Motor-Schutz Division, 5th German Army

1. *Poland: Unrest in Poland. Polish Solidarnosc has called for its 10-million members to initiate a period of civil unrest. Martial law has been declared, but the army are taking no action. Poland is in a state of paralysis.*

2. *Czechoslovakia: A second uprising is in progress in Czechoslovakia. The Czech army is withdrawing troops from Germany to ensure its internal security and protect its borders.*

3. *German Democratic Republic: Major discord within our borders. Severe backlash over casualties to National Volksarmee after nuclear strikes. Also street protests over the civilian casualties in the Federal Republic of Germany after the Soviet nuclear response.*

Orders:
1. *Cease all hostilities against NATO forces unless in self-defence.*
2. *Evacuate all military casualties to the German Democratic Republic urgently.*
3. *Prepare defence against Soviet military intrusion.*
4. *Take no further orders from Soviet Military Commanders.*
5. *Prepare withdrawal of all National Volksarmee forces.*

Urner
Generalmajor

1015, 12 July 1984. Ministerium fur Staatssicherheit, MfS state prison, Hohenschonhausen, East Berlin.

The Blue Effect +2 days

Bradley was back in the small room that had become familiar to him during his time spent being questioned by his interrogator. The man was sitting in front of him now, but the occasion was very different. In the last four hours, he had been allowed to shower and his uniform had been returned, tatty but cleaned and pressed. A uniformed doctor had also treated his wounds. A full plate of ham and pickled cabbage had been given to him to eat but after swallowing half, he brought it all back up. They'd helped him to clean himself up; then had given him some dark bread until his stomach was capable again of digesting anything more adventurous.

"Well, Mr Bradley." The major pushed a cup towards his captive. "I have been able to acquire some tea for you. Probably not as good as you have perhaps been used to, but tea all the same. I will stick with my coffee."

Bradley didn't move.

"Go on, take it. No tricks this time. Only tea." He smiled.

Bradley reached out and picked up the cup. There was no milk, but his first sip tasted like elixir.

"Good, good. That's more like it." There was a pause and then the major leant in towards him. "Events have moved very quickly in the last couple of days."

"24388749, Bradley Reynolds, Sergeant, Royal Corps of Transport."

"Ha, ha, ha," laughed the MfS major. "No need for that, Mr Bradley. Those days are over. You are still in our custody, but you are to be released soon."

Bradley's mind raced, but he kept control of his emotions. He thought back to his R2I training and the tricks that were played on him to gather information. An interrogator posing as a Red Cross representative, asking him to sign documents to prove to his family that he was alive. Tricks. *Is this a trick?* He thought. He was still at Hohenschonhausen, the MfS prison, a prison used by Ministry of State Security.

"Herr Bradley. Truly. Your government know we have you in custody, and your exchange is being organised as we sit here with our drinks and chat. So, please relax."

"24388749, Bradley Reynolds, Sergeant, Royal Corps of Transport."

The major leant back in his seat and lit a cigarette. "I understand, Sergeant Reynolds. My men will take you to a room with a bed where you can get some sleep. As soon as an exchange has been arranged, I will call for you again. Good day to you, Sergeant."

1130, 13 July 1984. The Kremlin.
The Blue Effect +3 days

General Secretary Baskov crashed down into his low-backed leather armchair, shocked at the latest news from the battlefields of West Germany. "Comrade Aleksandrov, tell me this news is false."

The head of the KGB, the *Komitet Gosudarstvennoy Bezopasnosti*, the Committee for State Security, probably the second most powerful man in the Soviet Union, Yuri Aleksandrov, nodded his head. "It is true, Comrade General Secretary. The Polish army is pulling back in both the north and south, and the *National Volksarmee* is doing the same."

"Our forces are holding?" Baskov asked, fiddling with his favourite toy: a model of an artillery piece.

"Yes, Comrade Secretary, 2nd Guards Tank Army and 20th Guards Army are consolidating along with the divisions of the Northern Army, but they have had to pull back to Hamburg and east of Hanover as they are under threat from the north and the west. The West German Army, along with the US III Corps, is on their heels. The British are consolidating, but Intelligence tells me that they are getting ready to push for and cross the River Leine. 3rd Shock Army no longer exists."

"Reinforcements?"

"Yes, the Military Districts are starting fill the gaps. Further south, it is stalemate, but the French forces are building up, and more and more Americans are being shipped in."

Baskov stroked the metal pin in the shape of a Soviet flag on the left lapel of his grey suit. "We must attack again, Yuri." The squarish, jowly face smiled. "We have a powerful army still. Tactical nuclear weapons."

"But not the ammunition and supplies to support it, Comrade Secretary."

"What, you want to sue for peace, give up on the ground we've taken?"

"Let me pour a drink, Comrade Secretary."

"Yes, yes, if you must."

Aleksandrov proceeded to pour two cups of coffee from the decorated slender coffee pot, his hand passing over his Politburo leader's drink, the white powder from his ring masked as he added sugar to the Soviet leader's china cup. He placed the cup and saucer in front of Baskov who took a long drink from the now cooled coffee.

Aleksandrov passed across the plate of biscuits. Baskov's hand was shaking as he went to pick one for himself. His face reddened as the batrachotoxin quickly took effect. Found on the skin of the very small poison dart frog, the toxin attacked the General Secretary's nervous system, opening the sodium channels, paralysing the large man, and shutting down his body's systems. Baskov's eyes widened as he fell forward out of his chair, collapsing onto the floor in a heap. A few twitches and he was dead.

Aleksandrov called out, and Baskov's secretary opened the door letting Marshal Obraztsov and Marshal Dolzhikov into the room.

"Comrade Baskov is unwell, Marshall Obraztsov. Please have him taken for treatment."

"Yes, Comrade General Secretary, straightaway."

"Marshall Dolzhikov."

"Yes, Comrade General Secretary."

"Let's get down to business. We need to initiate peace talks and to find away of getting the Motherland out of this mess."

Vulcan XH558 is the sole remaining airworthy example of Britain's V-force of over 300 aircraft that once stood on alert as the UK's contribution to the NATO strategic deterrent during the Cold War period.

Today, she is also the last all-British designed and built four-engined aircraft still flying from the period when Britain led the world in aviation design.

The awesome sight and sound of XH558 in the air may currently be seen at various air displays throughout the country in the summer, or close up on the ground in her hangar at Robin Hood Airport near Doncaster.

When sadly XH558 ceases to fly, she will form a centre-piece of a completely new type of inspirational centre, specifically designed to encourage more youngsters to choose an engineering career.

If you would like to find out more, then visit the website at vulcantothesky.org, sign up for free newsletters or follow XH558 on Facebook and Twitter.

Just search for 'Vulcan XH558' and you will find us.

VULCAN TO THE SKY
HONOURING THE PAST, INSPIRING THE FUTURE

For more from Harvey, including maps, photos and background information visit his website at www.harveyblackauthor.org.

Lightning Source UK Ltd.
Milton Keynes UK
UKOW04f0057020315

247081UK00002B/31/P